S0-AGK-485

WHO WILL ANSWER THE CALL TO ARMS?

What will war be like in the future? Will we find enemies or allies on distant worlds, species so different that there is no common meeting ground, others so similar that they become rivals for the same kinds of planets and resources? Will war in the future be totally bloodless or cause the destruction of entire civilizations? Or, when we finally make our way to the stars, will we find that war has at last become obsolete?

Discover what the future may hold in these ten thought-provoking tales of the perils and the promise that await the human race the day after tomorrow.

FUTURE WARS

LOGAN-HOCKING
COUNTY DISTRICT LIBRARY
230 E. MAIN STREET
LOGAN, OHIO 43138

More Imagination-Expanding Anthologies
Brought to You by DAW:

WONDROUS BEGINNINGS *Edited by Steven H. Silver and Martin H. Greenberg.* The writers included in this volume are a real "who was and who is" in the field of science fiction, from such masters of science fiction's Golden Age as: Murray Leinster, L. Sprague de Camp, Hal Clement, and Arthur C. Clarke; to a number of today's hottest-selling and award-winning authors such as: Anne McCaffrey, Gene Wolfe, George R. R. Martin, Orson Scott Card, Lois McMaster Bujold, and Stephen Baxter. How and where did these writers get their start? Now you can find out by reading the stories that began their careers, along with an introduction by the author which offers insight into the genesis of both the particular story and the individual writer's career.

ONCE UPON A GALAXY *Edited by Wil McCarthy, Martin H. Greenberg, and John Helfers.* Fantasy and science fiction writers know that technology and magic are far more closely linked than many of us care to admit. And some of the most fascinating novels in the genre are the ones that have taken that premise to a variety of intriguing conclusions. Now such top writers as Gregory Benford, Stanley Schmidt, Michelle West, Fiona Patton, and Tanya Huff offer us their own unique versions of classic fairy-tale themes in fourteen highly original and innovative stories. In some cases the original source is unmistakable, in others half the fun will be guessing what fairy tale inspired the current story.

SOL'S CHILDREN *Edited by Jean Rabe and Martin H. Greenberg.* In sixteen original stories, such master explorers as Timothy Zahn, Jack C. Haldeman, Kristine Kathryn Rusch, Mike Resnick, Roland Green, and Michael A. Stackpole offer an unforgettable guided tour to the adventures that await us on the and around the various planets of our own solar system. From a Martian sting operation into the most closely guarded bastions of wealth . . . to a conflict between life-forms at an observatory on Io . . . to an impossible space race to reach all nine planets in nine days . . . these are orginal stories filled with the allure of action, adventure, and discovery that marks the finest science fiction.

FUTURE WARS

edited by
Martin H. Greenberg
and Larry Segriff

DAW BOOKS, INC.
DONALD A. WOLLHEIM, FOUNDER
375 Hudson Street, New York, NY 10014

ELIZABETH R. WOLLHEIM
SHEILA E. GILBERT
PUBLISHERS
www.dawbooks.com

Copyright © 2003 by Tekno Books and Larry Segriff.

All Rights Reserved.

Cover art by Gregory Bridges.

DAW Book Collectors No. 1254.

DAW Books are distributed by Penguin Putnam Inc.

All characters and events in this book are fictitious.
Any resemblance to persons living or dead is strictly coincidental.

If you purchase this book without a cover you should be
aware that this book may have been stolen property and
reported as "unsold and destroyed" to the publisher. In such
case neither the author nor the publisher has received any
payment for this "stripped book."

The scanning, uploading and distribution of this book via the
Internet or via any other means without the permission of
the publisher is illegal and punishable by law. Please purchase only authorized electronic editions, and do not partici-
pate in or encourage electronic piracy of copyrighted
materials. Your support of the author's rights is appreciated.

Nearly all the designs and trade names in this book are registered trademarks. All that are still in commercial use are
protected by United States and trademark law.

First Printing, April 2003
1 2 3 4 5 6 7 8 9

DAW TRADEMARK REGISTERED
U.S. PAT. OFF. AND FOREIGN COUNTRIES
—MARCA REGISTRADA
HECHO EN U.S.A.

PRINTED IN THE U.S.A.

ACKNOWLEDGMENTS

Introduction © 2003 by Larry Segriff.

Bifrost Crossing © 2003 by Barry B. Longyear.

Faith on Ice © 2003 by James H. Cobb.

Sparks in a Cold War © 2003 by Kristine Kathryn Rusch.

Los Niños © 2003 by William H. Keith, Jr.

An Admiral's Obsession © 2003 by Kathleen M. Massie-Ferch.

Ranger © 2003 by Bill Fawcett & Associates.

The Vacation © 2003 by Ron Collins.

On the Surface © 2003 by Robert J. Sawyer.

Air Infantry © 2003 by R. J. Pineiro.

Toy Soldiers © 2003 by Robin Wayne Bailey.

To the memory of
Kathleen Massie-Ferch
(1954–2002)
A true warrior.

CONTENTS

INTRODUCTION

by Larry Segriff

MANKIND is many things. We are a race of poets and dreamers. We have taken our first small steps off this rock we call home and have dared to reach—however tentatively—toward the stars. We give to the poor, take care of the elderly, and care about the fate of the whales, the spotted owl, and the rain forests.

As a race, we have come a long way. We've harnessed the power of the atom. We've stood upon the surface of our moon and looked back at the Earth. We've peered into the tiniest crevices of the universe, and gazed into the farthest reaches of space.

But we also have our dark side. We murder and rape and steal. We cheat our neighbors or turn our backs on our brothers. We divide ourselves based on race, creed, nationality, or whatever other arbitrary category seems convenient.

And we wage war. Brother against brother, neighbor against neighbor, man against man. For causes both noble and ignoble, glorious and dishonorable, for humanitarian reasons and for greed. We've had holy wars, world wars, and the war to end all wars. We've honored our warriors, making them kings and presidents and emperors, erecting tablets and statues and pyramids to remember their names and their deeds.

War. It's a part of us. A part of our heritage. A part of our history. It's a bright scarlet thread running through the tapestry of our past. And it hangs over our future like a pall.

As far as we've come, as much as we've grown in the ways of peace and love and honor, we've walked even farther down the path of death and destruction. We've increased immensely the number of people we can feed from a single acre of farmland, but we've also increased exponentially the number of people we can kill with a single weapon. We've advanced the art of medicine to where a single doctor can save untold thousands of lives in a single career, but we've improved the art of war to where a single general can kill tens or even hundreds of thousands of people in a single war.

Mankind. We've come a long way in a short time. We have much to be proud of, and much to look forward to. But as much promise as tomorrow holds for us, as many bright, shiny dreams as we can look forward to—expanding our presence in space, finding new frontiers to explore, inventing new cures and new technologies and new ways to help more people—we cannot escape the promise and threat of war. It's our past. It's our present. And it is our future.

BIFROST CROSSING

by *Barry B. Longyear*

Hugo and Nebula-award winning author Barry B. Longyear is best known for the novella "Enemy Mine" which
was made into a movie in 1985. Other novels of his
include *The Homecoming* and *Infinity Hold*. A freelance
writer for more than twenty-five years, he has also written several books for the *Alien Nation* syndicated televi-
sion series. He currently lives in New Sharon, Maine,
with his wife, Regina.

*I*T *was aimed at him, as so many others had been aimed
at him. It found its mark, as so many others had found
their marks. He died, as—*

"At any point in time," interrupted the psychiatrist, "you are who you are and you are where you
are."

A soft voice, half-bored, reciting the party line,
moving space debris through his office pod, doctors
crazier than their patients. If there was anything Jere
Suiter knew, it was that he wasn't who he was and
he certainly wasn't where he was.

> *Endless frost, colorless, deep and killing,*
> *Gales that blacken skin, the Sun defeated—*

"Where are you, Jere?"

Jere Suiter forced his eyes open. The doctor was behind his transparent titanium desk. His uniform was
deep blue with iridescent stripes of mother-of-pearl
across the left shoulder. Medical captain. Frazier.

Something wrong there, though. It was as if Jere had always known the psychiatrist but had just figured out his name. It was as if he had always been sitting in that chair, but just noticed it. It was as though he was where he was, but where that where was wasn't where it was—

—or something like that.

A line or two of poetry: "As if through a dark glass—" he muttered, shaking his head. No, he thought to himself, concentrating, chipping the scale from ancient memories:

> *As if through a glass and darkly,*
> *The age-old strife I see.*
> *For I fought in many guises, many names,*
> *But always me.*

Confused images of the Stone Bridge, a jungle trail or two, the hell of that French forest, that smell along the west wall in the summer, calling out the watch signs that long, lonely night in Beth-horon, knowing the morning sun would bring with it torture, death, and desecration.

"But men!" he heard an ancient voice cry. *"We are soldiers! We are warriors!"*

And the voice was his.

Somewhere, a gleaming white bridge across a star-dusted abyss—

It was home, thought Jere. My home. The home of my fathers. That's where I'm supposed to be.

But was home the jungle, the forest, the prison, the Stone Bridge, that gleaming white bridge? All of them? None?

Someplace other than this, that was for certain. Jere was supposed to be elsewhere. Perhaps the else in elsewhere, the when in somewhen, had got misfiled. Then is then, now is now, but he wasn't persuaded. His certainties were breaths in a fog.

The walls of the office pod were flat gray. Dr. Fra-

zier kept his walls opaqued. But they told Jere that
if he believed them to be clear, they would be clear.
They were opaque because Jere believed them to be
opaque, which was so much butt blow, thought Jere.
They are opaque because that's the bloody way Captain Frazier bloody well keeps his bloody walls.

Jere looked from the walls to the psychiatrist.
"Doc, there's a poem. I can't remember the poet's
name. It goes like: '—The age-old strife I see./For I
fought in many guises, many names,/But always
me.'"

"You're hanging onto the past, Jere."

"If you don't know who wrote it, Doc, just say so."

"It was written by George S. Patton, Jr."

"Patton. The general from the twentieth century
wars?"

"Yes."

Jere Suiter shook his head and rubbed his temples.
"Am I crazy, Doc? Dumb question, considering
where I am. How crazy?" He lowered his hands and
glanced up at the doctor. "Am I going to come
back?"

"You've had a nasty shock, Jere, that's all. Give it
some time."

Jere giggled. Black Pulse; nasty shock. Like telling
Marie Antoinette she just had a little crick in her
neck.

"Why did you want to know who wrote those
lines?"

"It was in my head." Jere glanced around the office, seeing nothing. "It's all these thing in my head:
Places, names, wounds, burial grounds—the lines
just came to me. Seemed like a key of some kind."

"I see." There was something sad in the doctor's
face. The eyes. Jere knew the eyes from somewhere.
"It's simply taking you some time to sort things out,
Jere. You are going to have to let go of those other

times and places, though. If you couldn't have been
there, then you weren't there. Got it? Start getting
used to that. If you can't accept that, I have serious
doubts about a full recovery. Try, Jere. Make the effort." There was a sigh, more sadness than disappointment.

The doctor nodded at something above and behind
Jere. As he did so, Jere noticed an expression in the
doctor's face. One of those knowing looks to another
in the know, the knowledge being kept from the
third party because they don't know what he'd do if
he knew.

The chair pulled back and turned as Jere decided
it was just as well that the knowing ones kept their
precious secrets to themselves. He wasn't certain he
wanted a straight answer.

Someone was moving the chair, escorting him back
to the ward pod, the hiss of the plastic floor beneath
the chair's tracks. Think about it, the doctor had said.
Jere shook his head. He couldn't remember what it
was he was supposed to forget. He couldn't forget
what it was he was supposed to remember, that
smell along the west wall making everything seem
filthy. A filth that could never be cleaned.

He looked at his knees, asking himself, the west
wall of what? Thin orange bathrobe covering his
knees. He frowned because he had expected to see
blue. Beyond his knees, the floor. Multicolored transparent floor plates shooting vertically beneath the
chair, the Whatever Nebula below depicted in blues,
yellows, reds, and greens, depending on the panel.
As he tried to remember the name of the nebula, a
pair of pale blue trousers bloused above issue blue
gravs walked the other way.

"The doctor's right, you know," said the female
voice from behind him. It was Val, the morning
nurse. Stunning beauty, he had overheard some of

the other patients say. Jere didn't know himself. He couldn't recall ever having seen her. He turned his head and looked up over his shoulder. Beautiful, yes. Although the kind of powerful woman one might call "handsome." Never cute or pretty. Her uniform was pale blue, a double red stripe across her left shoulder. Field nurse lieutenant. She was one of the ones who go down planetside to pick up the scraps that still twitch and weep. Easier to kill than do that; still easier to die.

She smiled down at him, her large almond-shaped eyes deepest blue. "You are who you believe you are," she said. "You are where you believe you are. That soldier who just passed us going the other way, Jere. Who do you believe that soldier to be?"

"I only saw boots."

"And?"

"Well, they're blue and bloused. That means he's all Bucked up." He frowned at the phrase. The blue-bloused boots were Space Rangers. Space Rangers, Buck Rogers, Rogers Rangers, Dumb Bucks, all Bucked up. And what did the Buckups call everyone else? Dirt. Dirt grunts.

"So, what are you, Jere? Who do you believe you are? Where do you believe you are?"

"Dirt infantry." He looked at the access tube: one spoke of many in a great wheel suspended in space. "Okay. This is the military hospital complex on some space station. Either that or I want to talk to someone about my eyes."

"Which station?"

He raised an eyebrow. "Eagle Five USEF Base, en route to . . . someplace."

"Ruga Sector."

Jere nodded and faced forward. The chair slowed slightly. There were no reflections from the surface of the tube. There seemed to be nothing between Jere and the universe of stars except for the next access tube from the next ward to the office ring. That tube was opaque. Infinite distances.

He shut his eyes. "The walls bother me."

"Change them."

Jere glanced up briefly, saw stars, and closed his eyes. "The walls *are not* opaque!"

"That's because that's what you believe, Jere. The same applies to you. You are who you believe you are."

"That'd be one hell of an army, Val. Eight million generals and no privates."

"Do you think there are eight million privates in the army who believe they're generals?"

As they approached the opening to the ward pod, the hatch plates dilated. Jere felt himself doze off, the endless death within the pine log walls now more taste than smell.

—Now. Not the prison, not the Stone Bridge. It was now; it was the jungle trail following Snake. The trail was at Aytak Na on that planet—planet—

Whatever it was called. The prison was in Georgia. The Stone Bridge was at Bull Run.

Manassas.

Manassas where we lost our asses—

—the walls morphed into wood grain and vertical lines, the Old Dutchman on the wall looking down at the dead soldier hanging on the deadline, the Georgia State Militia private, smoking rifle in hand, standing at his side, Gerald, afraid to stare, afraid to cry out in protest, afraid to draw attention to himself. He slumped down against another prisoner, looked to apologize, then let it pass as he saw the man's fixed stare above a toothless mouth, the cold smell of death about him.

—*the death of Mercy's heart,*
The trees glisten with icicles of blood.
The monsters gather—

*   *   *

Things teetering; something on his arm. He opened his eyelids to mere cracks, reality bar coded by his eyelashes. Blue-gray walls of undressed stone, the mortar black and glassy. Stone arched ceiling. Walls extending forever. Vein-laced glistening pods every few meters along the walls looking like massive jellyfish. Center of each jellyfish, a two-meter-long blue maggot. Jere was in a jellyfish, too. The maggot closest to Jere's right leaned in his direction, its sightless face all mouth and goo. "Hey, Suiter," it said. "You okay?"

Jere closed his eyes. "Oh, yeah. I'm just fine."

"Suiter," the voice insisted as the creature removed its appendage from Jere's arm.

"What?" Jere forced himself to open his eyes. Stars spread out over him. The blue stone walls were gone. He looked at the next bed. Doaks was sitting on the bed looking back: short black hair, eyes too close together, pale blue cast to his skin, but the skin was human. Below the overhead, the side plastic walls of the ward pod were tan opaque, privacy mists surrounding most of the beds.

"What is it, Doaks?"

"What is it? What is it with you? You seemed okay for a couple of days, then you bubble out on me. You okay?"

"What they tell me, I'm okay if I believe I'm okay. Saves a bundle in compensated medical discharges."

Doaks raised his eyebrows. "Frazier's laying that stuff on you, too, huh? So, who are you, where are we, and what time is it?"

"I'll play," answered Jere. "When is this? What year?"

Doaks held out his hands. "Twenty-three thirty. Isn't it?"

"It sounds right to me, but, then again, I'm in a psych ward."

Blue maggots and jellyfish pushed a thought into

Jere's mind: one more reason to regard reality as a suggestion. "Hey, Doaks, what if our words are the same as the walls? What if they are what we believe them to be? Say, in your head it's eighteen sixty-four, and you say it's eighteen sixty-four, but I believe it to be twenty-three thirty, so what I hear you say is twenty-three thirty. So what year is it, really? What did you answer, really? How can we tell? Or is there such a thing as a year date that means anything?"

Doaks brought down the corners of his mouth and shook his head. "Man, I just wanted to know how long it is to chow time."

There was the sound of soft swearing. Gilcrest and Hernandez were across the aisle on visitors' chairs between their beds working their jaws. Gilcrest talking again about the battle that had put both of them in the hospital: Ikina Ron. A major CF on a Class Four slated for a heavy drop. Two heavy weapons groups slaughtered before the mistake in orders had been detected. The attack zone almost collapsed, six thousand more lives poured in to keep it open. All those computer-generated medals and letters. Ikina Ron had happened on the other side of the sector, though.

Aytak Na, Jere reminded himself. That was where he had got his. He glanced around the ward. No one else there from Aytak Na. A minor CF. They only killed a few, as far as Jere knew, which was good. The thing that was not so good, as far as Jere knew, was that he had been killed with them.

Gilcrest and Hernandez seemed to have recovered from their wounds, but had landed slots in the mental ward anyway. He looked at the others. Mostly dirt grunts. A couple Bucks. No one in the ward carried a physical wound.

Moving his head and neck, Jere tried to make it hurt the way it ought to hurt. If what he remembered was what had actually happened—

Staring at Snake's back, trying to keep up, all of them knowing as they hustled down that cold valley trail that they were asking for it. The Daks—the Sydaks—had to be waiting for them. Dry flat-gray skin stretched over a batlike skeleton, deep alizarin eye sockets, hearts bereft of pity, devastating energy weapons, minds clever beyond imagining. The field detectors didn't work on the Daks. What to do?

Well, the solution came right up from USEF HQ: Run a point squad in there, draw fire, hope not too many get sent back into the matrix as random electrical impulses. Can we have a few volunteers for this important mission?

Yeah, right. Get on the hump, dirt grunt.

"This is stupid," say more than a few. More than a few use more multihued terms. The answer is always the same, though, the panacea for all "why?" questions—the great military tautology: Orders are orders.

Yeah, orders are orders, and burned marshmallows are burned marshmallows. So what?

So, on the hump, dirt grunt. Snake volunteered, though. Snake had the spirit, the fire, the hunger for glory.

Jere spent yet another humid gray morning cleaning and charging his piece. Then crowded onto the sky sleds for an hour beneath the darkening clouds, followed by the rains as the company worked its way into the brownish-green jaggedness of Curo high country. When they approached the mountains, felt the rain grow cold, they saw the head of No-name Valley.

No-name had a name in Sydak, Jere remembered: it was *Luvak-ah*. *Luvak-ah* meant No-name. It wasn't that the Daks had run out of names, Jere surmised. Instead, some ancient bat-faced explorer must have paid big for entering the valley and refused the place a name, it was that bad.

"Hey, Gooba-gooba," one of the bat-cats might've said to the returning explorer, Loos'n'Clahk, "Hey, what's the name of that valley you discovered the other day? Thought I'd check it out."

The other bat-cat shakes his antennae. "*Luvak-ah*," he answers. No-name. "You stay outta there, man, unless you want to be splattered all over the great giant windshield. *Luvak-ah* sucks. Big time."

No lie there, thought Jere. *Luvak-ah* sucks.

On foot, through the brush and mud and over the slippery root knobs for chilly, endless hours, the sweat condensing on the insides of their rain gear, soaking them anyway. A bend in the trail, the green grayed down by the falling rain, a pause listening to the drumming of the raindrops on broad leaves, then in half a second the valley was gone and a giant fist drove Jere into the next dimension.

Black pulse. Landed right in the middle of the squad. When a black pulse hits, everything within ten meters of it disrupts on the quantum level. If you see it happen, it just looks like a piece of reality turns to mush and then drains away into nothingness. You don't heal from a black pulse. You become not.

"Hi, there," Jere whispered to himself. "I'm Not, from No-name. Howjadoo?"

Aytak Na was Jere's battle, the Sydak Police Action his war, the twenty-fourth his century. "So," he asked himself, "why am I here thinking about General Ambrose Burnside?"

Jere frowned as he shook his head. Burnside. A nineteenth-century American Civil War general. A Civil War battle. "I still can't let go of that Stone Bridge thing." He held out his hands in explanation to nonexistent listeners. "But Burnside couldn't have been that stupid. No one on or off Earth could've been *that* stupid."

Over four hundred years ago. He couldn't have

been there, he insisted to himself. Leaning back, he filled his sight with stars. A maintenance shuttle high above the station appeared as a cluster of bright stars traversing the heavens. There had been different stars in Beth-horon.

Jere felt something connect in his memory: "Burnside. That's why he sticks in my memory. Burnside was like Cestius Gallus. Still can't forgive Cestius for Beth-horon. The shame of the Twelfth. The sacrifice—" He glanced about to see if anyone had overheard. Gilcrest and Hernandez were still making jaw music. Doaks was looking at a handheld magscreen.

"Beth-horon," Jere whispered to himself. "That was when it all began going bad: Beth-horon." He looked down at his hands, clenched against the orange bed coverings. "I know I couldn't have been there either. That was thousands of years ago."

"Are you all right?"

Doaks again, the magscreen on his bed.

Jere dried his eyes with the heels of his hands. "I'm used up, man. My soul is all used up." He faced Doaks. "So, who are you? Where do you go when you need a good maggot rub or a used jellyfish?"

The man in the next bed raised his eyebrows. "I'm almost certain I didn't understand that."

Jere shrugged slightly. "Maybe my tongue has a kink in it. Things're a little fuzzy."

"That's the verazine. Now that you're talking, Heidrun'll lighten up on it."

"Heidrun?"

"The meds nurse."

An image drifted through Jere's mind. "Face like a goat?"

"Aren't you a sweetheart."

"It is what it is." Jere's gaze wobbled about the ward. "Isn't it?"

Through a clear screen on the opposite wall, he

saw that in the other ward pod, a patient was standing before one of the screens looking back. The patient seemed to sense Jere looking at him and the screen he had been looking through opaqued.

All the way around to his left, through the pod wall behind him, Jere could see another ward against the stars. It looked crammed with wounded, midnight-blue uniformed doctors working feverishly; one by one, the patients getting up and moving to the right, through the access tube, toward the center of the station.

"Man, they are really pushing the meat through that other ward."

Mangled bodies, missing limbs, sense organs missing or destroyed, yet there was something in Jere that envied those soldiers. They were getting up, moving toward the center of the station, going home.

He looked toward the center station access hatch set in the mostly opaqued wall at the end of his own ward pod. Next to it was the nurses' station. Heimdall, a male nurse who looked like a bouncer, was back there, fingering his screen, doing charting, glancing up every now and then to make sure some wigout didn't get to the locked hatch. Muscular, heavy, his red hair cut down to virtual bald, his uniform was pale blue with dark blue med chief's slashes high on his left sleeve. The signs above the station and on the tube door both said Ward 271.

Jere looked in the opposite direction. At the opposite end of the pod was the hatch he had come through earlier. That access tube led to the office and treatment ring where Captain Allen Frazier cast his spells. Jere frowned. He couldn't understand why he had this feeling—this need—to please Frazier.

He looked down at the pocket on Doaks' orange bathrobe. A golden caduceus flanked by a golden "U.S." on the left and an "E.F." on the right.

Beneath the snakes it said in bright red: "Ward

271—Escort Required." It said the same thing on
Jere's own bathrobe pocket. And across the front of
his pajama tops. And across the front of the right leg
of his pajama bottoms. No one wanted the folks in
Ward 271 to get loose, to get into the center of the
station.

Maybe twenty patients, a couple of hundred, perhaps thirty thousand. The numbers seemed to change.
Three quarters of the beds filled in 271.

Memories filled Jere's mind like corrupt down-
loads through an intermittent modem. Walls, flashes
of fire, reflections off burnished metal, every bone so
weary. He leaned over on his right side, lowered his
head to the pillow, and put his feet up on the bed.
Doaks came within his gaze.

"Thanks for being here for me, man," he said to
Doaks.

The man shrugged self-consciously. "No sweat."

"We ever serve together, Doaks? It's like I know
you from somewhere, but I can't place it."

Doaks shook his head. "I don't think so. I was with
the 117th Assault. You?"

"Seventh Recon attached to Gold Corps, Aytak
Na." Jere frowned as he realized he couldn't remem-
ber any faces from the Seventh. Only the back of
Snake's head.

"No," said Doaks. "I don't think we ever served
together. You're familiar to me, though." Doaks settled back on his bed and looked up at the stars.
"Maybe back in training—"

"Hey, Doaks. Do you remember a battle group
commander—I mean, a legate from a long time ago—
named Cestius? Cestius Gallus? Governor of Syria?"

"Syria? What sector is that in?" Doaks looked at
Jere, his eyebrows raised. "I never heard of him before." He rubbed his eyes. "Strange, but I'd bet a
year's haz pay on it."

"On what?"

Doaks held up a hand. "I never heard of Cestius Gallus, but I know I hate his guts. See?" He reached out his hand and placed it on Jere's arm.

As the verazine pulled Jere back to sleep, he caught a glimpse of those blue stone walls again, that big blue maggot sitting in the middle of that huge glistening jellyfish, his gut filled with contempt and hatred for an old Roman governor who had turned to dust thousands of years ago. Puzzled look on his face—puzzled look for a maggot. "Now that I think about it, Suiter, I hate Cestius Gallus worse than Burnside, and I really hate Burnside."

Jere felt himself falling to sleep before he could ask about the Stone Bridge.

—Sun and Moon eaten,
The stars drop from Heaven, the mountains clash—

The light, the heat, the smoke, the ear-smashing thunder surrounded Gerald and filled his mind. Henry Streeter's ear was shot off and when Henry bent over to pick it up, canister and grape made a crowd out of him. Calvin Boyle caught one that ripped off his right arm above the elbow. Blood everywhere.

The screams. My God, the screams.

Gerald was trying to wipe the blood and pieces of flesh and bone from his face when a horse and rider crushed him against the bridge.

Couldn't breathe. Blue legs. They hurriedly stepped over Gerald for a time, ricochets buzzing about him like angry hornets, a caisson wheel rode over his ankles, crushing them, then frantic hands lifted him and tossed him over the wall down into the stream.

Drowned.

The end of the universe. The end, but not the end. A vision: *The Great Hall, holding up his drinking horn,*

the golden mead falling into it from the center of a blind-
ing galaxy of stars—

A jolt. Hand pushing him awake. The feeling that
an awful mistake had been made.

"On yer feet, yank."

Gerald opened his eyes to see a handsome reb private looking back, his rifle held crooked in his arm
like a fowling piece. He looked very familiar. "What's
your name, reb?"

"Now, that ain't none o' yer business, yank. Move
'long. You got lots t' do befo' yo' sleep t'night."

Jerry stood and looked through the open gate.

First, the smell: Feces. Filthy bodies and feces mixed
slightly with the smell of pine.

Then sight: mud, acres of improvised shanties and
blanket tents, living skeletons staring from sunken
eyes at Gerald and his comrades from the 16th
Connecticut.

Gerald wanted to ask the guard the name of the
place, but all the Union soldiers knew it: Camp
Sumpter, Georgia. Near a little village called Andersonville.

No big blue maggots inside those pine walls. A lot
of little white ones, though. Two prisoners dragging
a body to the gate. The reb guard, said to Gerald,
"They average one a day, yank, but that's goin' up
soon. Gettinn' mo' prisoners now."

The 16th Connecticut's "ninety" was assigned a
spot next to the foul-smelling swamp. There was a
man watching them. No boots, no shirt, only tatters
of once-blue trousers. Yellow stripe. Cavalry.
"Leastways they didn't rob you." Gerald reached
into his pocket to share the bit of hardtack he had
left over from the last prisoner rations he had received before going through the gate, but one of the
members of his regiment held his arm. "You're goin'
t' need that fer yerself, Suiter."

Gerald turned and looked at the big blue maggot who was giving him the advice.

Doaks.

Doaks hated Burnside, Gerald—or Jere—repeated to himself. He couldn't have been at the Stone Bridge or Andersonville any more than me, but Doaks hated Burnside and he hated Cestius Gallus more than Burnside and he was a big blue maggot, and just how many big blue maggots were in the 16th Connecticut? I mean, as enlisted men?

Bone tired. Soul weary. Running on empty.

—the wolf freed from its chain, the serpent up from the sea—

Jarl's dream moved, and he felt the horn in his right hand, the slab of Saehrimnir in his left, the grease dribbling from the corners of his mouth into his fierce yellow beard, the laugh of his lord shaking the immense trunks that supported the ceiling of the Great Hall. When the lord laughed, all laughed with him. Not for fear but because no one could help himself. To be a part of the lord's joy was to be alive.

The lord was happy, pleased with them all, fiercely proud, and that was the warm glow within Jarl's chest: gathering the praise of his fellows, pleasing the lord. He stamped his feet with the others and bellowed with joy as the hall thundered, shaking the universe. Thousands in the hall. Millions. Countless. The feeling: ecstasy-home. Home is a feeling.

A pause in the revelry, then it was time again: Jarl watched as a few of the other men put down their meat and drink, took up their weapons, and called out their battle cries as they moved toward the doors.

One final quaff of mead, and Jarl put down his own meat and drink, took up his mighty sword, and followed the Einheriar through one of the four hundred and twenty doors, singing of glory and the endless reward . . .

"Have you been having any dreams, Jerry?"

Jerry giggled. Captain Frazier leaned back in his chair, his khaki shirt sleeves rolled above his elbows, the end of his black necktie neatly tucked in between the second and third buttons of his shirt, his silver captain's railroad tracks hanging tacked to his collar. The green window shade was pulled down.

"A few. A few dreams, Doc. Oh, yes." The giggles bubbled up and he forced them back down. I'm a loon, he thought. I am as crazy as a bloody loon.

He noticed his bathrobe. Pale blue. Something vaguely wrong there. Pajamas, too. The medical insignia on the bathrobe's pocket was maroon. USA. He had expected gold. Gray-green asphalt tile on the floor. Cheap fiberboard walls.

"Anything you care to share?"

"Sir?"

"Your dreams. Would you care to share them?"

The giggles drained away. "How about a couple of CFs in the Civil War?"

"CFs?"

Jerry studied Frazier, wondering himself why he had used the term. CF. "A mess, Doctor. A really fouled-up situation. Snafu cubed. Cluster f—"

"I think I got it, Jerry. What happened in your dream?"

"Burnside, the commander, ordered us to cross the stream—Bull Run—at the Stone Bridge. There were other places to cross, but he made us cross there, even after he knew the rebs were waiting for us. Even after they began chewing us up—"

"Us?" The psychiatrist held out his hands. "How old are you, Jerry?"

"It's what I believe it is, right?"

"How old do you believe you are?"

"Twenty. I'm twenty years old." He frowned and

focused on a warp in time. "When we fought at Aytak Na, I was twenty." He shrugged away the psychiatrist's questioning look. "On another planet." He felt himself giggling again. "Yeah, about three hundred years from now. Bring on the rubber jacket."

"How old were you at the Stone Bridge?"

"Seventeen. At the Stone Bridge, I was seventeen." Jerry held up his hands and let them fall to his lap. "I was thirty-one when we stood the long watch at Beth-horon." The psychiatrist frowned. "The Jewish War," explained Jerry. "Palestine. The thirteenth year of the reign of Nero." He nodded to himself. "That was the mother of all CFs. A bunch of us—four hundred—were left behind in Beth-horon at night to keep the campfires going and call out the watch signals so the rest of the army could escape under cover of night."

"What happened to the four hundred? What happened to you?"

"What difference does it make? It's only a dream."

"What happened?"

Jerry raised a hand and let it fall to his lap. "We died! We all died." He rubbed his eyes and shook his head. "All those men, those boys. My hundred. All of what they were, who they were, their stories, all gone. No one will ever know their names."

"Was there anything else?"

Jerry looked up. "What? In my dreams?" The doctor nodded. "I was a prisoner of war. At Andersonville."

"The rebel concentration camp?" asked Frazier.

"Yeah. Crazy, huh? I mean, I died at Bull Run when I was seventeen. How could I be a prisoner at Andersonville?" Jerry frowned. "I was twenty-nine at Andersonville. The war was only four years long, wasn't it?"

"I believe so."

Jerry nodded and thought better of telling the doctor about the big blue maggot in the 16th Connecticut.

"Do you remember Vietnam?" asked the psychiatrist.

"Wasn't there a trail, some grass, a hot sun, another ambush? An Hoa, or was that Aytak Na? Do you want to hear the rest of the dream?"

"Please."

"I died and I went to heaven." Jerry pressed his lips together and looked down at his hands. "It wasn't heaven like everybody talks about: You know, wings, playing harps, sitting around on clouds in nightshirts singing 'Amazing Grace.' It was more like, you know, those old Viking sword-slasher vids. Opera. Wagner."

"What did it look like?" Dr. Frazier asked with false calm, leaning forward, his eyes eager—and strange.

"Doc, do you have a glass eye?"

"No. What did heaven look like?"

"It was all smoke-blackened hand-hewn logs, bigger than redwoods. The place was huge, bigger than this space—I mean, this hospital, this base. Damn near as big as this island. The logs were like miles long and thick as battleships. Huge roaring fires, and the hall was filled with men. Thousands. Maybe millions. Big men, muscled, scarred, blond-, red-, and black-haired, huge beards, great silver buckles, thick leather belts, furs, weapons like something out of chipvids—comic books. All of us drinking this stuff—wonderful tasting stuff. I don't know."

"Go on."

Jerry rubbed his eyes as the taste of the meat came back to him. "This meat I was eating, Doc. Tender as spring lamb. So rich it seemed to fill you with life.

It had a name. Not like beef or pork. A name, like Jones, or Smith—Saehrimnir. The meat was Saehrimnir. And you could eat all day and it would never run out. It grew itself back every night. It was a god." He leaned back in the chair and held up his hands. "How's that for a dream, Doc? God is a pork chop." He let his hands fall to his lap.

"Was there anything else?"

Jerry let out his breath. "There was someone there. A huge man, blond. A chief of some kind. A lord. It was like—it was like he was my father—more than a father. All of the men there. Sworn to him. We were all honored to be sworn to him. It was like he was a father-god. We all fought for him. We all . . ."

Jerry stared at the pulled window shade. A crack of light came through from outside and he thought he saw the flash of a passing car.

"What are you feeling right now, Jerry?"

He could feel the tears burning his eyes. "Doc, I know I'm here in the Camp Kue Hospital on Okinawa. I'm twenty-two years old and this is nineteen sixty-nine, but my head is buzzing with old fights, future battles, and right now all I want to do is capture that feeling of being in that hall, that meat and drink in my belly, at my lord's side."

"How do you feel?"

"How do I feel? Homesick. I'm homesick." He shook his head. "What's happening to me, Doc? I hate war, but I'm all caught up in some kind of Germanic myth."

"Name it," ordered the doctor.

"Valhalla." Jerry sat forward in the chair. "That's it. Doc, do you believe that at one point in time some people's idea of heaven was to die in battle, go to this big hall, eat, drink, tell stories, then hack each other to pieces and be reborn the next morning to do it all over again?"

"What do you feel about that?"

"Feel about it?" Jerry slumped back in the chair. "Feel? How do you think I feel about it? It's stupid. It's dumb. Childish. Getting hacked to pieces hurts."

"What about the glory, Jerry? What about the Glory?"

"You keep talking like that, Doc, and they'll put you in a home, too."

Frazier sat back in his chair. "Okay, Jerry. Stupid and dumb aren't feelings. How do you *feel* about Valhalla?" Frazier sat back in his chair. "Think about your answer between now and your next session. Okay? We did some good work, today. I'm encouraged."

Jerry nodded numbly, stood, and turned, opening the tan wooden door behind him. He stepped out into the hall, the side opposite the offices lined with double-hung windows looking out upon an irregular quadrangle formed by the covered ward access ramps on both sides, the ward buildings, and at the far end, the windowless wall of the central hospital. The space was brightly lit by the harsh sun, dull green grass, scrubby little trees. A mamasan was preparing to trim the grass with one of those stupid little Okinawan sickles.

Val was waiting for him in the hall to escort him back to the psych ward. Today she was dressed in fatigues, her dark hair pulled back in a bun. She'd be going back in country with her team to bring back more mental cases—more filberts for the fruitcake.

"How was your session, Jerry?"

He shrugged and began walking toward the access ramp to B-71, his issue slippers slapping against the plank floor. "I don't know, Lieutenant. The clearest thought I have right now is that I'm a conscientious objector who fantasizes about being a Viking warlord."

She smiled warmly. "Actually, Jerry, that means you're getting better."

Before he could laugh at her, her face, the hall, Okinawa, and the universe grayed out.

—Roaring death, they advance upon the bridge—
—Sword of Fire, the world in flames—

"Are you awake?" German artillery rumbled in the distance. The voice continued: It was the American. He wanted to talk again.

"Yes." Gérard opened his eyes. Past his toes, he looked through the diamond-shaped leaded panes of the chapel's windows. Where the tiny panes remained, the glass distorted the view of the next wing. Another American, Gilcrest, was sitting on his bunk putting on his puttees. He was getting released from the hospital. Sam Brown belt, single silver bars on his shoulders. Back to the trenches for him, and who's insane now?

It was growing light, touches of blush on thin gray clouds. In Gérard's mind the great lord's hall faded as wispy memories of Okinawa, the prison, and the Stone Bridge touched him, then faded to a face he could never have seen: Cestius Gallus. Ratty little beard, the belly of a senator. All robe; no guts. The Twelfth. *Legio XII Fulminata*. Vespasian banished the Twelfth to Melitene, carrying Cestius' shame in their baggage train. What a swine. The Third Hundred of the First Cohort, heroes every one.

"Suiter, do you dream?"

Gérard looked over to Doaks. Pale skin, blue eyes, light brown hair. A brow creased by worry.

"I dream."

"Do you have any judgment in your dreams?"

He leaned on his elbow and turned toward Doaks. The man had an olive drab blanket wrapped around his shoulders. "What do you mean, judgment?"

"It doesn't matter how silly a dream gets, I never stop in the middle of it and say, 'My God, this is really insane,' and then change it. Instead, I wake up later and I can't believe I didn't question the foolishness while it was going on."

Gérard looked at the upended packing crate to the right of his bed. A glass of water on it. He couldn't remember if he smoked, but he felt like he needed something. "I suppose I don't really question much of the insane things that happen to me in the real world, my friend. The whistle blows, they call us, time after time, up out of the trench, right into the barbed wire, the gas, the shells, and machine guns. When we're lucky, we take a few meters of mud from the Hun. Tomorrow they take it back. Nothing's changed except the number of dead."

"What about your dreams?"

"I do the same in my dreams. Perhaps it's all dreams. Why?"

"Heimdall. Look at him."

Gérard looked at the chief orderly seated at the chapel's locked entrance. Beneath the hand-stenciled Ward B-71 sign, he was at his usual place, behind the rickety wooden desk, scribbling on the paperwork. Master sergeant stripes on his American uniform. He glanced up, checked to see if any of the shell-shocked fellows had got too close, then went back to the paperwork. "He looks just like he always looks."

"Exactly. Did you ever notice that he's always there? You never see anyone else take a shift."

Gérard frowned and thought on it, trying to remember that desk without Heimdall's face behind it. He shook his head. "I'm not awake very often, Doaks. I'm not really awake right now."

The reason why, Nurse Heidrun, was at the medicine cabinet next to Heimdall preparing potions and another groggy evening for her charges. Gérard tried to remember. He'd awakened last night, his head filled with battles, the only light down at Heimdall's desk. He'd been there, scribbling and checking. One time. So, maybe all he was doing was covering for a friend. It was the ugly nurse that interested Gérard, though. Her name was Sally Heidrun. Ugly, but he felt as though he had loved her longer and more than any woman he had ever known.

Gérard glanced at Doaks. "I do not know, my friend. It is a shell-shocked ward, after all. Maybe . . ." He twirled a finger aimed at his own right temple.

Lowering his hand and swinging his feet to the floor, Gérard stood, waited a moment for the universe to settle down, and then headed for the lone water closet, just to the left of the locked entrance. As he went down between the rows of beds, he paused, trying to remember if he had ever used the water closet before. All he could remember involved foul-smelling ditches and an anus so inflamed he could hardly walk, skeletal soldiers in ragged blue drawing drinking water from nearby.

"No," he said to himself as he drove the memories ahead of him through the morphine. "No. That was Andersonville, and I couldn't have been there."

"What you have to do," said a voice, "is aim for moderate madness. Avoid the extremes."

Gérard looked and it was Hernandez advising Gilcrest as the first lieutenant continued to dress, his face glum. Hernandez was dark-haired and thin, his eyebrows turning up at the ends.

"What do you mean, moderate?" asked Gilcrest.

"Look, say you act like you just found all your marbles. You're sane, right?"

"Yeah?"

"Well, then, that makes you insane."

"How?" demanded Gilcrest.

"They're sending you back to the front, right?"

Gilcrest nodded. "I see what you mean."

Hernandez held up a hand. "That is not all, my friend. If you act very crazy—you know, hitting people, cutting yourself with razors, drinking out of the toilet bowl—they put you in shackles, fill you up with dope, and put you in a padded cell. You never see the sun again. A little crazy is the way to go."

Gérard laughed, but paused as he felt guilty about laughing. He frowned because he agreed with Hernandez. Anyway to get far from the front was the way to go, but there was a piece of him, something inside, that felt betrayed—that felt himself to be a betrayer—for encouraging Hernandez's behavior. He looked at the rafters above the beds. Beyond them the sky was blue and dotted with tiny white clouds. He frowned, wondering if the chapel roof was missing, or if he only believed it was missing, and did it even make a difference. The sky grew very dark and he felt himself being pulled into bottomless soundless depths.

"Doaks!" he cried out. There was no answer, and Gérard, remembering what Doaks said about judgment and dreams, tried to force the thing his way.

—*Advance on the bridge. The Sword of Fire, the world in flames*—

Major Frazier sat at his stout wooden desk in the corner of one of the hospital's tent wards. A dirty white flap had been pulled over the end to keep out the sights of the hospital compound. The smells and sounds—gangrene and screaming—were unfettered.

"The guard said you fainted. Suiter? Do you hear me?"

"Yeah. I hear you."

The doctor pushed thin white fingers through his lengthy blond hair. There was a respectable blond beard and mustache on Frazier's face. He had a patch over his left eye. "Well, what about it?"

"Are you mad? It's called exposure and lack of food, Major." Gerald shook his head slowly. "I don't get it."

"You don't get it?"

"We're dying by the hundreds in there. Starvation, dysentery, exposure, guards taking potshots at us. I faint, and I'm the one you call in here?"

"Earlier you were saying something about China, Siam, or something."

"No. Vietnam."

"Where exactly is that?"

"Southeast Asia, but I don't know when they started calling it Vietnam, if they ever did, or do. I don't believe I'm really here, Major. What do you think about that?"

The Confederate officer leaned back in his chair and folded his arms across his chest. "What about your Germanic myth?"

"My what?"

"You remember: The Great Hall, the warlord, the meat and the drink. Valhalla, the home of the heroes slain in battle."

"Yes." Gerald looked down at his emaciated legs, arms, and body. The hunger was very real. "Yes, the dream. We ate from a pig that grew itself whole overnight, we drank mead from a vessel that never went dry. The goat. The goat brought the mead. That's why the nurse looked like—" He stared at the reb officer's eyes, seeing once again that familiar thing. "I think I know you. Why?" asked Gerald. "Why do you do this to us?"

The rebel officer glanced away and pursed his lips. "There's not much else I can do, soldier. But it will get better. You'll see. It will be all right. In the end it will be all right."

He nodded at the militia guard and the private poked Gerald's back with the muzzle of his rifle. Gerald turned and stumbled from the closed off area into the street between the tent wards, the rows of skeletal bodies lying on the bare ground, some moaning, most too weak to even complain.

"This isn't really here, but, good Christ, reb! What kind of creatures are you people to do this to your fellow man?"

"Do what, yank?"

Gerald, astonished, turned and looked at the guard. "Do what? Valke, or whatever your name is, do you not have eyes in your head? Can you not see? Can you not smell?"

"What do you see, yank? What do you believe you see?"

Pulling himself upright, Gerald turned without answering and remained silent as he was led back to the main compound, the gate closing behind him. There was a guard on the wall above the gate, a fat Georgia State Militia private carrying a bugle. "Heimdall," muttered Gerald. "It's Heimdall. It's always Heimdall guarding the bridge."

Doaks, thin as a rail, was waiting behind the flag line. "What did Frazier say this time?"

"It doesn't matter." Gerald shifted his gaze to his comrade, stopped walking, and held out his arm. "Touch me."

"What?"

"With your finger. Touch me."

"Why?"

"Because I asked you."

Warily Doaks raised an arm and touched Gerald's hand with a bony finger. Light became dark, pine logs became undressed blue-stone mortared with black glass. From the depths of his healing mound of living jelly, the big blue maggot, his appendage coiled around Gerald's, waited expectantly. Gerald noted his own state of existence.

"All right," said Gerald. "Let's go back to the tent. We need to discuss escaping from here."

"What, from the prison?"

"From that, from time, from the All-father, from Muspelheim."

Gerald sat, his back against the dugout wall, looking at Doaks and Hernandez from the Union's 13th Tennessee Cavalry. He asked Hernandez, "Do you see things as others see them?"

A shrug, Hernandez's sunken eyes confused. "Who can say?"

"Know any poetry?"

"Some."

"Do you remember anything about a bridge?"

Hernandez closed his eyes. "Man, I tell you this: It is impossible that you were at Bull Run at seventeen. You were seventeen and dead. Now you are twenty-nine and alive."

"It's possible."

"How? You telling me Bull Run happened twelve years ago?"

Gerald looked at Doaks. "Go on. Touch Hernandez. With your finger."

After a pause and a compliant shrug from the cavalryman, Doaks reached out and touched Hernandez on the arm of his jacket. "No. Move it down to his skin."

Doaks moved his emaciated hand down over Hernandez's and touched it. The cavalryman's eyes widened as his mouth opened to a silent scream.

"He isn't breathing," said Doaks. "Hernandez. Breathe."

"It doesn't matter, Doaks," said Gerald. "We never die. We once lived, but we never die. Not really. Go ahead, pull back your hand."

Doaks did so, and Hernandez pulled in a ragged breath, staring first at Doaks, then Gerald, then at the shelter, then back at Gerald. "What is this? A trick?"

"Reality is a trick, my friend. You are not here. We are not here. All those thousands out there in the compound died hundreds of years ago. That part of each of us we all call 'I,' all of us used to be here, in the past. We were all in lots of times and lots of places."

Hernandez rubbed the back of his neck and shook his head. "Man, you been smokin' a Chinese pipe? *Dios*, what was that bad-looking blue worm?"

"Go on," said Gerald to Doaks. "Touch him again."

Hernandez pulled a length of sharpened metal from within his jacket and held it threateningly toward Doaks. "You keep that spooky finger away from me, *gringo*." He shifted his gaze to Gerald. "Okay, Suiter, what was that? The big blue worm in that shiny blob?"

"That, my friend, is how someone from another race sees himself, sees us, and sees this moment and place." Gerald looked at both of them. "We see and hear, taste and smell what we need to see, hear, taste, and smell to fit within a particular reality. That's how we can get used over and over again between battles, between wars."

"You have lost me," said Doaks.

Gerald held out his hands. "We're all in Andersonville right now, correct?"

They both nodded.

"So, how long ago was the American Civil War?"

Hernandez nodded and held out his hands. "It pretty much looks like it's going on right now, *compadre*. Eh?"

"When? What year?"

"This is eighteen sixty-four. They fired on Fort Sumpter in 'sixty."

And Doaks mumbled something, too, incomprehensible.

"What was that again, Doaks? Real quick, before we can adjust and make what you say what we need to hear.

Doaks opened his mouth and out of it came a curious hissing, garbled chirping. He tried again and said, "It began in eighteen sixty."

Hernandez's eyes moved rapidly as his conclusions chased his observations. "Man, you telling me we a bunch big fat blue worms?"

Reaching out his hand, Gerald grasped the cavalryman's hand and held it. "See any big blue worms?"

The man stared for a moment, then shook his head. "No."

Releasing his hand, Gerald leaned back and spoke more to himself than to his two companions. "We came from distant stars, diverse universes, infinite dimensions. Even so, we all have been here before: our souls, our life forces. Doaks was with me at Bull Run. I'm not certain, but I think he was my corporal. We were together in the Twelfth before Jerusalem. He was in my hundred. We stood the watch at Beth-horon."

Gerald closed his eyes. "I think Doaks fought in the Argonne, but not with me. He was in the hospital with me. I can only guess at what these names, sights, and experiences were to Doaks."

"What do you mean, Suiter?" Doaks protested. "What do you mean? They mean the same to me as they mean . . ." He frowned and looked at his own naked feet, not seeing them. "But Cestius, I hate him. The watch." He looked at his hands and shook his head. "The watch. I've read about it, or heard about it. I recall a centurion. Nireus. Named after a Greek king." He looked down and focused his memory on a feeling. "Nireus. I honored him—" He looked at

Hernandez. "On the beach, in the great city, in the jungle, do you remember? We were together."

Hernandez blinked his eyes, stood, looked around, and sat again. "Cortez. I thought it was a dream. You." he nodded at Doaks. "I mean, we fought them—"

Doaks held his hands before him, his eyes closed. "What does any of this have to do with big blue worms? I am a human."

Gerald nodded. "And, Doaks, we hear you say what the All-father would have us hear. But when you touch me, I see us all as different. When you touched Hernandez, he saw us all as different. We saw us and saw you as you see everything. Doaks, do your people speak by touch?"

"Don't be absurd. All we do by touch is allow another—" and his words became garbled, incomprehensible.

"All you do by touch," completed Gerald, "is to let another see as you see."

"Certainly. I do not lie, and I touch you. You see, you trust my word and my sight, and we are in agreement. Every child learns this."

Hernandez stared wide-eyed at Doaks. "That is what you see? A blue rock prison full of shiny blobs and fat blue worms?"

Doaks shook his head. "Now I can't understand what you're saying."

"It's what we believe," said Gerald. "I am who I believe I am. I am where I believe I am." More to himself, he muttered, "And maybe it might work back the other way. After all, as you see us, we can do that."

"Do what?"

Before Doaks could figure out what he meant, Gerald reached out and touched the back of the man's hand with the tip of his right index finger. Gerald saw no change, except in Doaks. The man's face grew ashen, the eyes wide. He studied Hernandez, then Gerald, then himself. Slowly his gaze came back to Gerald.

"What is this filthy hole? What are you?" He looked down at himself. "What are we?"

"This is what we call human form, my friend," said Gerald. "This hole is what Andersonville looked like when we were imprisoned here four centuries ago, through my eyes. Your blue rock prison never looks any different to me, though. I'm guessing all of your changes are on some other level." Gerald removed his hand and sat back against the dugout wall. Doaks wrapped his arms about his knees, his gaze darting wildly about. At last he calmed, looked at Hernandez, and held out his hand.

"What?"

"You touch that hand. You touch me, as well."

Hernandez touched Doaks, and instead of the expected look of horror, Doaks grinned and nodded, looking at Gerald. "Oh. That's what *gringo* means." Hernandez broke contact, rubbed his eyes, and looked at Gerald.

"What you mean about poetry?" Hernandez asked Gerald.

Gerald nodded. "See if anything sounds familiar to you, fellow warriors: 'Come the God's Twilight, the Fimbul-winter/Snow falling from all corners of the world—' "

Hernandez frowned and joined in: " 'Endless frost, colorless, deep and killing/Gales that blacken the skin, the Sun defeated/Nine years, the world white and barren—' "

Doaks spoke with them: " 'Brother, to eat, takes sword and slays brother,' "

A strong voice from outside the shelter said, " 'Parents, children, the death of Mercy's heart.' "

Gerald stood as more voice from outside joined in:

> " '—*The trees glisten with icicles of blood.*
> *The monsters gather, Sun and Moon eaten,*
> *The stars drop from Heaven, the mountains clash,*
> *All above, between, and below shattered.' "*

All along the West Wall, the voices took up the words:

> " '*The Wolf Fenris, freed from Gleipnir, its chain,*
> *And the Midgard Serpent, up from the sea,*
> *Roaring death, they advance upon Bifrost Bridge*
> *Following Surtur and his sword of fire,*
> *And the sons of Muspell, the world in flames.' "*

The entire camp, prisoners, slaves, sutlers, and guards, spoke the words:

> " '*Across the bridge, upon the Vigrid Plain,*
> *Ranks positioned for the Last Great Battle,*
> *Wait mighty Surter, the Sons of Muspell,*
> *Fenris and Jormungand, their sire, Loki,*
> *Their sister Hela and the race of Giants.*

> " '*Standing in Asgard's Gate, Heimdall sees them,*
> *And takes the Giallar-horn to sound warning,*
> *With all the Heroes, the Gods gather there,*
> *In front of Valhalla, Odin's Great Hall,*
> *To march on Vigrid Plain, to kill and die.' "*

Surtur raised his flaming sword above his head, blanketing the dark hills with light. The fur-clad giants on the black cliffs and ledges donned their armor and took up their weapons. Hard it was for Doaks to let go of his world, but soon Gundic of legend stood before Surtur. Still, he had a question.

"Master." He stared about himself in wonder, the familiar cliffs and rivers bringing him home once more, the gleaming white bridge beyond, beckoning. "Surtur, what has been done to us? We are the heroes slain in battle, the Einheriar, taken from the field of battle by the Valkyries to come to sit at the All-father's table in the Great Hall. We have always been there to fight the giants. How do we find ourselves on this side of Bifrost?"

Surtur reached out and touched Gundic's hand with his index finger. "See this, now, Gundic. Hear me now, Doaks. We are broken heroes. We have had the battle lust broken from us. Now we are the giants." He turned to the ocean of upraised faces. "Valhalla is across the bridge and now we are the giants!" More quietly, he added, "And now comes the dusk."

He saw his midnight-black steed pawing the air in anticipation of battle. Beyond the great animal was the universe of darkness, at the edge of which was Bifrost, the sparkling white bridge that spanned the night sky. At the other end of the bridge, beyond the Vigrid Plain, the Great Hall.

As he mounted the black stallion, a roar came from behind him. Surtur turned and beyond his army of giants were the Great Wolf and the Midgard Serpent.

He raised the fiery Sword of Victory and called to them, "Sons of Muspell, brothers of Darkness, bite down hard upon your histories and follow this flame! Our enemy is war itself!"

There was a hand that held his reins and it was not his own. Surtur looked down and saw Gundic-Doaks holding his steed. "Speak! What is it?"

"Surtur, what if this is all another illusion? We were in a madhouse—mental hospitals, weren't we? Aren't we? What if we are mad?"

The sentinel of darkness placed his hand upon his

comrade's. "If we are sane, we are spirits of war used and abused each time a king, a general, or a frightened soldier invokes us, again and again, through time, through the universe, until the end of forever. If we are sane, we deserve to be insane."

"But to cross the bridge, Surtur! To war with the Einheriar! What if none of this is real? What if we are mad? What if this is a hospital and—"

"What can they do, Doaks," interrupted Surtur. "Shoot us again? Burn us again? Crush us again? Starve, slash, and disintegrate us again?" There was a sound and Surtur held up his hand. "Listen!"

The sound of a great horn filled the universe. "The gods have been warned. The heroes will be gathering upon the plain. This," Surtur carved an arc in the heavens with his sword of fire, "This is the last great battle! This is Ragnarok!"

As Heimdall blew the Giallar horn to warn the gods of the giants' coming, the Einheriar put down their meat and drink, took up their weapons, and sang the call to war as they went down to the plain to fight one last time.

As the last of the giants crossed it, the Bifrost Bridge crumbled into a dust of diamonds. The Wolf and the Serpent tore into the gods and heroes as Surtur used his sword to clear the way to the Great Hall. As he approached, his steed's legs drenched in the blood of heroes, the greatest of the doors opened. Standing there was Great Odin, the one-eyed, clad in his sky helmet and his sky cloak, deepest blue spotted with clouds. From behind him came the smells, the sounds, of the Great Hall. As they pulled at Surtur's heart, the sentinel of darkness took the Sword of Victory and thrust it through the heart of his lord and god.

—surrounding them there was no Great Hall, no Vigrid Plain, no giants, no pig, no mead. All was suspended in a dimension of eternal liquid movement. Doaks . . . Gundic was little more than a warp in a rising bubble of blue. The others, specks of light swirling around a tiny creature, smaller than any of the specks who were the giants. The creature's head had a single eye below a thin mouth. Its head was supported by a tiny neck attached to a writhing mass of hair-thin tentacles. A pink ooze drained from the center of the mass.

"He is so small," said Gundic.

The eye looked in Surtur's direction. And now Jere recognized the look in Frazier's eyes. "Father, we are all here."

The eye looked through and beyond the battle souls who hovered there. "All of my children," it said and its eye looked upon Surtur. "Why, my son? Why have you lost your heart?"

"We haven't lost our hearts, Father," whispered Surtur as the life force left the ancient creature. "We grew up."

The lights, the universe of heroes slain in battle, looked in Surtur's direction. "We are the gods of war, now," he said looking at the universe of universes. "Find your homes. All of you, find your homes and tell your comrades that war is over."

As the tiny lights flew into myriad directions, Surtur stayed for a moment, wept by the All-father's side, and vanished.

"This one is dead, under-commander." The rain in No-name Valley only seemed to grow colder. Too weary to fly, Nathsi, the Sydak squad leader, pulled himself over to the side of the human corpse by his wing hooks. The human corpse was missing its face, the front of its chest, and its legs. Ki, the pulse gunner, turned away and prepared to cocoon in the relative dryness beneath a tree. Nathsi almost ordered the gunner to stop, but he didn't. Gunner Ki was close to cracking. Black pulse is supposed to be clean, quiet. The enemy is there, then the enemy is not there. But the human had made gurgling and crying sounds for moments—forever, it seemed. And then it was done. He died. The war. It was over, for now.

Margat slung his weapon between his wings and glanced at his leader. "On the edge of a pulse, Nathsi. What a terrible way to die. And just moments before the truce." He held out his hand. "Here. It's the creature's identity chip."

Nathsi took the blackened chip, rubbed the thin film of blood-ash from the tiny screen and read: Jere Suiter, his rank, and his service number. In the under-commander's pouch he already carried the identity chips for the others in the human's unit who had died; four of his own soldiers, as well. Stupid of their squad leader to run his squad down this trail. Before Ki fired the pulse into them, the human called Snake was driving them down, urging them on, dying gloriously much more important than living intelligently, it appeared. He hung his head for a moment, for he had once been much the same.

"To be the last one to die in a war," said Margat, "what a terrible thing."

"Perhaps," answered the under-commander. "Perhaps not, if war dies with you."

"Is that possible, Nathsi?"

Nathsi programmed a graves beacon with Jere Suiter's ID chip, set it beside the human's remains, instructed his soldiers to gather up Gunner Ki's cocoon, and began the long trek out of *Luvak-ah*.

FAITH ON ICE

by James H. Cobb

A lifetime resident of the Pacific Northwest, James H. Cobb is the author of both the Amanda Garrett techno-thrillers (*Choosers of the Slain, Sea Strike, Sea Fighter,* and *Target Lock*) as well as the Kevin Pulaski suspense mystery series (*West on 66*). When not writing or re-searching his next book, he is a dedicated Route 66 "Road Warrior," and can usually be found somewhere on the two lane highway, collecting the legends and lore of both the Mother Road and of the classic American hot rod.

"THE Fall of Presidente Marisole Valdega of the *Federacion Economico Del Sud* might be upheld as an example of what was once called the 'Peter Principle,' the promotion of a formerly successful individual to a level of authority above their capacity to succeed.

"Ms. Valdega, who had been a dynamic and effective Minister of Interior Affaires under Presidente Juan Morisco, was elected to the *Federacion* presidency in 2080. In the term and a half that followed, she not only erased the bulk of the impressive gains made by the prior administration but came close to shattering the entire *Federacion* itself.

"Her reversion to a rapid trade protectionism not only drained the life from the South American economic rebirth, but set her at odds with every other major economic alliance on the planet. So did her jingoistic insistence on *Federacion* parity in orbital weapons systems. The final blow fell when she pursued the lost dream of Antonio Sparza, seeking Antarctic natural resources and *Lebensraum* in the second South Polar Confrontation.

"The *Federacion*'s abrogation of the Antarctic Treaty and its deployment of military units within the South American polar territories precipitated an explosive reaction on the part of the global community. Condemnation was universal and trade embargoes slammed down. The North Atlantic Free Trade Alliance, deputized to act by the UN General Assembly, deployed counterforces into the region and a literal game of 'freeze out' began.

"On the night of April 19, 2086, with the *Federacion*'s economy and her own personality cult in ruins, Marisole Valdega made her last and greatest poor decision."

"We Called Them Newsbytes"
The Memoirs of the Last AnchorWoman
Valerie McKinley/Athena
Lunar Com/CyberMedia, Dawn City 2201

45 Kilometers South (Antarctic Navigational Grid Reference) of the Ellsworth Mountains
2207 Hours, Greenwich Meridian Time; April 19, 2086

I guess as wars go this is kind of a pretty one.

My copilot Buck and I hovered our skim up behind the nunatak we were using for cover. Extending our sensor masts over the crest, we took a long good snoop and scan before pulling our next sprint.

We had clear skies and little wind. Very not standard for Antarctic plateau country. We had to be under a transitory hole in the perpetual polar superstorm that's been going on down here since the last ice age. This was good in a way. I could actually see through the cockpit canopy and eyeball vision, even night-bite enhanced eyeball vision, is a refresh from operating under full Virtual Reality.

It was also an awful lot bad, though. If we could see, so could the Feds.

The Sentinel Range of the Ellsworths was off along the northern horizon. Scoured bare of glacier cover by a couple of thousand years of hurricane winds, their ridges glowed steel blue under the starlight, while the ice on the flats before them was a sheening blue gray. And the stars, Lord and Lady, you have never seen such stars, so clear and bright it hurt your eyes to look up at them.

There was a lot else going on up in the sky, too. A wispy green-and-gold aurora wavered like a torn curtain beyond the Sentinels, providing a backdrop for the biggest fireworks display in history.

A couple of hours ago, the *Federacion*'s Madball Mary had started the orbit wars.

The intels figured that she'd planned on risking just a sniff of space-based weaponry, just enough to wipe out our polar bases. Then she was going to jump back and say she didn't mean it. It didn't fly. NAFTA's Strategic Space Command had been waiting for her. Now the *Federacion*'s orbital assets were being peeled out of near-Earth space, right down to the last weather eye, science platform, and commo relay.

Battle sats, K bombers, and sky forts were slugging it out up there, and hardware worth a couple of trillion of any monetary unit you care to choose was raining back to Earth in a dazzling man-made meteor shower. Every few seconds a new fire trail arced across the heavens.

"Fantastic," Buck commented. "You ought to see all the different colors under the multispectrum scan."

"I can guess."

I'll affirm it was an overload of pretty. The only thing was that some of those burning things falling out of the sky had people in them.

Off to the northwest, something hit atmosphere and began to curve down in an incandescent parabola too clean to be just another piece of space junk. Just as it reached the zenith, another glowing streak, this one die-straight and instantaneous, lanced from over the eastern horizon. It intercepted the first, and a baby sun flared in the heavens, making the ice glow orange for an instant. A reentering metastate warhead, a big one, had just been ripped by one of the Polecat Base's point defense HEL beams.

More good-bad. This demonstrated that Polecat Base, formerly the Scott/Amunsen South Polar Science Complex, was intact and in the fight. Buck and I still had somewhere to go home to. Good.

The bad was a reminder that we had yet to achieve space supremacy. The Feds still had operational weapons overhead. While that state of affairs continued, we groundies were nothing but a bunch of cockroaches being hunted by a guy packing a sledgehammer.

"Buck, try and pull up Polecat. See if we have clearlink yet?"

I slouched in the skim's pilot seat as Buck diddled with the communications, praying that we'd still have crud on all channels. It was scary out here, but I didn't want that direct recall order I wouldn't be able to ignore.

". . . at . . . . uni . . . enemy act . . . .
reform . . . . 267th . . . . co ord . . . . . .
olecat repeat . . . unit . . . break . . . .
Refor . . . . acknowledge . . ."

We had an aurora and even nowadays that means bad commo on the ice. And tonight, between the sat nets being chewed up and a crap bag full of high intensity miljamming going on, things were still beautifully shagged up.

"Buck, you hear anything addressed specifically to Teal Ace?"

"I don't discern our specific call sign in that particular transmission," my copilot replied cautiously.

"Then you agree nobody's given us a mission diversion yet?"

"Don't try to push this off on me, Lars. The regs say the decision making is all on your side of the loop."

"I'm glad we agree. We're staying after 'em. Do we have anything new?"

"We have one point five seconds of crisis beacon and a hit scream from Sanda bearing grid reference northwest and that, brother, is all we have."

"That's good enough. Kick it."

When you're out looking for friends lost in the Big Cold, you go with what you got.

For the twenty hours prior to the Fed attack, Job Clarendon and I, along with our copilots, had been sprinting and spooking along the Teal Check Line, supplementing our robot sensor pickets. The Teal Line is NAFTA's forwardmost patrol station, covering the passes that lead up to the Hollick-Kenyon Plateau from the *Federacion*'s Antarctic Peninsula territories.

Some of our squadron humorists also refer to it as "chopping block station" because of what was likely going to happen to anyone on it when the shagging and fragging started.

Well the F and S had started, and my patrol mate must have been about the first NAFTA groundie to have the sky fall on him.

Job was a good guy, a Brit contingenter, from somewhere called Yorkshire. He had a funny kind of

accent that his copilot Sanda was always aping for
the humor quotient. I was Teal Ace and he was Teal
Deuce and we were partners. I mean we're not blood
brothers or he mates or anything, but for the past six
months we'd worked, sworn at the weather, and
gone ice crazy together and maybe split a few up-
sides along the way.

He and Sanda were *team*, like Buck, you know?
You don't lurch on your teamies and you don't leave
them out on the ice to die. Not while there might be
a chance.

Buck and I bobbed over the hogback of the nunatak and accelerated hard for the next patch of terrain cover.

We were running the Hawker/McDonnell AGE-
16C Tactical Ground Effects skimmers on the Teal
Line. Skims are one of the rigs that popped up to
replace warplanes after HEL beams made combat
flying a real bad idea.

To survive around High Energy Lasers you have
two options. You either fly real high, i.e., orbital, so
you have enough atmosphere between you and the
bad guys for thermal bloom to kill the beam, or you
stay real, real low, so you can duck, dodge, and hide
behind things, breaking the line of sight and fire.
Skims are good at this latter tactic.

Technically, the Hawker McDonnell is a Wing-in-
Ground-Effect aircraft, a twenty-two-meter-long
arrowhead of armor-composite. Its single, large central lift fan produces a bubble of high-pressure air
that's held trapped under its down-angled delta
wings. The skim rides atop this ground effects bubble, half airplane and half hovercraft.

You can pull better than six hundred K topped out
in a combat skim, but you're never more than fifty
meters off the deck when you're doing it and mostly
you're a lot less. Even with your autoterrain avoid-

ance up, it's very brisk living, but it does keep you breathing. At least until the orbitals get taken out of the box and they start dropping crowbars on you.

That's why you sprint and stealth. You ground or hover only in broken terrain and you cross open ground only at absolute max accel and with lots of randomized jinks and jags thrown in. Maybe you can throw off the space-based targeting systems, and if not, maybe you can get out from under the KAT swarms or warhead scatter pattern after the drop is committed.

Maybe.

Just before the Feds had committed to their strike, Job and I had been out on either end of our patrol sweep. Buck and I, as Teal Ace, were to the south by Antarctic navigation grid reckoning, down on Pine Island glacier while Job and Sanda as Teal Deuce were to the north up here at the Sentinels. Sanda had reported a sensor abnormality at her extreme range and Job had said they were going to investigate just before the ceiling had fallen in.

We heard Sanda scream, and then our commo link with them had gone down.

Perdition! All of our links to everybody had gone down and then the sky had lit up.

After we found that we couldn't get through to Polecat base or to squadron control, Buck and I set out to do the only constructive things we could think of: A, find Job and Sanda and B, find out what was going on in the northern sector. Now, two hours later, we were closing with Teal Deuce's last known waypoint.

As the ice blurred away under the skim's chisel-shaped nose, I let Buck handle the controls while I set myself up for possible action. Unzipping the forearm of my environmental suit, I peeled off the transdermal sustain patch I'd been wearing. It was the green standard patch, good with nutrients and anti-fatigues for a twenty-four-hour continual operating period. Just in case, though, I was going up to the yellow heavy operations patch. Along with a normal water intake, this would give me another forty-eight hours of stay awake and alert at the penalty of a bad hangover afterward. If things really got bad, I could go up to the red crisis patch which would be good for another hundred and fifty hours but would also require about the same amount of time in hell and hospital to recover.

Nobody likes going red patch.

I was just resealing my sleeve when things zoned on us. We came zooming up on an ice ridge, just a little buckle in the ice cover, and Buck, who's a Lord's awful showoff at heart, elected to ski jump it. He blipped the lift fans just as we reached the foot of the slope and we soared over the ridge, just for a second of honest flight.

"CRAB!" Buck screamed and turned us inside out.

At least that's what it felt like. He translated us around a full hundred and eighty degrees in midair, nosed down, fired bursts both from the chin and spine turrets as well as from the hypervel rocket pods, reoriented back to our line of advance and caught us on our air cushion again, all within one second flat. My eyeballs almost bounced off the inside of my helmet bowl.

"Lord and Lady, Buck!"

"Sorry, brother," he apologized. "We had a Crab laying doggo behind that ice ridge. We went right over the top of it."

I visioned the rear scanners and saw only a steaming crater falling away behind us. When Buck kills something, he likes to kill it extremely dead.

In the vernacular, a "Crab" is a *Federacion* ENGESA/AVIBRAS *Lancero* strike/recon rover. Essentially a cheap, dumb robot gun platform, with just enough AI to be marginally self-deployable on simple missions. If you stumble across a Crab, it issues a shrill scream of electronic delight and charges you, pinking away with its 30mm ELF mount. It's a nuisance rather than a real threat, but it gives away your position and you still have to kill it before it kills you, expending time and ammo.

There's another thing about Crabs. There's never just one of them. You find flocks of them scurrying around the flanks of larger and more sophisticated *Federacion* elements.

What did you find out here, Job?

"Buck, did that Crab get a chance to yell?"

"Of course he did. But with the gooey commo, I can't say if anybody heard him. Orders?"

"Stand on, but max the sensors."

"Doing it."

As we closed with the Sentinal Range, the ice grew more broken and buckled, the pressure ridges rippling away under us like waves on a pond. This country would have been pure hell for the old-timers with their dogsleds and Caterpillar tractors, for us it only put a mellow bounce in our ride. Buck was keeping us trimmed down tight on our cushion, lateral thrusting around the higher ice stacks and keeping the ice spikes flickering past barely a meter under our belly. I was used to it, but it's still kind of puckery at three hundred plus KPH.

How much did we owe Job and Sanda? The Feds were up to something out here. They had to be and Teal Deuce patrol had sniffed it and had got snuffed for it. Ipso facto, we were heading into that same something. Buck is no faster than Sanda and I'm no smarter than Job so the odds were that whatever happened to them was also due to happen to us, and at any second. The smart thing would be to break away and come back later with friends.

Lord, why is it so hard to be smart sometimes?

Okay, we were already beyond the approved check line of the patrol. Job and Sanda had to be close or they were nowhere. I elected to give them another thirty seconds on this bearing, then Buck and I would reverse out. Twenty . . . fifteen . . . ten . . . We found them.

I was thrown into the seat harness as Buck lifted the skim's nose and braked back hard with the bow thrusters and the main lift fan. The nose dropped as velocity zeroed and we bounced into hover.

"Ah, shag it all entirely, Buck!"

"Yeah," he replied awed, "the fraggin' Feds didn't drop crowbars on 'em, they dumped fence posts!"

Almost an entire square kilometer of polar glacier looked as if it had been run through a giant party ice crusher. There wasn't a single block larger than a meter square on a side. And about twenty meters out into the devastation, the crumpled aft thruster assembly of a skim protruded above the stark jumble, looking like a skewed gravestone.

Only space ordnance can make this kind of a mess. Job and Sanda had been nailed from orbit by a *Federacion* K bomber or a KATsat, a Kinetic Attack satellite.

It takes a Lord's worth of energy to move a kilogram of mass from the Earth's surface to Earth orbit against the planet's gravity pull. If that kilogram of mass falls back down Earth's gravity well from orbit to the surface, all that energy comes back. An aerospace plane or bulk hauler barge bleeds this energy off by atmospheric deceleration, the kinetic energy inherent in the mass is converted to thermal energy through friction with the air. That's why spacecraft glow white hot during reentry and why they need heat shielding.

Orbital kinetic attack projectiles, on the other hand, are designed not to decelerate during reentry. They punch through atmo like a needle through gelatin, hitting the bottom of the well still carrying most of their energy load.

A standard tactical K-kill dart, or a "crowbar" as we call them, will strike the Earth's surface traveling at about eight kilometers a second. This gives it as much energy potential as about two hundred kilograms of old style TNT. On impact, *all* of that kinetic energy is converted to thermal form *instantly*.

Or in other words, KABOOM!

A crowbar will punch right through fifteen meters of solid steel reinforced concrete or just about any other physical structure you can name. "Fence posts," intermediate kinetic strike projectiles, are the next step up, weighing about a hundred kilograms each, and we don't even want to talk about "telephone poles."

The Feds had been serious about killing Teal Deuce. They'd used a swarm of fence posts. When the K rounds hit atmosphere, Job and Sanda must have been doing a sprint across the flats. When Sanda caught the ionization flare on her sensors, she must have braked hard in the couple of seconds she had, trying to force the swarm to overshoot. She almost made it—but not quite. A couple of megatons of ice must have been blown into the air right in front of them. She and Job must have slid right under the airborne avalanche that followed, and they'd been buried alive.

"Buck! Full sensor! Is there anything in there?"

He snapped the sensor masts out to full extension. "Scanning . . . scanning . . . can't tell . . . scanning . . . Maybe, very hard to say. There are waste heat leaks . . . There's a trace modulation . . . Maybe it's Sanda, maybe just dying board. I can't call it. This requires a command pilot decision."

"Right," I snapped. "Stealth and ground. I'm going out there."

"Remember the Crab, brother. We got Feds in the neighborhood."

"Frag the Fraggin' Feds! Stealth and ground!"

"Doing it."

We whumped down on our landing jacks and the bottom dropped out of the cockpit as the pilot's seat lowered on its rails to ground level. I popped the decouple pad and my environment suit's locks and connectors disengaged from the seat back. As my suit came under independent power, I heard the heater element relays close; click . . . click . . . click . . . click. It was cold out here! Like maybe eighty degrees below zero Fahrenheit, and that's still air!

I had about ten paces of smooth surface to run across, then it was all crawl and scramble over jagged and tumbled ice. Behind me, the skim hunkered down on the edge of the impact area. Buck used the variable hull camouflage system to merge us into the terrain as much as possible and kept the lift fan moaning softly on auxiliary power, trying to keep our thermal signature dispersed. If he could figure out a way to sweat, he'd probably be doing that, too.

After about a century, I rested a hand on the crumpled rear armor of Teal Deuce. In the flickering auroral glow, I could make out that the skim had flipped onto its back and had angled in at about fifty degrees. That would put the cockpit about twenty-twenty five meters under the ice. There wasn't anything more to see . . . except maybe for a black gap under the skim's spine, a space where the fuselage was holding up the ice like a roof.

I lifted the bottom edge of my helmet bowl visor and yelled down into the darkness. "Job! Can you hear me? It's Larson, we're here to get you out! Talk to me, brother!"

I couldn't hear anything except the thin piping of the plateau winds and the moan of Teal Ace's idling fan. After a few seconds, as my lips started to frost burn, I had to slam the visor shut again. Lord, but it was cold!

It would be colder down there under all that ice. It was going to be a tight fit in an environment suit, but I squatted down and shoved my legs into the hole.

"Hey, Lars, that's not a good idea!"

"I know it, Buck."

"Lars, if something goes wrong, I can't get to you! I can't get you out!"

"It's okay, Buck. I know you can't. If I get hung up or drop out of the loop, return to base and report. That's an order! Until then, maintain overwatch. I'll make this as fast as I can."

I wonder if this is what being swallowed alive feels like?

I wormed my way down into the black between the fuselage and the ice, feeling my way with my boots. I halfway hoped I'd come on a dead end so I'd have an excuse to quit and get out of there. But there was always a little more space, a little darker, a little more claustrophobic. A little tighter to squeeze into, a little harder to get out of and all the light in the universe came from that little handful of stars in the mouth of the gap.

I'd just worked my way past what had been the ring mount for the spine turret when Buck whispered in my earphones. "Lars, we got trouble plus. Double trouble plus!"

He sounded scared, and when he exhibits like that, you had better pay attention.

"What's hitting?"

"Ground traffic on the sensors. A lot of ground traffic moving fast, east-southeast along the foot of the Sentinels. Twenty-K range. It's got to the be Feds! Assessing now!"

"Stay on it and report." As I already wanted out

of that hole in the worst way possible, Buck's words didn't have all that much immediate effect. Job and Sanda had seen something, probably a *Federacion* advanced ground scout and we'd got here just in time for the big show.

I writhed down another meter. Why not? We were probably dead anyway.

"Lars," Buck's voice was deadpan emotionless now. "We got long-range artillery hogs, metastate tactical missiles, rail guns, the works. A whole regiment with heavy warbot escort. Heading confirmed east-southeast at 120 KPH."

All of a sudden I felt tired. Yellow patch or not, I was so tired I had to let my helmet bowl clunk against the ice. Shag it entirely, we were going to be dead, me, Job, Buck, Sanda, all of us, and I was the one who was going to have to kill us.

It was easy to figure the Fed strategy. The check lines had been established to keep the *Federacion* far enough back so that they couldn't use ultra long-range artillery against our prime installation, Polecat base. But now, under cover of their orbital attack, they were trying to rush their long tubes into range. Polecat's point defenses would be saturated by a barrage of metastate shells and submunitions. Polecat would go down and the Feds would take the strategic center of the whole continent.

We couldn't let it happen of course. This was why we were out here, to sound the alarm. To give our people warning. And, as with all scouts throughout military history, the warning was the important thing, not the survival of the scout.

"Buck, transmit an immediate sighting report in clear on all channels and follow it with real-time targeting data for whoever might be out there. Maximum power, update, and repeat for as long as possible."

"Doing it, brother. I'm arming up now. As soon as they get actives on us, I'll go to hover and start counterpunching. They'll know they've had bad times."

"Good deal, Buck. I'll finish up down here."

I might as well.

Abruptly I slid down another couple of meters, and, as I groped around, my glove closed over shattered transposit and the aft cockpit frame. I'd made it.

"Job, you hear me? Talk to me!"

Twisting onto my side, I reached into the empty space, straining, and my hand closed on another hand reaching back.

An unmoving hand, its fingers already frozen stiff in its last desperate claw for life.

"Ah, damn, Job."

I gripped the hand for a second, telling him I was sorry and that I'd see him again on the next go round. There was nothing else to do.

"You find him, brother?"

"Yeah, Buck. Dead one. Going for Sanda now."

"Better make it fast. We got trade coming."

At the other end of the tunnel I heard the skim's lift fans spool up as Buck went into combat mode. I started to writhe upward, going for the copilot's compartment aft of the cockpit.

Light glared through ice as Buck cut loose with his hypervel pods.

"Engaging! Lars get out of there!"

Maybe it was a zoned move but, perdition, I was going to get somebody out of this! I clawed at the scarred composite searching for the quick release indent.

"Sanda, can you hear me? Clear your hatch!"

Nothing. Maybe she was dead, too. Or maybe she was scavenging in the cold with everything shut down to absolute minimums to preserve her battery power.

Topside an explosion roared, then a second, Buck raved back with the skim's turrets. Ice shuddered and a trickle of frost crystals showered over my helmet bowl. After a forever of fumbling, I found the manual indent and the hatch seals parted. I wrestled the slab of armor down and groped inside for the T grip lever of the primary decouple.

WHAM! That one hit close. For a hideous instant I felt the ice close around me squeezing. Then it fell away again and my hands closed around Sanda.

"Buck, I got her!"

"Then get out of there," he screamed back. "I'm losing!"

I climbed! Lord and Lady and every step of the Dance but I climbed! Getting past the jagged edges of the spine ring I tore the environment suit. That's supposed to be impossible, but I managed it. I didn't even feel the cold. I don't even know how I managed to climb lugging Sanda the way I was.

I emerged from one kind of hell into another. The ice was burning, waves of incoming fire converging on us from half a dozen different points. Buck had the skim airborne, dodging and weaving and expending ammo at virulent rate to maintain a point defense against the incoming shells and missiles.

The second he spotted me, he lunged, literally scooping me into the extended pilot's chair. Without waiting for me to reconnect, he slurped me, Sanda, and about a hundred kilos of flying snow and ice up into the cockpit. Spinning around, he blasted off at max acceleration burning the throats out of the skim's thrusters.

Out of position, the acceleration jammed me across the seat. But in the rear screens fire waves were overtaking us.

"Buck?"

"I'm sorry, Lars" he replied softly. "We aren't going to make it. Magazines are almost empty. Point defense failure in ten seconds."

"Yeah, well, we tried, Buck. Thanks for staying, brother."

"It's what we do, brother. See you next go round."

And then the Lord and the Lady spoke over the land.

A hundred and sixty clicks up, as we later learned, Mission Commander 1st Class Cassin Torry and her copilot, Hercules, in the NAFTA Space Command Venom class K Bomber *Virgin's Revenge*, spotted action on the ice. She hadn't picked up Buck's targeting call. Given the clagged commo, nobody had, but the Feds gave away their position when they opened fire on us.

She had half a dozen pods of crowbars and fence posts aboard, meant for the Fed Naval Base on South Georgia Island, but, being slightly brilliant as well as gorgeous, talented, and saintly, she realized that the Fed artillery column was the priority and she emptied her bays.

The entire sky went as bright as white hot steel as several hundred kinetic attack projectiles hit air, and that air, Lord, how to describe the way it rang as the swarms descended!

Then the shock waves hit us, both from the impacts and from the Feds metastate magazines going up, and Buck almost lost it in a nose-for-tail tumble.

When he got us restabilized, there was nothing to be seen behind us except for a titanic mushroom cloud of steam silhouetted against the aurora.

I let Buck drive on the way back to Polecat base.

Cradling Sanda in my lap, I jacked a couple of leads into her auxiliary ports, giving her access to the skim's power and sensor nets. Her casing wasn't cracked and her check lights were on, indicating that there should have been enough power left in her internal emergency cells to keep her personality matrix from collapsing.

"Hey, Sanda, you in there?"

"Larson? Is that you?"

Whoever set up her basal programming had given her a real pretty voice and she has kind of a wistful little identity to go with it. I hope that whoever gets her next will appreciate her.

"Yeah, little pretty, it's me. Buck and I have you. We're going home."

"Situation update please?"

"I guess we just won the war."

"And Job?"

"He didn't make it, Sanda. We lost him."

She was quiet for a long time. "I'm sorry," she whispered finally.

I patted the gray metal case. "It's okay, little pretty. It wasn't anybody's fault. It's just the way it played."

The cyberphriques who developed the copilots say that they made these portable Artificial Intelligences mimic human behavior and emotional responses to smooth out the Human/Machine interface. They only seem to have self-awareness and individualized personalities, they aren't really people. We warriors who live and die with them wonder sometimes, though.

Either way, we'd kept the faith with Sanda and with Job. I guess that's about all you ever can do in a war. That and to hope that someday it will make some kind of a difference.

I peeled the yellow patch off my forearm. Closing my eyes, I rested my head against the seat back.

SPARKS IN A COLD WAR

by Kristine Kathryn Rusch

Kristine Kathryn Rusch is an award-winning fiction writer. Her novella, *The Gallery of His Dreams*, won the *Locus* Award for best short fiction. Her body of fiction work won her the John W. Campbell Award, given in 1991 in Europe. She has been nominated for several dozen fiction awards, and her short work has been reprinted in six *Year's Best* collections. She has published twenty novels under her own name. She has sold forty-one in total, including pseudonymous books. Her novels have been published in fourteen languages, and have spent several weeks on the *USA Today* bestseller list and *The Wall Street Journal* Bestseller list. She has written a number of *Star Trek* novels with her husband, Dean Wesley Smith, including a book in the crossover series called *New Earth*. She is the former editor of the prestigious *The Magazine of Fantasy and Science Fiction*, winning a Hugo for her work there. Before that, she and Dean Wesley Smith started and ran Pulphouse Publishing, a science fiction and mystery press in Eugene, Oregon. She lives and works on the Oregon coast.

THREE Earth hours later, they sat on the styro-platform in the center of camp, pretending that nothing happened. They were lithe, thin, and strong, reedy in the way that athletic women were, and not nearly as brittle as they looked.

Bryer turned on the perimeter, then punched a button which raised the UV roof. He had a lot of work ahead of him, not the least of it protection against the Cuiesto. And if the Alliance heard what happened this afternoon, they would make sure he never worked again.

"No roof, Bryer." Audra straightened her long legs and leaned her bronze face toward the blazing sun. "I'd like to experience the elements."

"You've been experiencing the elements all day." Liv walked toward the semipermanent canopy stretched between the three main tents. "I think we've had enough of experience."

It was the first reference to the day's events, and the first quiet dig.

"I don't care if we're protected or not," said Keely. She was the smallest of the three and, Bryer had noted, the strongest. "All I want is a beer."

Bryer had been with these three long enough to recognize that statement as a command. He ignored it.

The perimeter wasn't going to keep them safe for long. It would hide their presence and, with the roof up, make it impossible to fire a weapon at them. But it also blinded them. An ambush could be set up outside—gliders floating above the cutgrass, perhaps, or something more sinister—and he wouldn't know until it was too late.

"I thought we weren't going to drink until the sun set," Audra said.

Keely's face flushed. "I thought we weren't going to bitch about anything."

"Too late," Audra said. "Liv already started."

The roof finished closing with a loud click. Keely jumped as if someone had shot at her. Liv gazed upward.

Audra sat up. Her dark eyes met Bryer's. "I said no roof."

"Yes, you did." He crossed his arms. "And I said no shooting without my permission."

She shook her head. Her red hair, wrapped in braids around her skull, made her look as if she were wearing a helmet. "You're as bad as the others."

"No," he said. "I'm worse. I'm the one who has to save our asses."

"You make it sound like I committed a crime."

"You did." Keely got out of her chair and walked toward the cook camp. He heard the portable refrigerator beep as it dispensed her beer.

"We're all committing a crime," Audra said, leaning back and closing her eyes. "That's part of what we're paying you for."

Technically, she was right. Extreme Safaris took their clients to unsanctioned or dangerous worlds, trips that could result in serious fines or, in Bryer's case, the loss of his ship's clearance for those areas. So far, Bryer had managed to avoid the fines simply by having his clients sign a document that said they had insisted on a trip to the unsanctioned area. He had never had his clearance removed, but he figured it wouldn't be a serious problem. He could always charter another ship.

"You shot a sentient being," he said. "You didn't pay for that right."

"Oh?" She tilted her head toward him. "Is there a higher fee for that?"

He didn't trust himself to answer her. He could barely restrain himself from crossing the styroplatform and wringing her neck.

"Audra, enough." Keely squeezed her beer. The cap levitated off and deposited itself in the recycler. "Mr. Bryer is doing his best."

"If he were doing his best," Audra said, "he would have let me take my trophy."

"Your trophy would have been the head of someone's child." His fists squeezed tight, but he held them at his sides.

"Everything we kill is someone's child. And sometimes, sentient or not, those creatures miss that child." Audra stood up, dusted off her light, crease-free shorts, and headed toward the refrigerator. "You're being a hypocrite, Mr. Bryer."

She passed him as she said that and gazed into his eyes, challenging him.

"As I said before this trip started, there is game and there are natives. We don't hunt the natives." He wasn't sure why he was arguing with her. Probably because it was preferable to killing her.

"Kind of makes you guilty of false advertising, doesn't it?" Audra bent down, grabbed a can of white wine, and pulled it out of the refrigerator. She squeezed the can, and the cork popped, pausing before her so she could inspect it before it got recycled. "After all, the word 'extreme' implies something out of the norm."

"My company doesn't sanction murder," he snapped.

"Really?" she asked. "Is that what you think happened this afternoon?"

She had an odd look on her face and he suddenly felt uncertain. He had thought the afternoon's events had been an accident, but he had never been able to get a clear read on her.

She and her two partners had approached him, as all of his clients did, and they had paid his exorbitant fee like everyone else. He never knew who his clients were. As long as they could pay and abide by his rules, they could go on his safaris.

He hadn't regretted that rule until this trip.

These women, though, seemed uninterested in the various places he had taken them and he had sensed no thrill at the hunt. He had thought it was because he failed them, failed to bring them game that challenged them.

But something in her gaze made him wonder if he had been wrong. If that afternoon, something had happened he hadn't entirely understood.

* * *

They had used glider cars with their screens down to reach the Range, a wide-open section of grassland and youngling trees where gracela could be found. Gracela had several features that made them perfect for a safari geared to humans.

First, the gracela were hard to find. They were scattered throughout the Range, but their mottled coats blended with the browns and greens of the landscape. They were among the fastest creatures in Alliance-controlled space. When spooked, a gracela could hit speeds of over a hundred-and-fifty kilometers an hour. And they were ferocious if cornered. He'd seen a gracela turn on a hunter, and shred the man's skin off his bones using only teeth and hooves.

But most important of all, the gracela were elegant creatures. Long snouts, wide dark eyes, angular ears that gave the face a beauty not found in the game in this far sector of the galaxy. Hunters who liked to follow the ancient tradition of hanging the head as a trophy would have something beautiful for the wall. The other hunters, who didn't have such barbaric instincts, usually had still holos made of themselves with the carcass. A stunning kill was always more impressive than a big ugly one.

He'd brought the three women to this part of Mgasin almost in despair. They were the best hunters he'd ever traveled with, taking down game as difficult as the nazon and the guyn with barely any work at all. Audra kept pushing him for a challenge, and finally he thought of the gracela—fast, beautiful, and vicious—rather like the women themselves.

But they'd killed two thirds of their quota of gracela in less than an Earth hour and it was only on the trip back that they had run into the young Cuiesto.

That was when everything changed.

*   *   *

Audra was watching Bryer. She leaned against one of the support columns, its cheap plastic distorting her reflection.

"We wanted a challenge," she said softly. "You couldn't provide one. So I had to do the work myself."

He stared at her. She had known exactly what she had been doing. Somehow that made everything worse.

It took only a second for that thought to pass through his mind, for his hand to find her throat and pull her toward him. Her expression didn't change—or perhaps it did, filled with amusement at his reaction.

He squeezed like she had squeezed the wine can, and part of him wondered if her head would float toward the recycling bin like the cork had.

Keely grabbed his arm, her small fingers warm against his skin. "Let her go."

He continued to squeeze, watching little bloodshot lines forming in Audra's eyes. Her face was turning an unbecoming shade of red.

"Let her go," Keely said again, then she reached around his side, grabbing for the stunner.

He caught her with his free hand. He held both women for just a moment, to see if Liv would come to their aid. Liv watched from the other side of the styroplatform.

She didn't move.

Bryer let Audra go. To his immense satisfaction, she staggered backward and coughed, putting a hand—involuntarily, he guessed—to her throat.

"You little fool," he said. "You didn't make this challenging for you. You made it challenging for me. I'm the one who has to get us out of here."

She smiled at him, still hunched over, her fingers

playing with her neck. His hand left a red mark there that was beginning to bruise.

"Then maybe you should pay us," she said, her voice hoarse.

He cursed and lunged toward her, but Keely held him in place.

"Stop it, Audra. Stop baiting him now. We need him."

Audra stood slowly, her face filled with hatred. He wondered how he ever thought her beautiful. "We don't need him. We can manage without him better than we'll managed with him."

"Fine," he said and twisted himself free from Keely's grasp. He strode toward the organizational tent, reached toward the easy access controls and shut off the perimeter.

Around him, the cutgrass spread like an ancient lake, the sharp blades glittering in the sun. The very edges of the grass pushed up against the Range, outlined like waves against a beach.

He had just revealed their presence to the Cuiesto, and a large part of him no longer cared. He nodded mockingly at Audra.

From inside the tent, his assistant cried out a warning. Nendre must have realized the perimeter was off. Bryer heard the slither of tentacles and knew that Nendre would soon join him.

"I thought you were going to leave," Bryer said.

Audra laughed. "Why should I? Things are about to get very interesting."

He walked toward Audra. She smiled at him, and let her hand drop away from her neck.

"I figured you'd want to play," she said. "This makes everything so much better. We're not hiding here. We become visible, we let them come to us, and then we act. I suggest we take down the camp, go as far as we can, see if we make it before the Cuiesto find us—"

He grabbed her arms. She let out a small startled shriek, which surprised him. He didn't think anything made her cry out. Then he shoved her backward, so that she fell off the styroplatform and into the cutgrass.

Keely screamed. Liv continued to watch. Nendre had come out of the organization tent and was unfurling a tentacle so that he could reach Audra.

"You stop," Bryer said.

"But, Jack, we cannot do this." Nendre's voice sounded even more mechanical than usual.

Audra struggled in the cutgrass. She was smart enough not to move much. Any movement she made would slice her skin. She had on no protection at all.

"You bastard," she shouted.

He watched from the edge of the platform. He'd shoved her hard and she'd flown at least five meters away. The clear grass was down near her. He was surprised a blade hadn't sliced through her back.

"Turn the perimeter back on," Bryer said to Nendre.

"You'll kill her," Keely cried.

He reached inside Audra's tent and found her laser rifle—the very thing she had used to kill the poor Cuiesto. He tossed it to her, making sure it landed at least a meter away, so that she couldn't pick it up and fire it at him.

"Turn on the perimeter," he said again.

Audra got up slowly. She looked toward the rifle, then to the camp. Blood dripped off her left arm.

"Regulations, Jack—"

"Regulations." Bryer covered the five steps toward the easy access controls. "We are so far outside of regulations now that this one more case won't matter. In fact, killing her might stand in our favor."

Audra used a booted foot to stomp down a section of cutgrass. She was moving across it quicker than he had expected.

Nendre hadn't moved, his hulking round frame,

tentacles coming off all sides, filling the organizational tent's doorway. "We can't do this."

Bryer had had enough of can'ts and should haves and regulations. "We can do anything we damn well please."

He reset the perimeter. With a hum, it shimmered into place, cutting off Audra's angry scream outside.

"Let her back in," Keely said.

His fingers found the rest of the controls. He set the security protocol. Now no one could touch the perimeter except him.

Keely pushed at him. "Let her back in."

He caught Keely's fingers with his own. Her eyes narrowed and she struggled, but he held her fast. She may have been the strongest of the three women, but he was stronger than anyone else here.

"Maybe I'll let her back in," he said softly, holding Keely fast. "In a few hours. By then she might understand what it feels like to be hunted."

"You have no right," Keely said, jabbing him in the stomach with her elbows.

She had knocked some of the wind from him. "I have every right," he said, letting go of her hands and stepping out of her way. "Audra gave it to me by changing the rules. Either you do things my way, or you join her in the cutgrass. And, if that happens, I promise I'll give you the challenge of getting out of here all on your own."

Keely opened her mouth as if she were going to respond and then she dove for the easy access panel. When her fingers touched it, the security system gave her a electronic jolt.

She cried out and backed away.

"Touch it again," he said, "and the jolt will be twenty times higher."

She held her fingers against her chest, staring at him like a chastized child.

"You'll do things my way," he said, not just to her, but to Liv and Nendre as well. "Or you won't get out of here alive."

Even if they listened to him, he wasn't sure any of them would get out of this place alive. Audra had put them in a terrible position.

The Cuiesto were one of Mgasin's sentient races. They were at war with another sentient race, the Viotu. The Viotu were a highly technical race who subdued the planet the way that humans had once subdued Earth. The Cuiesto were the only other group on Mgasin that had any technology at all. But they utilized it differently. They made it blend with the environment, used it to preserve or improve the life that they had always lived.

The two societies had been at war with each other for the past twenty Earth years. The war had been a cold one—no action yet, but with the possibility of total devastation. But in the past five years, threats on both sides had increased.

A lot of private companies outside of the Alliance had been monitoring the situation. A non-Alliance war meant profits for the arms and munitions industries. And then there were the terrorist factions, which looked at a hot war on a planet like Mgasin as a way of roping the Alliance into a role it didn't want—that of choosing sides.

Finally, a year ago, the Alliance decided there had been too many close calls. It decided to broker a peace. For the past nine months, the only humans allowed on Mgasin were peacekeepers and diplomats. The worry was that all other humans would confuse the issue and possibly ignite the hostilities.

A Cuiesto, murdered by a human, could do just that.

*   *   *

Bryer had elected to leave the body where it had fallen, in the thick brown grass of the Range. He was beginning to regret that decision.

If he could keep that body from being found, they all had a better chance of getting off Mgasin alive. The problem was, he didn't want to be caught with it at camp or anywhere near his equipment.

The Cuiesto, for all their show of being simple people, were anything but. They had elaborate tests for finding the slightest thing that didn't belong—scents, genetic markers, a mere sliver of skin that would reveal someone's DNA. The Cuiesto could prove, beyond a doubt, that a person had been in an area six months after he left.

Bryer was always careful when he was in Cuiesto country, but this afternoon, he probably hadn't been careful enough. And he knew that, in addition to getting out of here, he had to cover his tracks.

The first thing he had to do was destroy the evidence of the murder. He sat deep inside the organizational tent, going over the digital. Nendre, always competent, had made copies of the day's work—without viewing it, of course. Nendre had long ago stopped watching the events of a day's hunt. He found most of it repetitive and uninteresting.

Bryer took the original disk and placed it in the machine. He was about to hit delete when the image appeared before him—not a still holo at all, but moving, just as it had that afternoon.

The gracela exploded out of the brush, disappearing toward the west. Audra raced for a glider, but Bryer caught her arm.

"We don't hunt out of vehicles," he said.

"I do," she said.

He remembered the feeling he'd had then, the anger. She had signed an agreement. She understood that his safaris were a specific kind and he had his rules. He even explained them to her verbally: no hunting out of vehicles because it gave the humans an unfair advantage—it was their job to outthink their prey, not simply to outrun it; no explosive weapons that would either destroy the prey or the nearby area; no contact with the natives; and a complete agreement to abide by the bagging limits set by Extreme Safari.

"This is why you exiled the woman?" Nendre spoke from behind him.

Bryer froze the holo and turned. He hadn't heard Nendre enter the tent. Nendre's eyes had moved forward, the stalks that hid behind the eyeballs completely visible. He examined the frozen hologram from all sides.

"She did something, hey? I knew her coldness would clash with yours."

"I thought you knew," Bryer said. "This was set to play."

"I heard the fighting outside. I decided to look. That was when you shut off the perimeter." Nendre pulled his eyes back and they went back into the center of his body. He folded two tentacles before him and wrapped the end filaments together, imitating the way Bryer templed his fingers when he was thinking. "You know she will die out there."

"That would be the best thing for all of us."

Nendre raised two other tentacles in surprise. "You freely admit to committing murder? You would make us all accomplices, then. I am not certain I wish to be one."

Bryer unfroze the holo.

A Cuiesto slid out of a youngling tree and glanced in their direction. His slender six-foot height marked him as young himself. He turned toward them, the golden feathers covering his naked body glistening in the sunlight.

Bryer had thought the Cuiesto was looking directly

at him, but it seemed now that the Cuiesto was watching Audra. As if there might be recognition in his scarlet eyes.

He stretched, his tail tucking upward against his spine. His crest rose, scarlet and gold to match his eyes and feathers, and then he poised to run after the gracela.

Audra turned her rifle on him.

"This is not possible," Nendre said.

Bryer grabbed her arm, but the whir of the shot already echoed in the Range.

The yellow light of the laser was hard to see in the bright sunlight, but the results were clear: the shot left a hole in the Cuiesto's torso, and he fell forward into the brush.

Bryer snatched the rifle away from Audra, and she didn't seem to care. Instead she went to the Cuiesto, crouched over him, and grinned at them.

"He's dead," she said, removing her flaying knife. "Do I take my trophy here or wait until camp?"

Bryer froze the holo again. He couldn't look at the fight that ensued. All the markers they must have left, traces of themselves. He should have killed her there, left her, the digital, the rifle, and the Cuiesto for one of the natives to find.

But he hadn't. He had taken her back against his own better judgment, and she had been angry at him for not allowing her to take her trophy.

Nendre was staring at the woman, crouched over the Cuiesto. The Cuiesto's crest was already wilting and his colors were fading. He would be nothing but bones and feathers come morning.

"What do you plan to do with this?" Nendre asked.

"You mean the holo or the women?" Bryer asked.

"All of it."

Bryer turned to his companion. He and Nendre had gone on a hundred trips in the past ten years, most of them illegal as Audra had charged, all of them extreme. He'd taken aliens from various parts of the sector, although his main clientele was human.

Most of the hunters were fine, interested in prey, interested in a trophy or two, interested in a grand adventure that would become the center story of their lives. A few were exceptionally cruel and needed great tending.

None had ever committed a crime like this.

"I'm getting rid of the digital and all the copies," Bryer said. "Then I'll worry about the others."

Nendre studied him, four more tentacles joining the first two. "Throw the original out with the woman."

Bryer started. He hadn't expected Nendre to help him. "I think it's better to destroy it."

Nendre waved his tentacles left and right, a gesture that mimicked the shaking of a human head. He'd learned it early in his association with Bryer, and humans always appreciated it.

"The Cuiesto will already know that we are here. Even if you had not left evidence of yourself in the Range, which I am sure you have, you shut off the perimeter. That will come up on someone's monitor. Then there is the matter of Runners."

Runners were the term the Cuiesto used for their young hunters. From the Cuiesto's fifteenth to twentieth years, they hit their speed spurt. It lasted no more than five years, sometimes less, and it was the only time they could successfully hunt gracela.

"What about Runners?" Bryer asked.

Nendre let his tentacles drop. "They always work in pairs."

So time was even shorter than Bryer imagined. He kept the original as Nendre had urged him to do, but he destroyed the others. Then he began the shutdown procedure that would lead to the breakdown of camp.

He didn't like the idea of traveling in a Mgasin night, but he felt they had no choice. He had left the ship two hundred klicks from here, in a sea cave that was accessible only from the air.

If there had been a second Runner and he had gone to his people, then the Cuiesto were already looking for the hunting party. The perimeter kept them from being noticed on Cuiesto equipment but if the Cuiesto had been searching when he tossed Audra out, then they would know his position.

He couldn't take that risk.

He covered himself with weaponry—two laser pistols at his side, his laser rifle strapped against his back, and an old-fashioned hunting knife hidden in his boot. He also had over a hundred explosives, all smaller than his fingernail and powerful enough to destroy a village, tucked, along with the digital, in a pouch against his stomach.

No one was preventing him from getting out of this hellhole.

He left the organizational tent. Keely was waiting for him just outside the door, arms crossed, face fierce. "You said we could get Audra."

"Audra's dead," he said, "and if she's not, she will be soon."

"You can't just leave her here."

He stared at Keely. Was she going to be as much trouble as Audra? He had no idea how the other women felt about the afternoon's events.

"Yes," he said after a long moment. "I can just leave her here."

"I won't let you."

He made sure his smile was cold. "You can stay here with her if you like."

Keely flushed. She grabbed his arm with her strong

hand; he looked down at it. If she didn't move, he would rip her hand free and give her what she wanted. She would die here with Audra.

After a moment, she removed her hand and stepped aside. He walked past her.

Liv was eating a dinner she had cooked herself. The smell of roasted game made his stomach rumble. He grabbed a piece of meat off her plate and ate it as he walked to the glider.

He could feel both women looking at him. Nendre was probably watching, too. None of them seemed to realize just how precarious this situation was.

Bryer could feel the time ticking away. Fortunately, he had designed his camps so that they could be broken apart quickly. The last thing to go would be the styroplatform and the perimeter. He pressed the computer controls near the glider's flank, finishing the shutdown.

The entire camp shook. Then he could hear snapping sounds as the interiors of the tents packed themselves. The packed bags traveled to their places in the glider as the tents folded in on themselves.

Liv let out a squeal of protest as her plate rose, dumping its contents in the recycler, and flew to its own packing crate. Her chair and table followed, folding themselves down to their traveling weight so that they went into the glider as well.

Keely kept her place on the styroplatform. Nendre stood beside her, all of his tentacles down. He seemed to be watching Bryer with great disappointment.

Bryer didn't care how they felt about him, so long as they got out of here alive.

He flicked on the glider's engines, felt the rush of warm air beneath it. Now he wished he had brought a glider built for speed, not one large enough to hold the equipment. He turned on the other two gliders as well, and punched the last of the computer controls, sending some of the equipment to the third glider. Normally, he and a client rode in the third glider, with the other clients in the second and Nendre with the equipment in the first. This time, he would have his own glider.

If need be, he would leave them all behind.

"You coming?" he said to them.

They stared at him, none of them moving.

"Because once the perimeter goes off, I get into the glider and take apart the styroplatform. You'll fall into the cutgrass and you'll no longer be my responsibility."

Liv walked toward him. Nendre shrugged all of his tentacles and followed, heading toward the first glider as he always did. Only Keely remained in place, staring at Bryer as if he had become some kind of monster.

Maybe he had. But his survival was at stake. A man had the right to do anything he could to survive.

The last of the equipment packed itself in the third glider. After he shut off the perimeter, he had to take the small generator apart by hand. It only took a few minutes, but during that time, he would be vulnerable.

Then he would pack it, get into his glider, and go.

Nendre reached the first glider and, using his front tentacles, levered himself inside. Glider seats weren't built for his anatomy, but he managed, as he always did, to spread himself nearly flat and yet be able to reach the controls.

With an unreadable glance, Liv passed Bryer and climbed into the second glider. She didn't even look at Keely.

Bryer shut off the perimeter.

The cutgrass glowed in the dying sun. The grass had its own luminescence, a quality that he had once enjoyed. This time, he saw it as a liability. Their presence would be obvious as dark spots against the blades.

He heard the rustle before he caught the movement. A laser rifle raised out of the grass like an arm waving for help.

"Audra!" Keely called, her voice full of triumph. "Bryer, you've got to—"

The shot reached him, long and yellow, in such perceptual slow motion that he actually believed he could escape it. He leaped toward the third glider, his hand going to one of his own laser pistols, as the beam caught him in the left boot.

Heat seared through the rendisian leather, igniting the steel reinforced toe. He cursed, landed, and hit the disconnect on his boot. It pulled off his foot slowly, damaged by the blast.

So Audra was still alive. She was smarter than he had given her credit for. He had thought she would try to find a way out of the cutgrass, adding to her wounds and speeding up her death. Instead, she had remained in the same place, unmoving, until she saw the perimeter go off and the camp reveal itself.

Although that shot must have cost her. All of that movement would have resulted in more cuts on her skin.

Then he felt a muzzle against his back. Keely. Of course. She would help Audra.

He rolled into Keely, knocking her down, and removed her laser pistol from her hand. Then he pointed it at her chin.

"Stop being an idiot."

"Give me a glider," Keely said. "I'll get Audra out of here on my own."

He considered for a very brief moment. On the face of it, hers was a simple solution. Except that they'd meet him at the ship and he'd have to take them off planet.

He wasn't going to do anything else for Audra.

"No." He grabbed Keely's collar, pulling her up. Then, still crouching, he dragged her toward Nendre. Liv watched the entire thing as if it amused her.

Bryer knew that Audra could hear everything, and she could probably see them move beneath the gliders. But she was waiting for another clear shot. Too many movements, and she'd be too cut up to shoot that rifle.

When Bryer reached Nendre's glider, he offered Keely up like a carcass. Nendre took her in four of his tentacles and held her against the glider. Then he wrapped a fifth tentacle around her neck.

"Try anything," he said, his voice sounding even more mechanical than usual, "and I will squeeze."

She glared at Bryer. He didn't care. She was the least of his problems.

He went back to the third glider, rose above it, and saw the darkness in the cutgrass. This time, Audra didn't shoot at him. But he knew that, like any good hunter, she was biding her time.

She wanted him inside the glider. She wanted to shoot him down so that she could use the glider to escape. If he was dead, she'd get off Mgasin. If he lived, she wouldn't.

They both knew that.

He wasn't leaving this place until she was no longer a threat. But it would take a risk on his part. Still, it would probably work. She didn't think him all that bright. She might fall for the trap.

Bryer moved around the glider, keeping his feet on the styroplatform. His left foot throbbed and his balance was off, but he wasn't willing to remove the right boot. He had reached the very edge of the platform, pistol at his side, finger at the ready.

He had made himself as perfect a target as he could.

Behind him, he heard a familiar click and whir. He

ducked just in time. The shot came over the center of the glider, disappearing into the darkness.

Liv. Liv had shot at him from behind.

He swung his pistol around, fired, hit the computer control on the back of Liv's glider, and saw it light up.

They had less than a minute.

Nendre, knowing what was going to happen, launched his glider off the platform. The glider, unbalanced by Keely's weight, tilted precariously toward one side.

But Bryer, still crouching, didn't watch Nendre. Instead, he searched the glowing cutgrass for the dark area that marked Audra's position. He found it right where he sensed it would be and fired. The shot went wild, severing a swath of cutgrass.

Liv was struggling with her glider. Its sides had sealed like they always did when someone tampered with the back controls, holding her inside. She couldn't get out, although she was trying to force the interior controls to let her.

Audra's rifle rose above the grass, and Bryer shot again. The beam hit her in the belly. Her body flew backward, landing even deeper in the grass.

This time, he knew she was dead.

He only had a few seconds left. He dove into his own glider and hit reverse, going off the styroplatform backward, away from Liv's glider. She was pounding against the clear walls, screaming at him, but he looked away.

The cutgrass was illuminating Nendre's glider from beneath. It looked odd, the shadows making the bottom seem uneven instead of flat. The glider was level now, and Bryer didn't see Keely's head against the sky. Nendre had probably let her fall into the cutgrass. She wasn't as resourceful as Audra. If the fall hadn't killed her, the grass would.

Bryer banked his own glider, heading toward the edge of the grass. At that moment, Liv's glider exploded, sending plumes of fire and light into the darkening sky.

If the Cuiesto didn't know where he was before, they knew now. He had to hurry. But first he had to make sure Nendre was all right.

Bryer eased his glider beside Nendre's and gasped.

He was looking at the glider's flat bottom. The glider was flying upside down.

Bryer lowered his glider, so that he could see underneath Nendre's. Bryer hoped to find Nendre clinging by his tentacles.

But Nendre wasn't there—and neither was Keely. The glider was empty.

Bryer looked down. Nendre was flat against the cutgrass, his body deflated the way his people's bodies did when they were dead. A few meters behind him, Keely lay broken in the grass.

They must have struggled, upset the glider, and fallen to the grass below.

Bryer cursed. He and Nendre had been together a long time, working well despite their differing philosophies. They had been friends.

He hadn't meant to get Nendre killed.

Although Bryer couldn't do anything about it now. Nendre was dead, but Bryer wasn't. And he still had time to get out of this godforsaken place. He nudged the glider forward when he noticed something odd at the edge of the Range.

Runners, dozens of them, stood in front of him, holding a weapon he recognized as a cross between a laser rifle and an old-fashioned projectile gun.

He turned, saw shapes in the darkness all around the cutgrass. His glider's scanner confirmed what his eyes took in: hundreds of Runners, some visible, some not, waiting for him. He couldn't fly away from this. Even if he tried, they'd keep up with the glider. If they fired at him, those weapons would do serious damage because his glider was not armor plated.

Bryer hovered, safe as long as he was above the cutgrass. No Runner could venture inside—and they wouldn't shoot until they were sure he had seen them. Unlike Audra, the Cuiesto had ethics.

He had one chance. He fingered the explosives he had stored in his pouch. If he used them, he would be able to get away. He would probably make it to the ship and off Mgasin.

But he would leave behind hundreds of dead Runners and the first volley in a two-pronged war. The uneasy truce between the Viotu and the Cuiesto would end, and no human could broker a peace. In fact, the war would probably spread to the Alliance, since humans would have been the trigger—the spark that made the cold war hot all over again.

It was just what the terrorist factions wanted. They wanted to destroy the Alliance by involving it in a war that would divide the member nations. Such a war would show that the Alliance only talked about peace.

Audra had known about the dangers of coming to Mgasin illegally. In fact, Bryer had explained them to her before the trip. But as he had spoken, she had watched him with faint amusement, amusement he had taken for contempt at the rules.

It had been contempt at the information.

He finally understood what he should have seen all along.

She hadn't been here to hunt gracela. She had come here to start a war.

She was a terrorist, the Mgasin equivalent of a suicide bomber, whose desperate act had a small probability of survival. Even if he hadn't killed her, the Cuiesto would have—after she had told them lies about human involvement in a war the Alliance didn't even know they were going to be part of.

His hand left the explosives. Instead, he fingered the digital in his pouch—the digital he had nearly destroyed. As it existed now, it could be what he wanted it to be. Audra wasn't alive to explain her motivations. He would use the digital to show Audra hadn't meant to start a war—only that she was mean-spirited and selfish, a hunter who didn't understand the sanctity of sentient life.

But he did. He always had.

And if he killed the Runners just so that he could escape, he would be no better than Audra. In fact, he would be her pawn for the rest of his miserable life.

Bryer cursed softly to himself. He was guilty. Guilty of coming to Mgasin illegally. Guilty of so many tiny things. He had never thought that such small guilts could have such huge repercussions.

Strange that he always considered himself a moral man. Stranger still to discover here, in this place, that he had never acted like one.

It was time to start.

He raised his hands and, in broken Cuiesto, surrendered.

Everything.

LOS NIÑOS

by *William H. Keith, Jr.*

William H. Keith, Jr., is the author of over sixty novels, nearly all of them dealing with the theme of men at war. Writing under the pseudonym H. Jay Riker, he's responsible for the extremely popular *SEALS: The Warrior Breed* series, a family saga spanning the history of the Navy UDT and SEALs from World War II to the present day. As Ian Douglas, he writes a well-received military science fiction series following the exploits of the U.S. Marines in the future, in combat on the moon and Mars. Recent anthology appearances include *First to Fight II*, *Alternate Gettysburgs*, and *Silicon Dreams*.

"*H*EADS *up! Six Mikes!*"

Lieutenant Siegel's voice over my headset was shrill, edged with excitement and maybe some cold fear as well. That was okay. I was scared, too. Hell, we all were. Three minutes to show time . . . *if* we made it through the Greenie-Meanie defense net, and that was a pretty damned big "if" right now.

The APL bounced and jolted, riding the shock waves of a triplet of high-KE blasts from somewhere up ahead. I let my seat harness take the shock, gripping my 120 tightly in armored gauntlets and muttering something unpleasant about the parentage of the F's driver.

Marine Armored Personnel Landers aren't built for

comfort or for looks. Outside they look like big, black, flat beetles with surly attitudes; inside, it's damned hard to tell what they look like because you just can't see much. With twenty-four battle-armored leathernecks wedged in shoulder to shoulder, crammed in between a low, pipe-tangled overhead and a steel grate deck in red-lit, claustrophobic coziness, they can't do much but stare at the backs of the Marines in front of them.

The APL jolted hard again. "Fuckin' slimers," Private Bedecker muttered over the company channel, using another of the more common epithets for the Greenies. "They won't fight once we get down there and start kicking ass."

"Hey, Malone!" Corporal Slattery called out. "Greenies don't have noses. How do they smell?"

"Terrible!" several of the Marines in the compartment chorused. An ancient joke.

"That's th' Goddesses' own truth," Sergeant Reingold said. She laughed. "And a good thing, too. We'll be able to smell the turdlickers comin' a klick away, even when we're buttoned up!"

"Yeah," Private Rodgers added. His voice sounded eager and terribly young . . . and maybe just a bit scared. "Anyone know why Greenie-Meanies eat shit?"

" 'Cause they're friggin' *cannibals*, man!" Private Delambert shouted back.

"Cannibals that can fuck themselves," Wilcox added. "Man, do they know how to have a good time on a Saturday night dinner date or what?"

As the banter continued, Private Malone signaled a request over the private NCO access channel. "Hey, Gunnery Sergeant? Can I ask you somethin'?" He didn't sound scared, exactly. More thoughtful than anything else.

"Go ahead, Malone. Present and fire."

"They say the Meanies only fight when they got

odds in their favor of ten t' one, that they'll scatter as soon as we land in force."

"What's your point, Malone?"

"Well, that's right, ain't it? I mean, everybody says the Meanies're just born cowards, and no good in a stand-up fight. They've all been sayin' this assault'll be a damned walk in the park, y'know?"

I'd heard the same scuttlebutt, and I didn't like it one bit. "Malone, if I catch you thinking anything that goddamn stupid," I growled at him, "I'll have it out of your hide. You know better than that."

"Yeah, Gunny, sure. I guess I'm just wondering how good the turdlickers really are, is all. *Uh!*" The APL thumped hard, lurching sideways as a shock wave thundered past. "And how come they're puttin' up this kind of fight *now*, if they're supposed to be such cowards!"

"The Greenies are the *enemy*," I told him, speaking quietly and with what I trusted as authority in my voice. "They're different from us in lots of ways, different philosophies, different customs, different ways of looking at things, but all you need to focus on is that they're the enemy. Any animal'll fight back if it's cornered, right? The Meanies'll kill you if they can, so when you hit the beach, you be damned sure to kill them first. Got it?"

"Sure, Gunny. I got it."

"Good."

I switched back to the company channel and listened in for a moment. The discussion had moved, inevitably, to the fact that the Meanies were hermaphrodites, each with the sex organs of both male and female. Marines seemed to find this single xenobiological fact endlessly entertaining.

"So how many Meanies does it take to screw in a fresh MHD charge coupler? Only one, but it has to *really* like itself. . . ."

"Yeah, it's gonna be a real pleasure to tell those slimy freaks they can go fuck themselves."

"Hey," Private Huseman called out. "I heard a good one on the *Vandergrift*. A Meanie goes into this singles bar, see, and . . ."

"Secure that crap, Marines!" I barked, using my best D.I. grinder voice. "Comm silence!"

We weren't actually under communications silence protocol, but I wanted to listen to the chatter between Regiment and Battalion, and be able to pick out the bits that pertained to us. Not my job, yeah, but I believe in staying up-to-date. I'd done a bit of quiet, strictly contra-regs hacking to gain covert access to officers-only channels. Hell, the more information I had, the better able I'd be to keep myself and my people alive.

"We've taken damned heavy casualties already," Captain Elliot was telling someone at Battalion. Her voice was tight and hard-edged, showing stress, not fear. *"Three APLs are down. Heavy fire from the objective. . . ."*

"I've got heavy ground fire from Sector Five," another voice added, one of the other company commanders, I thought. *"Taking hits . . ."*

"Sky Base! Sky Base! This is Silver Three! We're hit! We're hit! Do you copy?"

The chatter washed over me like the incoming tide. Actually, I wished I'd gone ahead and let my people talk. Jokes, wisecracks, even heartfelt bitching helps relieve the tension just before grounding. I couldn't back up now, though, not and preserve some semblance of command dignity.

Another jolt, a bad one. Delambert cursed. The worst of being aboard an Armored Personnel Lander in a combat drop is not being able to see out. You're strapped immobile into a hard, narrow seat, no windows, nothing to look at but fellow Marines and your helmet HUD, feeling every bump and bounce as the pilot jinks and turns as he tries to avoid incoming fire and the turbulence of particle beam wakes, knowing, *knowing* that some damned little four-eyed green monster somewhere on the planet's surface below is drawing a bead on your craft with anything from a hand gun to a 510 cm skytorch to a pocket nuke.

At least I had a tactical feed through my helmet display, along with the unauthorized comm link. As topkick of Alfa Platoon, 24th Regimental Drop Team, I got to see what was going on in case the Boss and his exec both bought it going in. Information, all I could eat. And it kept my mind off that green monster with its thumb-analog on the trigger to a SAM with a fractional kiloton warhead. So far, though, my helmet feed wasn't showing me much but dark. We were coming down on the objective planet's night side, and nothing was showing up ahead but midnight pierced by stuttering white flashes, like lightning.

We'd been released from the transport *Alexander A. Vandergrift* in low planetary approach ninety klicks up, hitting atmosphere in a blaze of ionized plasma, chaff, and radar-blocking EMP bursts, over two hundred APLs deployed in a full MPEF assault drop on the Greenie capital. The 24th was tasked with hitting an objective known as "The Citadel," a massive, black-walled structure on the southeastern outskirts of the city complex, rising in two stages, a steep-sided tower perched atop a flattened pyramid. We were coming in from the east, three hundred klicks out at eighty thousand meters, angling in for a landing on the open plain below The Citadel's walls.

S2 wasn't sure what The Citadel was, but to judge from the recon holos taken from orbit, it was definitely military and definitely tough, with massively fortified outer works, heavy weapons emplacements, and support facilities that suggested a large garrison on-site.

No one could tell us, though, just how many

Greenie-Meanies we were likely to find down there, or how ready they were to face a Marine space assault drop.

It was a bit unsettling just how little we knew about the Meanies, even after three years of warfare. We knew they were a technic species, but still a couple of centuries behind us. They had space flight, but didn't seem to aggressively colonize. They didn't seem to think that way, and except for research outposts and such, pretty much kept to their own world, which we called Gamma Pavonis IV and they called Khaharesh. The dominant philosophy or religion or whatever it was had to do with some kind of oneness-of-the-universe crap, which might have accounted for the notion of their being a race of cowards.

We knew they called themselves the *Mi-hie-nyees*, which was supposed to be their word for "people" or "us" or whatever. Somehow, that became "Meanies" in Marine-speak, and since their coloring was a kind of an overall olive-drab color, with black stripes, that evolved into "Greenie-Meanies."

I'd always been fascinated by the rifleman's unflagging tendency to dehumanize his enemies . . . not that that was all that difficult with beasties that were decidedly nonhuman in every way. Oh, the Meanies stood upright and had the rough shape of a human, but they weren't even remotely mammalian. Neither warm- nor cold-blooded, their circulatory fluid was copper-based and ran at variable temperatures depending on the need, neither warm nor cold. Their sun was an F8, a lot brighter than Sol; they sported two sets of eyes, great big ones for seeing in the dark, and tiny, deep-set ones for the dazzling light of day. Hermaphrodites, each individual could bear live young, and fed them their own wastes. According to the xeno-bio boys and girls aboard the expeditionary force flagship, there were some rare elements necessary for certain catalytic reactions in their biology . . . niobium and thallium, I think? Something like that. Anyway, the stuff passes right through them after helping those reactions along, and they get concentrated doses by, well, engaging in some personal behaviors and feeding habits that are pretty damned disgusting by human standards. That might explain why they eat their own dead, too, though that, of course, was cloaked in some kind of religious significance.

So it wasn't all that hard dehumanizing the *Mi-hie-nyees*, to think of them as animals, no, as *things* rather than as intelligent beings with a principal planetary civilization at least as rich and old as anything Earth had to offer.

It made them easier to kill.

My helmet vid-feed was showing a bit more, now . . . the rectilinear crosshatching of city streets brightly illuminated . . . and the broader, random glows of fires flickering beneath palls of smoke. I could see The Citadel now, a vast, black, truncated pyramid blocking the background glow of a thousand fires. City, Citadel, and horizon were canted sharply to the left as the APL banked into its final approach vector.

"All right, Marines!" I shouted over the tac channel. "When we grab gravel, I want a clean exit, by the numbers, do you hear me?"

"Right, Gunny!"

"Loud and clear!"

"Yo!"

"You will disperse, cover, and *move*. I don't care what you've heard about the Meanies, or how primitive their technology is, or what they eat for dinner. You *will* move smartly, you *will* take your assigned objectives, and you *will* kick Greenie ass!"

"Ooh-rah!" they roared back in chorus, the ancient battle cry of the Corps.

The Citadel was much closer now, looming huge on my helmet display, its black walls cracked and broken by near hits from the orbital bombardment. What I wanted to know was why they didn't just drop a high-velocity kinetic-kill slug onto the top of the thing. A ten-to-the-fifteenth joule impact would have turned the thing into fused rubble strewn about a glass-bottomed crater. No muss, no fuss, house-cleaning while you wait, the Navy way.

But orders, as they say, are orders. Someone a hell of a lot farther up the chain of command than I was wanted The Citadel more or less intact. Maybe they were hoping to find documents in there, or maybe they were just going to use it as an advance base for the invasion force that was building up in orbit.

To tell the truth, I wasn't even all that sure what the hell we were doing on Khaharesh in the first place. The official story was that the Meanies had wiped out one of our trade missions to the planet, but most of us suspected that this was another war fought for the greater glory and profit of PanTerran Industries and the other interstellar megacorps: trade with us on favorable terms, in other words, or we send in the Marines. In a way, it was a reprise to the bad old days of the Banana Wars of the twentieth century, when the Marines were used to enforce the imperial will of the United Fruit Company. Not moral, no . . . but then who ever claimed that war was moral? Some are just more popular than others. . . .

We lost our stomachs as the APL suddenly swooped. Our driver had just pulled up sharply, and was arrowing now in level flight across a torn and fire-swept nape-of-the-earth. On my helmet display, I could see clouds of white-and-yellow plasma tracer rounds rising to meet us, punctuated by the sharp stab of particle beams and the flash of explosions against the night. I watched the display with a kind of nightmare detachment; this was always the worst part of an assault, the waiting dragged out across endless minutes, sealed inside a flying metal box, helpless, unable to move, and feeling like the biggest, juiciest target in the sky.

A loud bang rang through the compartment, and the APL shuddered like it had slammed into a mountain. My HUD static-fuzzed to black, and I felt the momentary gut-dropping sensation of free fall. "We're hit!" someone yelled.

"*Blue Three! Blue Three!*" I heard our driver yelling over the comm channel. That was our call sign. "*Blue Three is hit and going down!*"

"Brace for impact!" I yelled, wondering if it would do any good. Everything depended on just how high we were and how hard we hit going in.

We hit and we bounced, then slid through rubble with the sound of an avalanche. All of us were shook up pretty badly, but the APL's troop restraint system kept us more or less intact in a somewhat elastic web of straps and support pylons. We lurched to a halt, deck canted sharply nose-high and to starboard.

"Any casualties?" I yelled. "Anyone hurt?"

There were grunts, grumbles, and groans, but no takers. That had been a pretty decent touchdown, as things go, and I decided I owed our driver a big kiss, assuming I survived the next few minutes.

Smoke was filling the compartment in a red-lit parody of hell, as the restraints let go and the aft hatch cycled open. With the lander's data feed knocked out, I had no idea where we were, but Lieutenant Siegel yelled, "*Let's go, Marines!*" and we began scrambling down the ramp and into the flame-shot night of Khaharesh.

"You heard the man!" I bellowed over the tac channel. "Move! Move! Move!" This was the deadliest part of the assault landing, if you don't count the possibility of getting shot down on approach. Twenty-four of us were packed together so tightly that one lucky rocket or plasma burst would splatter us all over the lander's troop compartment.

I clanged down the ramp and jumped, landing on a sharply-sloping clutter of black ferrocrete slabs. The APL had actually come to rest partway up the lower side of The Citadel, on the flat slope just below the rim of a ragged, fifty-meter breach in the east wall.

No plan of battle survives contact with the enemy, and this assault was no exception to that ancient law. The other APLs had come down all over the landscape; we'd missed ours by a good kilometer or more. Still, sometimes there are lucky plan miscarriages, and this looked like one of them. Our objective was The Citadel, and the driver had managed to drop us right on the wall. This could be a good thing or a bad, depending; the idea had been to land the entire company below The Citadel and move in together, looking for a way in. We seemed to have found the way in, but there were only twenty-four of us, no support, no reserves.

Three parallel streaks of flame suddenly appeared to the west, slanting out of the sky and blossoming sun-bright on the horizon—another salvo of high-KE slugs from orbit. The naval task force was laying down a bombardment designed to wall off the objective, and keep the enemy from reinforcing it. I counted silently to myself, then bellowed "First Squad! Duck and cover!" The shock wave hit a second later, rolling across the rubble-blasted terrain and causing The Citadel itself to tremble.

We started climbing, then, making our way up the slope of The Citadel. This part of the wall was only at a twenty-degree angle or so, but the going was still slow, the footing uncertain. High-velocity gauss rounds slammed into the side of the APL and struck sparks from ferrocrete, as enemy gunners opened up from the breach above us. A private in Third Squad, Owens, got tagged by a hypersonic slug that sliced through his combat armor and shredded his right leg, leaving him shrieking and writhing on the ground. Private Karpowski was hit an instant later, the round taking off her helmet and head together in a crimson splash. Sergeant Meier's whole upper torso exploded in orange flames.

"First and Third Squads, cover fire!" the lieutenant yelled. "Second and Fourth, move in! Nail those shit-licking snipers!"

Battles are won by the unexpected, the surprise, by daring and initiative. If Fate had dropped us here on the Enemy's doorstep with the door wide open, we were going to take advantage of it. Hell, we couldn't stay out *here*. A marine could get killed that way.

I was First Squad, so I hustled up the slope to the rim of the breach, threw myself down, and trained my arc gun into the hole. I flipped my helmet display to show the IR feed off my weapon's sight system. In infrared, the hole was a soft black walled in green, while heat sources glowed in yellow and white. The Meanies were in there, all right, and they were coming out.

They kind of looked like frogs, if frogs could walk on their hind legs—long-legged and digitigrade. They were skinny, though, not fat, with long, un-gainly legs and arms that were somehow graceful when they moved, and large heads set on flexible, almost snakelike necks.

And those critters could *move*, dashing forward in a rush that nearly swept over me and the five people in my squad. These guys had boosted their metabolisms until they glowed white-hot on IR, and when they moved it was bent over low to the ground, and so fast I swear they were blurs.

I racked the charging lever on my arc gun and triggered it, sending a pinpoint of dazzling white-and-purple energy searing into the breach. Greenie-Meanies vanished in roiling clouds of greasy smoke, while others flopped and twisted and shrieked with those odd, mewling, two-throated voices they have. The rest of my squad opened up as well, Kenzie and Slater with their big fusion-bolters cycling on full-auto, the others with M07 HELguns powerful enough to boil through combat armor, to say nothing of the naked hides of the charging natives.

Face it. Without combat armor, the life expectancy of any flesh-and-blood organism on the modern battlefield is measured in scant seconds. All of those nasty chips and shards of hurtling rock and metal, the plasma bolts, the laser and particle beams, even the high-rad back-scatter from our own weapons add up to one very unhealthy environment unless you're sealed into at least a Mk. I battlesuit. The Meanies went naked, except for a kind of identifying uniform, like crossed cloth brassards sporting ornate knots tied in blue-and-silver cord. We cut them down in bloody, burning, thrashing heaps.

But they kept coming . . . and coming.

Third Squad joined us on the rim of the breach, adding their firepower to ours, but as fast as we burned them down, more were crowding ahead, meeping and mewling and firing their weapons blindly. The Meanies carried a variety of weapons, from explosive crossbow bolts up to a kind of over-the-shoulder rocket launcher that was bad news if the warhead caught you full-on, armor or no armor. Most common were gauss rifles, complicated looking weapons a meter and a half long, that used an intense magnetic field to hurl a steel-jacketed slug at something like Mach 7. Primitive stuff, really, technology a couple of centuries out of date . . . but a freaking *club* can still kill you if the bad guy can get close enough to you to swing it.

Second and Fourth never made it beyond the rim of the breach. Private Larry Malone took a gauss slug through his chest; I saw it explode out the back of his battlesuit in blood and fragments of armor and bone turned to shrapnel. Three more Marines edged forward and were cut down, and pretty soon the whole section was lying at the lip of the opening in the wall, cycling rounds as fast as we could.

"Keep firing!" I yelled. "Pour it on 'em!"

Rounds hissed and snapped overhead, or exploded among the black slabs and rubble. We kept up a heavy covering fire, burning down the Meanies as they rushed forward, burning them down until the gaping breach in The Citadel's wall filled with oily smoke. Sergeant Costler shouted a warning, then he and Slattery lobbed a pair of M990s into the opening. We all flattened out on the ground an instant before flames blasted from the breach, searing the tortured air just above our heads.

The alien horde made it all the way to daylight, struggling ahead over the charred and smoking bodies of their comrades. For a horrible moment, they were all around us, too close for us to use our energy weapons for fear of hitting our own forces. We fought hand-to-hand, clubbing them down with the butts of our weapons, driving them back until we could open up with arc gun and laser.

More Marines were arriving on-site, struggling up the slope from the plains below, where their APLs had touched down. All sense of platoon organization had been lost, however, and the assault was balanced on the ragged edge of chaos. The newcomers rushed into the fray, joining us for a moment in the seesaw struggle at the breach rim.

And then the swarming hordes were gone, the breach empty save for smoke and the mounds of bodies shattered and charred by the firestorm.

But there was no rest, could be no rest, not yet.

"Gunnery Sergeant Aguilar!" Lieutenant Siegel called over the private NCO channel.

"Yessir!" I snapped back.

"Take three squads forward into that hole! Find a defensible position a few meters in and hold it." He must have heard my thoughts, which weren't exactly pleasant. I was tired, I was shaken, and the idea of leading my people into that black hole sounded more like group suicide than an exercise in small-unit tactics. "Don't sweat it, Gunny. Reinforcements are on the way up."

"Aye, aye, sir!"

In other words, keep those damned snipers away from the breach opening, so the rest of the landing force could get organized for the main assault. It was a descent into the proverbial lion's den, but at least there'd be more cover inside. I felt damned naked on the outside slope of the wall. Hell, my section had taken thirty percent casualties in a little over two minutes.

"First, Second, and Third Squads!" I called over the platoon tac channel. "With me!" Rising to a low crouch, I scrambled over the lip of the breach and plunged into the smoky gloom.

The breach opening ran back into the pyramid for thirty meters, sloping gently downward into a tangle of smashed-open corridors, stone-walled chambers, and rubble. It was pitch-black, but we moved ahead with our helmets set for infrared viewing. There were bodies everywhere, some of them still moving. As we neared the far opening, red-lit and eerie, our surroundings took on the nightmare aspect of some ancient religious hell.

Complete with demons. Sudden movement sent broken rock clattering to our right, and three Greenie-Meanies stumbled out of a side chamber. *"Ch'yeem myee-hee!"* one cried. *"Gh'yavaeet n'yeej!"*

Corporal Baedecker triggered his arc gun, sending the eye-searing pinpoint of plasma lancing into the attackers. One exploded as the bolt penetrated its body; the other two shrieked and dropped, twitching. "What the hell does 'cheem mee-hee' mean?" Baedecker asked, laughing.

I had my translator program running, of course. Only E-6 and above had them loaded in their suit AIs, of course, since the damn things could be distracting, but you never knew when you might need to speak the local lingo in the field. Words were scrolling up on my HUD, overlaying my visual feed:

CH'YEEM: EMPHATIC. PERTAINS TO YIELDING OR SUBMISSIVE BEHAVIOR, OR A DESIRE TO TAKE A DIFFERENT PATH. SURRENDER?

MYEE-HEE: PERSONAL PRONOUN, GENDER-NEUTRAL. LITERALLY "THIS ONE OF THE PEOPLE."

GH'YAVAEET: UNTRANSLATABLE. POSSIBLY RELATED TO "GH'YEET," TO STRIKE, OR TO "GH' YA' HAYEET," TO KILL.

N'YEEJ: NEGATION. REVERSAL. MANIFESTATION OF SOMETHING UNTHINKABLE. NEGATIVE STATEMENT. DO NOT?

PROBABLE INTENDED SENSE OF STATEMENT, RELIABILITY 76%: "I YIELD. DO NOT KILL."

Damn. The Meanies had been trying to surrender.
I took a closer look at them. One was obviously old,
its face gnarled and wrinkled like ancient tree bark.
The others, what was left of them, seemed like ordinary Greenie-Meanies . . . but none had been armed,
or wearing brassards.

"I think those three were civilians," I told the platoon. "Heads up, people. Don't get careless . . . but
check your damn targets, okay? Headquarters wants
prisoners."

We continued our advance, as the corridor became
narrower and more difficult. At last, though, we
reached an area of passageways where the avenue
opened up into a high, dome-ceilinged room. There
was light here, a pale twilight filtering through the
dusty air in a luminous haze from fixtures on the
walls.

And there was another Meanie, an armed one, this
time. It was standing alone on the far side of the
chamber, its back against the stone wall alongside
the mouth of another passageway. It wore a double
brassard and knotted cords, and was holding a slender weapon taller than it was. It goggled at us as we
emerged from our corridor, swinging the weapon up
to bear on us. "*Sh'ghyee!*" it shrilled. It was smaller
than the ones that had just emerged from the passageway, and paler in color.

"*Ch'yeem!*" I shouted back, reading from the choice
of phrases appearing on my HUD.

"*Sh'ghyee! Sh'ghyee!*"

My HUD provided the translation.

SH'GHEE: EMPHATIC. STOP. HALT. CEASE ACTIVITY.

It triggered its weapon, and a Mach 7 slug exploded Private Huseman's upper chest and right arm
in a gory explosion. Corporal Benkowski fired his

M07, the higher energy laser pulse popping a bright green hole through the Meanie's torso. The critter slumped against the wall, but fired again, taking off Benkowski's leg and splattering my armor with blood.

Half a dozen HELgun bursts ripped at the creature's body. It keened something untranslatable, killed Private Wilcox, then smartly shouldered its weapon and sagged to the floor, its torso still propped up against the green-splattered wall at its back. I almost fried it with my arc gun, but held my fire when I saw it die.

"This is our firebase," I told my people. It was a good, sound, defensible position, the flanks anchored on solid rock walls, and I didn't care to push much farther into this maze, not if the four-eyes were going to hold their positions like *this*. "Get those bolters set up here . . . and over there. Cover those passageways to left and right. Rest of you, start piling up rubble . . . debris, whatever you can find and haul. Move it, now!"

It didn't take long for my boys and girls to erect a wall of loose rubble a meter high and a meter thick. Lieutenant Siegel came in with some more leathernecks—a couple of squads from Charlie Platoon—and took over organizing the line. "Go help Doc with translation, Gunny," he told me.

"Aye, aye, sir."

I made my way back to the opening of the breach. Meanie bodies and pieces of bodies were everywhere, piled six-deep in places, and scattered so thickly on the chamber floor it was impossible to walk without stepping on them. I found HM1 Yaegar, our company corpsman, in the mouth of the tunnel. He'd finished patching up our people hurt in the battle, and now was trying to help some of the alien wounded. Obviously, though, he was baffled by the alien biology.

"I don't know what to do, Gunny," he told me, looking up. He was kneeling above a squirming frog-shape, its bluish-green blood coating the gloves and gauntlets of his battlesuit. Its eyes, two big ones on the outside of its head, two little ones deep set one above the other in the center, looked glassy and blind and very much in pain. "I can stop obvious bleeding, maybe make them comfortable . . . but damn it, I don't dare try giving them painkillers, tranqs, or O_2 circs. Those'd poison 'em for sure."

"Do what you can, Doc," I told him. At the moment, I wasn't that interested in saving Meanie lives. The bastards had hurt us, bad. "Headquarters is going to want some intact Four-eyes for questioning."

Yaeger didn't answer, but his silence was eloquent. For him, patching up wounded enemy soldiers was as much a part of his job as patching up wounded Marines, though he always took care of our people first. I noticed the wounded Meanie had stopped moving, and realized how frustrating Doc must find this.

He rose from the lifeless body and moved to the next one, a slender Meanie, with lighter skin.

Another Marine was standing guard nearby, shin-deep in green corpses. "Welcome to the Meanie banquet hall, Gunny," he said, a grin in his voice. He nudged a green body with his boot. "The turdlickers're gonna eat well tonight, huh?"

"Stow it," I snapped. I was tired. I was frayed to the breaking point. I didn't want to hear stupid *machismo* bravado, not now. Too many good Marines had died taking this damned hole in the wall.

"Hey, Gunny?" Doc called. "Take a look at this."

He was kneeling by the light-skinned Meanie. "Watcha got?"

"I'm wondering if we've got a custom job, here."

I took a closer look. The Meanie was still alive, its eyes, large and small, tightly screwed shut. Its left arm was missing, burned away to judge by the charring, and Doc was applying a tourniquet. I thought one of its legs might be broken as well, but the alien articulation might have been fooling me. Its two mouths, one above the other on the top of its big, smooth head—the one for breathing and speaking, the other for eating—were opening and closing spasmodically.

A custom job? Shit. That was what we called the Shar Kiiar warriors, in that nasty little dustup on Wolf 1421 IIC a few years back. Their technology, such as it was, had evolved along purely biological lines. They *grew* their buildings, their vehicles, their weapons, rather than building them. Their warriors were specially bred, deliberately mutated, I guess, to be bigger, stronger, faster, and more deadly than your ordinary, garden-variety Sharkie. Three thousand Marines died on that ice ball before PanTerra got the trade concessions it wanted.

I could see what Doc Yaeger was getting at. This Meanie was a good ten percent less massive than the others we'd seen, and its leathery skin was smoother and quite pale, almost yellow instead of olive.

The Meanie guarding the corridor up ahead had been of the same type. I looked at the bodies filling the cavern, and realized that perhaps half, or even more, had the same light-hued, smooth-skinned features.

I wondered if I could talk to the thing.

I used my translator to pull up a likely phrase: *"Chook yeem nyee?"* That was supposed to be a request for identity.

"D'haii . . . u . . . yeegh . . ." the Meanie squeaked through its top mouth. The eyes opened, all golden-brown with round, black pupils.

D'HAII: PREDESCESSOR. PARENT. FORERUNNER. PROBABLY RELATED TO *HAA'IIYI*, "LIFE-GIVER."

U: MODIFIER PRONOUN. REFERRING TO SELF. I. ME. MY.

YEEGH: INTENSE DESIRE. NEED. WANT.

PROBABLE INTENDED SENSE OF STATEMENT, RELIABILITY 85%: "I WANT MY PARENT."

"*Chook yeem nyee!*" I shouted. "Damn it, answer me!"

The small eyes closed. The large ones blinked. "*Sayeesh nya gh'd'vyeem,*" it told me quietly and with intense concentration. The eyes closed again, and the being died.

SAYEESH: VERB. TAKE. HAVE. USE.

NYA: MODIFIER PRONOUN. REFERRING TO OTHER. YOU. YOUR. YOURSELF.

GH'D'VYEEM: UNTRANSLATABLE. POSSIBLY RELATED TO *VYE'EEYEM*, "CONJUGATION" or "JOINING."

PROBABLE INTENDED SENSE OF STATEMENT, RELIABILITY 59%: "YOU JOIN YOURSELF."

A biological weapon? A made-to-order warrior? I didn't think so. In fact, I was pretty sure that I knew exactly what the smaller Meanies were.

I didn't have time to follow through on my theory, though, because an instant later, Lieutenant Siegel was dead, and Corporal Logan from Charlie was calling for help on the company tac channel. The Meanies had regrouped and were attacking again, wave upon wave of them thundering out of The Citadel's tunnels and hurling themselves against our fire position. I reached the wall in time to add my arc gun's fire to the fusillade of high-energy weaponry burning down the green hordes.

We held the line, shoulder to armored shoulder, for a full forty seconds, until bodies and fragments of bodies were stacked up in front of us waist-deep, and the survivors were crawling across their own dead to reach us. Nearly all, I saw, were the smaller, lighter breed of Greenie-Meanie; most were armed with gauss rifles or crossbows and most were in "uniform," such as it was, but many were unarmed, and some were waving knives with wickedly curving blades, or throwing rocks.

Knives and rocks could not penetrate battle armor, but high-Mach gauss slugs could. We took eight casualties in those forty seconds, and when we lost Slater and the hammering firepower of his bolter, we started falling back, step by agonizing step. The guys with HELguns were running low on charge packs, and my arc gun was running so hot I thought the barrel was going to melt before I had a chance to swap it out.

At some point during that horrible retreat, a gauss slug smashed through my guts and I was killed.

I woke up aboard the *Vandergrift*, in orbit, and they told me over two weeks had passed. Well, it took that long to tease what was left of me into growing a new lower torso and a pair of legs. It took a bit longer for the memories to start to surface; my brain had been blood-starved for a long time before they finally recovered my body, and it takes a while to retrace the neural pathways within newly revived brain tissue.

I was luckier than a lot of Marines. I heard later we lost sixty-eight hundred people in the invasion, half of them irretrievables . . . and over three hundred in taking down The Citadel itself.

"Catharine?"

I opened my eyes to see a kindly-looking major peering down at me out of the glare from the overhead light panels.

"Gunnery Sergeant Aguilar, sir," I said, trying to sit up.

"At ease, at ease, Marine," he told me. "Don't get up. I'm Major Weiss. I brought a little something for you."

He handed me a velvet-covered box. Inside was my purple heart.

"You've also been recommended for the Silver Star," he told me. "That's still being processed through channels, but it's a done deal. You're going to get it. The way you took charge of your unit after Lieutenant Siegel's death and led them in a fighting withdrawal undoubtedly saved their lives, and inflicted so many casualties on the Greenie-Meanies within The Citadel that they could not resist our second assault."

"I don't want the Silver Star," I told him, bitter. "Not for fighting *Los Niños*."

"Who?"

"Children, Major. *Kids*."

His smile faded. "You figured that out, did you?"

"It was pretty obvious, talking to them. I had a translator program, you know. What was The Citadel . . . some kind of military school?"

"We didn't know that going in. We thought it was a major military fortress. We now think it was an academy of some sort. A training center for their armed forces."

"For kids, they put up quite a fight."

He nodded. "That information is still compartmentalized and top secret," he told me. "Need to know only. I don't want you telling anyone else, once you return to your unit. That's an order."

"Why the hell not, sir? Our people should know what's going on."

"The information could, ah, deleteriously affect morale. The Meanies are putting up a stubborn defense of Gamma Pavonis IV. There's a lot of tough fighting yet to do. And the people back on Earth might not react, ah, favorably to stories of kids fighting to the last against Marines."

"*Children*," I said, turning my head away. "Wave after wave of *children*. . . ."

The history of war is filled with children's crusades . . . heroic assaults and valiant defenses and just plain stupid wastefulness with children cast in the role of warriors. Twelve- and fourteen-year-olds helped defend Germany in 1945, the infamous *Hitler Jugend*. Cadets from the Virginia Military Institute charged grizzled Union veterans in a raging thunderstorm at the Battle of New Market, in 1864. Fifty-six kids out of a class of 225 died taking those Yankee cannons.

But at the moment I was thinking of *Los Niños*, heroes from my own cultural past. My grandparents, you see, moved to the United States from Sonora fifty years ago.

On September 13, 1847, U.S. troops—including U.S. Marines—stormed the castle of Chapultepec. Built on the site of the palace of Montezuma, Chapultepec was the last *Mexicano* fortress guarding Mexico City . . . and the "Halls of Montezuma" remembered in the Marine Corps Hymn. Among the defenders at Chapultepec, the last defenders of the Mexican flag, in fact, were cadets at the Mexican Military Academy. Their heroism is one of Mexico's most cherished traditions. There is a painting—I've seen it—of young Vincente Suárez, who refused to leave his sentry post guarding a stairway and died with his musket still at shoulder-arms.

They were called *Los Niños,* the Children.

I thought about the way humans always caricaturize the people they happen to be in hate with at the moment. Gooks, slants, wops, chops, gringos, krauts, and worse. Call the other guy something derogatory and it was easier to bring yourself to kill him, a kind of shorthand to represent the feared, the hated, the *unknown* stranger. The tendency became even more pronounced once we made it to the stars and found strangers out there unlike anything we'd ever imagined back on our own small, overcrowded world. Sharkies, Greenie-Meanies, four-eyes, turdlickers, cannibals, slimers.

Give them a funny name, and you don't feel so bad when you kill them.

So it hurts when your nose is rubbed in the fact that they share something in common with you. That they're *people,* no matter how many eyes or mouths they have, what color they are, or what they had for breakfast.

"You can take the Silver Star," I told Weiss, "and stuff it."

"Catharine," he said, "don't be like that. You're a *hero.* And we need heroes in this war. The Meanies have been inflicting heavy casualties on our forces. We need heroes . . ."

"*Mi-hie-nyees,*" I said.

"What?"

"Not 'Meanies,' sir. *Mi-hie-nyees.* PanTerra may be trying to take their home world away from them, but damn it, they deserve our respect."

"Gunnery Sergeant Aguilar, do I need to remind you that they are the *enemy?*"

"No, sir, you do not."

I was thoughtful for a long time after he left. The

Corps is everything to me. Mother. Father. Family. Since I lied about my age and joined at seventeen, the Corps had been my home.

But I was beginning to wonder who the real enemy was.

Damned PanTerran grifters. Suits. *Lawyers*. . . .

AN ADMIRAL'S OBESSION

by Kathleen M. Massie-Ferch

Kathleen M. Massie-Ferch was born and raised in Wisconsin. She worked her way through college, earning degrees in astronomy, physics, and geology-geophysics. For twenty years she worked for the University of Wisconsin as a research geologist. Massie-Ferch made short fiction sales to a variety of places, such as *MZB's Fantasy Magazine*, *Sword and Sorceress*, *Warrior Princesses*, and *New Altars*. She coedited two historical fantasy anthologies for DAW Books, *Ancient Enchantresses* and *Warrior Enchantresses*. Kathy passed away in 2002.

*C*URRENT *Action, Part 1—Planet Qu'Appelle Prime*
   I handed Admiral Catherine Westmoor a tumbler of juice. She took a swallow, then quickly looked from her glass to me, her eyes narrowed slightly. I shrugged. The admiral took another drink as she glanced around the reception hall. Dinner would begin soon.

   "An interesting lack of bite to this brandy, Captain Barclay."

   "Actually, I'm following your husband's orders. He insisted we take caution whenever Senator Devon is near."

   "Ah, I must remember to *thank* him for this useless deception."

I couldn't help but smile. "If you hadn't promoted him over me, this wouldn't have happened. I trust you."

"I've had a long day and thought I earned a stiff drink."

"Yes, but then you would tell our new senator just what you really think of him."

"Barclay, I don't see the harm in that scenario. Truly, I don't."

"Well, it would be the best entertainment we'd likely see tonight. Devon had at least two robust drinks before you got here. Both of you drinking would make for some very lively arguments, excuse me, discussions."

"But did you actually think I wouldn't notice if—" She stiffened as she listened to her earpiece. In the next breath she deposited her glass on the nearest table, not caring if it stayed there, and pulled out her data-link as she hurried across the room. A quick jab at the wall's sensor with her link and the door to the adjoining room whisked open. I followed closely. Many in the reception hall were moving toward the Communication Center, including Senator Devon. This had to be a general alarm, if all ten admirals were alerted.

The Comm room was small, but it had direct communications to our orbiting station, including a small transference pad. Admiral Westmoor activated the comm-link while the room's technician bristled nearby in dismay. He was employed by the Council and not the Military, so his professional instinct was to stop Westmoor, but his survival instinct wisely overruled. The admiral soon had visual for the orbiting station.

"You delayed relaying that message by ten minutes!" Admiral Westmoor exclaimed to the Station's Comm-tech. "Ten minutes!"

"Yes, sir." When the admiral used that tone, no one made excuses. No one.

"What's going on?" Senator Devon asked even as other admirals and Council members crowded the room.

Admiral Westmoor ignored him and continued checking data on the space-net connection before her. "Activate the MCT from Prime to Station now," she ordered the Council's tech officer. He didn't move. I started to follow Admiral Westmoor's orders, but Devon deliberately blocked my path.

Westmoor changed the Comm address and the image of the Station's trans-officer filled the screen. "Ensign, charge Station's main MCT! Run the *Farpoint* protocol with the latest updates and set up a high-energy transference. Mark fifteen minutes from now, one transfer. Followed twenty minutes later by the second, single-step transference."

The ensign paled. Even I felt short of breath and I had expected that order. Several Council members behind me asked simultaneous questions.

"Catherine," Admiral Swan outvoiced them all, despite her advanced age. "That's just too far. You can't solve enough of the fifth order derivatives."

"We've no choice." Westmoor glared at the Council's tech. He stepped aside. She initialized the program for Prime's small MCT and turned to Senator Devon as the power was surging on the transference pad. "The *Aeneid* has found your father's virus. Or, rather, it has found the *Aeneid*. They're under attack."

"Ridiculous! This virus has been dead for centuries. It's a dead system!"

"Still, they're under attack, and we can't shut down *Farpoint*. This is your fault. If you hadn't countered my orders with legislation, we could destroy *Farpoint* from here."

"Destroy a new space station, not to mention abandoning our best research ship and all of her crew? Only you would expect us—"

"Listen to me! There is now a direct path from

there to here. Direct and open to whatever is attacking them. If the *Aeneid* fails, that attacker will be here soon after, perhaps in days!"

"An alien virus! Not much of a threat."

"I have no intentions of finding out. It can't have that option."

"Yet you're planning on mapping the way by going there first?"

"That won't happen, not with my program."

The pad was at full energy, so Admiral Westmoor simply walked away and onto the MCT platform. I followed as did several others, including Admiral Swan and a hurrying Senator Devon. I barely reached the center of the pad when Westmoor activated it with her data-link. I felt the power tingling along my nervous system, and then the energy mist cleared and we were walking out of the Station's transference device.

The MCT's alarm stood at yellow and colored the room in its warm glow. The only admiral to follow us had been Dayel Swan, and she immediately descended on Senator Devon, grilling him about his legislation, as if she had just learned of it. Westmoor had already swooped down on the main computer net.

This was the Station's largest transference center and it was crowded with hurrying women and men. A select crew of eighteen tech-soldiers would make the first transference to *Farpoint* Space Station with Westmoor and myself. The other ten tech-soldiers in the room were our backup insurance and would follow us soon.

Devon ignored Swan. "This could not have all started in the last five minutes. You're running a preprogrammed sequence."

"Of course it's preprogrammed," Westmoor answered. She took a survival pack from an aide and strapped it on, even as I did. Her eyes never left her computer screen. I watched the program's progress as well.

"On whose authority?" Devon demanded.

"My own. I've been concerned this would happen for the past week. Now, go away. I have work to do."

"I'm going with you."

"Too dangerous."

"If it's safe for you, it's safe for me. Who else can keep you honest?"

She shook her head. "Your skin!"

Devon looked around. "Where are the weapons? None of these soldiers are armed."

"Hand weapons against a virus?" Swan asked, her voice oozing sarcasm.

I looked up. "We can't risk their energy stream in a transference field."

"Admiral Westmoor transferred weapons with MCTs all the time during the war," Senator Devon countered.

Westmoor finally looked up from her data-net. "Can you really understand so little? This is the longest single transference in our history, with the exception of the jump that brought our ancestors here. And even you should remember your history of that disastrous event." Westmoor looked down again and pointed to the program's status. "Looks within parameters. Seven minutes," she then told the room of busy techs.

I brought up some of the deeper derivatives. "It looks really good, actually. Not many variations since our last update, just before I left for dinner."

I keyed in my code and sent a personal message to my wife, one I had made several days before, just in case, and then touched the alarm circuit and spoke into it, knowing everyone on Prime's Station heard me. "Captain Denver Barclay, here. High-energy transference in five minutes. Code red, lockdown beginning now."

I heard the solid thump as automatic doors closed all over this portion of Station, isolating it from the living and office spaces. At the moment, this complex had no surface in common with Station. If an error occurred, they would be safe and only the MCT would be lost.

Red light filled the room since we were at a higher alert status, adding a tension that hadn't been there a moment before.

I moved away from the data-net, and knelt beside some of the other gear to examine it. The poly bags all contained explosives. And not just any kind, this was specially designed to travel through the MCTs safely. The latest toy from the research groups—Admiral Swan's special project. There should already be enough explosives on hand at *Farpoint*, I had sent the material there myself, but Westmoor wanted more. For all we knew, Devon could have ordered that first shipment of explosives spaced.

Admiral Swan touched Westmoor's elbow. "You could travel in two transferences if you went to Bocelli's Station and then *Farpoint*. Each transference would be shorter and safer."

"We looked at that option. Bocelli is unmanned and was stripped to the bone. Its automated pad has a very small power plant. We're moving a large mass, I can't be sure it'll provide enough energy. And the total travel time would be over seven hours. We may not have that much time. I know this program will work."

"You're right, about the power being limited. Especially after Senator's Devon's spending cuts," Swan said. "I agree, your plan is the best. Be safe."

Catherine Westmoor nodded in the direction of

Station's central hub. "Watch after my kids, would
you?"

"It'll be my pleasure."

I knew both women were referring to the Station
as well as Westmoor's three-year-old twins. The
older woman turned.

"Good fortune, Captain Barclay," Admiral Swan
wished me.

I nodded to her as I adjusted the weight of my
survival pack, then picked up one of the last poly
bags not already claimed by a tech-soldier, and
walked to the transference pad beside Westmoor.

Admiral Swan addressed the entire room. "Good
fortune and may you all return safely from *Farpoint!*"

Senator Devon grabbed a survival pack for himself
and hurried after us into the energy mist as the
power was already coursing along my spine. Damn,
he wasn't going to let Admiral Westmoor out of his
sight. He had guts, but not too many brains.

Four Months Earlier—Prime's Space Station

I checked the time and then toggled Prime's commuter MCT. "This is Captain Barclay. How long before Admiral Westmoor's party arrives?"

"Judith Barclay on this end. I suggest the captain
get his butt over here if he doesn't want to be late
to greet his admiral."

Normally her tone would have brought at least a
smile to me, but I just wasn't in the mood today. I
had been up most of the night, and I still couldn't
see the top of my desk. My specialty was mapping
MCT shipping routes, a skill my commander ex-
ploited incessantly. "Of course, Judith. If Ensign
Orham is there, I'd actually like his report."

A young man's voice interrupted Judith's next
reply. "The admiral's party is sixteen minutes out,
sir. All trace readings appeared normal when they

passed the last Trans boost. There is no honor guard here. Does the captain wish me—"

"Negative, Ensign. The admiral is merely returning from a long weekend."

"But, Denver," Judith interrupted again. "She's an admiral. She deserves some pomp. At least a few guards?"

"That's an order, Ensign! I'm on my way."

The station was quiet. Being the middle of the week and midmorning, it should have been busy, but then Westmoor was the first admiral returning from holiday. By week's end all ten admirals would be in residence and many of the Council's members would start returning to Prime. Even though the full Council session wouldn't start for another two weeks, the Council couldn't abide a full complement of admirals without an equal complement of their members close by. The discussions, or should I say arguments, about the Brightman Cluster would start soon after and then everyone's holiday would be over.

I glanced up at the planet hanging like an orange-and-rust jewel in the black sky, Qu'Appelle Prime. It was far from the most beautiful planet in the twenty colonized systems, but it was our first and it was still rich in minerals and ores. Perhaps the richest.

I entered the MCT's receiving room. Judith let out a steady stream of French the moment she saw me. I knew the court language, somewhat, from what she had taught me in the eight years we had been married, but I didn't know it that well.

"Slow down. I couldn't follow half of what you just said. Or speak Common."

"You're impossible. Why no honor guard?" She interrupted me before I could answer. Damn, but I loved her accent when she was worked up like this. "And don't say this is what she wants. She deserves respect."

"I won't argue." I spoke softly as I ushered her off to the side of the room, and away from the busy techs. A transference from this far out had all of their attention and a good portion of mine. It was very reliable technology, but most people didn't trust it as Westmoor did. Anyone else journeying from so far away would have spent the day traveling and made at least three transfers. But then few truly understood the physics of the MCT, Mass and Communication Transference device, as Admiral Westmoor did. It was the lifeblood of our culture which is why her grandfather, the late king, had insisted she know it so well.

"But?" Judith persisted.

"She'd have my head. No show, especially in front of the children. Plus an honor guard will point out the fact she wasn't here. And then some may ask where she was?"

That pulled some of the T-cells out of her. "But she owns Thames."

"How many admirals, or for that matter even senators, own their own planet?"

"She lets anyone who wants go there. To vacation or live, without even a permit."

"And to answer my question, none. A few wealthy may own an asteroid, or a small moon, but she owns a good-sized planet and has the right to charge taxes."

"But she doesn't. Well, not very much tax."

"Thames is far enough away that few think of it very often, and despite its beauty, few covet it. And she travels in one transference to play down the fact she goes there at all."

"But she's worked so hard for the Service," Judith spoke in a whisper. "My cousin is loyal to the core."

"The war's memories are deep wounds, even after twenty years. I fought beside Catherine and Andrew, so I know they are loyal. Others haven't seen that side of her. There are no holos of her fighting against her grandfather, or her slaving over the data-net since then, and far too many holos of her as the darling of the Royal Court. Becoming a full admiral is not exactly disappearing into the military structure. She has lots of power. Some say too much. Councilman Devon is not happy—"

"I'll take that man and—"

I had to laugh and kiss her forehead. "Spoken like the Mad King's granddaughter all right." Judith was very much like her cousin Catherine. But whereas Judith was strong-willed and could weather any storm as a young tree might, Catherine was more like the storm itself. But then Catherine had been bred to rule from generations of rulers—descended from the original Station commander—as had been her grandfather, Mad King James. Only his own son and granddaughter could unravel his genius and ultimately defeat him. Many tried to put young Catherine Westmoor, the beautiful princess and war hero, on the throne in his place. She declined. Now she was twenty years older and some saw her rise to this new military position as a way to take back power.

I knew better. Catherine Westmoor wanted nothing more than to explore space, finding new worlds, and perhaps that elusive prize—Earth. But in the 220 years since the Separation, we still didn't have a clue as to where our first home was. Most scholars believed it still existed. The disaster that sent our original MCT off course was isolated and couldn't have destroyed Earth, too. Others disagreed.

"Captain Barclay," Ensign Orham began. "Admiral Westmoor's trace is very strong. It'll be here in a moment."

Already the air above Transference Deck began to glow bluish white with the raised energy levels. The force field separating that portion of the receiving room from ours strengthened and shielded our eyes from the brightening energy. After two minutes that room was back to normal and there stood my boss with her family.

She was taller than Judith and more athletic, but the cousins had the same honey-brown hair and sea-green eyes. Catherine sported a deeper tan and wore a long beach dress and, depending on how she moved, left more uncovered than covered. She carried little Athena and Andrew carried Jason.

Andrew Welton wore the casual dark blue uniform of a ship's captain. The children were talking rapidly as only three-year-olds can. As soon as their parents set them down, they ran to Judith. Both were speaking a stream of French. Judith swept the children up in a hug.

"Uncle Judith," Athena exclaimed. I lost much of the rest in the quick gibberish. Catherine groaned softly.

I looked at Andrew. "Something about a monster fish on the beach?"

"Judith, I'm sorry," Catherine began. "I thought we had this aunt versus uncle thing fixed."

Judith kissed Athena again. "Anglais, anglais, mon petit urchin. It's all right, Catherine. She'll get it soon enough. They speak French so much better now!"

Catherine shook her head. "The people of Thames swear they will never speak Common. Even my household staff!"

"Loyalist?" I asked Catherine softly, though the MCT tech was too far away to hear us.

"No, stubborn and harmless supporters of tradition."

"Or they're just trying to be different," Andrew added.

"You never did like French class," I teased Andrew.

"You all look rested. How was your trip?" Judith asked.

"Too short!" Andrew exclaimed as he picked up one case, and I picked up the other two off the transference platform. The children were still going on in a combination of French and Common, finishing each other's sentences and holding onto Judith. I listened as we walked through the station to the admiral's quarters.

"A sea monster?" I asked.

Catherine nodded. "A very large squid-type thing." Andrew tried unsuccessfully to interrupt. "I don't care what its technical name is. It was trapped in a tidal pool. Since there are so few of them, some of the servants, under Andrew's expert eye, worked very hard to keep it out of the sun and wet until the tide returned."

Andrew covered Jason's mouth briefly, slowing down his excited jabber. "That was two days ago and the children have been down to the beach every day since, hoping for another glimpse of one. No bodies washed up, so it's likely we saved it. By the way, it was a *cephalopod molludermata.*"

Catherine shook her head. "Never take a biologist to the ocean for a vacation. Do I have to report right away, Denver?" she asked. "Or might we get some lunch first? And I need to change. Not a single one of my uniforms made it in my travel bag, although I placed several in there. If it weren't for the fact I had some old clothes from my school days there, I'd have spent the weekend in my beachwear or my nightshirt." Judith merely smiled. "Fortunately, Judith, you never had access to my work pouch."

I ignored the dark, but good-natured looks that passed between the cousins.

"The Station is deserted. You're the first admiral back."

"Really? Have we heard from Professor Kendrick yet?"

"Surprisingly, no. That's right, she was supposed to either call in or transmit her report by now. I'll help you take this luggage to your rooms and then go—"

Catherine interrupted. "You take the luggage while I go to my office and contact her, then I'll be back for lunch." She started to move away when my wife spoke up.

"You mean Klaefer Kendrick?"

"Yes." I answered. "How do you know her?"

"Oh, she sent a longish thing to Catherine's personal data-net in the apartment."

"When?" Catherine asked softly. She stopped in the middle of the walking path.

Judith being Judith, she just ignored the soft intensity in the admiral's voice. There was an undercurrent of anger very carefully restrained in the older woman. It usually sent most people dashing for safer ground. But Judith could weather it, as could Andrew.

"Oh, early yesterday." she answered brightly. "And if I had sent it on, you would have spent all night reading and not with your family. And the nightwear I placed in your bag was anything but a simple shirt!"

"It is a very important report," Catherine answered softly.

"Of course it is. It's a very thorough discussion." She bent down to tease a smile out of Jason and then started forward again. They began a nursery rhyme. I wasn't certain, but it sounded like something they were making up on the spot, and spoke of large sea monsters and of course was in French. I exchanged glances with Andrew.

"She's a civilian," Andrew told his wife. "And is more like you than you know."

"She has the clearance," I added.

"I know she can hold her tongue, otherwise I'd throw her into holding myself. Reading my correspondence!" Catherine started forward again. "Like me, you say?"

"Very much," Andrew answered.

"Except she doesn't worry about anything."

Andrew shrugged. "It's a good way to stay away from politics. Something you seldom manage." That won him a dark look from his wife. I tried to maintain a straight face.

When we got to the admiral's rooms, Judith started lunch while Catherine, Andrew, and I went to her study. We found two copies of the data-pac on her desk, next to the original. We started reading. Sandwiches appeared at our sides and I ate without thinking. When I finished reading, I found both Catherine and Andrew staring off into space. Judith was leaning against the doorjamb waiting. I could hear the children in their room, playing and singing.

"The planet Kendrick's on now has the oldest ruins in the Brightman Cluster," Catherine said.

"Do all show such violent destruction?" Judith asked.

Catherine regarded her a moment. "Yes, all nine of them. But this world's is the most chaotic, almost as if it took them one world to learn how to destroy their own planets."

Andrew and I looked at each other. He got the words out first. "Who's them? You don't really think the death of these planets is anything other than accidental?"

Catherine answered. "I don't know. I have always felt the virus and destruction were more closely connected than Professor Devon believed. His discovery of the virus, as discussed in their literature, was a brilliant jump in logic. It was years before it was proved. But nine destroyed worlds in such a small area of space? And there's something about how each planet looks. I restudied the holos from Kendrick's previous reports a lot over the last few days."

"Instead of resting?" Judith asked. "And playing in the warm sand?"

Catherine looked at her cousin. "This is very important. You've studied tactics under the best teachers. What does this report tell you?"

Judith sighed. "Yours is a reasonable conclusion. There is no other advanced species near their space, but for us. This culture had not known conflict for many, many generations. Yet the pattern of the violence appears as if they were using explosives as a surgical tool. However, it did not work, since they couldn't halt the virus' progression."

"Do you really see a pattern?" Catherine asked.

"Yes."

"Then look at these." Catherine reached into her work pouch and handed over many enlarged pictures. Judith studied each holo.

I saw a side of my wife I seldom saw. In public Judith played the content and happy teacher of the very young, but now I saw that other side, the one of restrained power, weaker than Catherine's, but then Judith was nearly ten years younger. In another ten years?

"Why?" the admiral asked.

Judith shrugged as she continued to scan the holos. "Perhaps because you were the last admiral to leave. Because you spend so much time looking at Kendrick's many reports and you needed your rest in order to think more clearly about this new report. Your family needed you and you needed them. I can find other reasons, but the strongest is this: once you send Andrew out, you won't see him for months."

"You're not my nurse or nanny."

Judith shrugged again as she sorted the holos into various piles. "I'll not apologize for doing what was right."

"Am I going somewhere?" Andrew asked. He looked from Catherine to me. I could only shrug in turn.

"Probably," Catherine answered as she activated her main computer. Her fingers moved rapidly over the touch pads. In another moment a hologram of the Brightman Cluster and its nine star systems, all dead, danced in the room before us. Our own twenty-star cluster was farther toward the galactic center. Judith circled the holo-display. Catherine came from around her desk and did the same. It was strange seeing my commander in a beguiling beach dress and not the standard uniform. I wondered how Judith, with her rounder curves, would look in that dress.

"Where is this planet? The one that died first?" Judith asked.

Catherine touched the control pad. "I'll scale it with the oldest destruction in deep blue, the newest in red. Their prime or Alpha as we called it, is somewhere in the mid-range of dates."

It took just a moment and we could all see the pattern. The ages swept out from the oldest world in a spiral. I reached for the computer, requesting details on other worlds near the Brightman Cluster.

"What are they?" Judith asked as the display changed.

"Star systems within the Brightman not considered dead," I answered. "Although that is a debatable condition. We surveyed them a few years ago and found they never contained higher life-forms. So they are, in fact, dead worlds. They just were always absent of advanced life, or in some cases, any life."

"What's the time of first destruction again?" Andrew asked.

I looked for the data on the screen. "That would be six hundred eighty-five years, plus or minus fifteen years. The second is from six hundred seventy-five years ago, with the same differential."

"What is the most recent?" Judith asked.

"Six hundred and fifty years ago, plus or minus six years."

"All much older than our appearance in this part of the galaxy," Andrew commented.

"Thirty-five years to destroy billions of *people* on nine worlds? And with space travel?" Judith asked. "That is a long time. No?" We all looked to Andrew for the answer.

"For them, it may be a swift movement through their worlds. But you're right. For us, thirty-five years would be slow for a wild plague to sweep through. MCT travel would spread things much more quickly. Probably in one month, but that depends on the incubation time."

Catherine began. "These four worlds! We found them lifeless, low in minerals, so we never did a detailed study because they were not worthwhile for expansion." Catherine turned to me. She was my admiral again, even out of uniform. "We have to return and do detailed studies. Captain Barclay, you need to break the news to Professor Kendrick."

"News?" I asked.

"She's not going to get a holiday. I want her crew ready for the next site within ten days. The specific world will depend on another rapid study when she gets there. Andrew, you need to get my ship ready. The *Aeneid* will shuttle Kendrick and also set up an MCT closer to those systems."

I took notes on my handcomp. "Kendrick'll complain she's not finished with her work on the current planet."

"It's a dead society. It's not going anywhere anytime soon. She can go back later. I need a rapid survey of those other worlds. And a time line of their death, if she finds ruins."

"You're sure they contained life at one time?" I asked.

"No, but if that space was ours, we'd have at least one station around each of those worlds." She was back at her desk and brought up the stats for her old ship. "We should be able to make transference by—"

Andrew came forward. "Admiral, do you mean to take back my command from me?"

She opened her mouth and then closed it again. Judith chuckled softly, but then stopped after one look from her cousin.

"Dearest, that's the price of your promotion," Judith said softly. "You knew it would come to this, some day. Just be glad you now have the power to send out the *Aeneid*, or any other ship, without authorization. Not from Council or other admirals. Your word is law now."

"As long as I don't go myself."

"Yes, it was an unfair bargain between the Admiralty and the Council, but you'll become used to it," Judith said. "Councilman Devon and his friends were desperate to have you off that ship and the power it holds. If he could, he would take it from under your command completely."

"I wish I was as fearsome as he seems to think I am," Catherine said. The rest of us had everything we could do to keep from laughing.

"You do have your moments," Andrew said softly.

"I'm going to get your children ready for a nap," Judith said. "They'll be wanting hugs and kisses from all three of you in not more than five minutes."

"Why don't you like old Professor Devon's theory?" I asked the admiral.

"That's my question, too," Andrew interjected. "It's sound biology. And passed stiff critiquing years ago."

She shrugged. "It's a little too convenient. Any form of illness, viral or bacterial, would have left some survivors on some of the planets. But every race dead? Every planet dead of all higher, land-dwelling species?"

"Professor Devon also thought they destroyed each world, one at a time, to save the others from the illness. As Judith said, surgery by explosive. An energy pulse is very effective killing."

"It was a good theory, until there was only one world remaining. Why destroy that last one? Was the virus so horrendous they'd rather die than contract it? Or face the results? We started with a broken space station and a few hundred survivors and now we are twenty star systems strong in two hundred years. Their society had space travel, but they couldn't outrun it?"

"All of those species were genetically related," Andrew said. "As if they began from the same roots. Perhaps that base just wasn't as hardy as humans."

"Perhaps."

I went in to find my wife. Admiral Westmoor was already at her computer working on finding the answers she could believe. Captain Andrew Welton was working beside her.

Prime's Space Station

Captain Welton had left for the *Aeneid* nearly five weeks before and it seemed as if all I did since then was listen to the Admiralty argue with the Council. Sometimes it took place on Qu'Appelle Prime, other times Councilman Devon sought out Admiral Westmoor to pick up the argument where they had left off, usually because Westmoor had been called away and actually had the nerve to leave him in mid-argument. This was one of those days where he had followed us to the Station and then to Westmoor's office.

"Councilman, I thought you were the protectionist?" Westmoor asked. The coolness of her voice sent a shiver up my spine. Didn't he feel it, too?

"I am, when it is appropriate," Devon answered. "This new MCT site is fully funded and built. Why aren't you seeing to its deployment? Instead you're playing with that research ship. If it's beyond your abilities, we can find someone else."

"Beyond my abilities to deploy a string of Transference probes in a quiet region of space? Please, Councilman, surely even you can formulate a better insult than that?"

"Then what are you trying to avoid?" Devon's aide asked.

Admiral Westmoor was unshakable today. "I am the military's expert on MCTs. Like it or not, we launch the next phase of this mission when I say the area is secure. Nothing you do can change that."

"Are you sure?" Devon asked.

"Yes. We currently have a science mission evaluating that system and its viability."

"It was your report that recommended expansion," the aide pointed out.

"Actually, it was against my conclusions that the Council decided to fund this project."

"Is this what's bothering you?" Devon asked. "We didn't listen to the great war hero and now you're trying to make us suffer?"

"Yes, Councilman, you understand me perfectly!"

"Each delay costs massive revenues," Devon said after a brief pause.

"With no chance to recoup those moneys," his aide added.

"This is the first system we are trying to take over that was once inhabited by another, intelligent, space-faring species. Perhaps a little delay is warranted?"

"A long-dead people," Devon added.

"Still, are we sure of what we are entering?"

"The biohazard was evaluated and dismissed."

The admiral nodded. "I know. I'm reevaluating it."

"Ridiculous! Possibly we should take this expense out of your personal wealth?"

"If you want my wages, take them," Westmoor answered evenly.

"That's not the source I had in mind."

Admiral Westmoor merely smiled. "Try it." With that the councilman and his aide walked out. I closed the door quietly behind them.

"Why make him angry?" I asked, as Westmoor turned to her data-net. "He can cause some real trouble. He's days away from being elected a senator."

"It'll keep him busy."

"But if he looks too closely at what we're doing—"

"He's not stupid. Perhaps he'll learn a few things, once he stops listening to that fool who shadows him. He might even come to agree that his father was not totally right about the source of the Brightman's demise."

"His father? His personal hero is wrong and you're right? Not likely since it was your grandfather who killed that hero."

"That was an unfortunate event, especially since I could use the elder Devon's help just now. The professor was brilliant."

"Admiral—"

"Captain Barclay, you worry too much about my career. You have your own problems to examine. Just let me know if Captain Welton signs in."

"What makes you think he'll check with me before his wife?"

She actually smiled. "Get to work, Barclay. I want those safeguards in place before the *Aeneid* leaves her home base MCT."

And of course she was right. Andrew Welton did

contact me first. "Barclay, what the hell is she thinking?" Welton asked. "These extra relays in the MCT will add hours to the data transfer. Narrowing the transference width will make communication a royal pain!"

"She insists we keep the signal from being followed through the nodes. This narrow band with a complex route will be nearly untraceable, in part because of the rapid decay. She calculated a delay of about fifteen minutes."

"Bull!"

"I agreed with your take on it, but Lieutenant Markum backed up her figures."

"Captain Welton, the numbers are accurate."

I nearly jumped out of my seat. I hadn't heard the admiral walk up behind me.

But Captain Welton wouldn't back down. "Admiral Westmoor, this doesn't give us leeway to maneuver if there is any equipment failure. It leaves only enough transference space for communications, none extra for crew movement through the MCT."

"Agreed," she said evenly.

"Admiral," I began. "Everyone on Council already knows where the *Aeneid* is. Why conceal it further?"

Welton interrupted. "Wait! Catherine, this looks suspiciously like that gambit Mad James made. The one where he abandoned his fleet to us and—"

"No, Captain, it wasn't a move of abandonment, but rather one of sacrifice."

"Same difference," Welton answered tersely.

"No, it meant that even though we had control of all of our space, we had to search another two years to get to him, personally."

His eyes narrowed slightly. "Why are you so worried over these desolate worlds?"

"If they're truly barren worlds, they won't concern me, but if they were destroyed? That's another problem. Nothing should cause so complete a destruction of life. I want guarantees that whatever killed the Brightman Cluster is now harmless. Is Kendrick there?"

"Yes, Admiral." The compact woman walked into the camp's view. She looked tired and old, every bit of her eighty-four years.

"Doctor, you mentioned in your very first report from thirty years ago—a different species, and not a new derivative of any of the existing species."

"Yes, ruins and bio-remains for that one species appeared only on their Alpha world. All other species occurred on at least one other world."

"You're sure of it?"

"Yes, but I don't see how that matters."

"Could this have been the first intelligent species in the system and all others derived from it?"

"No, this was the only species living in a hivelike society. Derivations would also be hive dwellers. It was likely a bio-engineered species to manage certain crops or control pests."

"You mean something like our Colonial ants or bees?" I asked.

"Yes, but most of the members of this species, when full grown, were nearly as tall as you are, Captain. We don't know a lot. King James pulled the detail before we explored their nest too far. He thought we were in their zoological exhibit."

"If I can interrupt," Welton began. "Barclay, you're right. This species is very similar to Colonial ants in one important feature, that each hive is a hive of near clones. On Brightman there was only one hive that we ever found, and all of its members were virtually identical to each other."

"How does this matter?" the admiral asked.

"Well, first because of how rapidly an advanced intelligence can communicate when it's a cloned hive.

It's a great defense mechanism since anything not of the hive is an enemy. And of second importance, because creatures this large had to eat so much to survive, we should be able trace their presence, or absence, on any of the destroyed worlds by looking for their bio-signature."

"After all this time?" I asked.

"These planets have very little bio-turbulence going on. Once we identify the sediment horizon of the pre-disaster, we should be able to scan for their existence in the sands and building residue."

"Captain Welton," Westmoor said. "When will you have the initial MCT nodes in place?"

"They're in place now and sending back data from the first world we want to explore. In another day we'll have enough data to allow us to send a full scale MCT to that placement. We can transfer the *Aeneid* the day after."

"Excellent."

"Admiral, I don't need to remind you that if something happens to that end-point MCT, we'll be stranded a long way from home. It'll take us years to actually pilot the *Aeneid* back to *Farpoint* and its large MCT."

Westmoor smiled. "Yes, I'm counting on it. But don't assume we wouldn't come and get you. It would take us a few weeks, but we would."

"Glad to hear that, for a minute I was wondering if you wanted a divorce."

"No, Captain, you're stuck with me for the near future, as both commander and wife."

"Wouldn't have anything else. Give my love to the children."

The Comm-net shifted back to data transfer from the *Aeneid*. I made sure all the proper stations were moving smoothly and turned to the admiral. She was still leaning over the screen and watching several of the data streams.

"I've seen Judith almost this paranoid, on rare occasions. Does it run in your family?"

She thought for a moment then laughed. "I prefer the term 'focused.' But yes, I believe it does. And fortunate for you that it is so. Otherwise, James would still be king, I would be dead, and Judith would never have known you existed, since she would be his heir."

"Just because that level of caution worked for you during the war, doesn't mean it'll work now. The enemy is a dead virus."

"You're right, Captain, I am who I am."

The *Aeneid* moved through the MCT. It was still a tense time whenever something that big transferred. I always wondered, just for a moment, if another MCT mishap would occur. But she materialized in space on schedule. The main end-point MCT transferred back to *Farpoint*, leaving the *Aeneid* with only a Comm-node MCT. Data flowed from the planet's surface to ship and then to headquarters with a maddening delay of twenty minutes, one way, instead of its usual few seconds. Captain Welton wanted to start survey teams on all four systems at the same time. Admiral Westmoor immediately rejected that idea.

Minimal presence, and only in one system at any given time. Never leave traces of visitation in any system. Only small teams and in enviro-suits at all times. Protective screens up on all sides of the ship, except for that portion of the ship facing the planet, thus allowing instant communication with the ground team and there were other restrictions. Captain Welton and Dr. Kendrick were frustrated by the slowing restrictions.

I arrived at my office one morning to find the admiral still in her dress uniform and watching incoming data. I thought she had gone down to the Council session on Prime the night before. Senator Devon had invited her personally. It had been an important affair.

"Was it a pleasant reception?" I asked.

"No, poor liquor and silly food. I stayed only a short time. And just for you, I was nice to Devon. I even danced with him."

"What's bothering you?"

"If I knew that, I'd not have to waste so much time poring over endless data files. Contrary to general gossip, I really do find this boring. I'd much rather be setting up the next MCT station or opening the next star system for exploration. Endless holograms of broken or melted artifacts are not very interesting either. I can't even piece together the purpose of half of what Kendrick found."

"Why do you need to?"

"To understand their enemy and ours."

"Our enemy? All of these worlds are dead!"

"Show me one world partially dead, or only partially destroyed during their *cleansing* that died slowly, later on, and I will stop worrying."

"Finding living aliens will make you happy?"

"Oh, yes. Because then we'll be able to see how they got to where they are. We'd be able to better understand why they destroyed all of their worlds."

I didn't have an answer for her, but then she wasn't waiting for my opinion. Already she advanced the next image. What did she see? What connection was she looking for? I went to answer some routine questions, and when I returned it looked as if she hadn't moved.

"Admiral," I began. "Is there something I can help with?"

"I'm now tracking the patterns of explosions. If it is a primary destruction, it gets a red code. If it is a secondary explosion, it is coded toward the blue end, depending on the delay. Purple has less delay."

"Secondary?"

"Yes, those areas that blew up because of the triggering, first explosion. Without that initial event, which was most likely some form of energy pulse, there would have been no other problems."

"Can we know the sequence that clearly?"

"Not even half the time, but it is a big planet. We should get enough pieces to get a sketch. As advanced a culture as they were, they would have enough objects in their everyday lives to cause a chain reaction, if the igniting energy is high enough."

By the end of the week we had pieced together enough data for the destroyed worlds. Westmoor ran the simulations over and over, each time faster. World after world. She looked at me after the last run.

"Each of those worlds was destroyed from space," I said. "By massive energy pulses, not surgical pulses."

"Yes. Which explains why the destruction was so complete."

"That doesn't mean it was done by an outside force. It still could have been as a preventative measure to stop the spread of disease."

"True."

"But you don't believe it?"

"I am willing to be wrong, but what illness can be that bad?"

"I don't know. Depends on their point of view, of course."

"We'll have to wait till Andrew brings in these four new worlds."

Every so often Senator Devon would arrive, and hover in operations, watching the telemetry from the *Aeneid*. And he listened. Westmoor never banned him, as if she had nothing to fear. Hell, I worried enough for all of us, especially after Devon started legislation that, if passed, would hamper our efforts. Admittedly, I didn't see the value in this exercise that

Westmoor did. But Mad James himself had trained her in tactics. How could she not know what she was doing?

And of course Devon arrived on time, and uninvited, for the summary at the end of the *Aeneid*'s exploration of the first planet. Finally Devon asked his questions. "Was this world destroyed by biological agents? Was the biology menace more fearsome than any physical destruction? If so, how was it so terrible?"

While we waited forty minutes for the *Aeneid*'s reply, I searched recent files from Kendrick for data we might already have to answer the senator's questions. Westmoor looked as if she was writing her latest report to the Admiralty. The senator paced.

Captain Welton spoke first. His deep voice filled the room with his presence. "This planet was destroyed by energy pulse. We are no closer to determining why it happened either. That notwithstanding, we did learn something new. We think it is important and may hold a clue as to their destruction. Their technology was bio-based. Meaning that each wiring component or circuit was alive, organic as well as part inorganic. Our optical wire is just a wire spun of silica, but their wire could get a cold. It could also heal itself, if broken or cut. It would be like sending a message through a living plant. If their technology had the same genetic base as their own biology did, and I think it did, then the virus could destroy the technology, along with the populace. The survivors would have been sent back to their preindustrial days."

"Or," Kendrick added. "The virus caused a form of mass insanity. And in their insanity they destroyed themselves."

"Although I don't see any evidence for that," Welton said.

"I'd think destruction of the whole cluster is evi-

dence enough," Kendrick added. "The possibility we
might respond as they did is something we must
prepare for."

"As you can see, we're not all in complete agreement
on what we're seeing."

Their new information on Brightman technology
surprised us. But Devon was grinning as he walked
out of the room.

Admiral Westmoor recovered quickly. "Captain Barclay and I ran some simulations. The major worlds were
clearly destroyed from space, though this doesn't negate
what you just said, but it adds to the puzzle. Why didn't
we see this aspect of their technology before?"

Again while waiting for their long reply, both Westmoor and I searched the computer files. We wanted
to know if there was any chance we had just missed
this data before.

Captain Welton's voice again filled the room. "Because this moon is devoid of an atmosphere. Always
has been. They spaced whole sections, I suppose to
try and stop the spread of the virus. The vacuum
preserved the components very well."

Kendrick added, "We found some more of their
writings. Some of the best since the first ones translated by the senator's father, Professor Devon. What
he translated as virus could also have been read as
death."

I looked at Westmoor.

"I don't see as how that makes any difference one
way or the other," she answered.

By the end of the day, I knew Westmoor was just
as frustrated by the communication delays as Captain
Welton, but she wouldn't budge on her restrictions.

Current Action, Part 2—Farpoint *Space Station*

I had experienced long transfers before, but they
never prepared me for the transfer from Prime's

Space Station to *Farpoint*. I was very glad I hadn't had anything to drink at that ridiculous dinner party. And I was betting Admiral Westmoor was just glad she had only had juice. However, Senator Devon had been drinking. I was wondering how sick he'd be when we got to *Farpoint*.

This was not a simple, commuter transference. Twenty-one people and their gear was a significant mass and it meant nearly four hours of energy teasing every nerve in our bodies as if with sharp needles. I was very relieved to finally arrive at *Farpoint*.

The transference pad was bathed in a steady red light, indicating the space station's status was one of highest alert. There was no sound in the empty room but our own breathing and movement. Admiral Westmoor motioned for two tech-soldiers to take point at the door, and for me to access the station's datanet as she handed me her data-link. The bright stick was warm in my hand. Senator Devon started asking a question, but Westmoor waved him silent. The station's data-net activated with the link's slight touch. At the same time, two techs, Walters and Simmions, began unloading their explosives and placing them around the transference pad. Everyone else crowded around me and the room's data-net.

"Admiral," Senator Devon whispered. "What are they doing?" He pointed to Walters and Simmions.

"Insurance," she answered softly as she looked over my shoulder at the screen indicating the station's full status.

"Ten persons in the command center," I said. "The rest likely went with the *Aeneid*."

"Any alien life-forms?" Westmoor asked.

"None reported, there has only been communication with the *Aeneid*. The main MCT is currently parked outside, right where it is supposed to be."

"Good," Westmoor looked at the techs. "You all

know what your jobs are. Get to them. If you encounter anything odd or alien, send word immediately as you are leaving the area. Seal those sections off. Do not investigate. Get to a safe place and hold for instructions. Simmions, you wait here for the rest of our crew. This room stays staffed at all times. Move out. Senator Devon, you're with me. Don't touch anything and keep out of mischief."

"I—" Devon started to speak.

"No discussion. Follow orders, or I'll have you tied up and put in a corner."

The admiral walked from the room as the techs began to disperse. I motioned for Devon to precede me as we followed Westmoor. He looked pretty steady on his feet, despite his alcohol consumption. The admiral and I wore soft-soled shoes, but Devon's were harder and his rapid pace was just about the only sound we heard until we entered the command center. I went to the Comm port.

"Admiral!" Lieutenant Sawchuck said. "Am I happy to see you. The *Aeneid*'s in trouble, and Captain Welton won't let us send the MCT back. We were just trying to raise them again."

"Captain Welton knows what he's doing," the admiral began. She placed her hand on the younger woman's shoulder. "You're doing great. Relax. When did your crew last eat?"

"We're fine, sir," Sawchuck answered.

"Good. The MCT, is it rigged?"

The lieutenant barely glanced at Senator Devon or even paused. "Yes, sir, just as your specs required."

"Admiral," I interrupted. "Our second group of techs just arrived. And I'll have the MCT to the *Aeneid* opening in five seconds."

She hurried to the port beside me and waited as the link became alive and Captain Welton's face filled the screen.

"Catherine! Where in hell are you?"

"*Farpoint*. What is your status?"

"Dead in space." He turned to his left. "Jerry, get those log files and download them to *Farpoint* now. Rapid compression on the data band." He turned back to us. "We were opening a new passage on that large moon. It was intact. Kendrick was ecstatic at the thought of whole objects."

The scene of Kendrick's crew approaching a door and opening it, played on a second screen. We watched as her crew, dressed in full enviro-suits, approached the small object.

"Is that a scout ship?" Westmoor asked.

Welton answered. "That's exactly what it was. It was also a trap."

We saw Kendrick's assistant open the ship's hatch. Immediately hundreds of spiderlike creatures spilled from the inside. But these creatures were the size of a small dog and had too many legs to count. Then the picture stopped. I looked up and saw Sawchuck had killed the vid-link.

"Don't watch it now," the lieutenant said, but her voice was almost a pleading.

"She's right," Welton said. "One of Kendrick's people got his hands on several dead critters. They're bio, and they're from that hive. Same genetic code. This is old Devon's virus. But he was wrong. It's death, pure and simple."

"Wait," the admiral said. "Kendrick said that species was human-sized."

"And the main ones are, but these are the worker's worker. Same species, dwarf-sized. And no, we don't know if they had a giant size, too."

"What happened to Kendrick? The short version."

"These beasties spread out. When at least one had attached itself to every member of the landing party and covered their craft, an energy pulse arrived from space and was channeled through the beastie until death occurred. Sometimes it wasn't real fast either. Pulse source is still unknown, otherwise we'd have a little surprise for them, too. Do you remember your military history?"

"Are you saying these are smart bombs?" Westmoor asked.

"Yeah, or very close to it. The people of Brightman weren't as peaceful as we thought. There was fighting among the species toward the end, and their main weapon outlived them." He checked his datalink. "You've got all of our data now. An hour ago we sent a probe toward that Alpha planet and the original hive."

"Via MCT?" Westmoor asked.

"Yeah, but a very small one, and it's rigged to blow soon after it transmits its data. I want to see these creatures. See where they live. If we have to die, I want it to be worth something."

"Die?" Devon interrupted. "Why can't we send the main MCT to get you and ship out of there?"

"Because we'd likely be bringing back lots of them with us. They hide very well, as we found out when some of Kendrick's people managed to escape and returned here. We've killed every critter we saw, but every so often they try sending another scout ship at us, so one or more beastie must be hiding here. It could even be on our outer hull. One of these times they'll sneak a ship past us. We can't take the chance and come back. Who knows how far they can communicate with each other. You're safe. They can't travel the Comm signal."

"And *Farpoint* will be gone very soon, too," Westmoor added.

"Those were my orders to Sawchuck," Welton added.

"I gave orders to destroy all explosives," Devon said.

Welton smiled. "So court-martial me for not following legislation! But the explosives are solidly in place, if anything bigger than a photon gets back to you, it all goes up. But it's a manual trigger. Otherwise Devon's aide would have been onto us."

"Understood," Westmoor answered.

"Where is my aide?" Devon asked.

"Here, out of trouble. Admiral, this was the best we could do." He smiled. "You gotta stop being right, Catherine."

"I'll keep that in mind," Westmoor answered softly.

"Admiral, this space is starting to feel crowded. How many people do you have there?"

"Too many. But we need to see your data from the hive. How long till return?"

"An hour, maybe a little more. I also want to see their response to a purely non-bio machine. Will they view it as a threat? And soon after that, it blows. Then I'm blowing all MCT tech on this end and aiming my ship for a little planet we noticed. There is no guarantee we'll get there and survive, but I owe my crew that. We'll have to see if I can get this baby away and if we're followed. That probe is small but very high powered, if you know what I mean?"

"Yes, I trust it's one of Swan's little toys?"

"Yep, these little beasties liked energy pulses, so they might not recognize this for what it is. I doubt it will kill them, but it may hurt them. I'm hoping for the mother nest."

"You are hopeful!" I added.

"Might as well aim for the top spot. I've gotten precious few breaks with these beasts. And they are just that. They're like biological robots. A Colonial ant with a wired brain. Definitely bioengineered by the Brightman races as a weapon. I'd be surprised if most of those races weren't engineered. The primary race loved playing. And they were very good. Technology that repaired itself! Amazing! But they got new genetic material from somewhere else and it appears as if they fought over access to that material. Kendrick thought the beasties were limited in their extent. That perhaps they only have one queen. But it seems more subtle than that. I'm betting they're bio-machines with simple tasks, and one is to protect against invasion."

"With the result of all the other life-forms being the invaders," the admiral added.

"Yes, even the one they were supposed to protect. When they sense no threat, they lie dormant and don't even procreate, but the minute their sensors detect something new, they swoop in and destroy. That's why there are no large land animals on any of these planets."

The admiral nodded. "And the lunar colonies the Brightman set up?"

"They were likely safe havens, until they grew too large and left a signature on the space around them."

"Or maybe they thought they had managed to destroy the beasties, or the beasties had died naturally, and came out of hiding."

"But the beasties show no signs of dying. We awakened them thirty years ago with the first expedition. It has taken them this long to get a large enough presence to attack us."

"Are you suggesting they're immortal?" I asked.

"No, but what is the life span of a hibernating computer? They'll have an attrition rate from natural events—storms, earthquakes, and the like, but who knows how long they were designed for."

"Any clues on their genetic source?"

"None."

"If we could remove their space travel abilities?" Westmoor asked.

"And their space ears, whatever they use, then

they are trapped on their world and will die out naturally. Or they could learn to evolve and learn how to repair and create their own technology."

"That's a cheery thought," Senator Devon added.

"But we've seen no new technology on any Brightman planet. I'm guessing they haven't evolved yet," Welton said.

"That's good news," I said.

"Very good news. What would send them over that threshold and trigger evolution?" Westmoor asked.

"Don't know. A large enough population might trip them over the edge."

"Which would only be achieved if they felt threatened enough," Westmoor said.

"Can they even evolve?" I asked.

"They're alive, so why not? Or perhaps the Brightman didn't add that mechanism in their genes."

"We can't be sure?" Westmoor asked.

"No."

The admiral turned to me. "Captain, round up all the kids and get them home, along with those data files." She looked at the station's crew. "You folks get to go first."

The ten women and men looked at each other. "Sir, we want to stay till the end, just in case," Sawchuck said for all of them.

"There is no 'in case' of anything. All crew here are going home. You've earned it. Go." She turned back to me. "Captain Barclay, I want a very tight stream back. Five crew per packet should be a good size. An hour between transfers will allow the energy signature a very rapid decay. Faster than any of these beasties can possible see, if they even know where to look."

"That makes sense," I agreed. "Or we could take Swan's advice and go back via Bocelli's station."

"I considered that. Bocelli's power plant design is

still a problem. It was never meant to transfer anything more than small research groups observing the planet. The power plant is marginal at best for this large a mass, even in small packets. We'd have to send most of our people planetside for days while waiting to get us all cycled through."

"That planet is primitive," Devon interjected. "We can't stay there!"

"It's preindustrial, but has the basics to survive, by most accounts," I added. "We'd have to pay for the right to stay there, of course."

Admiral Westmoor shook her head. "No, we all go to Qu'Appelle Prime. It's safer. Five crew per packet."

"But that tight a beam can't be done automatically. Someone will have to process all transfers."

"Not a problem."

"Until the last transference."

"Yes, but I'll take the last transfer by myself and then the bandwidth will be great enough to allow me to return via auto setting."

"It sounds reasonable."

"I thought so," she said with a slight smile.

I ushered the ten crew out of the command center and pulled Devon with me as Westmoor turned back to the screen.

"Why do I have to help you?" he complained. "I want to see what else Welton has to say." The bridge's door closed behind us.

"Because I think it would be decent to let a husband and wife say good-bye in private, don't you?"

"Oh," he had the good sense to look a little pale. I noticed Sawchuck and a few others looked more than a little upset. I wondered if some of the *Aeneid* crew were more than just friends and shipmates. I addressed them. "You can stop by the Comm Center, if any of you want the same privilege. It'll take me a few minutes to set up the transference." Most of the faces before me looked immediately relieved. We all hurried.

I set up the first transfer of five soldiers with the data packet as an extra kick, and then the second transfer an hour later. As I was waiting for the third window to open, I scanned the station's data banks and stripped everything not essential to the next few hours. During this exercise, Andrew Welton's image appeared on my Comm screen. He smiled and cocked his head, but his blue eyes were sad.

"Can you take care of them for me?" he asked.

"You know we will. Did you download that planet's coordinates?"

He shook his head. "Are you alone?"

"No, but all of *Farpoint*'s crew are on their way home."

"There is no planet. But I wanted them to have some hope till they got home. But all of my crew here have agreed that if we're a big visual ball of destruction, these beasties might go back into their sleepy mode. Then, in a few years, you can aim a probe right for their nest. Destroy the planet if need be."

"And if they don't shut down?"

"Don't know, but I don't see them as explorers. Just stay away from this space and keep your eyes open and heads down."

"There has to be a way. Any prospect of—"

He shook his head. "I've just had this argument with Catherine. Watch the file of how Kendrick and her people died. You'll know why there isn't a chance we're going to risk that. I agree with the Brightman's choice to destroy themselves." He touched his hand to the screen as I placed mine over his. "Take care and give my love to Judith. Tell her I'm sorry I can't be there to see if her babies have green eyes, too."

"Peaceful journey, friend," I said softly then the

screen went blank. Someone's hand rested on my shoulder in comfort, but I had a hard time seeing anything just then. I went back to clearing data from the station's net when we felt the whole structure shake.

"The large MCT just blew," someone called out. "Good job, too. I doubt there's a piece even as big as my hand."

A short time later Catherine Westmoor came into the station's MCT receiving room. We were getting ready to send the fourth group back home.

"Admiral?" one tech began from where he stood on the pad.

"Good journey," she said. "Tell them to put the coffee on, we'll all be right behind you."

The next few hours were quiet. Some of the tech-soldiers stretched out on the floor and napped, others went in search of better food than the rations we had brought with us. But it was a quiet time. No one wanted to say too much. Westmoor sat near me and drank some hot soup in a mug.

"What did the probe show?" Devon asked her. It took her a moment to come out of her distant thoughts.

"Beasties. Lots of them. They didn't like the probe much. Their hive is very active, unlike the first report from thirty years ago. The planet overall shows no land animals, but has lots of vegetation and some insect life. It looked pretty. I'm not a scientist, I'm sure I missed a lot. The experts will have to decipher it when we get back."

The quiet stretched on and then Devon spoke again. "Why did King James kill my father?"

Westmoor looked at him and thought for a moment before answering. "Your father was the best linguist and historian I ever met, and my teacher. And my grandfather didn't like his lessons."

"Which were?"

"That the monarchy was obsolete and restrictive."

"Was my father trying to brainwash you, or something?"

"No, it was a lively discussion. He took pro, I took con."

"Yet you swore you held that very opinion!"

"Professor Devon was an excellent teacher and a brilliant thinker. Whether I agreed or not didn't matter, until he died because we had a silly discussion over cold drinks on an oceanside terrace on a hot day. He was also my father's best friend and dear to me. We both had to avenge his death. I guess you could say Professor Devon's death proved he was right."

"Are you saying?"

"That your father destroyed the monarchy? Yes."

"Why has this never come out before?"

"The professor's last words to me were *Revenge is a poor motive for revolution and will not sustain change.* My father agreed, so we found a stronger, but no less true, reason. Insanity. It has held for twenty years. Long enough for the new government to survive under its own weight. Plus you never asked me."

I listened to the conversation, but I was also looking at the net screen when a small blip on the scanners caught my attention. I got up and tuned the instruments to a deeper sensitivity. It took a few moments to recognize it for what it was.

"Admiral, we've got a problem."

She was at my side in a heartbeat. "What?" She tuned the signal again.

"An energy pulse," I answered.

"Yes, and to get from there to here, this fast, it has to be traveling at much greater than the speed of light."

"Not possible."

"I know," she answered.

"Did they send it through an MCT?" Devon asked.

"Not possible," Westmoor answered.

"A closer source?" I asked, as I reached for another screen and tried to locate the source.

"Has to be." She looked for a targeting solution. "Blast, it'll be here in four-point-six hours. Is that enough time to get us all out of here?"

I looked at the clock. "Just barely. Four transfers left to go, including the solo packet."

"Can't we just all go now?" Devon asked.

"Not and keep the signal noise down. We can't leave a trace for them to follow."

"How do we know they can follow?" he asked.

"We don't, but then I would have said this energy pulse was impossible ten minutes ago and here it is."

"Send the transference back faster!"

"Same problem. It would be just a matter of them connecting the traces from here to home. No, the size and spacing of transfers is designed to cause the smallest ripple and to keep the ripples from adding up to form a wave pattern. We stay the course and get as many back as possible." She looked at the clock. "Next transfer?"

"Ten minutes."

We waited out the next three hours and we were down to six left, including Senator Devon, Westmoor, and myself. And the next window was rapidly approaching.

"Catherine," I began. "I want you to go next. I'll stay and—"

She smiled and shook her head. "This is a commander's prerogative. Besides the last transfer will be very close to the blast waves. I don't want to face my cousin if you don't make it back."

"But your children?"

"—Will be fine. You and Judith will see to that. Besides, Judith is probably a better mother than me any day. But I'm intending on being back home an hour after you."

This woman had been my commander, and friend, for over twenty years. She had married my best friend. I wanted to believe I'd see her in a few hours, but I was beginning to fear it might not happen. I reached out and pulled her into a hug. She hugged me back.

"Andrew would want you to go on," I whispered.

"Of course he would, and I intend to. Watch for me, I'll be there. It'll be tricky. This station is rigged to blow in one hour fifteen minutes and that pulse beam will hit here at almost the same time. But in either case I intend on having my nerves massaged to nearly the screaming point, by both shock waves."

"Is that a promise?"

She smiled. "Yes, Denver, I promise. Now will you go and stop making a scene."

The others were already on the transference platform, except for Senator Devon. He faced Westmoor. "I'm sorry about Andrew Welton. He was a good man." She barely nodded. "And I was wrong about you, you're not two women, a public face and a private face."

"But I am. You just don't know either of those women."

"Then I look forward to meeting them. And thank you for telling me about my father. Good fortune." And he held out his hand to her. She didn't hesitate as she shook it.

"Go! The longer you stay, the longer I have to stay here, too."

Soon the energy was coursing along my nerves. By the time I got back to Prime's Station, I wanted to never step into another transference flow again. It took several minutes for me to even get any voice out. Two such longer transfers in so few hours were just too much. Judith was there waiting for me, as was Admiral Swan. I couldn't answer their questions and I didn't even want Judith to touch me. She understood. We stood watching the signal net. It showed all of the old, rapidly fading traces and one trace still approaching. I took a deep breath.

"She did transfer," I finally said.

Devon let out a loud sigh. He had collapsed into a chair.

"Why wouldn't she?" Judith asked.

"Andrew destroyed the *Aeneid*, with all aboard."

Judith's green eyes went wide, then she nodded. She wouldn't cry, not in public. Damn, but she was just as tough as her cousin. Admiral Swan drew her into an embrace, but Judith ended it after a moment and stood very close to me as I reached for her hand and held it briefly. I studied the trace. Twenty minutes passed. I enlarged the scan.

"Something wrong?" Devon asked me.

"Her trace is off track."

"That's not possible," Devon said.

"You're right, Captain, it is off," Swan agreed. "Can you compensate and draw it in with a magnetic pull?"

I surged the power. I had Prime Station's entire power plant at my disposal and that of Prime below us. I sent as much as was possible, trying to attract it back to the proper course.

"Did it correct?" Swan asked.

"I don't— No!" I said as the trace ended.

Devon actually tapped the screen. "Where did it go? Did it disperse?"

"Even I know it can't do that," Judith said.

"Then where is it?" Devon asked.

I increased the screen's magnification. It showed the mass distribution between here and *Farpoint* in three dimensions. "Bocelli! She went to Bocelli! She might even have made it before that shock wave hits."

"Get that Comm-node open," Swan ordered.

But Admiral Westmoor was ahead of me. Her tired voice filled the room. "Strong shock wave will destroy Bocelli's station. Brace Prime for a lesser shock wave. I'm transferring planetside immediately, equatorial zone, main continent, via temp node. See you when you get here."

I didn't bother answering, and instead looked at the data stream with her message, hoping to learn more on the station's status.

"Aren't you going to answer her?" Senator Devon asked.

"She had left Bocelli's Station before we even heard the message," Swan answered. "How long till the shock wave gets here?"

"Less than an hour." I reached over to the general alarm. "This is Captain Denver Barclay. I'm ordering a Class One lockdown. Clear all transference traffic. All personnel will clear the MCT pads on Station, mark fifteen minutes from now."

The room turned a steady red glow as the alarm went into effect. Everyone in the center quickly left as I ushered Judith, the senator, and admiral before me. Once outside the main transference center we checked the status screen.

"It's evacuated." I announced.

"Lock it down," Admiral Swan ordered.

Again I heard the comforting thump of the transference core being separated from the rest of Station. We moved deeper into the heart of Prime Station and safety, though I wasn't worried. I knew we could weather this shock wave. We had built Prime to be strong.

"Why did she go to Bocelli?" Judith asked.

"Because she could get there before the shock waves. They would have left her packet unstable, she must have known there was that chance. Then her packet might have been pulled off course or damaged."

"What could pull her off course?" Devon asked.

"Any large mass, a star or large planet, could easily do that."

"Can you figure out where she transferred to on Bocelli's surface and find her?"

Swan nodded. "We'd have to rebuild Bocelli's Station first. Even if only a temporary node like the kind the *Aeneid* used at Brightman."

"We have to do that." Devon's voice was steady.

"Wouldn't that be rather costly for a princess?" Judith asked the senator. Her voice was icy, a good copy of Catherine Westmoor's coolest tone, if ever I heard one.

Devon nodded. "I deserved that. Especially since I've been trying to shut down Bocelli's Station for two years now. And I suppose once we get her back, I'll still be suspicious of her, as always, but she doesn't deserve this. She should be here, with her children, not stranded out there."

My wife shook her head.

"What is it, Judith?" Admiral Swan asked.

"I remember reading reports on Bocelli Prime."

"Catherine will survive," Swan added. "The desert people of the equatorial zone are some of the more friendly."

"Or at least less hostile to our researchers," I added.

"She is going to be playing in the sand for this vacation, I think," Judith said. "How long? What should I tell the children?"

"It'll take a few weeks to rebuild Bocelli's Station and find her location," I said.

"She'll need that time," Judith added softly.

"I wish I could give her a long time to rest," Admiral Swan began. "But we have to build a barrier between us and these beasties, and we need Admiral Westmoor for that. Can you get legislation through quickly, Mr. Senator, to rebuild Bocelli?"

"Yes, I'll do that. Are we going to have to pay to get her back from the Tribes?"

"Absolutely." I answered.

RANGER

by Bill Fawcett

Bill Fawcett has been a professor, teacher, corporate executive, college dean, game designer, author, agent, and book packager. Bill Fawcett & Associates has packaged over two hundred books. He has also designed almost a dozen board games, including Charles Roberts award winners such as *Empire Builder* and *Sanctuary*. He has written or collaborated on several novels, mysteries such as the Authorized Mycroft Holmes novels, the *Madame Vernet Investigates* series, *Making Contact*, *It Seemed Like a Good Idea*, *Great Historical Fiascos*, *Hunters and Shooters*, and *The Teams*, the last two oral histories of the SEALs in Vietnam.

THE air screamed like a banshee as it rushed through the cracks in the ranger's padded helmet. How appropriate, Joel thought. If he made even a small mistake, they would all be dead in a few hours. The lanky, dark-haired ranger had been in free fall for what seemed to be a very long time. He glanced at his altimeter, and then at the ground. Still far below approaching desert waste was more a threatening darkness than it was just dark, the formless black had a presence of it own. The few stars he could see assured Lieutenant Joel Nyman, U.S. Rangers, that he was falling upright and in the correct position for his chute's deployment. The team had jumped from over 40,000 feet and the time it took for them to reach their 800-foot release height was well over a minute. It was a standard HALO insertion such as he had practiced dozens of times. But this time it was for real and that made all the difference. Despite the buffeting wind, the fall seemed almost slow, taking painfully long. Ten thousand feet read the altimeter. There was still plenty of time for the young officer to view the scenery and worry about some old-fashioned militia type getting lucky and blowing him away as he fell defenseless.

A short distance away he could see the tiny red lights of the other three rangers on his team; as team leader his own was blue. They had to stay bunched, but remain far enough apart that they didn't tangle each other when their chutes opened. The young officer had checked their positions every few seconds since they had jumped. This was the first time he had commanded a real strike mission and Joel knew that constantly checking details was an indicator of just how nervous he was, but that didn't stop him from looking again at the end of the thought for each of the little red lights. The tiny LCDs would be invisible from the ground, or even from more than a few dozen meters away, but stood out in the blackness. Their spacing was perfect, he would have been surprised at anything else. These were experienced men, men who had sent the elephant. He was the untested element in the team.

There were some few clouds, and the air already tasted of dust and sand. In the distance Lieutenant Nyman could see the lights of Rhyabab, the capital of the Jihadic State and the large, highly lit building that held their target . . . his target. He was proud of that, his steady hand and gentle touch had made him the top shooter in his class and that had got him this mission. After nearly thirty years without a real

shooting war, any combat mission was a coveted
prize. And strike missions were the ones every
ranger trained for. If they didn't have a tendency to
turn deadly, the U.S. Ranger Lieutenant suspected he
would be less concerned and more excited about the
mission. But there had been a lot of "accidents"
lately, despite the Peoria Accords that banned most
of the overtly lethal weapons. Rangers died and apo-
logies were sent. So there was a good justification for
the core of fear that was forcing masses of adrenaline
through his system. He patted the .45 auto against
his hip for reassurance. If things did go wild, he was
ready. Though the ranger knew that if he used deadly
force the mission was a failure.

The 800-foot level was approaching. Not realizing
he was holding his breath Joel grasped the manual
release. If the auto failed, he had about 2.4 seconds
before splattering into the Jihadic Desert. Even as the
ranger's fingers tightened on the rip cord, his para-
wings were opened by the quarter-sized altimeter
and minicomputer. With a whump that was painfully
loud even though Lieutenant Nyman wore a padded
helmet, the chute opened and snapped Joel to attention. Working the straps, he led the team to the
drop area.

Thinking of the briefing made the ranger smile.
Their drop area was the desert a dozen kilometers
outside the city. This section of the desert was empty,
too dry and broken for even subsistence farming and
the powers that be in Rhyabab preferred their capital
closed and isolated. Basically they were to simply hit
the desert just about anywhere and go from there.
Not a vary hard task for jumpers trained to land in
an eight-foot circle in thirty m.p.h. winds. Except for
the distant city there was nothing but emptiness
below them . . . he hoped.

As he neared the ground, the lieutenant changed

from visual mode to the starlight viewer on his helmet. The darkness below was replaced by a green landscape with sharp edges and no shadows. There was a risk to starlight viewers. Even a bright flashlight would be magnified to such a brightness Joel would be flash blinded for hours. Nervously he switched to infrared and back to starlight, but there were no heat sources below. None that was large enough to be a human anyhow.

The ground came up with a familiar rush. Joel had just a second to react and pull up his legs to avoid a ditch. Then he was automatically struggling out of his chute looking around for the three men in his command. All were in sight and taking their stations as planned, a good start Joel felt, finding reassurance in the well rehearsed pattern.

Pascal Pochol, a thin-faced man who looked too slight to be anything as deadly as a ranger until you noticed the smooth grace of his walk, was gathering up all of the chutes and pouring on the plastic a chemical that would dissolve the tangled mass in seconds. Dave Potter and Franco Rinaldo were both facing out into the, hopefully, empty desert by the time the lieutenant had pulled out his field computer and established their exact location. Big men, with years on the Teams, they both had seemed confident in his leadership when selected for the mission. To Nyman, this put even more pressure on him to succeed.

"Let's get going," Lieutenant Nyman ordered in a low voice. They were all wearing radios, but there was always the slight chance they would be detected. Talking was safer, if you were sure no one else could hear you. These were the only words anyone had spoken since they had jumped.

Signaling Sergeant Potter to take point, they walked single file toward the lights of Rhyabab and the heavily defended palace that contained their target. Staying passive, using their starlight optics only, the four rangers easily crossed the gully and boulder-strewn waste and soon found themselves walking through painfully straight rows of small trees. A small red dot on the tiny screen of the rangers' computer indicated their position and the surrounding terrain as recorded a few days earlier from a satellite. According to the map in the small computer they were approaching a road.

"Rally." This time they were too spread out to hear a spoken command, so Joel used the radio built into his helmet. The message was actually stored in a chip and was sent as an incredibly brief digital burst.

Potter was the last to arrive, silently signaling he felt the area was secure.

"Okay, all of you must have guessed or heard scuttlebutt on the mission by now," Lieutenant Nyman began. Nods affirmed that as usual the noncoms were better briefed than their officer. "We are here because the grand high muckety-muck of this mass of desert and oil has been making nasty noises again."

That drew a chuckle from Rinaldo. At least Joel hoped he was chuckling at the comment and not the quaver the young officer was sure they could hear in his voice.

"We are to penetrate and prove to the Ayatollah he, too, is human." The lieutenant wasn't sure they caught his reference to Roman practices, but the meaning was obvious. "This is an important one. This guy is in a position to cause us a lot of trouble. We still need some oil from these parts, not to mention there is a rumor he's hiring Chinese nuclear scientists who were trained before the Commie state fell apart."

It was Potter's turn to smile. He was the oldest on the team and had been on some of the missions that caused the Chinese Army to decide the Communists were a liability.

"Tomorrow is the Ayatollah's birthday and he always makes an appearance. We all know how paranoid this guy is, so this is literally our only shot at him. I am the designated shooter, but if I go down, continue, and one of you try for the hit. I'm expendable, the mission comes first." Joel tried to sound selfless and determined while discussing his own death or lengthy imprisonment, but suspected he just sounded like the cliché he was using. Still, Joel was encouraged by the soft Hu-Yah he got from Pochol.

"We'll be going in parallel to the road less than a klick ahead. At 0900 we're to penetrate a tall manufacturing facility that has a view of the palace grounds and take the shot. Of course we don't know what they make in the building, or what we will find there; hopefully it is the palace laundry, though the briefing has listed it as an administrative center, possibly for the Jihadic Inland Revenue Service. Recon says it is the least active piece of real estate near the palace, so they hope the staff will have the birthday off. Piece of cake." No one laughed at his final attempt at humor.

"We are operating under the Peoria Convention," the lieutenant reminded them as they stood. Potter groaned. His preference for the "bloody old days" was well known.

"That will get you back on point," Nyman responded with a smile acknowledging Potter would have been on point in any case. Still the sergeant groaned again for effect before trotting to his position twenty paces ahead of the other three rangers.

For the next two hours Joel discovered that it was possible to be bored and on edge at the same time. Sunrise was approaching and in the gray light of false dawn the ranger could see the little puffs of dust that rose with each step. The paved road a hundred meters to their left was becoming visible. The lieutenant had just checked the map when Potter froze and raised his hand. Instantly the other three rangers sank to their knees and remained motionless.

Slowly the sergeant raised three fingers and pointed. The morning breeze began and Joel shivered as it cooled the sweat that had appeared on his back. With a deep breath he signaled Pochol right and Rinaldo left, crawling with slow patience up to where Potter crouched behind the scant cover of a browning bush.

Again, no word had been spoken.

It seemed a long time before everyone was in position. The sun was edging up over the horizon. Still they had to wait. Only two of the guards who manned the barricade across the road were visible. The other was inside the small building and Joel hoped the soldier wasn't sleeping. They only had a little more than two hours before the Ayatollah's appearance.

Finally the last guard strolled, stretching, from the shed.

"Now," Joel spat the order and he steadied his heavy weapon and fired. With a "phut" the riflelike weapon fired a two-inch doughnut made of rubber and something much like what superballs had long been made of. He could almost follow the flight of the large missile. When it hit the guard he had chosen, the center one who had just appeared, it threw the Jihadite against the wall. To either side the other men fell, equally stunned.

Standing, the lieutenant motioned to them to approach. The men might only be out a few minutes. He was pleased to see all were still alive. A blow from the stunner in the temple could be fatal and what they did to a face was almost as messy. He had taken only a few steps, relaxed by the action after the hours of suspense, when a face appeared in the open door of the guard shack, looked startled, and withdrew from sight.

There had been a fourth. Instantly Sergeant Potter rushed forward, pumping stun rounds through the open door. The brown-haired noncom followed his fire through the door. Everyone else stood shocked at the development.

Moments later the sergeant exited, shaking his head, "He was jabbering on the radio when I got him. No telling how much he said." His voice trailed off as he looked across the flat, empty terrain toward Rhyabab.

For a long minute they all stared at the dark road leading to the Jihadic capital. They all knew it would take some time for the message to move through channels and a response to appear, but the urge to watch for some instant result was strong.

"So much for the element of surprise," Rinaldo commented ruefully, breaking the stillness, as he wired the legs and wrists of the unconscious guards with plastic restraints.

Doing his best to appear as calm as the other rangers, Joel Nyman's mind raced. They were screwed. The entire plan had been to enter the city without being detected. He could hear those often repeated words of Senior Instructor Docery as he forced his students to create alternate plan after alternate plan for every contingency: No plan survives contact with the enemy. Well, they had made contact, and their plan had not survived. When he was finally released, in an exchange or after twenty years or so, he'd have to tell Dorcery he'd been right . . . damnit.

It was time to take a deep breath, and review their assets and see what they inspired. Each man was a veritable armory of high-tech weapons. But they would soon be overwhelmed by sheer numbers. Therre were at least three battalions of Elite Guards adjacent to the palace itself. There was no real cover. The only real building for three miles was the guardhouse itself and that was where any avenging force would race to. He could see some small structures closer to the city. From the photos intel had provided at their briefing, Lieutenant Nyman knew they were a veritable maze of new single- and two-story brick housing provided to the palace staff and lesser Jihadic officials. They formed a crescent that ran halfway around the city. If they could get into them, there might be a chance. They would be expected to go to ground. If they kept moving, it would take hours for the bad guys to check out all the apartments. Time enough to slip past and complete their mission. Maybe even get away again. Maybe.

They did have transportation, of a sort, an old Chevrolet sat behind the guard shack.

"They're forming up, sir." Rinaldo had climbed onto the top of the building and was using a digital amplifier to watch the road where it emerged from the buildings. His voice came clearly over Joel's headset. "There is a tall major leading a column of six APCs. No, wait. Make that eight APCs, and . . . yep, they're upset, two T-eighty tanks."

"So we have them outnumbered," Pochol broke his radio silence to add. The lieutenant almost reminded him to stay off the air to avoid detection, then realized just how absurd that would sound at the moment.

The armored column was their first concern. It had to contain over a hundred infantry. More than enough to neutralize a few men, even rangers. The tanks were a compliment in a way. They had to know there were only four of them, but had sent them anyhow. A reputation can be, he realized, a two-edged sword.

"Rinaldo, get down and check out the Chevy. See

if it will run. Potter, help him search these guys for
the keys to that car. Pochol, trash that radio and then
turn on this light," Nyman finished, pointing at a
large light that must be used to illuminate the barricade at night.

Putting down the stun rifle, Joel studied the map
in his microcomputer. He chose a spot as far from
them as possible but where the approaching column
would still be within the effect radius. Changing helmet frequencies, he superimposed a target grid over
the spot and spoke.

"This is Rover One. I have a priority fire mission.
I need one instant dark, repeat instant dark asap at
GL, George Light, grid two-four-three-B. Repeat instant dark at George Light, two-four-three-B. Please
confirm." When he tripped send, the signal went out
in a burst that lasted less than two tenths of a second.

"Darkness has left the hawk," came the reassur-
ing reply.

Rinaldo was holding up a set of keys and smiling.
Pochol watched the dust raised as the column hurried forward.

"Don't start it yet, just in case. Dark coming."
Nyman was surprised that he sounded so calm.
"Once the flash passes, be ready to rev her up and
we'll see how she does cross-country."

They heard the small missile as it passed almost
overhead. Joel suspected that it had been programmed to follow the road. Seconds later, he could
hear the rapid fire of a 40mm trying to knock the
missile down as it passed directly over the speeding armor.

There was a pop, not really a bang, and a flash of
light so brief it was barely there and yet so bright it
couldn't be ignored. The light over his head remained lit. Good. They had remained just outside the
range of the EMP burst. Inside its radius everything

electrical would have been literally fried, bursting into sparks and flames in the best B-movie fashion. Ignitions gone, the Jihadic APCs and tanks slowed to a halt. Targeting computers were useless, radios even worse off.

"Mount up," Nyman ordered jumping into the front passenger seat. "We just burned off about six million tax dollars. Let's get past them while they are still dazed."

A bumpy ride later they were among the "suburbs" of Rhyabab. To the rangers' amazement, no one at first noticed the battered Chevy containing four camo uniformed U.S. Rangers. Surely, he thought, the city would be in an uproar. Then he thought about the Ayatollah and his reputed ego. Perhaps the man didn't want his birthday spoiled. But that ego was why they were there, to teach the man a little humility. Enough to make him think twice about the very personal result of any further adventurism against America's allies.

Having knocked out an entire armored column, the Elite Guard knew they were in the city. Their best chance was to direct the Guard's attentions to where they were not. Troops that wouldn't be in their way later. Joel worried that they might actually have to cause a scene to get noticed. He had met the eyes of several civilians as they drove past, but not one raised an alarm. It came to the lieutenant that they were so repressed, they would do nothing to attract the attention of their police . . . not even acknowledge an enemy as they entered their own neighborhood. Their worried looks and furtive glances as they turned away reminded Joel why there were rangers and why they did what they did. These were not the enemy. In a real war they would simply be victims of one side or the other.

Finally, when they slowed for a light, a brightly uniformed soldier directing traffic noticed the car's unusual occupants. Pulling his sidearm, the man fired into the car. Joel felt a blow against his shoulder. There would be a bruise there in a few hours. He didn't have to look down to know the ultra-kev had stopped the round. A guy could get killed here, he realized again and felt yet another surge of adrenaline bring on its artificial alertness.

"Don't fire back," Nyman cautioned. "We need him to report we are here. Now let's get elsewhere."

Pochol spun the wheel and turned into the alley.

"We need a new car. They'll be looking for this one," the ranger lieutenant observed rubbing the sore spot on his shoulder.

"A less drafty one," Rinaldo joked causing Joel to turn around.

The back window had been pierced by three shots, their holes clear among a spiderweb of cracks.

"Look for something like a van," he ordered.

"Cripes, sir," Potter protested lightly. "Twelve years as a ranger and I'm back to lifting cars. That's why the judge suggested I enlist."

Laughing felt good after being shot at.

Rhyabab was a new city, built with the wealth of oil for the convenience of the peninsula's new leaders less than a decade ago. The blocks built for the lesser classes already had a worn look about them with cracked tiles and empty windows on every block. On any surface more than a few meters across there was a mural of the Ayatollah. The ordinary citizens were plainly dressed, the women totally swathed in dark clothes and veils. Joel wondered how they could stand it in the sweltering heat. The men were mostly dressed in slacks and white shirts that could have come from the Sears Catalog.

The buildings they passed, those not set aside for the leaders or government offices, were plain to a fault. There were those with three stories of boring unpainted standstone brick, with four doors and four windows facing the road, and those with two stories and six doors and six windows. He suspected if you got inside, every one would have the same floor plan. The city smelled of exotic spices and the pungent tang made Joel momentarily grateful that he hadn't been forced to eat a local diet. Had they been inserting into a rural area, they would have been forced to eat only food from their target area until their body odors wouldn't have tripped odor sensors that made a Big Mac a deadly deficit.

It took way too long to find a van they could use. All four rangers were sitting forward and scanning the street ahead nervously by the time they found one. Sirens seemed to fill the city, some passing within a few streets. The search was on and at any moment they could be discovered. The Renault van they found, marked as a delivery truck for a Halal butcher shop, was perfect. It even had tinted windows. The trouble was three soldiers armed with AK 52s could be seen sipping some dark liquid at a sidewalk café within a few meters of it.

"Potter, think you can hot-wire that van?" Joel asked as they slowly approached.

"Give me one minute. I'm a bit rusty, I suspect," the sergeant answered.

"Good to hear that," Pochol cracked. Joel remembered that the ranger took great pride in his vintage mustang back in Coronado. Then he continued improvising. There were too many civilians nearby to risk firing their stunners. They still packed a wallop, and the team didn't need to cause the accidental death of some kid who forgot to duck.

"Earplugs," Nyman cautioned, inserting his own. "One flash, one goaway..Right by their table."

As they slowed to a stop by the van, the two grenades sailed through the air only inches apart. They made a rattling sound as they bounced toward the soldiers' table. Then they burst, one causing a flash so bright it hurt even though the four men's eyes were closed. The sonic grenade simply started screaming at a pitch that sent literal chills up even the rangers' spines.

Blinded and confused, the three soldiers didn't even try to grab their weapons, stumbling away amid the crowd of panicky bystanders. Pochol had slammed on the brakes and jumped from the Chevy the instant the flash had passed. For good measure, he threw two more of the sonic goaway grenades up and down the street. That kept the rest of the curious locals moving away. They were all rolling away in the van being driven by Potter, who was smiling proudly at his own skill, before the second goaways ran out of power.

They had better hurry. There was less than half an hour until the Ayatollah's birthday appearance.

The sirens faded into the distance as they approached the building chosen as their shooting platform. As promised, the entrance to the modern glass-and-steel building was unguarded. Something about that bothered Joel. The large grass-filled courtyard that separated the six-story complex from the housing contained only a large bronze statue of his target, looking nobly up to heaven. The Elite Guard knew they were in the city; certainly every approach to the palace should be crawling with members of the Elite Guard. Yet, aside from an easily avoided roadblock, this area was bereft of any military at all. Why?

Psych had said even if detected they were to continue the mission. The fanatic leader would never allow a mere threat to interfere with his promised appearance. The loss of face might endanger his hold over the generals. Joel hoped they were right. In the distance the sirens of scurrying security vehicles continued wailing. From the location he guessed they were still searching near where they had abandoned the bullet-holed Chevy.

The unknown and unexplained are never welcome in combat. All his instincts told Joel to stop, run away, go back, and do anything but enter the innocuous-looking building at the edge of the palace. Duty and the desire to win fought with instinct—and instinct lost. There was less than ten minutes until the scheduled appearance. No time remained for them to do anything but push ahead. The team was undetected and unharmed; he could never abort.

"Leave the van here and let's cross the courtyard in a rush."

"Your show," Potter answered pulling into an alley only a few doors down from the open area. The young lieutenant wasn't sure if the older ranger's reply was a criticism or acknowledgment. He hesitated for what seemed a long time, but nothing more was said. Finally he opened the door and got out. The others exited as well and stood waiting for his orders.

"Two waves. Pascal and I go first," Lieutenant Nyman ordered. It seemed calm in the alley. Even the sirens in the distance had quieted.

The four rangers burst into the open and ran. Pochol was a few steps ahead of Nyman, with the others ten paces back. The lieutenant had almost made it to the door when a small section of the wall to their left simply fell forward. Behind it stood three men in the uniforms of the Elite Guard. There were popping sounds and Joel dropped to the ground. With a hissing whistle, the sticky net continued through the space the young officer had just abandoned and wrapped itself around the legs of the dictator's statue.

At almost the same instant there was a painful gasp and Joel realized that either Rinaldo had dropped too slowly, or one guard had aimed low. In either case, the ranger was out of this firefight. Pochol, still lying flat, began pumping doughnut rounds into the gap in the glass wall from his stun rifle. Two of the Elite Guards fell almost simultaneously. The other guard panicked and dropped the net thrower. The lieutenant thought the man would run, but instead he drew a revolver and the echo of real gunfire filled the half-acre courtyard.

The young ranger's first reaction was to draw his own sidearm and fire back. But before he could open the flap, a black cylinder flew toward the shooter. Instead of drawing his own weapon, Joel rolled and then ran as far and as fast as he could away from the shooter and, incidentally, into the building.

There was a muffled whistle and then a slightly louder blast. Knowing that the way was clear, the officer tried to look calm when, after making sure no one was rushing down the corridor toward his back, he returned to the concrete and grass open area. The scene inside the trick wall was about as he expected. The sonic device Potter had tossed was a miniature version of the truck-mounted Nitrogen Neutralizer that had been used as far back as Desert Storm. It had the same effect, exciting the molecules of any nitrogen-based chemical into exploding. In this case the effective radius had been small. Which was fortunate for him, or the thirteen rounds in his own sidearm would have also gone off in a single explosion along with every other nitrogen-based compound in the area affected. You didn't throw one of these into a warehouse full of fertilizer, the explosion would be seismic. The six-inch cylinder had landed right at the Elite Guard's feet. Potter was already using one of their restraints as a tourniquet to stop the blood pumping from what little remained of the young jihadic soldier's hand.

At this point the lieutenant realized that Pochol was cursing with more vehemence than normal as he tried to cut Rinaldo free. The fourth ranger was just lying there, unmoving. A small pool of blood was forming by one leg. Without thinking, Joel rushed to their side. The net was almost free, sticking mostly to the back of Rinaldo's jacket. Carefully, as the wounded ranger winced, they cut the jacket away and pulled him free. There was a deep wound in the big ranger's right leg just below the knee. From the blood covering his camos below the wound, it was deep. Rinaldo tried to pull himself up and fell back, uttering a short, anguished cry.

"The bone is shattered," Rinaldo announced, recovering some of his color as the pain blockers Pochol injected him with took effect.

"Pochol, get him to the pickup area. Use the butcher's van again," Lieutenant Nyman found himself ordering. It was the way they did it. No ranger was ever left behind. Even if a team member was killed, the body was taken along or hidden and recovered. The only way anyone saw a ranger was by shooting at them.

Silently, but carefully, the smaller man picked up Rinaldo and slung him over a shoulder. He seemed almost lost beneath his more massive burden, but still managed to jog back to the protection of the residential crescent and was lost from sight.

Less than a minute had passed since the guards had appeared. Hurrying toward David Potter, who was in the guards' hidden station, Joel saw a dim red light suddenly activate in the back of the opening. Changing direction, he dived inside the doorway just as the antipersonnel mine, one of their own antiriot claymores from the sound of it, exploded, sending several hundred rubber balls across the courtyard, some striking the Ayatollah's statue with a twanging ring.

"More coming, that TV camera over my head showed them that someone is left moving here," Potter transmitted as Joel regained his feet. "But I was below it, so maybe they are going to look for only one more ranger. You're the shooter," the sergeant finished, "I'll lead them off."

There was no time to debate. Given any luck he could buy Joel the time needed. With a sinking feeling, the young ranger realized he had made quite a hash of it. One man was down, the nitrosonic almost killing one of the opposition, and the rest of his team either out of it or on the run.

Even so, aborting wasn't an option. He had to get going before the target returned to his bunker. With a sense of determination, and maybe just a slight sense of doom as well, the ranger ran for the nearest stairs. He glanced at his chrono, the local time was 8:57. On the far side of the building he could hear the crowd roar. Great, this time the Ayatollah just had to be early. Joel hoped it would be a long speech. A second roar sent him sprinting up two steps at a time.

The ranger knew he needed to be at least four stories up to get a shot, so he hurried past the first two landings. He was almost at the fourth floor's door when he heard the ground level door slam open and the sound of several voices . . . the loud, annoyed voices of men on an urgent mission.

Pausing only for a second Joel literally jumped back down to the landing below and after cracking open the membrane dividing them into two parts, the ranger threw two small pellets, neither more than an inch across, down onto the still empty steps between the second and third floor.

Even prepared for it, the odor alone nearly caused Joel to retch. He actually felt a bit sorry for the men below. The second pellet had been nausea gas. From the disgusting sounds echoing up the stairwell, it was safe to assume that approach was blocked for the next few minutes.

He had just turned back up the stairs when the foam began to surge from nozzles in the ceiling that the lieutenant had mistaken for part of a sprinkler system. Each step upward became more difficult as the foam began to harden into an ankle-deep, then a knee-deep gel. This type of foam had been used by nuclear plants to slow or detain terrorists for well over fifty years. There was nothing to do but get out of it as soon as possible. Even as he was forced to concentrate mostly on just taking the next step, the young ranger wondered why it was deployed in what his briefing had described as a minor admin center. The last steps that took him out of the hallway and into the fourth floor came so hard they brought tears to Joel's eyes.

The fourth floor consisted of a single open area running the full thirty meter length of the building. It was divided into cubicles only by chest-high temporary panels. There seemed to be a computer on every desk. Panting, the ranger began to move toward the far windows as yet another cheer rose and he could now make out his target's voice. Automatically, the lieutenant pushed the button that caused the translation chips in his helmet to activate.

". . . chosen one . . . foreign devils. . . . Coming holocaust." The unit could only understand part of the what the dictator was saying, his mountain accent being simply too different from the highly educated voices used to program the device. Not that Joel really cared what the Ayatollah was saying so long as he kept talking.

It was now 9:04. The Ayatollah had a personal rule

to never appear in public for longer than fourteen minutes. It took fifteen minutes for a cruise missile launched from the nearest border to reach Rhyabab. No Mideast leader could forget, even after three decades, the ten-missile salute that had spelled the quite messy and rather spectacular end of Osama Bin Laden.

Gaining speed as he hurried toward the windows, the lieutenant suddenly stopped. A sound behind him caused him to duck and whirl, stun weapon ready. But the Oriental-looking man who made the sound was not only unarmed, but was visibly frightened. Surprised to see a Chinese in the capital of the horribly racist Jihadic State, he hesitated. With a squawk, the other man spun away and ran into the same stairwell Joel had just nearly been trapped in. His plaintive cries when the Chinese man discovered he was stuck a few steps beyond the door were almost amusing.

A quick glance confirmed what Joel had suspected. On several of the desks were pictures of families or girlfriends, all Oriental-looking. He had stumbled into the computer research center where the old Commie scientists were trying to re-create neutron bombs for the Jihadic State.

Before turning to complete his main mission, the ranger couldn't resist the opportunity. Pulling one of the two EMP grenades he had brought from his harness, the lieutenant set it for maximum delay, six minutes. This small unit was a thousand times weaker than the missile they had watched disable the armored column, but when it went off, every computer within twenty meters would be wiped. Joel allowed himself a slight grin as he flung it casually into the center of the room.

Another cheer from the mob and Joel was at the window. For the first time he could actually see the ocean of turbaned heads facing away from him and toward the raised platform from which the Ayatollah spoke. The palace grounds were a good half mile across and held thousands of the Ayatollah's most devoted followers. The podium was directly across the parade grounds and behind a solid phalanx of Elite Guards six deep and facing the enthusiastic crowd. Banners flew from every corner and a three-story picture of the dictator dominated the wall of the palace behind the speaker's platform.

Once he had cut away a small circle of glass, the Ayatollah's voice was less muffled. The translator now worked perfectly and what the voice said first froze the young ranger then started him digging madly in one pocket to extract one of the special rounds that had been prepared for his mission.

"In conclusion," the Ayatollah had been saying, "you have heard the rumors that American Rangers are in the city."

Hisses and protests filled the air.

"There is no truth to this," the ruler assured his followers. "They know better than to defile our sacred city. Soon they will fear our wrath too greatly to oppose us anywhere."

With a passing concern for his team, the ranger continued loading. If any of them had been captured, they would have been on display before this mob. So maybe they were safe, so far anyhow. Cursing at his own clumsiness, Joel finally inserted the oversized round. More easily, in one rehearsed motion, he pulled the barrel extension from the pocket on his calf and screwed it on the end of the weapon. The Ayatollah continued to exhort the crowd, obviously enjoying their adulation.

"I am the chosen one. You have only to follow me and Paradise will be yours," the dictator's voice rose with charismatic flair.

Carefully the lieutenant poked his extended stun weapon through the hole he had cut and sighted through the digital scope on top of its thick barrel.

"Like me, you will be immune to the Yankee bullets. Protected by the holy power that has been given me," the head of the Jihadic State continued.

As he continued to speak, the face recognition system built into the sight outlined the speaker's body in red. There was no question of Joel hitting the wrong man by mistake. The range was long, several hundred yards, but he had regularly hit six-inch targets that far away on the range. Trouble was this wasn't on the range; the young officer looked up from the sight and found his hands shaking.

Taking a deep breath and holding it, he cleared his mind. Then he stopped. He was forgetting something.

"Join me on the Jihad, and we will rule the world!" There may have been more, but wild cheers were untranslatable. The speaker stood there, arms raised, drinking in the cheers that rose in volume the longer he stood silent.

There was one more goodie. The ranger had almost forgotten it. Quickly Joel opened a pouch and turned a dial until a certain light on his radio-linked helmet turned green.

Surprised now at how calm he had just become, the young ranger centered the barrel on the Ayatollah's chest and then compensated for range and windage. Holding his breath, he fired.

His target stumbled back from the podium and ended up sitting a few meters back, a look of shock replacing his earlier smiling superiority. The Ayatollah was covered with bright Day-Glo green dye from his waist to the top of his head. Watching through the sight, Joel saw the leader's expression go from rage to disgust as he became aware of the smell.

The reaction of those around the Ayatollah to the combination paint round and stink bomb was almost immediate. Some froze; several turned and fled, jumping into the crowd below or pushing each other off the single set of steps. One elderly cleric threw up on the floor a few inches from where the head of state was sitting.

Knowing a little confusion wouldn't hurt his chances of escape, Joel took the opportunity to launch a few more stinkers and some riot buster sonic grenades into the thousands of silent, stunned Jihadites staring at the bright green figure of their "invulnerable" leader.

Before they even landed, Joel smiled and tied into the local public address system and announced those words the U.S. Rangers had made so famous after every successful hit, "Tag, you are it."

Author's note. As you may have guessed by now, every piece of nonlethal equipment described in this story really exists. The EMP missiles, the foam, the screamer grenades are there now. The nitrogen exploder fills a heavy truck and has limited range, but was available during Desert Storm. The real problem with nonlethal weapons, as shown, is that they can be lethal.

THE VACATION

by Ron Collins

Ron Collins' short fiction has appeared in several magazines and anthologies, including *Dragon, Return of the Dinosaurs, Mob Magic, Flights of Fiction,* and *Writers of the Future.* He lives in Columbus, Indiana.

"LOOK," Muriel said, "isn't that the longest nose you've ever seen?"

Frieda squinted against the noonday sun. Individual rays broke through openings in the mesh of her straw hat to highlight her wrinkled face. She ran her handkerchief carefully over her brow, bemoaning the handkerchief's sopping wrinkles and the way the color was baking out of its flowered embroidery.

"I don't care if Vega's light is silver or not, this place is still too damned hot in my book."

Muriel grimaced. Fifty-eight years of friendship and a heat stroke be damned, she wasn't going to let Frieda ruin this vacation. "I said, isn't that the longest nose you've ever seen?"

Monument Plaza was flat and expansive. Its pavilion floor was an interlocking pattern of brown-and-yellow bricks inlaid with black planets and nebulae the color of sun-dried peppers. Monuments dotted the space, sitting testament to the bravery of men and women of two races that fought in the bloodiest and most decisive battle of the Transgalactic War.

Muriel wore a white linen jumpsuit with a checkered pattern along one side and an orange sash that cinched her waist. Yes, she had lost a lot of her figure since her working days, but the jumpsuit made her feel like she was still a viable crew member. Waistline be damned, she would wear what she wanted. Frieda's outfit was a gauzy, ankle-length navy skirt and an ivory cotton blouse. Both women carried oversized travel bags with big handles and wore straw hats held to their heads with pieces of violet ribbon tied under their chins.

A gusty breeze picked up dust and debris in short-lived dust devils. The statue was tall enough they both had to bend backward to take it in. It was carved of smooth gray rock that looked a lot like granite to Muriel, but that the locals had called abradite.

The guide chip chirped against Muriel's ear. *"This is Dengara, the Vegan system's most able general. He was the Grand Commander of all Vegan forces, and led the freedom fighters' charge over Galleo's Agridale Field to drive the last of the Teg Empire from system Vega. Hence this ground is considered forever hallowed."*

"Did you hear that?" Muriel asked.

"Humph," Frieda said, the brim of her straw hat quivering. Her own tour chip clung to her ear. "He wouldn't have been anything without our help."

"You are, of course, quite right," their hovervan driver said from across the way. He was short, average for a man from the Vegan system, but coming only to the bottom of Muriel's chin. He wore a tight-fitting suit of reflective green material, and a wide-brimmed hat that made him look like Gumby at graduation. A large name tag noted he was to be called Adar. The hovervan stood silently in the distance behind him, draped with banners announcing tour stops, its doors folded open along its side and its landing mechanism splayed out at its feet, making it look like a giant cockroach. "Galleo could not have won our freedom without the very able and—might I personally add—gratefully received, support of our human neighbors. We are a proud race though, ladies, and General Dengara was a brave leader. Believe me when I say that while your help was invaluable, we would never have given up. Without your help, we would still be at war."

"Not much to boast about," Frieda said.

Muriel pulled at her friend's elbow and led Frieda off in the direction of the tomb of Kadea.

"What's the matter with you today, Frieda? You're making a total ass of yourself."

"What do you mean?"

"You know darn well what I mean. Don't do this to me, all right? All I wanted was a nice vacation and you're acting like you do when Beth Ann's been cheating at bridge club—only now you're taking it out on innocent bystanders."

"I am not," Frieda answered in a huff.

The muscles around Frieda's seventy-seven-year-old face clenched, making her look like a blanched coconut with blue eyes and a cashew nose. Her gray curls were damp against her temple and stuck out in clumps from under the hat.

Muriel gave her the glare of infinite patience they had each perfected over the years. Never mind that Muriel had just lied, that inside she was secretly hoping for a lot more than simply a nice vacation.

They had come to Vega because they had both lost things to the war. Frieda, of course, had lost both her sons, Arnold and John. As a result, Muriel had lost her best friend to a sustained bout with anger and eternal sadness. Cal, Frieda's husband, turned bitter over the years, sour and unable to forgive the loss of his children, blaming everyone from God to the Solar

Council to the Vegans to the Teg Empire. Frieda stayed by his side, never talking about her own feelings, holding on instead and never putting it behind her.

But the war had been over for a very long time, and Cal had passed away three Earth-standard years ago. When Muriel suggested Galleo as their next vacation spot, she was only partially surprised that Frieda agreed without debate. Before their departure, both Muriel and Frieda had pretended the planet was just another tourist stop.

They both knew better.

Still, Muriel wouldn't let Frieda embarrass herself with ill-timed rudeness if she could help it.

"Ach," Frieda said, surrendering with a sigh and a wave of her bone-thin hand. "It's nothing, really. Let's just have a good time."

"That's more like it."

"It's just . . ."

"Just what, Frieda?"

"I . . ." she said, seeming to choke on her thoughts. She mopped her brow again, then sighed. "Nothing."

Muriel shook her head with frustration.

"You know what I want?"

"No, Frieda, what do you want?"

"Lemonade."

"Lemonade?"

"Yes. Pink lemonade. Just like they used to have at the state fair. A tall glass, frosty, and served in a plastic cup that will glaze over with sweat."

"You want pink lemonade? On Galleo?"

"Tart as I can get it."

Muriel turned her eyes up in exasperation, then scanned the horizon. The plaza went from one edge of their world to the next. Galleo, the fifth planet in the Vega system, was three quarters the size of Earth, resulting in the horizon's curvature being noticeably more pronounced. The star was hydrogen rich, and therefore cast light that was far more silverish or white than that of Sol. In addition, the star's intensity was far greater, and the heat was almost unbearable.

Opposite Dengara's monument was a small stand with signs that listed prices and sales.

"Well, I can't imagine we'll find a lemonade stand around here."

"But that's what I want."

Muriel cringed. Frieda was stubborn as a cat sometimes. She had seen her friend once work her way through five shop clerks and a floor manager to get a sale price on an old coupon. Now she had that same look in her eyes. Vega or no Vega, Frieda was going to get her lemonade and that was that.

"We could try the gift shop," Muriel offered.

"All the way over there?"

"Come on, ya spoiled old biddy. You've gotta expect to do *some* work if you want lemonade on a planet twenty-six light-years from lemons."

"Oh, all right," her friend grumbled.

They padded along the rope, heading toward the stand. The wind was dry and warm, kicking up the brims of their hats and exposing their faces to the silver-toned sunlight. Frieda was right. It *was* too hot. But at least it was a dry heat—good for her knees.

Muriel held her hand along the edge of her canvas bag and glanced at Frieda.

They had been friends since they had roomed together at the University of Wisconsin—Frieda studying agricultural engineering, and Muriel studying mostly the anatomy and physiology of football players.

She blushed a bit at that memory.

Frieda had married Cal, and Muriel, having somehow managed to graduate with a degree in mechanical technology as well as an interest in diving, had taken a post doing underwater maintenance on Europa. It was a good job, really. Lots of work, good pay. Hard on the knees and elbows.

It wasn't her fault that she had never met the right person, was it?

Those had been the days, though, days before the war, before humans even knew for sure that other life-forms existed.

Muriel looked at Frieda now and saw the lines of her face and the hunched curve of her back. Her brittle fingers clutched at her bag and at the linen handkerchief, reminding Muriel of the hours they had sat together over the past few years, knitting, doing needlepoint, sipping at Darjeeling tea, and chatting while turning out quilts and napkins and pillows with frilly designs and San Francisco tucks.

When did they get to be such old ladies?

A thin line of sun-resistant lipstick remained on Frieda's lower lip, the upper having already worn off. It was hard to believe there had actually been a time when no one knew the Vegans or the Teg Empire even existed.

"Hey, Frie?" Muriel said, motioning to Dengara. "What do you think Cal would have said if he saw this guy's monument?"

A glimmer came to Frieda's eyes. "Oh, he would probably walk up and piss on the thing's big toe."

Muriel laughed out loud to cover her grimace. She shouldn't have brought Cal up at all. Getting Frieda to travel while her husband was alive had been like prying stone from asphalt. But since his death they had traveled together often.

"We've had some good trips, haven't we, Frie?"

"Yes, we have."

"What's your favorite, so far?"

"Probably the forests on Centauri Three."

"But that's where I got that incredible food poisoning!" Muriel said, involuntarily rubbing her hand over her belly and glancing at Frieda.

Her friend was smiling.

"Got ya."

Muriel chuckled. "You're a sour old woman, Frieda."

"Not sour. Tart."

"My two favorites were the lunar caves, and Mars Colony Crater."

"Those were good ones," Frieda agreed, the tip of her pink tongue running over her upper lip.

Despite that not-so-little gastric problem on Centauri Three, the past few years were, in some ways, the happiest years of Muriel's life. Back when she was working, she had leaped from one job to the next, supporting the war. Rebuilding afterward. Someone always wanted something built. It was a good life, but very hectic. After all that planet-hopping, Muriel found it nice to have someone to be with again. It was nice to have a home, and a friend to travel with.

They drew near the shop.

It was smaller than it looked from across the plaza, pentagon-shaped, with windows on each side filled with vid-signs in Vegan and English. Digicam: 212 GC. Shirts: 2 for 900 GC. A doorway stood propped open, and the warm smell of something that might be spiced popcorn came from within.

If travel throughout the galaxy had proved anything to Muriel, it was that gift shops are the same everywhere. A mother picked through rows of overpriced, poorly sewn clothes stamped with images and slogans. Kids argued over candy and desk ornaments made of rocks embedded in Flexiplast. Games, posters, puzzles. The entrance was lined by a row of e-card machines direct-linked to the galacticnet. *Send images straight to your loved ones*, a sign read.

Frieda's jaw tightened as she strode past the machine.

Muriel untied her hat and removed her sunglasses, then used the hat as a fan. At least the building was cool and out of the sun.

A Vegan, dressed in the same type of suit as their guide, stood behind a counter that came to the level of the women's thighs. His tag read "Yemminy."

"How I help?" he asked in a singsong tone, struggling slightly over pronunciation.

"I want lemonade," Frieda said firmly.

"Lemonade?" Yemminy replied.

"Yes. That's what I said."

"I am terrible sorry, Miss. You describe what that might be?"

"It's a drink. You squeeze lemons and add sugar and water."

The Vegan's face broadened, his lips growing wide in an expression of regret. "I am sorry so. Would cola be accept?"

"No," Frieda replied.

"I have water, in more," Yemminy said.

"Well," Muriel said before Frieda could go completely outer rim. "I guess it'll be cola, water, or nothing."

"Then I'll have nothing," Frieda said, crossing her arms in her most belligerent fashion and leaning backward like she was preparing for a tug-of-war.

Muriel rolled her eyes. "Come on," she said, stepping toward the exit.

Frieda stomped off, bustling through the doorway with one hand holding her hat to her head, leaving a rack of shirts flapping in her wake.

Muriel had to scoot to keep up. Her knees began to ache as she jogged alongside her suddenly spry friend. "Come on, Frie. We've come all the way here. What's the matter?"

"I'm hot, Muriel. I'm sweaty and grimy all the time. The air is so dry my elbows are cracking and the inside of my nose is raw. The hotel is made for people half my size. They put an eight-story monument up for a general that couldn't lead a penful of pigs to slop. The people here are tiny and condescending and . . . and now—" Frieda turned and glared at the gift shop.

Frieda's halt caught Muriel off guard, and she continued on for a step before turning back herself.

"Now they can't even have the common decency to serve a glass of lemonade!"

Muriel put her arm around Frieda's shoulder and realized her friend was shaking.

"There's nothing here, Muriel," Frieda mumbled. "Nothing."

"Come on, Frie. Let's get back in the hovervan and see if we can get the driver to take us back, okay? Maybe we can relax a little there. Maybe they could even wrangle a glass of your lemonade."

Frieda nodded and let Muriel turn her around. "I've got a headache."

Slowly, the two friends strode back.

As they neared the hovervan, the driver came to check on them.

"Can we return to the hotel?" Muriel asked as kindly as she could, pushing Frieda onto the bus in order to keep her from talking.

Adar smiled widely. "The tour bus does not leave the site for another thirty Earth-standard minutes," he replied with a small bow.

"I know. But we really need to get back now."

"But—"

"I'm sure you have a schedule to keep. But if you were to call another hovervan in right now, they could get here in time to pick up the tour and take them to the next stop, couldn't they?"

"Well, yes."

Muriel leaned in and said in a lower tone of voice, "My friend is really not feeling well. Could you maybe call them and see if they would do that?"

Adar seemed perplexed for a moment then, seeing Frieda plop wearily into her seat, nodded and pressed the com button on his communicator.

"I understand," he said to Muriel, waiting for someone on the other end to answer. "I've seen it before. Sometimes it's best to forgo the sites." He exchanged a barrage of Vegan with the operator, then turned back to her.

"Please," he said. "Get in. I'll take you back."

Having her choice of the entire van, Muriel settled in next to her friend. She reached over and took Frieda's hand in hers, and there they sat like a pair of eight year olds as Adar closed the doors and started the jets to raise the hovercraft off the ground.

"I'm sorry," Frieda said softly.

"It's all right."

"No. It's not all right." Frieda shook her head. The straw brim of her hat quaked. She stared vacantly out the window. The plaza slipped past, monuments sliding silently by the pane. "This was the day Johnnie was killed," she said in her most matter-of-fact voice.

Muriel's heart dropped. She had forgotten that.

"I'm so sorry."

"It was thirty-eight years ago: Earth-standard," Frieda replied, the last two words falling as if they were a burden to the sentence. "No reason you should have remembered."

Muriel held Frieda's hand.

The hovervan took off.

"I used to drink lemonade with him," Frieda said, staring out over the brilliant white landscape as it whirred by. The hovervan traveled at over 450 kilometers an hour, if you believed the vacation brochures. "He would sit beside me with Cal's old Brewers hat on and he would sip lemonade through a straw. He would chew the tip of the straw, too. Enough so that no one else wanted to drink out of it."

Frieda smiled.

"Used to drive me crazy."

Muriel pursed her lips. *I should have remembered*, she thought. *A real friend would have remembered.*

"He volunteered, you know."

"I know," Muriel said. "They both did."   ·

Frieda nodded. "I remember the day they walked out the door together, Arnie to Fighter School, Johnnie straight to his assignment on *Miranda*. They were both so handsome. So young."

Miranda had been the first battle cruiser to enter the Vegan system and had been primarily responsible for shutting off supply lines to the Teg Empire.

A noise came from the back of the hovervan. The engine whined differently, and Adar turned his head quickly to look out the back of the vehicle.

"*Taga!*" he cursed in his own language as the van slowed.

"What's the matter?" Frieda said.

"Not to worry," the driver replied. Adar's English was far better than the shopkeeper's had been. "We've lost an engine. Don't worry, though. We can still travel. It's actually better this way. Better that you wanted to get home early."

"Why is that?"

"Losing an engine with just the two of you here means there's less weight to carry back. Better an engine go with two passengers on the way home than with thirty on the way to a distant stop."

Muriel nodded.

"Of course, my service manager will still be angry." Adar grinned.

Both women sat back into their seats. The van continued.

"Did I hear you right?" the driver said over his shoulder. "You had family on *Miranda?*"

"Yes," Frieda said, her hand tightening in Muriel's.

"I'm sorry to hear that." Adar's expression showed sincere sympathy as he turned to guide the hovervan again.

Frieda's jaw clenched. Darkness crossed her expression like a veil of misted lace, a veneer that stiffened her cheeks and dulled the shine of her eyes. It was an expression Muriel had seen a thousand times, the one crushed under a man's unrelenting anger and sadness, the expression of a woman who never spoke of her pain, who pursed her lips and stared into space as if nothing was happening behind her gray eyes.

Muriel had failed.

They would still be friends. They would meet for bridge club, and do their embroidery on the porch. But Frieda had held her anger for so long that to lose it was more terrifying than keeping it. Muriel would never know her true friend again.

The hovervan slowed further.

A row of houses came into view, low to the ground, rounded in the style of Vegan culture, and built of dried brick and a plastic compound. They turned down another street.

"This isn't the way to the hotel," Muriel said.

"I'm going to stop a moment and let the engines cool," Adar replied.

The van stopped alongside the road. A collection of young Vegans were playing a leaping game in front of a house.

Adar stood up and walked down the aisle to sit heavily on a bench seat across from them. The sound of the ventilation system hummed from the background as the engines wound down. The Vegan's cedarlike aroma filled the enclosed compartment.

Adar balled his fingers into a fist, put his elbows to his knees, and looked into Frieda's face, seeming impervious to the fact that Frieda's gaze slipped to the side more than it came at him straight on. His face was rounded, his eyes dark, but glistening with reflected sunlight.

"When I was very young," Adar said, "my father came home and grabbed me up in his arms. I remember him yelling to my mother and brothers and sisters."

Frieda's hand grew tight in Muriel's.

"He held me to his chest and he ran. My legs, they were jangling up and down." Adar waggled his arms, looking almost comical as he tried to describe the movement. "Corners and walls flashed by like they were battering rams. I was afraid my father would hit me against them. But we made it out of the house. There was smoke. And screaming. Very loud screaming. Black battle vans, tanks I think you would call them, rolled from the hillside leaving orange dust hanging in the air."

Frieda stared at the Vegan with steel in her eyes.

"A missile fell, whistling like the wind as it came in. My mother and siblings died. I saw it happen. My father and I hid in a cellar. But the Teg soldiers found us."

Silence built.

"What do you want me to say?" Frieda whispered in her reedy voice.

"Nothing," Adar replied. "Nothing at all. But I would be most honored if you were to look outside the hovervan. See those four young children?" He pointed.

"Yes," Frieda said.

"Those are my little ones," he said. "Well, three of

them are. The fourth is one of their friends. You see, lady. Teg soldiers executed my father while I watched. But I was small, and maybe . . . how do you say . . . inconsequential at the time, maybe. I don't know. For whatever reason, they did not pay enough attention to me, and I ran away after my father was killed. I hid in a cellar. From there I watched as the human warriors came. I saw them fight. They were brave men, lady. And they fought well.

"In the end, a Teg warrior found me.

"Late at night, if I sleep just right, or maybe just wrong, I still see the barrel of the blast gun as it leveled at me."

The cabin was deathly quiet. A muffled voice came from outside.

"It was a tall man from *Miranda* that saved me."

Muriel's heart beat like a hummingbird's wings.

"Do you know," Frieda asked, "what the man's name was?"

Adar shook his head. "No, sadly, I cannot say that I do."

Frieda could not hide her disappointment.

"But," the driver said, "I am alive because *Miranda* was there. As are the children you see here. I do not know the name of the human who saved me. And it has always haunted me that I did not know it. If you do not mind, I would like to think it was your son."

Frieda's face remained stony. Her cheek quivered once.

"Johnnie," she said, her voice firm. "His name was Johnnie."

When it became obvious that Frieda would say no more, Adar nodded, went back to the driver's seat, and started the engines.

They drove back in silence, neither Muriel nor Frieda commenting on the fact that all the engines were working fine.

* * *

"Turns out they don't have lemonade," Muriel said as she sat down at the table across from her friend. "I got you grapefruit juice instead."

She slid the can across to Frieda—processed pulp with water added locally.

"It's all right," Frieda replied.

They sat in the hotel's restaurant, a room with a panoramic view of the southern face of the planet. The landscape rolled smoothly away toward Agridale Field and Monument Plaza. A tangled forest of Galleo's viny trees grew to their right, a gray-green river flowed to their left.

"What do you say we change our ship out?" Muriel said. "I think we can get a trip tomorrow."

"I think I'll make them a pillow," Frieda replied.

"What?"

"I think I'll make Adar's family a pillow. No, a pair of pillows. They'll need at least two to throw at various ends of the couch—do Vegans use couches?" she added quickly.

"Oh, I suppose so," Muriel replied. "And if they don't, well I'm sure they can use them on their beds."

"I think you're right," Frieda said, glancing at Muriel with her eyes wide and open. "Everyone can use pillows."

Frieda ran a nail under the can's lid, then took a drink of her grapefruit juice.

ON THE SURFACE

by Robert J. Sawyer

Robert J. Sawyer's novels *The Terminal Experiment,*
Starplex, Frameshift, and *Factoring Humanity* were all
finalists for the Hugo Award, and *The Terminal Experi-*
ment won the Nebula Award for Best Novel of the Year.
His latest novel is *Humans.* He lives near Toronto.
Please visit his Web site at www.sfwriter.com.

"For once, at least, I grasped the mental operations of
the Morlocks. Suppressing a strong inclination to laugh,
I stepped through the bronze frame and up to the Time
Machine. I was surprised to find it had been carefully
oiled and cleaned. I have suspected since that the Mor-
locks had even partially taken it to pieces while trying
in their dim way to grasp its purpose."
— H. G. Wells, *The Time Machine,* 1895

THE Morlock named Grach had heard from others
of his kind what the journey through time was
like, but those words hadn't prepared him for the
reality. As he moved forward, the ghostly world
around him flashed, now night, now day, a flapping
wing. The strobing light was painful, the darkness a
bandage too soon ripped away. But Grach endured
it; although he could have thrown his pale white arm
in front of his lidless eyes, the spectacle was too incredible not to watch.

Grach held the left-hand lever steadily, meaning
the skimming through tomorrows should have hap-

pened at a constant rate. But the apparent time it took for each day-to-night cycle was clearly growing longer. Grach knew what was happening of course; the others had told him. Earth's own day was lengthening as the planet in its senescence settled in to be tidally locked, the same face always toward the sun.

Such perpetual day would have been intolerable for Grach, or any Morlock, except that the sun itself was growing much, much dimmer, even as it grew larger or as Earth spiraled closer to it; debate still raged among the Morlocks about which phenomenon accounted for the solar disk now dominating so much of the sky. The giant red sphere that bobbed about the western horizon—never fully rising, never completely setting—was a dying coal whose wan light was all concentrated in the red end of the spectrum, the one color that did not sting the eyes.

Eventually, as Grach continued his headlong rush into futurity, the bloated sun came to rest, moving not at all in the sky, half its vast bulk below the horizon where the still water of the ocean touched the dark firmament. Grach consulted the gauges on the console in front of him and began to operate the right-hand lever, the one that retarded progress, until at last all about him lost the ghostly insubstantiality it had hitherto been imbued with and coalesced into solid form. His time machine had stopped; he had arrived at his destination.

Of course, the invasion had been carefully planned. Other time machines that had already traveled here were arrayed about him in a grid, precise rows and columns, with every one of the squat saddle-seated contraptions, puzzles of nickel and ivory and brass and translucent glimmering quartz, packed close to each of its neighbors.

The grid, Grach knew, measured twelve spaces by ten: room for a hundred and twenty time machines, one for each adult member of the Morlock population. It had always seemed unfair that there were ten Eloi for every Morlock, but that was the ratio by which vegetarians typically outnumbered carnivores, by which prey had to accumulate in order to satisfy the appetites of predators.

There were still vacant spots in the grid, scattered here and there, where time machines hadn't yet come forward, or had perhaps overshot their targets slightly and would materialize an hour or two hence.

Grach took a moment to regain his bearings; this hurtling through time was unsettling. And then he dismounted, letting his narrow, curved feet sink into the moist sand of the great beach that spread out in front of him.

A leash of Morlocks shuffled over to greet Grach: in the odd red light it took him a moment to recognize Bilt and Morbon, females both, and the male Nalk.

Grach and his companions walked sideways, making their way out of the maze of time machines, moving out onto the great sandy beach. Grach found himself inhaling deeply; the air was thin. No wind stirred; no waves lapped the shore, although the vast expanse of water did heave slowly up and down, almost like a giant's heart.

And—now that giants were in his mind—Grach thought briefly of the giant who had come to them, apparently from an ancient past. Assuming the counting of years reckoned by the gauges on his machine had started with a "1" near his own departure date, the giant man had come forward some eight thousand centuries. And yet that gulf was tiny compared to the time Grach and the others had now leaped forward; millions of years separated him from the world of the Eloi and of the white marble sphinx and of the access portals to the Morlocks' underground domain, each protected from the elements by a cupola.

Grach's reverie was quickly broken as Morbon

shouted, "Look!" She was pointing, her arm appearing nauseatingly pink in the dim, ruddy sun. Grach followed her gaze, and—

There they were.

Three of them, off in the distance.

Three of the giant crablike creatures that by this time had dethroned the Morlocks from their dominion over the world.

Three of the enemy they had come to kill.

The crabs were each as wide as Grach's arm span, and looked as though they might weigh double what he did. They had massive pincers; supple, whiplike antennae; eyes atop stalks; complex multipalped mandibles; and corrugated backs partially covered by ugly knobs. Their many legs moved slowly, tentatively, more as if each creature were feeling its way along rather than seeing the ground in front of it.

And they were sentient, these crabs. That hadn't been apparent initially. Drayt, the Morlock who had mounted the first copy of the giant's contraption, who had originally traveled forth to this time, had returned only with wondrous tales of a world in which the surface was perpetually dim, a world in which Morlocks could leave their dismal subterranean existence behind and reclaim the day. Oh, yes, Drayt had seen the crabs, but he'd thought them dumb brutes and suggested that they might provide a superior substitute for the scrawny meat of Eloi haunches that had been the Morlock staple.

Others had come forward, though, and seen the cities of the crabs; their vile, ever-working mouths secreted a compound that caused sand to adhere to itself, forming structures as strong as those of carved stone. They communicated, too, apparently through sounds too high-pitched for Morlocks to hear supplemented by expressive waving of their antennae.

And although they had tolerated the occasional

Morlock visitor at first, when Drayt's proposal had been put to the test—when one of the ruddy crustaceans had had its carapace staved, when the white flesh within was sampled and found delicious—the crabs had behaved utterly unlike Eloi, for, unaccountable though it might seem, they *attacked* the Morlocks, decapitating several with neat snaps of their giant claws.

The crabs, then, had to be subdued, just as the Eloi had perhaps been centuries before Grach had been born. They had to learn to accept the honor of being fodder for Morlocks. It was, after all, the natural way of things.

Grach hoped the war would be short. If the crabs were sentient, then they should understand that the Morlocks would never take more than a few of them at a time, that the odds of any particular crab being that day's meal were slim, that there could be a mostly uneventful coexistence between the small population of subjugators and the multitudes of subjugated.

But if the war were long, if they had to slaughter every last crab, well, so be it. Grach and the other Morlocks had no desire to bring Eloi forward; they were tolerable as a foodstuff, but to share a reclaimed surface with those weak, laughing things would be unthinkable. Fortunately, this distant time had other life-forms that were agreeable to the Morlock palate: Grach had already tried samples of the giant white butterfly-like creatures that occasionally took to the dark skies here, wings beating against attenuated air. And there were other things that swam beneath the sea or made occasional forays onto the beach; many of these had also already been tasted and found most satisfying.

Grach looked behind him. Another time machine was flickering into existence, leaving only two unoccupied spots in the 120-position grid. Soon, the assault would begin.

There was little possibility for a sneak attack in this offensive, said Postan, the leader of the Morlocks. Day and night meant nothing here—one hour, or one year, was precisely like the others; there was no cover of total darkness under which to launch themselves against their foes.

And so, once all one hundred and twenty Morlocks were ready, they simply charged onto the beach, each one brandishing an iron club almost as long as a Morlock body.

The crabs either heard the attackers coming, despite attempts to restrain the normal cooing sounds of Morlock breathing, or else the crabs felt the footfalls conveyed through the moist sand. Either way, the crustaceans—twenty of them were visible, although more could easily be hidden in undulations of the geography—turned as one to face the charging Morlocks.

Grach had known battle once before; he had been part of the group pursuing the time-traveling giant through the woods outside the ancient palace of green porcelain. He remembered the huge fire blazing through the forest—and remembered the excitement, the thrill that went with battle. That night, they had been unsuccessful. But this time, Grach felt sure, they would triumph.

Morlocks learned quickly. They'd never thought of using clubs to attack other life-forms; it hadn't been necessary with the Eloi, after all. But that night—a few years ago, now, and a few million—when the Morlocks had fought the ancient giant, they'd seen him use a metal club, a large lever apparently broken off some old machine, to stave in skulls. And so the subterranean workshops weren't only set to the task of duplicating the giant's strange machine, its workings still not fully grasped but its parts easy enough to turn on a lathe or hammer out on an anvil. No, the factories were also set to making sturdy iron rods. Grach held his own rod over his head as he ran, looking forward to hearing the cracking sound of exoskeletons shattering under its impact.

The crabs' claws were each as long as a Morlock's forearm. They snapped open and closed, the sound oddly mechanical in this strange world of the far future. Grach knew to hold his rod out in front of him, and, indeed, it wasn't long before the nearest crab had set upon him. The creature's pincer tried to close tight on the rod, which rang in Grach's hands. But although the claws were strong, they weren't strong enough to cut through iron. Another Morlock, to Grach's right, was waving his own rod, trying to get the crustacean to clamp onto it with its other claw. And a third Morlock—Bilt, it was—had climbed atop the crab from the rear and was now straddling its carapace while pounding down again and again with his own metal rod. The crab's antennae whipped frantically, and Grach caught a glimpse of one of them bringing up a welt as it lashed Bilt's face. But soon Bilt managed a killing blow, a great *crack!* sounding as his rod smashed in the chitinous roof between the thing's two eyestalks. The stalks went absolutely straight for a moment, then collapsed, one atop the other, lying motionless on the broken carapace, liquid from within the animal welling up and washing over them.

The creature's many legs folded up one by one, and its lenticular body collapsed to the sandy beach. Bilt let out a whoop of excitement, and Grach followed suit.

It had been good to aid in the kill, but Grach wanted one of his own. Several of the crabs were scurrying away now, trying to retreat from the on-slaught of Morlocks, but Grach set his eyes on a particularly ugly one, its carapace especially rich with the greenish encrustation that marred the shells of some of the others.

Grach wondered if there was another way to defeat a crab. Yes, having his own kill to tell of would be good—but even better would be to have killed one in a way that had occurred to no one else.

There was but a moment to collect his thoughts: fifty or so Morlocks had veered off to pursue the retreating crabs; the others were in close combat with the remaining giant crustaceans. But, so far, no one had engaged the crab that had caught Grach's attention.

Grach ran toward his target; there was plenty of noise now to cover his approach—cracking chitin, whooping Morlocks, the harsh screams of the giant white butterfly-like beasts swooping overhead. The crab's rear was to Grach, and it did not turn around as he came closer and closer still.

When at last he'd reached the hideous creature, Grach planted his rod in the moist ground, then extended his hands. He got his flat palms underneath the left edge of the crab's carapace. With all the strength he could muster, he lifted the side of the crab.

The segmented legs on that side began to move frantically as they lost contact with the ground. As Grach tipped the creature more and more he could see the complex workings of its underbelly. For its part, the crab couldn't observe what Grach was doing; its eyestalks lacked the reach to see underneath. Still, its claws were snapping in panicky spasms. Grach continued to lift, more, more, more still, until at last the thing's body was vertical rather than horizontal. A final mighty shove toppled the crab over sideways onto its back. Legs worked rapidly, trying to find purchase; the forward claws attempted to right the crab, but they weren't succeeding.

After retrieving his metal rod, Grach jumped onto the thing's underbelly, landing on his knees, the hideous articulations of the limbs shifting and sliding beneath him. He then took his metal rod in both hands, held it high over his head, and drove it down with all his strength. The rod poked through the creature's underside and soon was slipping easily through its soft innards. Grach felt it resist again as it reached the far side of the shell, but he leaned now with both hands and all of his body's weight on the end of his pole, and at last the exoskeleton gave way. The crab convulsed for a time, but eventually it expired, impaled on the sandy beach.

The battle continued for much of—well, it felt to Grach the length of an afternoon, but there was no way to tell. When it was done, though, a dozen crabs were dead, and the others had fled, abandoning not just the beach but their fused-sand buildings, which were to become the initial surface dwellings of the Morlock race.

Of course, there had to be two great battles. The first—or second; the order of events was so hard to keep straight when time travel was involved—was the one that had already taken place here on the beach. And, naturally, no one would undertake the second battle (or was it the first?) until after the Morlocks had safely secured the far future for themselves.

It had taken Grach and the others quite some time—that word again—to comprehend it all, and perhaps their understanding of such matters was still faulty. But the reasoning they came up with seemed to make sense: first, ensure that the crabs could be routed in the far future, clearing the way for all the Morlocks to travel forward and live on the surface.

But, with the battle in the future over, the Morlocks couldn't simply leave the Eloi to make their own way in the past. After all, once the Morlocks had traveled forward, the Eloi would venture underground. Oh, surely not at first—months or even years might elapse before the Eloi decided the Morlocks really were gone, before any of those timid, frail creatures would dare to climb down the ladders on the inside of the access wells, thereby entering the underworld. But eventually they would—perhaps, Grach thought, led by that bold female who had narrowly survived accompanying the giant during so much of his visit— and just as the Morlocks were now about to regain the surface, so the Eloi would regain what had once been theirs, as well: equipment and tools, technology and power.

Simple experiments with the time machines had proved that changes made in the past would eventually catch up with the future. The time machines, because of their temporal alacrity, allowed one to arrive in the future ahead of the wave of change barreling through the fourth dimension at a less speedy rate. But eventually effect caught up with cause, and the world was remade to conform to its modified past. And so though the beach might now appear as Grach and the others wished it to, there was still a chance that reality would be further modified.

And that could not be allowed; the meek could *not* be permitted to inherit the Earth. For although the Morlocks enjoyed violence, Grach and the others couldn't imagine the Eloi ever fighting amongst themselves or with anyone else. No, with all aggression long ago bred out of them, their new technological culture might endure for millions of years—meaning they could still be alive, and hideously advanced, by this time, the time of the beach, the time of the crabs. If the Morlocks didn't take care of that loose end, that dangling thread in the tapestry of time, before permanently moving to the perpetual ruddy twilight of the future, then the Morlocks might find that future becoming a world dominated by Eloi with millions of years of new technology in their hands.

No, now that the crabs were dealt with, it was time to return to the past, time to launch the second offensive of this war.

Grach and the other Morlocks returned to the distant past, to the year that, according to the display they'd all seen on the original Time Traveler's machine, had been reckoned by him to be some 800,000 years after his point of origin.

Their fleet of time machines reappeared from whence it had been launched, one after the other flicking into existence inside the giant hollow bronze pedestal of the great marble sphinx, still arrayed in their orderly rows and columns, for although the journey through the fourth dimension had been prodigious, there had been no movement at all in the other three. Of course, there were only 117, instead of 120 machines reappearing. The others were sitting undamaged in the far future, but their riders had been casualties in the battle with the crabs.

There was barely enough room for all the time machines and their passengers within the sphinx's base, but although little air slipped in through the cracks around the upper edges of the vertical door panels, it still seemed richer than the thin atmosphere of the far future.

Naturally, they didn't have to wait until dark. Rather, they had timed their arrival to occur at night. No sooner had the last of the Morlocks returned back than the great bronze panels on either side slid down, opening the interior of the giant pedestal to the elements. The Morlocks spilled out into the night. Grach allowed himself a brief look back over his rounded shoulder; in the starlight he could see the white face of the great sphinx smiling on their venture.

Brandishing clubs, they clambered through the circular portals into the large houses in which the Eloi slept. The Eloi were used to the nighttime raids, to a handful of them being plucked each time to be food for the Morlocks. Those selected did not resist; those not selected did nothing to help the others.

But tonight, the Morlocks didn't want to carry off just a few. Tonight they wished to eradicate the Eloi. The weaklings' skulls yielded juicily to pummeling rods. To that, some Eloi did react, did try to defend themselves or get away—the brighter of these creatures clearly understood that all previous patterns were to be discarded this night.

But even the strongest of the Eloi was no match for the slightest Morlock. Those that had to be chased down were chased down; those that had to be hit with hands were hit with hands; those that had to be strangled had their larynxes crushed.

It didn't take long to dispatch the thousand or so Eloi, and Grach himself happened to be the one to come across the female who had associated herself with the original Time Traveler.

She, at least, had the backbone to look defiant as Grach's rod descended upon her.

The return to the far future had gone well. Many Morlocks had clutched infants or children of their kind as they'd ridden forward on the copies of the giant's machine. Others had carried supplies and goods salvaged from the deep prison that bright light had trapped them in.

As time wore on, Grach got used to the thinner air and to the red glow of the now-ancient sun. Mankind, the Morlocks had always known, had started on the surface, and only well into its tenure on Earth had one faction moved underground. Now the Morlocks had reclaimed their birthright, their proper station in the world.

Grach looked out over the beach. Morlocks had feasted on crab legs and the meat from the invertebrates' rounded bodies. But after that bounty had been exhausted, the broken carapaces were gathered together, making a monument to that glorious battle, and a reminder to any of the crab-beings who might consider reclaiming this beach what fate would await them if they tried.

Of course, Grach knew the world was eventually doomed. He had not made the journey himself, but others had told him of trips to the very end of time, when the sea would freeze and the sun, although bigger even than it was now, would give off almost no light and even less heat.

But that future was far, far beyond even this advanced time. For the remainder of the habitable span of the world, generation after generation of Morlocks would live here. Yes, there might have been an interregnum during which the crabs had been dominant, but that was over now. Morlocks ruled again, and, until the sun's red light finally faded for good, they would continue to do so.

Still, new changes were propagating forward. The large white butterfly-like creatures were now gone. Perhaps, mused Grach, just as the giant's kind had once metamorphosed into Morlocks and Eloi, so the Eloi themselves, flighty creatures at the best of times, had here in the far, far future, literally taken wing. But with no more Eloi in the past, of course no descendants of them could exist. A pity: the flying things had been delicious.

Grach looked out again at the blood-red beach, and he thought about the original Time Traveler, that giant from ages past. Had he found whatever it was he'd been seeking when he came forward from his time? Perhaps not in that year he'd numbered about 800,000. The injustice after all, of the best of mankind being damned to a subterranean existence surely must have disappointed him. But, Grach thought, if the Time Traveler knew what his machine had ultimately made possible—this wondrous moment, with the very essence of humanity on the surface—surely he would be pleased.

AIR INFANTRY

by R. J. Pineiro

R. J. Pineiro is the author of several techno-thrillers, including *Ultimatum, Retribution, Breakthrough, Exposure, Shutdown,* and the millennium thrillers *01-01-00* and *Y2K.* He is a twenty-year veteran of the computer industry and is currently at work on leading-edge microprocessors, the heart of the personal computer. He was born in Havana, Cuba, and grew up in El Salvador before coming to the United States to pursue a higher education. He holds a degree in electrical engineering from Louisiana State University, a second-degree black belt in martial arts, is a licensed private pilot, and a firearms enthusiast. He has traveled extensively through Central America, Europe, and Asia, both for his computer business as well as to do research for his novels. He lives in Texas with his wife, Lory, and his son, Cameron. Visit his web site at www.rjpineiro.com

1

YOU never quite get used to the implants, no matter what Federation Air Infantry surgeons tell you. Sure, the biochips, combined with hypnosis and injections, give you instant access to volumes of information, but the knowledge feels . . . foreign? Yeah, that's it. Fake. It's almost like sneaking out a cheat sheet during an exam, getting the answer you seek, and then stowing it away before anyone catches you. You get the right answer, but you didn't really know it. The only difference here is that you get to do tens of thousands of such transactions per second as your serotonin-enhanced brain interfaces with the implants lining the bottom of your skull.

That's just how the 3-D terrain map floating somewhere in my altered mind feels at the moment, as I fly in from the south, high above craggy mountain peaks that abruptly turn into a sea of green, a sea of vast forests and tundra.

I have to tell you, the view is incredible. Breathtaking blue-white glaciers and white-water rivers disappear into the hazy horizon as my HX-55 dashes across a misty Alaskan sunrise at four times the speed of sound.

Damn. You can easily lose yourself in the splendor and magnificence of glacier-carved cirques surrounding monumental walls that rise to snowy peaks, as seen by the dozens of optical sensors around my windowless craft, all interfaced via hyper-band wireless to the helmet of yours truly, where they connect to probes on the back of my shaved head. The implants, always filled with trivia, inform me that tundra and dark woods will ultimately reclaim thousands of eroded acres left behind by the passing glaciers as part of the geologic life cycle of this changing land.

My vessel dashes high above lakes and meandering rivers stained with vivid hues of orange and red by the looming sun's wan light; high above glaring mirrors of infinite shapes and sizes surrounded by rain forests, crystalline icing, and sleepy volcanoes; high above pure and sublime dying walls of ice approaching the harsh coast after years of scraping the ground and valley walls, before suddenly cracking and falling into the blue-green sea, marking the birth of new icebergs.

I take millisecond breaks in my high-tech sightseeing to review the mounds of data streaming in from

all subsystems of the forward-swept-wing fighter,
verifying no alarms. The craft's average skin temperature holds steady at 1085 degrees Celsius, peaking
to 1300 degrees where the low Radar-Cross-Section
mission-adaptive wings extend forward at a sixty-
degree angle to well past the cockpit, nearly touching
a set of low RCS canards, which also act as the vertical stabilizer of the fifteen-ton stealth fighter. Inward-
canted vertical fins at the tip of each wing provide
the horizontal stability needed in the absence of a
tail fin, and also contribute to the low radar signature
of the HX-55.

The extreme heat created by air friction raises the
interior temperature to about 175 degrees Celsius,
well within the operating range of the biomolecular
subsystems and the microrobotic units, but certainly
high enough to roast me alive. Rather than adding
lots of sophisticated cooling systems to keep a pilot
comfortable, as in previous generation fighters, which
not only added to the overall cost of the craft but also
made it heavier, the HX-55 designers chose instead to
bury the pilot in a Thermagel-filled, titanium-and-
graphite pod in the center of the jet. Resembling
more a coffin than a pod, the enclosure keeps me
well insulated from extreme ambient conditions while
also serving as an ejection module in case my HX-
55 gets hit while flying at multiple times the speed
of sound.

Turn to new heading, I think. *Mark one eight seven.*

Reading my thoughts through the optical probes
on my head, the on-board interface relays the command to thousands of microelectrode-optical actuators buried below the Flexible-Composite-Material
surface of both wings, vertical fins, and canards. The
actuators vary slightly the contour of all FCM surfaces in unison to bank the craft into a shallow left
turn. Leading and trailing edges move in an optically

controlled harmony under the command of my mind, the central processing unit of the advanced fighter. That's right, I'm the brain of this machine. Without a pilot, the HX-55 is just a sophisticated hunk of metal incapable of even taxiing out of the hangar.

As the vessel turns, the G-forces begin to pound the fuselage like the hammers from hell. At this speed, any maneuver, however subtle, really piles up the Gs. The HX-55 is built to take forty Gs. I breathe a sigh of relief when my pod's G-sensors automatically pressurize the Thermagel to keep my brain from passing out.

Eleven Gs—a walk in the park while inside my pod—flash in my mind before I order the FCM surfaces to return to their stable-flight configuration the instant the directional gyro feed reaches the correct heading. The whole process takes 3.6 seconds.

Fly-by-thought.

The HX-55 is everything my superiors promised it would be—and then more. Unlike the flaps, spoilers, slats, and ailerons of previous generation fighters, all of which would rip away when attempting maneuvers at these speeds, the Federation's new-generation fighter sports wings, fins, and canards that simultaneously change shape to provide the optimum air surface for the desired maneuver. Add to that my enhanced brain, my training, and my implants—all safely shielded in this handy little pod—and what you've got is an incredible war machine, far better than the best those damned Hominids can produce.

Hominids.

I frown, not understanding what in the hell our forefathers were thinking when they launched those Voyager satellites aeons ago into the far reaches of the Milky Way advertising the wonders of Terra—and including detailed cosmological directions to get here. It was only a matter of time before another civilization, probably one that had already spent the natural resources of their own planet, came knocking down our door.

They reached our solar system early in 2116, blasting our stations on Marte and Luna before reaching Terra orbit, disintegrating the old International Space Station before settling in this frozen region of the planet. Apparently the Homis like it cold. In any case, they pretty much took over the Alaska and Yukon Territories in weeks, sending the woefully-unprepared Federation troops in the region running for cover.

It was all actually quite humiliating. The Federation, the almighty world allegiance following the War of 2045, when our ancestors nearly erased our species off the face of this planet in a fifteen-minute nuclear and biological war, had subsequently ordered the destruction of all weapons of mass destruction on Terra, making it a safe place for humans. Of course, safe against threats from *within* our world. No one obviously considered at the time the possibility of an extraterrestrial threat.

But it came, catching us pretty much with our pants down. Our weapons, albeit advanced, were still all conventional, designed to deal with the unavoidable skirmishes that would flare up here and there around the globe each year, usually from leftover radical groups or rogue regimes still resisting Federation rule. So we couldn't just nuke Homi colonies at first. We had to go in and blast them with conventional munitions one at a time. We now have nukes again, but are unwilling to use them because Terra's still recovering from the environmental chaos of 2045. We don't want to repeat the mistake of our ancestors, whose actions created the global warming that raised ocean levels by several feet in 2046, pretty much swallowing thousands of square miles of land.

Places like southern Louisiana, the Florida peninsula, the Netherlands, Bangladesh, and a number of islands no longer exist. Since those days, we have come down from the exponential portion of the damage curve to the knee, meaning that the polar caps are still melting, but at a much slower rate.

Federation scientists are convinced that the 120 megatons that would be required to eliminate the Homis would push us back to the exponential portion of the damage curve, accelerating the process again.

So this is a conventional war all the way—one that the Air Infantry is committed to win before the end of the decade to meet the mandate from the Federation Council.

The Homis no longer have air power, but their land forces are formidable—though Federation regulars were able to contain them to Alaska and Yukon by the summer of 2117. Now, armed with weapons like the HX-55, we are slowly but steadily eliminating the nightmare that just earlier this year threatened to spread across Terra like the worst of plagues.

The Homis are real bastards. Trust me on that. During their one and only expansion, they took over entire towns and villages, fed on the men and children, and did things to the women that would turn your stomach harder than pulling twenty Gs. First off, this race is composed of only males, but they carry all of the necessary genes to form other Homis. They only need female hosts from a close enough species—and Homo sapiens women apparently do just fine—at least according to Federation scientists, who managed to capture some of the bastards alive. Yeah, you heard me right. As big as they are, roughly twice the size of an average man, they manage to impregnate our women during a ritual that a number of survivors from a recently-liberated village described as animalistic. The scientists surgically removed the growing embryos and managed to save some of the women, who required half a dozen additional surgeries—plus plenty of hypnosis and injections—to get over the brutal experience. The Homi gestation period is quick, about ten weeks, and they grow up to become adults in just three of our years, meaning their species can reproduce at a much faster rate—as long as there is an adequate supply of female hosts around. Our scientists projected that if allowed to exist unchecked, the Homis would outpopulate us within a decade.

I guess that's why in the Air Infantry we have a new motto: The only good Homi's a dead Homi. The fuckers have to be killed. Period.

Information from the fighter's sensors and avionics, organized both in time and in three-dimensional virtual space, gleam in my mind as I fly into a patch of fog. Forward-looking infrared sensors immediately take over, creating a holographic image of the landscape in a palette of greens according to their heat signature as detected by the IR sensors, the sensitivity of which has been adjusted for maximum resolution in such cold weather.

The projected image shows the optimum path across the sky to avoid beams of energy from Homi search radars. With minimal effort I keep the fighter in between these walls of energy resembling velvet curtains rising vertically from the ground and crisscrossed by green bands of tracking radars overhead, essentially leaving a tunnel through which I fly to minimize detection. The system also shows me the blue inverted cones rising up from the ground that foretell the presence of surface-to-air missile radar tracking stations. Although I doubt that the Homis can detect my HX-55 if it came in contact with the radar walls or cones, I can't accept the gamble.

Activate TATS, I think.

The Target Acquisition and Tracking System begins to display an array of information on my mind. The HX-55 sensors, linked with satellites in geosynchronous orbit, begin to select ground targets on the largest Homi stronghold in Alaska—the target of my sortie, a sea of domes on the foggy horizon.

Yeah, the Homis love those domes, and they all look alike, from their garrisons to their hospitals and living quarters. Domes, domes, and more domes, all sporting that familiar lavender color that matches the color of their skin suits—and their blood. And what's worse, the domes are electronically and thermally shielded, meaning we can't use our deep infrared or quantum optics satellite imagery to see what's inside, complicating our targeting prioritization process. There are obvious targets, of course, like the missile and laser emplacements, but as for the domes, the Air Infantry has a simple rule: burn them all.

Data arrives at lightning speed as my mind acquires each target, assigns it a number and priority level, stores the data in my implanted data banks, and moves on to the next. A counter somewhere in the recesses of my implants informs me that in the three seconds since activating TATS, I already have a deadlock on nearly two hundred Homi targets. I feed the range, speed, coordinates, and terrain elevation for the first target to the powerful laser gun I carry under the fuselage. The system replies with a READY TO FIRE message.

Go hypersonic and fire on command.

Twenty feet behind me, the dual turbojets' turbine blades, which I've been using from the beginning of my sortie to compress the air going into the combustion chamber to ignite the fuel-to-air mixture, stop rotating as engine inlet doors deflect the incoming air away from the blades and into a narrow tunnel below each turbojet. The tunnels use the ram effect of the supersonic wind to achieve combustion with injected fuel without using any moving parts.

Thermagel pressure increases to offset the powerful kick as airspeed jumps to Mach 6.7—a speed that would have melted the turbojet's turbine blades. Ramjets could carry the HX-55 from Mach four up to Mach ten, but the laser's accuracy decreases beyond Mach seven due to an oscillation problem that AI scientists are still trying to solve.

I climb for twenty seconds before leveling off at thirty thousand feet and starting a twenty-five-mile-diameter circular pattern. Even at such a shallow turn, and while immersed in pressurized Thermagel, I still experience a mild three Gs from the centrifugal force, but it doesn't matter at this moment. TATS is a go. The laser gun is a go. As forests and glaciers blend into a carpet of green and white surrounding Dome City, I release the laser to fire according to the list of two hundred targets now stored in my implants. The laser starts its rhythmic discharges, each spaced by the milliseconds it takes me to select a new target and feed its coordinates to the weapon.

On the third shot, the laser slices through the roof of a dome, incinerating anything inside. A moment later the dome is engulfed in a massive secondary blast of orange and yellow flames and billowing smoke.

Bingo. Explosives depot.

The laser shifts on to the next target, turning a missile station into scorched and twisted metal in milliseconds.

And so it goes, target after target in this virtual-reality-like game, ridding Terra of Homis, eradicating their parasitic kind from—

MISSILE WARNING.

MISSILE WARNING.

Shit. Eight missiles are heading my way. I see their contrails, like rivers of smoke, zeroing in on my ass.

Launch countermeasures.

Pods beneath the plane eject a dozen high-intensity flares.

As TATS reads twenty-six targets destroyed, I see confirmation data that the infrared brains of three missiles have fallen victim to the flares. The rest close in at Mach ten.

FIVE SECONDS TO IMPACT.

I'm holding Mach 6.7. Confirmed targets destroyed is up to fifty-nine.

Clinching, I break my laser run and shove the HX-55 into a steep climb. Twenty-seven Gs blast against the Flexible-Composite-Material skin.

God!

The pressure!

As my mind screams, Thermagel rockets to keep me from passing out, but the load on my chest is enormous. The image of a huge pink elephant materializes as it stomps on me. Some joker back at Air Ops has a sick sense of humor. My mind, however, never skips a beat, keeping the nose pointed at the heavens as I rocket past eighty thousand feet, outrunning the missiles, which sizzle off and fall to the ground.

I ease off the climb and cut back throttles, shifting from ram jets to blades. I level off at just over a hundred thousand while decelerating to Mach two.

Breathing a sigh of relief as the elephant vaporizes, I turn around to go for another—

FUSELAGE BREACH.

FUSELAGE BREACH.

Rats!

Telemetry on all vital systems pours into my mind like a raging river. The HX-55 grows rapidly unstable. A Homi laser has struck a direct hit against my left wing, disabling an array of micro-electro-optical actuators, forcing me to drop to subsonic speed, which over this land is as good as pointing a gun to my head. But some of the data doesn't make sense. The damage on top of the wing has a higher temperature reading than on the bottom, suggesting the laser strike came from above, not below. This high up that can only mean a strike from orbit, from a satellite. But that's impossible because Space Infantry took care of all the Homis up there three months ago, eliminating their orbital station and associated satellites.

Or did they?

Maybe they missed some. Perhaps they confused them with space junk. Or maybe more of their compatriots from across the galaxy have finally arrived. In any case, it becomes evident that the missiles were a diversion, something that forced me to climb into the stratosphere while bleeding speed, placing myself within the range of this well-hidden orbital weapon, which would had had a much harder time hitting me when I was at twenty thousand flying almost Mach seven.

Bastards ain't dumb. And those same bastards will vaporize me in seconds unless I . . . *eject*.

My pod shoots off the top of the fighter like a cannonball, sending yours truly into a long ballistic flight whose apogee skims the top of the heavens at nearly one hundred thirty thousand feet at Mach fifteen, fast enough to get me the hell away from danger but without shooting me into orbit.

One hundred ten thousand feet. Mach fourteen.

Quantum wireless data from the fighter ceases to arrive a moment later, meaning the Homis roasted it. The beacon in my helmet starts to broadcast a signal to the Unmanned Rescue Ship, which had been about a hundred miles away at ejection—per AI rules—but now it's getting farther and farther away.

Ninety thousand feet. Mach thirteen.

Wow. I'm really dropping in this thing, which now

has a mind of its own, following a preprogrammed ejection sequence. Its first priority is to get me the hell away from where I was shot down, and, unfortunately, also away from the URS.

Outside skin temperature's a cool three thousand degrees. Good thing the pod has plenty of titanium and graphite layers.

Since the pod lacks any outside cameras, I try to visualize what I look like, dropping from the sky like a flaming meteor in my first nonsimulated ejection that, so far, appears to follow the book. Let's hope that the rest of the experience sticks to the sim specs, otherwise there's going to be pieces of me from here to the North Pole.

The Thermagel is certainly doing its part, performing just as designed, not only holding my body temperature constant, but also keeping vibrations to a minimum.

At fifty thousand feet I peel off the first set of titanium-graphite layers, jettisoning them off with a burst of compressed helium. Outside the skin temp is just below a thousand degrees when the first parachute deploys. It's really not a chute but more of a metallic umbrella that slows me down to subsonic levels in a shove-your-guts-in-your-throat, ten-second jolt that even the Thermagel has difficulty cushioning, making me wish I'd never joined the damned Air Infantry.

Twenty thousand feet. Off bursts another set of insulating layers. By now my speed has dropped to a mild four hundred miles per hour and the outside skin temp is as frigid as the air over northern Alaska.

Eight thousand feet. My last insulating layer not only peels off, but it also breaks up into dozens of fragments designed to confused ground tracking radars. All that's shielding me is the cocoon of Thermagel, which continues to keep me nice and warm

despite the ten-below-zero outside temp in this sup-
posedly warm summer day at the Arctic end of
Terra. What a place to get nailed.

Seven thousand feet.

Five thousand.

Three.

One.

The fiber cocoon cracks like an egg, creating more
radar decoys, and in a flash the Thermagel flies off
in the slipstream, leaving me with just my Air Infantry all-terrain suit and my field equipment. One of
the decoys burns from a laser flash. There're Homis
nearby, which doesn't make sense because this area
is supposed to be deserted.

My main chute blossoms at the last second, as the
snowy ground comes up to greet me, slowing my
descent just enough to avoid breaking my legs, but
fast enough to minimize my exposure to ground fire.

The AI suit absorbs the brunt of the impact through
the thousands of micro-electro actuators sandwiched
between layers of Thermafoam and Flexalloy—the only
protection shielding my body from the harsh elements.

And from the Homis.

I come out of the roll and my mind switches from
pilot mode to infantry mode. I need to reach high
ground immediately.

I do so an instant later, jumping to the top of a
towering pine. The electro actuators interfaced to my
implants sense my brain's command to jump and
magnify the motion, allowing me to take a leap that
defies gravity, propelling my two-hundred-pound
body—plus another three hundred pounds of suit
and weapons—to a height of ninety feet, where I
snag one of the top branches with my free hand. The
other is already clutching my laser pistol.

I remain at the top for just a second or two, long
enough for the telescopic lenses built into my helmet

to confirm not only the reading from my implanted GPS receiver, but also from the multiple inputs of the helmet's sensors, which include an electronic nose far more sensitive than any creature on Terra. It can detect the scent of any living creature—including Homis—up to tens of miles away.

As I hop to an adjacent treetop, I compare the data to the 3-D terrain map stored in my implants and a moment later I know exactly where I am. I convey that information to the broadcasting beacon in my helmet to transmit the coordinates to the URS, and the transponder lets me know that it is at least an hour away.

All these fancy gadgets, though, tell me what I already know: I'm in serious shit, deep inside enemy lines with what appears to be about two hundred Homis converging on me, along with . . . I sense Homo sapiens in the vicinity as well. But that doesn't make any sense. There shouldn't be any this deep in Homi-controlled territory. I double-check the data streaming from my sensors and, sure enough, I sense about twenty red-blooded Homo sapiens.

Another message flashes in my mind from my suit's motion sensor: Keep moving.

In the Air Infantry, motion is life. You stick around too long in one place and you're bound to be fried alive by an enemy laser or even a bullet—though it would take more than a rifle shot to pierce the Flexalloy. In the AI they teach you to fight while in motion, to eat while in motion, and even to take a crap while jumping around like fucking Tarzan.

I spend an extra second on a branch, and as I'm about to hop to another one, it collapses under me, but not from my weight. Some Homi bastard has just sliced it off with a well-aimed laser shot.

I'm falling headfirst, but my gyro kicks in and straightens me up. My proximity sensor picks up two dozen Homis beneath me and no Homo sapiens, at least none in a five hundred-foot radius.

I land while shooting the laser with one hand and my flamer with the other, doing some serious damage to the picturesque scenery around me. A second later I'm jumping again, but never stop blasting away. I sense laser energy a foot off to my right, a near miss.

High-pitched shrieks behind me confirm that I nailed some of the purple aliens. Proximity sensors tell me that many are running for cover.

Ping!

A bullet has just bounced off my armored hide. I feel only a slight nudge because its kinetic energy is no match for my combined five-hundred-pound mass. You have to be careful, though, because these suits can give you the false sense that you're Superman. I've seen AI troopers get killed because they overexposed themselves to the enemy thinking that the suit would protect—

Ping!

Back on top of the trees I fire two grenades at the Homi mob taking potshots at me. The explosions rattle the clear morning, followed by more shrilling and grunting. Sensors report that there's now far fewer Homis in the vicinity than expected based on my strikes. Looks like the humans in the area are also killing their fair share of aliens.

I could keep on hopping toward the southeast and close the gap with the URS, but I can't stomach the thought of leaving my Homo-sapien brothers and sisters alone in this skirmish. I'm AI, damnit. I've been trained to kill Homis from the air or on the ground. I've taken an oath to protect the life of Homo sapiens on Terra. The time has come to put the Federation tax dollars that went into my infantry training and very expensive gear to good use.

As my beacon continues to broadcast my location

to the URS, I circle around, finally locating the gun-fight. The Homo sapiens are bunkered inside an old-fashioned log cabin. There's a mob of Homis all around it trying to get in. I see dozens of them sprawled on the ground amidst pools of purple blood. My species is nailing them—though it's not that easy with such primitive weapons. To kill a Homi with a rifle you've got to hit him in the head, preferably the face. Otherwise the bullets will just bounce off their purple armor—unless you happen to have at your disposal the Federation's latest gener-ation high-temp flamer or laser, both of which are designed to melt through their shield, in which case you just have to point in their general direction and blast away.

I come in from behind the main group, roasting them as I do a cartwheel over them, clearing their tall bodies by almost thirty feet while sweeping the flamer in all directions, turning their attack into a soprano concerto of out-of-tune trills. I spot a couple of humans on the cabin's roof turning in my direc-tion, probably not knowing who or what in the hell I am, but certainly realizing that I'm on their side. To them I probably look like a superhero from a comic book.

I land among tall figures running about in flames, and I cut them to half their size with the laser by doing a quick three-sixty at waist level, spilling their smoking purple guts across the frozen tundra. The smell would probably make me vomit, but the air-conditioning system in my trusty helmet not only warms up the air for me, it also filters out smoke and other undesirable particles.

And it is at this moment, as I'm feeling pretty fuck-ing invincible, that my sensors register a drastic in-crease in temperature on my back, just beneath my right shoulder blade.

I try to jump, but it's too late. A second laser

strikes the suit's primary battery system, just below the waist. The Homis either got lucky or the bastards have got hold of the suit design and learned its weaknesses.

The backup charge strapped to my chest kicks in, giving me partial motion. I jump while turning around, though not as high as I would have just seconds ago.

I briefly lock eyes with the Homi who shot me. He's an ugly mother, nearly ten feet tall and sporting orangutan arms and an apelike head—all dressed in one of those shiny lavender suits. I barbeque him, along with six of his plum comrades who make the mistake of stepping away from the surrounding woods thinking I've been neutralized.

I watch them turn into mobile pyrotechnic displays with delight. The only good Homi is a—

A bright flash of light engulfs me and I fall to the ground like a lead weight, landing on my back, light-headed, unable to move. My suit has been disabled and goes into lock-down mode. Shields automatically deploy to protect me from—

Intense pain shoots down from the top of my skull. Colors explode in my brain before all goes dark.

2

A rustic wooden ceiling slowly comes into focus when I open my eyes, blinking several times as I access my implants, which are powered by the natural juices in my brain when I'm awake but can hold their charge for about thirty seconds after I pass out. Like watching a movie in your mind, the implants replay the multiple blows inflicted on my helmet and suit—Homis trying to crack me open like an acorn. They are hammering me with everything they have, from laser shots and rifles to what feels like axes and clubs. Then, before the algorithm in the implants destroys the suit—and yours truly—to prevent it from falling into enemy hands, the pounding stops.

Slowly, almost painstakingly, I lift my head enough to see my naked chest and legs. The realization that I'm only wearing my underwear has a sobering effect.

Where in hell is my suit? My helmet? My weapons? For a moment I panic. In the AI you don't lose your gear—not to the Hominids, not to anyone—and survive. The implants are supposed to detonate the charges before anyone can strip you of your suit.

So what happened?

And where the hell am I? Did the Homis somehow manage to remove my suit after capturing me? I thought the bastards only took female prisoners for breeding and ate the rest. Am I being held pending preparations for their next luau? The image of a roasted pig with an apple in its mouth somehow worms into my mind.

Swell.

I just can't believe my luck—and refuse to accept the fact that I have allowed the enemy to take my suit.

Priorities. I have to keep things in perspective, have to figure a way out of this mess. First, I need to find out for how long and where I am being held captive.

Closing my eyes, I interface with the real-time clock in my implants, learning that I've been out of commission for over six hours.

I cringe.

Six hours!

Entire battles are fought in a third of that time.

I force both legs to the side of this small bed and somehow find the strength to sit up. As I'm about to access the GPS receiver in my implants, my head begins to spin from lack of blood to my brain. I've got up too fast and have to use my arms to keep from collapsing back on the bed.

Inhale deeply, I tell myself, filling my lungs with stale air that feels as if it has been breathed too many times. Exhaling through my mouth and breathing again and again, I force my cloudy mind back into focus, to the point where I can keep my balance, sitting up without the help of my arms.

I run a hand over my shaved head, my fingers feeling for the tiny optical probes surgically implanted there a year ago so that I can interface with the helmet. Other probes on my back connect the array of nerves in my spinal cord to the backbone of the suit. The message SUIT OFF pulsates in the far reaches of my mind.

My hand comes in contact with what feels like a bandage. Upon closer inspection I see other bandages on my legs and arms, and one on my torso. Someone has patched me up.

As I stretch my back and loosen my neck and shoulders, I inspect the room a bit closer while accessing the GPS, which tells me that I'm almost fifty miles away from the last location where I broadcast my signal to the unmanned rescue ship, meaning the URS reached that location, hung around for its programmed five minutes, and then RTB—returned to base.

Which also means I'm deeply screwed—unless my helmet is at this new location and has not been busted during the removal process.

Although not small, the murky quarters give me the impression of something built in a hurry. Planks of an assortment of wood grains were nailed against square columns that rose from the floor to meet crossbeams on the ceiling. Grayish paste fills the cracks in between the uneven planks. The room, although not particularly aesthetically appealing, provides adequate shelter—far better than some of the shitholes I've slept in since joining the AI.

A single gas lamp burning on a table on the other side of the room, next to the door, casts a depressing glow on the already gloomy interior. The general dimensions of the room and all of the objects in sight fill me with cautious optimism. They're all human size, not Homi. Still, I wish I had my helmet so I can smell out my surroundings and get a sense of who is holding me prisoner. During basic training you learn how to fight a Homi without any gear, just old-fashioned hand-to-hand combat. I can take three of them at one time with well-placed blows to the neck, which our scientists determined is a lot more sensitive than the neck of a Homo sapien.

The door suddenly opens. A bald man with broad shoulders and stocky arms holding a food tray stares at me for a moment before saying, "We were wondering when you'd be up." He sets the tray on the table next to the bed. "I'll tell Nizina that you're awake."

Before I get a chance to say anything, the stranger leaves the room, closing the door behind him. Puzzled, I start for the door but lack the strength to stand on my own and collapse back on the bed.

Crap. I'm a sad sight. Tens of millions of Fed bucks to make me a Homi killing machine and I can't even climb out of this damned bed. I'm glad my drill sergeant isn't here to see this.

I settle for the glass of water on the tray, gulp it down, and inhale deeply, feeling life slowly slipping back into me.

The door swings open again. A woman. Her harsh stare contrasts sharply with the delicate curves of her face. Her dark skin is accentuated by the large cheekbones and Asian eyes predominant in the Tinglit population of Alaska—according to the information streaming from my implanted encyclopedia. Tinglits are descendants of the tribe that once controlled the whole Alaska Panhandle, the Indian population that survived the brutal Russian military rule of the early 1800s just to endure an even longer struggle for ownership of the land when the white men from the American states came in 1867. The fur trade and the gold rush brought more people to this land than the original fourteen territorial Tinglit tribes could tolerate. The tribes were further eradicated during the modernization era of the early twenty-first century. Largely untouched by the War of 2045, the region prospered at a faster rate than the rest of the old United States during the recovery period of the late twenty-first century. Then the Homis arrived.

The Tinglit woman stands in front of me. Her skin lacks smoothness, probably robbed by the harsh climate and even harsher way of life. her lips are dry, coarse. I regard her tight-fitting clothes, small waist, full breasts, and shoulders a bit wide for a woman her size—shoulders that portray strength. As a soldier you're trained through implants and injections to get a feel about other people's fighting capabilities—info you use over and over while operating in suburban areas to weed out the threat from innocent bystanders. This voluptuous Tinglit woman's definitely a warrior. As a soldier in the AI, you're also given sexually-inhibiting injections to keep your mind focused on the job. The chemicals are still in my system because I feel nothing but the desire to retrieve my suit and helmet and get the hell back to my unit.

"I see that you've already met Junek," she says in a low and somewhat raspy voice that matches her tough appearance. "I'm Nizina Kluyek, leader of the Alaska Resistance Movement in this region."

"Resistance movement? The Federation's not aware of one," I reply.

She crosses her firm arms, thin muscles pumping beneath the skin as she does so. "You expect the people of Alaska to just sit back and watch Terra get ravaged by these raping cannibals?"

I'm not sure how to reply to that.

She added, "Are you with the Air Infantry?"

I nod. "Lieutenant Jake Gray."

"That explains the uniform we removed from your body—and also the way you fought off those creatures, which, by the way, saved our lives. We are grateful. In return we saved yours by killing off the last few gorillas before they picked you apart."

"About the suit," I say with some hope. "It's Federation property. I need it back."

She slowly shakes her head. "There wasn't much left of it by the time we found you. Like I said, the monsters were trying to dismember you. You're lucky to be alive."

"But . . ." I hesitate. The scuttle charges, as well as just about every other aspect of the suit—even its existence—is classified. However, the fact that I'm alive suggests that somehow one of them managed to remove the suit without setting off the charges, meaning that the suit itself has a weakness. "How did you remove it?"

Nizina grins ever so slightly. Her eyes widen as she says, "Very carefully. We know those suits are booby-trapped."

"You do?"

"The Federation is a very large and complex organization. Such conglomerates always have leaks."

I'm a bit stunned. "How did you get access to the specs?"

"That's my little secret." She winks.

Terrific. So much for all of the secrecy surrounding the development and deployment of the suit. The Homis know how to disable it and these Tinglit fighters know how to remove it without setting off the self-destruct mechanism.

Nizina's expression softens a bit. "How are you feeling?"

"A bit weak, but otherwise all right. What happened to my helmet?"

"Cracked open. The electronics were smashed."

"And my weapons?"

"Same."

"Damn."

"You must rest now, Lieutenant Gray."

"Rest? Are you kidding me? I need to get back to my unit. I need to get in contact with them."

"With this?" She reaches into her pocket and produces the radio transmitter that was built into my helmet as well as the backup transmitter in my suit.

I let go a heavy sigh.

"They're toast, and I can't afford to radio out. The apes have gotten quite good at tracing our radio sources. Where is your unit, Lieutenant? Somewhere in southern Yukon, I presume?"

"In New Seattle."

"Was there a rescue planned for you?"

I nod. "But it's no good now because we're not in the same location where you found me." I tell her our exact coordinates.

Concern films her brown eyes. "How . . . how do you know that?"

My turn to wink. "That's *my* little secret."

She makes a face and approaches me.

"Listen, Lieutenant—"

"Jake, please."

"Jake . . . this is my most secret of hideouts. If the Federation knows where it is, I have to assume that the apes might also know, and I can't afford for a few hundred of them to show up here like they did at my other safe house."

"The Federation doesn't know where this place is, Nizina. Only I do."

The puzzled expression tightens her features.

"Trust me," I add.

"All right," she says with a hint of resignation. "You did save my team, after all." She proceeds to sit next to me and puts her hands on my shaved head. "Now let's take a look at those wounds."

She pulls back the medical tape and says, "No infection so far."

"That's good news."

She adds, "You took quite a beating out there," and presses the dressing back in place a moment later.

"Tell me about it."

She moves to my torso, and then my thighs, her fingers groping my flesh.

I suddenly feel a little wood.

But that's . . . impossible. What in the hell happened to the sexual inhibitors that are supposed to keep my winky parked in neutral? Maybe it's the fact that I haven't gotten laid in over two years, ever since graduating from boot camp at Fort Hood and officially starting my training as an AI trooper. Not only haven't I had sex, but I really haven't even seen much of the opposite sex at all in that time. The Federation's dead serious about our training. They're not going to invest heavily in training, surgeries, and equipment for us to be thinking about anything but the job. And the injections are the ultimate insurance against everything from daydreams and wet dreams to masturbation. They expect *all* of our attention at *all* times.

Yet Old Pancho is getting as ramrod straight as my old drill sergeant as this Tinglit broad puts her hands all over me.

I try to think of my mother.

"Are these the cybernetic interfaces?" she asks, moving back to my head, running a finger around my probe points.

"Yep. But there're no good to me without something to interface them to, like my suit and helmet."

Nizina stands. "Rest tonight. We're moving west before dawn tomorrow."

"What's west?"

"We're not sure, but our informants think it might be an underground weapons lab."

My ears perk up at the potential military intelligence. "Weapons lab? What kind of weapons?"

"That's what we need to find out. Are you any good at fighting without all that fancy gear?"

The answer is absolutely yes. Before the implants; before the suits, helmets, lasers, and flamers; before the injections, I was—and still am—a leatherneck, trained to fight with anything, including my bare hands and feet if need be. I'm trained to survive in any type of terrain, to live off the land, to endure conditions that would make the toughest Federation Regular Army soldier pee in his pants. However, I'm not really sure what she meant by that question, so I ask, "Why is that important?"

"Because I need everyone in my group to be able to fight on his or her own with just simple weapons, like guns, knives, and explosives."

I try to stand—but quickly realize my mistake as my legs give out and I land back on the bed. So much for trying to appear intimidating. Nevertheless, I still manage to mutter the words, "What . . . do you mean 'in *my* group?' I'm with the Air In—"

"You're with the Alaska Revolutionary Army, Jake—for the time being, anyhow. We're the ones who saved you, and if you indeed know how to fight—and believe me, we'll test you first—then I need you to help us out, especially after losing so many volunteers back where you found us. This is war, and I must use every single asset within my reach to free my land. Besides, for the time being you can't go back because your unit doesn't know where you are."

The lady has a point. I ask the negotiation expert system in my implants, which has access to all external sensory inputs, including this conversation, for the best way to handle this situation. The artificial intelligence unit responds with a series of options depending on my intended outcome, and I select the one that has the greatest chance of getting me back to my unit the soonest.

"Okay," I finally say. "I'll help you out, but afterward I request that at the earliest opportunity you cut me lose with a radio and some weapons so that I can call for help on my own, without jeopardizing your team."

She shrugs. "Sure, Jake. But that's suicide in my opinion, unless your people can come in and rescue you right away. Otherwise you're likely to find yourself the object of the apes' undivided attention in no time. The bastards flock to any humans in their controlled territory like sharks to a bleeding prey."

That's a risk that my implanted mind is apparently willing to take, so I say, "We have an agreement, then?"

"Only if you're capable enough to pull your own weight."

"Don't worry," I say, though at the moment I can't even stand up.

"We'll see. Now rest and eat your meal." Nizina turns and leaves the room, closing the door behind her.

I gaze at the food tray. Not particularly appealing to the eye, but it seems eatable—certainly better than the stuff they made us eat at boot camp.

3

The meal and a good night's sleep have certainly done the trick. Dressed in ill-fitting and worn-out jeans and a sweatshirt I pace my room while Nizina and her clan confer in the room next door. I get the strange feeling that they're trying to figure out what in the hell to do with me.

The door swings open. Nizina and Junek walk in first, followed by the others, about a dozen of them, mostly men plus a few women who look as rugged as Nizina. I almost chuckle. The Federation spends millions to give its recruits the hungry look flashing in the eyes of all present. These are battle-hardened warriors, men and women who look capable of eating rocks in their cereal.

"Well?" I ask, refusing to be intimidated by this lot. After all, for the past two years I have seen my fair share of fighting—though always from either the confines of an HX-55 or with the added superpower of my AI suit. "What's the word?"

She looks at Junek, who makes a sudden move toward me, reaching for my throat.

Instincts take over. I shift sideways like a shadow, grabbing his left wrist, twisting it. The corpulent Tinglit makes a pained face as he flips in midair and lands flat on his side while I continue to twist before shoving my bare foot against his throat.

Junek's light moaning as he struggles to breathe is the only sound in the room. Everyone else is in apparent shock at my ability to best this man, nearly twice my size, in seconds. Then again, remember that I've been trained to handle Homis with my bare hands, and those creatures are bigger than Junek, who probably never saw this coming. Poor bastard. He doesn't know that implanted in my mind are a myriad of fighting programs that, combined with my conditioning, make me as deadly as the toughest man alive.

"Let him go," Nizina says, intrigue flashing in her eyes.

I help the stunned Tinglit to his feet.

"You fight well," he mumbles while massaging his throat, bowing respectfully, and stepping back.

"You learned that in the Air Infantry?" she asks.

"Among other things."

She gives me an approving smile before gazing over at her team. "Anyone else have any doubts about this man's ability to assist us?"

I quickly consult with my implants and come up with the appropriate thing to say in their silence: "I'm honored at the opportunity to fight by your side."

4

If you thought hopping around in an AI suit was exciting enough, you should try snowmobiling through the woods in the dark at forty miles per hour—with the lights off.

I'm asking myself what in hell I've signed up to do while I'm holding on for dear life to Nizina's waist as she floors the stolen machine while steering through a sea of pines.

What makes it worse is the fact that I lack any visual cues to prepare my body for an upcoming turn, or drop, or climb, rendering me as helpless as if I was a rollercoaster in the darkness. Only Nizina and the drivers of the other snowmobiles are wearing the night-vision goggles that prevent them from smashing into the tree trunks I see at the very last second, as we cross what seems like a heavily-wooded mountainside.

Strapped to the sides of the dark snowmobiles are

a pair of old automatic weapons. The trunk of each vehicle contains additional ammo for their guns in case they have a need for it, and some other gear, including hand grenades, a spare tank of gas, and whatever food and first-aid gear could fit in the left-over space.

These Homi snowmobiles are actually quite power-ful. I guess they need to be. The aliens are pretty big mothers.

The tractor belt underneath kicks snow to the side, helping Nizina make a tight turn. I pull myself closer to her and lower my head to keep my center of grav-ity lined up with hers as we clear what looks like a large boulder. I also duck to avoid decapitation by low branches. Keeping my head down, however, also means bending my back a bit, which puts a lot of stress on the ski jacket that Junek gave me earlier, which is a size too small but still better than freezing to death. The nylon collar cuts into the front of my neck while pulling down on a hood that leaves only my face exposed to the merciless wind. I now under-stand why these Tinglit warriors have leathery faces.

As the wind enjoys screwing with my face, I begin to feel respect for these people, a sense of admiration. They are the last of the real warriors, fighting against overwhelming odds to preserve their way of life, and doing so without fancy AI training, without surgeries and injections, without suits and laser guns. Concepts like ramjets, implants, and flamers are meaningless to these land warriors, who, according to what Junek told me after our brief wrestling match earlier today, use the land to live and to fight; use their own ene-mies as their supply of weaponry, transportation, and fuel—the reason at least one in five missions consists of a supply convoy attack, where extreme measures are taken to ensure the survivability of the precious cargo aboard those Homi transport vehicles.

The other missions are of the hit-and-run kind, meant to disrupt Homi operations, to be a pain in the ass to them, to let them know that they don't get to roam this land freely, without paying a penalty.

I hug Nizina even tighter as we go down a steep hill, the whistling wind and the roaring engine ringing in my ears, the smell of gas tingling my nostrils.

Nizina.

For a moment I wonder what forces compelled her to become what she has become. Was her family killed? Raped? Eaten by the Homis? Was her home sacked, destroyed? Junek had remained silent for a few moments when I asked him that question, finally informing me that it was not his place to respond to such personal queries about his leader.

Nizina steers us toward a bluff overlooking a large abandoned structure—a warehouse of some sort—apparently in the middle of nowhere. It backs into the side of the mountain opposite where we are, roughly a thousand feet away. A single road originating from the front of the structure disappears into the woods.

We stop but remain on the snowmobiles.

"That's the weapons compound?" I ask.

"According to my informant," she replies.

This doesn't feel right. "But . . . the Homis only like domes, and there're no guards, no perimeter fence, no obvious defenses to—"

"Exactly," she says. "It looks like nothing from the air to keep the Federation from bombing it. The place used to be an abandoned mine. It's now supposed to house an underground weapons lab."

"So, what do we do now?"

"We wait to confirm the intelligence."

"How?"

"You'll see."

I frown, hating to be spoon-fed information, though as

a grunt I should be used to it. The Federation also has the habit of telling us only what we need to know to accomplish a mission—and not a shred more. I find myself really missing my AI gear right about now. I could easily hop across the narrow valley separating me from the facility and just blast away with the flamer and the laser, cooking the place in the time that it takes me to take a dozen steps in knee-deep snow as we try to get a closer look.

Still wearing her night goggles, Nizina walks a few feet in front of me, carefully moving through the dense woods holding the same kind of machine-gun that I clutch in my gloved hands—a toy compared to my AI hardware, but the only weapon available to me at the moment.

An AI leatherneck makes do with whatever's available. Period.

We stop by a clump of boulders. Nizina checks her watch and says, "The trucks should be out within the hour."

"Trucks?"

"If my source was reliable," she replies, motioning her volunteers to stand guard fifty feet in each direction, before sitting down and resting her back against a trunk, letting the goggles hang loose from her neck. "Now we wait."

I sit next to her and pull out the stick of beef jerky that Junek gave me earlier. As I unwrap it, I access my GPS and store the coordinates of the warehouse in my implants for future reference.

"You have good people in your group," I say, biting an inch off the stick and then tilting it in her direction.

She shakes her head and replies, "They may not have your training, but they're loyal to the end."

After a moment of silence, she asks, "What's your story, anyway? I'm curious about how you became a trooper."

I almost laugh. "The short version: I didn't want to become a truck driver, like my father. I've always loved to fly but didn't have the money for lessons, so I decided to take my chances with the Air Infantry, where they put about a thousand applicants through endless weeks of hell to weed out those lacking the right combination of physical strength, spatial coordination, solid reflexes, and smarts. Only twenty of us made it through the course, and of those nine became pilots."

"Only nine out of a thousand?"

"Yep. Most went on to join the Federation Regular Army. Only the very best of the best get to join the AI. We're really a combination of a top-notch fighter pilot and an extremely well-trained soldier. An AI trooper in a HX-55 can do as much damage as an entire flight squadron in the old days. And on the ground, with my gear . . . well, you saw what I did to those Homis yesterday morning."

"We could certainly use a few troopers in our expeditions."

"Well, you've got one on loan for the time being—though not fully outfitted, but I think I can handle my share."

"I've noticed."

"What about you," I ask. "What's your story?"

Narrow beams of early-morning sunlight filter through the thick canopy overhead, making her face glow. She hugs her legs, leans her head back, and closes her eyes before replying, "After the apes burned my village north of Anchorage, my younger sister and I headed south, hoping to reach the Yukon territory. But the bastards caught up with us. They took us to Dome City and . . . raped us—and you really don't want to know how or how many times."

Nizina is staring at me now, anger glinting in her stare. I'm at a loss for words. I've read the Federation reports on the procreation methods of the Hominids, and I assure you they're the stuff that nightmares are made of.

"After impregnating us, they threw us in a cell, where they fed us three meals a day and kept us clean and healthy to maximize the chances of the parasites growing inside of us. There must have been a hundred or more women in that place, some of whom had given birth to one or more litters already. My sister and I were the new kids on the block and quickly learned of the terribly painful deliveries that resulted in the death of the mother three out of five times. There were also quite a few men, mostly for experiments and food. Junek was one of them. One day I got hold of a shard of glass, which I use to stab our cell keeper in the neck. I grabbed his keys and essentially led an escape. Forty-three of us made it to the forest, including Junek and my sister. All thirty women got together and unanimously made the decision to take our chances with field abortions rather than giving birth to those things. Most of us survived the rudimentary procedure. My sister and a few others didn't."

The wind is blowing from the north, swirling her hair.

"So that's the story of my clan, Jake," she continues. "We've all experienced firsthand the horror of the apes and will continue to fight them until they are gone from this planet—or we will die trying. So, why don't you tell that to your Federation leaders if you ever get out of here alive?"

I'm about to respond when Junek approaches us.

"Yes?" she asks.

"Trucks," he says. "Listen."

Barely audible, but I could still discern the engine noise.

"Let's take a look," Nizina says as we both get up.

Large front doors are now swung open and trucks are driving out, five of them.

She pats me on the back. "Let's go."

A minute later, I'm embracing Nizina again as the Tinglit warrior starts the snowmobile, which jolts into life with a forward jerk, kicking a blanket of snow behind, and nearly loosening a couple of my vertebrae.

She floors it while cutting right, doing a quick one-eighty, blasting another wave of snow behind us, and then we're off again. The wind cuts against me with the same intensity as before, forcing me to lower my head as trees, rocks, and branches rush by. A sudden turn, followed by a hard brake, nearly sends me flying over her, but I hug the seat very hard with my legs, keeping myself down.

The turn ends, and with it, I notice she slows down enough for me to risk lessening the pressure of my arms around her waist and take a glance and notice that we're riding parallel to the road connecting the presumed weapons facility to the main highway several miles away. Nizina points at the truck caravan, which she has let get about five hundred feet ahead while remaining within the protection of the trees to minimize detection.

"I hope they don't go too far!" she says loud enough for me to hear. "The range of these vehicles is about a hundred miles!"

"What, then?" I ask.

"Junek has two Terrain Cruisers stashed away for emergencies, but we prefer not to use them. Too exposed, plus they limit our getaway routes if caught."

"Makes—"

"They're slowing down," she says, while hitting the brakes and signaling the rest of the group following close behind us to do the same.

Junek, who rides at the tail of the single-file caravan, is the first to jump off his vehicle and comes running toward Nizina, who waits for me to get off before she dismounts.

"They stopped at a small clearing I saw on the way in," the Tinglit bodybuilder reports while putting a hand on the snowmobile handle. "It looked like some sort of abandoned excavation project."

Nizina waits for the others to make a small circle around her snowmobile before speaking. "I think we're on to something here. Junek, you take four men, go across the road, and cover the west side of the clearing. I'll take the others and handle the south side. Remember, we're just observing for now. Also keep in mind that the complex is only a couple of miles away. The informant claims that the apes usually keep over a hundred armed gorillas in there, and they could all be sent here in minutes. Keep your cool and don't turn this into another bloodbath. All with me?"

Heads nod.

"Good. Move out."

Nizina motions for me to follow her. Firmly clutching my submachine gun, I waste no time in falling single file behind the silhouette of another volunteer already following her. Sunlight breaks through the heavy branches enough for me to notice the space between Nizina and the second guy. I slow down until I have spaced myself by the same fifteen feet, and slowly scan the forest with the weapon.

The trucks have already stopped. The sound of Homi shrilling in the distance fills the air, chilling my body in the same way as the shivering breeze swirling through the foliage.

We reach the edge of the forest and take cover on either side of Nizina. The Homi group is less than a hundred feet away, and with sunrise just minutes away, I can see them walking toward the large pit in the middle of the clear—

A shot echoes across the frozen tundra. And another. And one more.

I tense, ready to jump in and—

"No," she whispers as I begin to lift my weapon over the underbrush to get a clean shot at the nearest Homi head. "They're firing at the bags they're unloading." She passes the binoculars to me and reaches for a small radio strapped to her belt.

I count eight Homis in addition to the truck drivers, who simply stand to the side while the rest drag long bags to the pit, where they fire their weapons sporadically.

"Junek?" she whispers into the radio.

"*Yes?*"

"Have your men line up the apes to the left of the trucks. We'll handle the drivers and the others. Fire on my mark."

"*But what about the warehouse? They will hear the reports.*"

"Do it, Junek. Don't argue. Run to the snowmobiles afterward. They won't be able to catch us."

I get ready to rumble.

At her command, the clearing becomes a killing ground, with most Homis dropping to the ground before they have a chance to react. Two aliens near the trucks manage to hide behind the rear tires of one vehicle and open fire on Junek's position, but that ends as soon as Nizina's crossfire blasts them from behind.

Then there's silence.

"Let's go! Everyone to the snowmobiles!" she screams as the volunteers do an about-face back to the forest.

The expert systems in my implants, however, have the sudden urge to find out what's inside those bags and convince me to head to the pit.

"Wait, where are you—"

I tell her as I trot across the underbrush and onto the virgin snow surrounding the old excavation site.

She catches up with me halfway to the trucks, just as I hear the snowmobiles cranking back up. We reach the first truck. Two of the bags are half open. The rest were still . . .

I freeze, my mind refusing to register the image that I have just seen: horribly mutated Homo sapiens.

In an instant I'm consulting my vast virtual library, realizing what I have just seen, coming to terms with the weapon the Hominids have created. The disfigured cadavers are silent testimony of the horrible pain inflicted on them by a weapon Federation scientists could never get to work right, could never achieve an acceptable yield for the amount of energy it took to operate. And even if it could, no decent civilization would ever even think of using it against another. No respectable general would ever dream of exposing an enemy to the lethal dose of high-frequency sound waves capable of altering the delicate molecular bonding of carbon-based systems, of living creatures, transforming the perfect architectural work of Mother Nature into a disarray of matter, literally melting its victims into themselves for the duration of the exposure. Whatever survived the waves wasn't expected to live for long.

The ultimate weapon.

I recall an AI general commenting once on the fact that such a system would leave machinery and buildings intact, as well as the environment.

"Oh, God . . ." Nizina says while pointing to one of the bags. "It's moving."

I lean down, tugging at the large zipper, opening it—and a hand grabs my wrist.

I pull back, terrified, dragging out an amorphous, fair-skinned creature.

"Kill . . . me . . . please . . ." comes a voice, almost like a whisper, a plea.

Nizina is paralyzed in shock at the holocaustic sight. I feel like puking but manage to regain control.

"Please . . ." the voice says again. "Kill me . . ."

Then I see the eyes—see his face. It has shifted down and to the side, near the area where the neck would normally meet the shoulder. There's an eerie leer forming as his lips move again.

"I beg . . . you. Oh, God . . ."

Curling my fingers around the alloy stock of my weapon, I press the muzzle against what's left of the man's gnarled face, against the inhumane results of a weapon that should have never been.

As I'm about to pull the trigger, words reach my throat, and I say, "I promise you I will do *everything* in my power to avenge this. You have not suffered in vain. You will not die in vain."

The gun goes off once. The hand releases its grip, and I see no further movement.

A sound to my left makes me look in that direction, spotting Junek and the others in the snowmobiles. But there's another sound behind them. My implants process the sound, and a moment later a word flashes in my mind.

Homi gunships.

But there aren't supposed to be any left. Federation forces had eliminated the Homi's air power months ago. Then again, they had also *destroyed* their forces in orbit, including the satellite that blasted me yesterday.

"Let's go. Move it!" I shout, grabbing Nizina by the hand.

Two purple hovercraft made a wide sweeping turn before coming around from the south side of the clearing, directly over Junek and his band of snowmobiles.

Explosions fill the air. The shock waves from the multiple laser blasts reverberate across the snow-covered field, nearly making us lose our balance.

We press on, trudging across the frozen ground toward the tree line, ignoring the gleaming lasers obliterating Nizina's clan. The cold air burns my throat as I take in lungful after lungful to keep up the pace.

She suddenly halts when a blood-curling scream echoes behind us. She turns around and starts shouting. The snowmobiles are now burning hunks of metal at the far end of this frozen clearing, amidst charred bodies.

I double back to get her, slip on the icy ground, stagger back up, and finally reach her, snagging her frame and throwing her over my right shoulder kicking and screaming.

"Let me go!"

"We can't help them!" I reply, reaching the pine forest, finding refuge.

Smoke spirals skyward before washing away in the downward thrust of the hovercraft as the Homis prepare to land.

I shake Nizina by the shoulders. "Snap out of it, damnit!" I hiss.

She blinks a couple of time but quickly drifts back into shock.

Out of choices, the Homi gunships almost on the ground, I slap her with the palm of my right hand.

"You son of a bitch!" she screams, immediately coming around. "Don't you ever—"

"Quiet!" I hiss, pressing a hand against her mouth. "Keep it down, or you'll get us both killed."

Our eyes lock for a few seconds, then she nods and I move my hand away.

Massaging her cheek, still a little dazed, she stares at the clearing while mumbling, "No . . . not this way . . . it . . . can't be."

Once more, I hold her shoulders. "Listen to me. They're gone. They died for the same cause that they fought for! You must let them go! It's the only way!"

She levels her machine gun at the Homi vessels.

"No!" I shove her muzzle toward the ground. "You don't stand a chance! All you'll do is telegraph our position!"

She snaps in my direction, her wet stare glaring like an angered beast.

Homis are jumping off the purple ships.

"We need to get out of here, and fast. Otherwise—"

I stop when I hear a new sound, a familiar sound mixed with that of the hovercraft—a sound that makes me smile. A moment later one hovercraft bursts into flames while the other flies away. The sudden inferno rumbles across the area, swallowing most Homis on the ground, though I do spot a handful making it to the forest across the clearing.

"Way to go, AI!" I shout, lifting a fist as the dark shape of an HX-55 zooms above the trees, going into a vertical corkscrew the moment it reaches the center of the clearing.

I grab her radio and quickly dial the standard AI operating frequency. "AI Oh Six, AI Oh Six requesting immediate pickup."

"Stand by, Oh Six," the HX-55 pilot replies. It actually isn't his voice, but the biosynthesizer translating his thoughts. A few moments later, "State your operational situation."

I provide him with the data stored in my implants, which marks the location when my fighter went down as well as the last set of telemetry. I follow that with my current location plus detailed data on my unit's group number and my own serial number. Nizina is still half in shock and quite confused, particularly at my apparent ability to recite so much alphanumeric information.

"Glad to hear that you're okay, Oh Six. We've been looking for you since yesterday. Do you need medical services?"

"Negative."

"Keep the channel open, Oh Six. The URS is right behind me."

"Roger that. I have a priority one request."

"Go ahead, Oh Six."

"Throw everything you have at the following coordinates." I provide to him the coordinates of the Homi weapons facility as well as a brief description of the weapon. "Not a nice place, if you catch my drift."

"Stand by, Oh Six."

I put the radio down and say to her, "He's running my request by AI headquarters in New Seattle."

"Roger that, Oh Six. Target is being acquired. Will be right back."

While the fighter heads toward the weapons facility, the oblong shape of the Unmanned Rescue Ship approaches the clearing from the east, making a wide circle over the area before landing in the center. A pair of smart machine guns on the starboard and port side of the URS begin to swing in every direction looking for the large shape of Homis.

"Let's go!" I shout, stepping away from the forest, quickly followed by Nizina, who stops after taking a few steps.

"C'mon! We ain't got all day!"

She shakes her head. "You go. I belong here."

"But your group. They're all—"

She's back to her normal self again. Her eyes are clear. "I'll organize another one," she says, extending a hand. "Take care, Jake. It was . . . interesting meeting you. Hurry now."

I stand there for a few seconds, not sure of what to do, not certain how to say good-bye to this woman. I glance at the hovering craft and know I have to hurry. Soon the Homis on the ground will catch up to current events and start firing.

Staring into her intriguing eyes, I shake her hand and take a step back, and another, then turn around and break into a run.

Fire erupts from the opposite side of the clearing. The starboard gun swings in that direction and begins to spray the forest with explosive rounds.

Just a few more feet, I think as the URS' powerful downdraft pushes down on me, the turbine noise ringing in my ears.

I jump in with both feet, landing on my side, glancing back just before the hatch starts to close.

Nizina has fallen on the ground. She's been hit and is dragging herself back into the forest leaving a trail of blood.

Instinctively, I punch the manual override button and keep the URS in place, jumping back out as machine guns continue to pound the forest, keeping the Homis at bay. I land on the snow, rolling twice before surging to my feet and running after her.

Nizina continues to crawl toward the tree line. I couldn't leave her behind like this, especially with Homis roaming loose in the area.

I reach her in seconds.

"What . . . are you—"

"You're coming with me!" I scream as I pick her up, as I press her against my chest, as I turn around and start toward the rescue vessel.

A shadow shifts to my right, between us and the tree line. It looks like the mother of all Homis, nearly twelve feet tall and probably in the neighborhood of six hundred pounds. He's holding a huge rifle, but he's not firing as he runs toward us in giant leaps, obviously thinking he can take us alive. The ape has closed the gap so quickly that the URS guns can't protect us against him without the risk of hitting us in the process.

With only a few seconds to react, I set Nizina

down while pivoting on my left leg, bringing my right one up, striking the incoming ape on his purple breastplate, just below the neck, missing my intended target but breaking his momentum.

He staggers back, confused. Our AI instructors claimed that Homis are not used to Homo sapiens fighting back without weapons, and thus would be caught off guard.

They were right. I take advantage of the precious seconds it takes the ape to react to my initial strike, and jump sideways to reach the right height while extending the heel of my boot toward the neck area. This time I connect. Cartilage and bones snap, and the jolly purple giant drops to his knees clutching his neck, his face a mask of agonizing confusion.

Feeling like David kicking Goliath's ass, I finish him off with a knee strike to the middle of his face, just as I have been taught, driving the nose bone up into the brain.

Purple blood and foam gushes through his flaring nostrils, but by then I'm already off to the side and picking up Nizina.

Snow explodes around us as other Homis by the tree line, obviously having witnessed my hand-to-hand skills, decide to just take us out with their firearms. The URS, smart enough to realize what's going on, opens fire on them, buying me time.

Focusing on the hatch, I ignore the gunfire, the strain on my arms and legs, the blood flowing out of Nizina's thigh, holding her as tightly as I have ever held anything in my life, until I set her down on the flight deck.

A moment later, as I leap inside, I feel multiple stings on my back and realize that I have just been shot.

The hatch closes, the turbofans whine up, and the armored ship leaves the ground. I black out a moment later.

5

I really can't remember a more peaceful sunset than the one I am witnessing as the crimson sun sinks below the St. Elias Mountains to the west. I watch it through the third story of a former Homi dome that the Federation has turned into the largest field hospital in the region, where URS vessels fly in the wounded round-the-clock from the front lines of this war.

A war that we're winning.

Nizina's intelligence resulted in the destruction of the well-hidden weapons facility, stripping the Homis of their last ace. Without their weapon of terror, the aliens only have conventional weaponry to defend their claim to a planet that was never theirs—conventional weaponry that continues to shrink at a staggering rate as more factories are hit from a combined space-air-land-sea assault. Federation supercarriers continue to deliver nonstop pounding to Homi factories and military bases in central Alaska while the Air Infantry hammers them with wave after wave of HX-55s and high-tech foot soldiers fighting alongside the Federation Army Regulars.

In spite of the burning pain that even the daily injections can't fully eliminate, I manage a thin smile. Soon there will be peace. Very soon.

The door to my room opens, and I see her face, her eyes.

"Hello, Jake."

I inhale deeply and gaze into Nizina's mesmerizing stare. I had not seen her since the day of the rescue—over a week ago.

"He–hello. How . . . how are you feeling? And how's the leg?"

"Good as new," she says, walking to my bedside without the slightest limp. "How are *you* feeling?"

I shrug. "Better, or so the AI surgeons tell me."

She sits at the edge of the bed and puts a hand to my face. "You're lucky to be alive. That was a very stupid thing to do. You should have left me there."

"I had no choice," is all I can say. I keep to myself the fact that one of the Homi bullets tore into my spine. Three long surgeries repaired most of the damage—enough to keep me walking, but my trooper days are over. I'm still looking at a couple more surgeries to remove the implants in my head as well as the optical probes, which in essence will turn me back to an average human—something that wasn't supposed to happen for another two years. My heroism in the field, however, gained me a promotion and an AI assignment in New Seattle, where I will very likely spend the rest of my military term while attending the local university.

She leans down and kisses me on the lips.

"What was that for?" I ask, caught off guard.

"For risking everything for me. Your superiors filled me in on your medical condition. I'm truly sorry."

I'm surprised that they told her. AI is usually tight-lipped about these matters. "The change will do me good," I say. "I'll be all right." I'm actually looking forward to a university degree and a more stable life. I've seen enough action in my two years of active duty to last me two lifetimes.

She stands. "I stopped by to thank you for what you did . . . and also to say good-bye. I'm glad you've made it."

"Wait, Nizina. Don't go."

She smiled. "I have to. The Homis are on the retreat, and your Federation has requested my help in finding their hideouts in the hills. We don't want to leave any hidden enclaves."

She's working for the Federation? Now, that's a surprise. "Maybe I'll see you again some day?"

Her smile broadens. I can tell she likes the idea. "Yes, perhaps," she says. "Maybe when this is over."

I smile, too, and take her hand, kissing it. "Take good care of yourself."

"So long, Jake Gray."

Nizina turns around and leaves, closing the door behind her.

I listen to her footsteps as she walks down the long hall, until they fade away, and a feeling of loneliness suddenly grips me.

A majestic Luna rises in the night sky surrounded by millions of stars, like a sea of burning candles shedding their light over this war-torn land.

I watch them through my tears.

TOY SOLDIERS

by Robin Wayne Bailey

Robin Wayne Bailey is the author of a dozen novels,
including the *Brothers of the Dragon* series, *Shadow-
dance*, and the new Fafhrd and the Grey Mouser novel
Swords Against the Shadowland. His short fiction has
appeared in numerous science fiction and fantasy anthologies and magazines, including *Guardsmen of Tomorrow*, *Far Frontiers*, and *Spell Fantastic*. An avid
book collector and old-time radio enthusiast, he lives
in Kansas City, Missouri.

Between the dark and the daylight,
  When the night is beginning to lower
Comes a pause in the day's occupation
  That is known as the Children's Hour.
> —Henry Wadsworth Longfellow,
> "The Children's Hour"

THOMPSON Eppers walked cautiously. The hairs
on the back of his neck prickled. He couldn't see
his watchers, but he knew they were there, hiding in
the night, in front of him, behind him. He could feel
their gazes like a chill wind. He paused, peered
ahead, glanced over his shoulder. The alleys, the
crannies, the dark and shattered doorways, the rooftops, all exuded a danger, some menace he couldn't
see.

He felt them, though, like a breath, like an itch, instinctively. He increased his pace, walking with a quiet, swift tread through Panperit's empty streets, his bootheels making soft sounds on the broken pavement. The splinter-gun hidden under his belt against the small of his back gave him little comfort. He clutched the hood of his thin cloak closer about his face and tried to blend into the shadows.

He wasn't quite sure when he'd become aware of them or how long they'd been following. Whoever they were, they moved as soundlessly as birds through the air, as mice in the gutters, observing, stalking him. More than one, he felt sure. More than two. He couldn't guess their numbers.

The dual moons in the sky overhead cast disconcerting shadows. He moved in and out of them, pausing sometimes in the blackness, changing his pace, even his direction, in the vain hope that he could shake his watchers. He walked down an alley, ran the next block, turned a corner, and pressed himself flat against the scorched wall of a burned out building. His heart hammered, and for a brief moment he squeezed his eyes shut.

With one hand on the butt of his small pistol, he listened, heard nothing. They had stopped, too, when he had stopped. He knew he hadn't lost them. They were still there. He felt like a target, sure that despite the darkness they could see him, and they knew exactly where he stood.

The night grew impossibly still.

Then, footsteps.

Thompson Eppers cursed silently and drew his weapon. His palms were damp with sweat as he crouched low. Farther down the street, from around a corner, a Kanamaran patrol appeared, six soldiers in full bug armor with TAZ-rifles. One of them carried a personnel sweeper.

He froze, but he was fucked, and he knew it. If the Kanamarans didn't spy him with the enhanced vision technology in their helmets, the sweeper's motion detectors and heat scanners surely would. He'd armed himself lightly for a quick-and-dirty recon mission. He wasn't equipped to take on a full patrol!

From the corner of his eye he noted a narrow alley opening only a few paces away. It might be a dead end, or it might not. The moment he made any move, the personnel sweeper would mark him, but if the Kanamarans weren't too alert and their reaction time was slow, he just might make it. In any case, it was his only chance.

Springing up from his crouch, he dived for the alley. But the Kanamarans weren't slow. The air around him crackled, and for an instant every cell in his body screamed as the blue flash of a TAZ-field fried his synapses. He bounced off a wall and hit the ground, nerveless, unable to move, barely able even to breathe.

With one unblinking eye turned toward the soldiers, he watched them rush forward. But before they could reach him, the thinnest line of red fire flickered from one side of the street to the other. The two closest Kanamarans touched it at almost the same instant, like runners at the finish line, but this finish line sliced them neatly, silently in half.

A vibro-wire!

From a rooftop someone dropped a flash grenade. The four remaining Kanamarans screamed as their vision shields clicked into place too late. A TAZ-rifle crackled, and a panicked blind man took out two of his own comrades. The personnel sweeper exploded in the hands of its operator as the intense electrical field scrambled its circuitry. The vibro-wire flashed once more as the final soldier lurched into it.

The night grew quiet again. Thompson Eppers

waited, unable to do anything else, staring one-eyed at the carnage. He remembered his watchers and felt them nearby, in the shadows, on the rooftops, though he couldn't see them.

Then he could see nothing at all. A soft shuffle close by on the pavement behind him, a hand on his shoulder, then the hood of his own cloak was thrown over his face. Someone searched him with calm efficiency and pried the splinter-gun from his unresisting fingers before they departed again.

He tried to think. What the hell was going on? Who could take out an entire Kanamaran patrol so efficiently, so silently? Why would they? He had to get up, had to get his ass back to the compound and report, and he damn well better do it before someone came looking for those dead bug-grunts.

When feeling finally began to return, he pushed the cloak away from his face and staggered unsteadily to his feet. The effects of a TAZ-field lingered like a bad hangover. He shivered all over, wanted to puke, but fought the impulse. For precious minutes, he leaned against a wall, knowing that if he dared take a step, he'd fall flat on his face again. He stared around. Even turning his head was painful. The shadows had shifted as the moons changed positions overhead. He guessed he'd been down less than an hour.

Was he still being watched? He didn't have that creepy sensation of eyes upon him anymore. Yet, with his nerves still jangling from the TAZ, he couldn't trust that he wasn't.

He stared down the street where the bug-grunts lay. Their armor had been cracked open. Ever the curious sort, he let go of the wall. His right leg didn't want to cooperate, so he half-dragged it as he stumbled closer for a better look. He stopped halfway, mindful of the vibro-wire. The stuff was hair-thin, impossible to see in the darkness unless you touched it, of course, but then it was too late.

The TAZ-rifles were gone. So were their sidearms and any other piece of weaponry or useful tech. Eppers fought the urge to puke again. The Kanamarans' helmets had been removed and cannibalized, and he could see some of their faces.

It made him half-sick to be reminded that they were human, too.

He turned away. He had to clear out of this area fast before these bugs were missed, and if his leg didn't wake up soon, he was going to have a hell of a time getting back to the compound. The ambassador would probably nail his ass anyway, and if the old man didn't, Major Raine certainly would. They'd all been explicitly warned about wandering around without official escort or attempting to leave the compound at night.

He'd barely limped around the next corner when another patrol rushed into the street where the ambush had occurred. Their curses and growls followed him into the next block and hurried him along. The whine of an air-car's engines suddenly filled the air, and he pressed himself against a wall. A pair of the vehicles appeared over the rooftops; blazing searchlights swept the streets. The wind from their gigantic rotors raised a storm of dust. Pebbles and stone fragments pelted him like hail. He drew his hood close to protect his face and melted into the deepest shadow he could find.

Just as the air-cars passed and he was about to start on his way again, another pair of bug-grunts stepped into the street. They carried TAZ-rifles and splinter-guns and were coming his way. At least they had no personnel sweeper. Thompson Eppers took quick stock of himself. His right leg was stronger, if not completely functional. He touched a tiny switch on the lapel of his cloak, triggering the microcircuitry woven into the fabric. The batteries wouldn't last longer than fifteen minutes, but for that period he'd blend perfectly into any background, like a chameleon.

He stood absolutely still as the pair walked right by him. If he'd only had his splinter-gun, he might have taken both the sonsabitches out. But he was weaponless, and there was little he could do against bug-armor and TAZ-fields empty-handed. He hoped he'd get another chance, though, another time.

When he was alone again, he flicked off the cloak's circuitry, saving the batteries, and hurried on. Twice more, air-cars hummed overhead—the same ones or different vehicles, he couldn't tell. He dodged their searchlights expertly as his strength and muscle control returned to him.

He sweated profusely, both from nervousness and from the heat. Ghora was a jungle world with a tropical climate, and even at night the temperature and humidity remained high. When a salty droplet stung his eye, he paused to wipe his face, putting out a hand to the nearest wall for support as he did so. To his horror, the charred facade crumbled inward at his touch, and a section of the low roof crashed down noisily, raising a cloud of old ash and dust. *Damn it to hell!* he cursed silently as he jumped back from the cascading brick and collapsing beams. Activating his cloak again, he ran twenty paces down the street, putting distance between himself and the ruin. A flash of light in the sky caused him to freeze motionless in mid-stride.

A bug-grunt landed suddenly on the pavement not ten feet from him and swept a flashlight around. Another soldier joined him moments later, leaping the rooftops, landing adroitly on exo-powered legs. While the first soldier held his flashlight steadily on the collapsed building, the second one approached it, TAZ-rifle at the ready. He peered inside with the buglike eyes of his helmet glowing. Then, with one hand, he lifted a fallen beam that obstructed the doorway and cast it aside as if it was a straw.

That was the power of bug-armor. Not only did it enhance the wearer's vision and auditory senses, it gave him an almost insectlike strength, as much as eighty times his own natural might. Bug-grunts could leap like grasshoppers, lift many times their weight like ants, and with the right weaponry, sting like wasps and spiders.

Thompson Eppers licked his lips and wondered how much power remained in his cloak's batteries. Caught in the middle of the street like this, his options were few. If he tried to run, the bugs would certainly hear his footsteps, and he'd already had one taste of a TAZ-field tonight, thank you very much. The second soldier emerged from the collapsed building and moved toward its neighbor. He didn't even bother with the doorway, just put his palms against the wall and flexed his arms. The entire structure caved in with a rumble.

The soldier with the flashlight backed up a step, then another, as his partner approached a third building. Eppers' attention focused on the splinter-gun the man wore holstered on his hip. It was a Peugh A-28 military model, larger and more powerful than the smaller concealable splinter-gun that had been taken from him in the alley. If he could make a grab for the soldier's gun . . .

A third building crashed inward under the second bug-man's assault. Dust swirled upward, filling the street. Eppers got an unexpected breath of it and fought down a cough that would instantly give him away. Were they really searching for him, he wondered, or was the stupid jerk just releasing some pent-up frustration? He eyed the splinter-gun again as the first soldier backed up yet another step, but this time when he stopped and directed his flashlight, he rested his hand on the butt of the weapon.

"Give it the fuck up, Ranzz," he called impatiently. "It was nothing! Half these places are just waiting for a good wind to knock 'em over!"

"There isn't any wind," the one called Ranzz answered gruffly from the ruins of the third building. He directed his TAZ-rifle toward another structure, then turned and stared across the street. "But I don't see a goddamn sign of anything. Let's catch up to the others."

They walked back up the street and around the corner, heading in the direction that would take them back to their dead comrades. Still unmoving, Eppers watched until they were out of sight. It was his turn to feel a little frustration. He'd itched to get his hands on that splinter-gun, certain that he could have killed them both. What a pair of dumb-asses! His cloak had kept him safe from their eyes, but observant soldiers might have noted the oddly elongated shadow that stretched down the middle of the pavement and wondered how it could emanate from nothing. His shadow would have given him away, if only the pair had looked!

He didn't know if he should thank his luck or the brother-sister pairings that must have produced such idiots. Before he could decide, the battery powering his cloak waned, reminding him that if he didn't want to be counted among the idiots himself, he'd better move his ass.

Patrols were everywhere now. Obviously, word of the ambush had stirred up the Kanamaran authorities. Weaving in and out of shadows, he left behind the devastated areas he'd discovered on the outskirts of Panperit, and made his way through better parts of the city. He skirted the glow from the well-lit starport, slipped past the walls of the Administration Palace, and approached the rear gates of the Ambassadorial Compound, which really was no more than a cluster of three small warehouses surrounded by a high stone wall.

Two Kanamaran guards stood duty at the gate. Eppers frowned. They hadn't been there when he'd left. But it was no matter. He wasn't really one for using gates anyway. He extracted a pair of *shukos* from a pouch he wore around his shoulders and slipped the metal claws over his hands. He gave silent thanks that whoever had taken his gun hadn't taken them as well. Effortlessly, he climbed the wall and dropped down inside. It was only a short dash to the nearest door. He put his ear to it, listened carefully, then gave a light rap.

The door opened. A hand shot out and grasped his collar, and he was yanked inside. He blinked his eyes in total darkness. Then the door closed behind him, and someone turned on the light.

Major Sharon Raine stood in the center of a temporary barracks, surrounded by a dozen uniformed Nebula-class warriors in various casual poses, some seated on cots, some leaning against desks or walls. They all regarded him with outward calm, but he could read the edgy nervousness in their gazes.

"You'd better bloody fucking have an explanation for what happened out there!" Raine said through clenched teeth. "Governor Teshak's with the ambassador now, and he's howling for blood. The compound's under lockdown, and you can bet all our asses are on the line!"

Major Raine, hell. Behind her back, the men called her a goddamn Storm. She was like that, a force of nature, taller than most of them, more muscular, too. Blonde, well-built, and better looking than a soldier of either sex had any business being. Most men couldn't keep their eyes off her. Eppers didn't even try.

"A bunch of bugs got squashed tonight," he answered coolly. "I can't take credit for it." He looked around at the other men as he wiped sweat from his face. Even without their weapons they were a tough looking bunch. Steel eyes and steel souls in battle-tempered bodies. A better lot of guys he'd never met. "Who's got a drink?"

Corporal Dave Killian produced a silver pocket flask and handed it over. "Regulation issue," he said.

Eppers knocked back a swallow of brandy and washed the dust from his mouth and throat. It was liquid fire, good stuff, and he took another before passing the flask back with a nod of thanks. "But if you ask me," he continued, "—and if you don't Ambassador Steed will—I think that Ghora's experiencing an untidy little guerrilla war, and the Kanamaran Occupation Force hasn't seen fit to mention it to the rest of the universe."

He watched her face as she digested that. It was an easy face to watch. "There's no one else here but Kanamarans," she said with a dubious frown. "Why would they be fighting among themselves?"

Eppers shrugged. "Beats the shit out of me, Major. But whoever it is, they're good. I mean damn good. And they've been throwing rocks at the hornets' nest for a long time."

An inner door opened, and Marc Perrault, the ambassador's aide, poked his head in. He glanced at Eppers with an expression of relief. "Thank God you're back!" he said, rolling his eyes. "Governor Teshak wants a count of all Terran personnel to make sure none of us have slipped out. There's been some kind of an incident. Some bugs—I mean, some Kanamarans have been murdered!"

"Perrault's always the timely one with information," one of the warriors said as he nodded to his comrades with an expression of mock-seriousness.

"Murder seems an awfully strong word," said another. "After all, they were Kanamarans."

Some low laughter and general grunts of agreement followed that.

"We come with empty hands and peace in our hearts," Eppers said softly in a passable imitation of Ambassador Steed's voice. He winked and they only laughed louder. It wasn't the first time he'd made them laugh with one of his vocal impersonations of the ambassador. Major Raine didn't discourage him either. She knew as well as he did that it helped to relieve some of the tension.

Unfastening his cloak, he folded it carefully and lay it on the pillow of his cot. The battery that powered its chameleon technology was photosensitive, and the light in the room was all it needed to recharge. He dropped his pouch on the floor and kicked it under the cot with his foot.

Perrault seemed to look right through him. "You don't seem to realize what you've done!" he persisted. "We're here on a peace mission!"

Major Raine caught the lapel of Perrault's jacket and lifted the aide to the tips of his toes. "Eppers hasn't done anything!" she said, bringing her face close to his. "Now shut the hell up before half the city overhears you. And go tell the ambassador that Governor Teshak can count us till his fucking cows come home. Tell him to come himself, and we'll sound off for him and curtsy and kiss his papal ring if he's got one."

Perrault gave her a stunned look as he stood with his arms dangling at his sides. Red-faced, he waited for the major to release him, and when she finally did, he backed away from her wordlessly and made a small show of straightening his collar. Backing out, he closed the door with an air of quiet dignity, but by that time the embarrassment on his face had turned to a look of barely controlled anger.

"Peace mission, my effing ass!" someone grumbled. "We oughtta just blow this sweat-ball off the star charts, then head for Kanamar and do it the same favor."

"Thank God for jamming tech," Eppers said as he lay back on his cot. He folded his hands under his head, crossed his ankles, and gazed at the ceiling. "God knows how many bugs the buggers might have hidden in this place." He raised up on one elbow long enough to cock an eyebrow at Major Raine. "I assume we smuggled in the jamming tech?"

"Enough to jam this whole damn planet in their ears," Corporal Killian assured him.

"All they're hearing are tapes of the corporal's shower room serenades on continuous loop," someone laughed.

Major Raine gave a rare laugh as she sat on the edge of a desk. "There goes any shot at peace, then. They'll kill us for sure."

"I've come close to fraggin' the corporal myself once or twice while he was singin'," another man admitted as he aimed his finger at the corporal.

Eppers listened to their good-natured banter with a certain wistful detachment. Though he knew them each by name and liked them, he wasn't really part of them. They were warriors, Nebula-class. They wore the honored black beret with the gold spiral cluster. They fought the battles on a score of different planets, stood toe-to-toe with the Kanamarans and their allies. They held the line.

But he fought a different kind of war as an Intel Op for the Terran Union. His battles were fought in the shadows, under cover and underground, in disguise and out of sight, and he was good at it, good enough to have earned a unique code name: Shadow of Darkness Falling. The ambassador knew, and so did Major Raine. But to the rest of these men, he was just another warrior with a few special skills that gave him some extra juice with their superiors. They accepted him. Still, he felt suddenly hollow in their company as he listened to them. Not inadequate or inferior. Just separate from them. And he found that he didn't much like the feeling.

He tried to tell himself it was only fatigue, but he knew it was more than that. He'd been careless tonight.

The inner door opened again. Marc Perrault reappeared in the entrance, his face pale. A pair of Kanamaran soldiers, out of armor but armed with splinter-guns, stood stiffly behind him. An instant later, the outer door also opened. "We shoulda brought some locks," someone said in a sarcastic tone as two more soldiers stepped inside. One of them held a TAZ-rifle casually. The other rested his hand obviously on the butt of his own holstered splinter-gun.

Every warrior came to his feet. Even unarmed, they were ready to fight.

"As you were," Raine ordered, and everyone settled back again. Only Corporal Killian remained standing. He took one big step forward, positioning himself directly in the path of the second pair of Kanamarans. Folding his arms across his broad chest, he flashed them a smile.

At the inner door, one of the soldiers put a hand on Perrault's shoulder and shoved him aside. With an attitude of arrogance, he strode to the center of the barracks, eyeing each of the Terrans in turn, almost daring anyone to make a move. On his sleeve he wore the double-star insignia of a Kanamaran lieutenant.

Raine hadn't bothered to rise from the desk. "Fourteen of us," she said with an undisguised sneer. "Fifteen if you count Perrault. The ambassador's in his office. He makes sixteen. We're present and accounted for, Mister. Next time you enter our quarters, you better knock first."

"A lady might not be decent," Corporal Killian explained to the two in front of him.

The lieutenant turned toward Raine, tried and failed to stare her down. "Despite the presence of your ambassador," he said smartly, "this is not an embassy. You're here on sufferance, Major."

"And you're still standing on your feet by sufferance, Lieutenant," she answered, poker-faced.

"Please, major!" Perrault wrung his thin hands nervously. "We all need to keep our heads and remember that we're not here to fight, but to discuss peace terms!"

Thompson Eppers snorted. They were here to establish the terms of Ghora's surrender. Everyone in the room knew it, even the Kanamarans themselves. In five days, seven carriers from the Terran Union Fleet would arrive at Ghora. The offer of peace terms was little more than a formality. They could surrender and retain their lives and maybe a shred of dignity. Or they could get stepped on—like bugs. Five days. That's how long they had to decide.

And that was how long Eppers had to solve another mystery.

A low, unmistakable rumble sounded outside, and beyond the open outer door the night sky flashed white. Eppers leaped to his feet.

Major Raine spun toward the door. "What the hell . . . ?"

The two Kanamarans near the door rushed outside followed by Corporal Killian. "Some kind of explosion!" he called back. "Looks like a big fire near the palace!"

A second explosion rocked the night, then a third and fourth in quick succession. Raine and the Kanamaran lieutenant exchanged hateful looks, then strode outside together. Snatching up his cloak, Eppers followed with the rest.

The Administration Palace was closest to them. Despite the high, surrounding wall, they could all see the pillars of fire and smoke that rose into the darkness. In the west, farther away, another flickering ball of orange illuminated the night. As they watched, there came a fifth explosion from the same area, and flame shot into the heavens.

"The starport," Eppers said stonily. He turned to the east where the glow of yet another fire shimmered beyond the compound wall. "And unless I miss my guess, that would be one of their power plants."

Perrault came running up to Major Raine. "The ambassador wants to see you immediately," he informed her.

Raine nodded and turned to the Kanamaran officer still at her side. "I'm sure you've got better things to do that stand around here, Lieutenant," she told him. "You know damn well my people are all accounted for." She beckoned to Killian. "Organize a lookout, but stay inside the grounds. There's no reason to think we're safe from these attacks. Everybody else, back inside!" She cast a glance at Eppers and snapped, "You're with me, soldier."

He followed her back through the makeshift barracks, down a brief hall that connected to the next warehouse and into the space set aside for the ambassador's office. It wasn't much of an office. A few chairs and a scuffed up desk had been hastily moved in, and a couch instead of a cot had been set up in one corner for the ambassador to sleep on. A lone window still blurred with dust and grime gave a view of the burning Administration Palace.

Ambassador Steed turned away from the window as they entered. His deeply lined face was stern, and he stood ramrod straight. For a man in his mid-sixties he cut an impressive figure, tall, not an ounce of fat visible on him. He looked more like a general than an ambassador, even in civilian dress.

His gray eyes blazed with worry. "I'm giving you the benefit of the doubt," he said, speaking past Raine directly to Eppers, "and guessing that this is none of your doing. But if you know anything, I want to know it, and I want to know it now. What in God's name is happening out there?"

Eppers rolled his eyes toward the ceiling. "This room secure?"

Raine nodded. "Swept and clean. There's an alpha-level jammer hidden in the desk."

"I took a look around tonight," Eppers answered. "Nothing more, just a little recon work. Whole sections on the outskirts of Panperit have been burned or bombed out. Sometimes it's entire blocks. Sometimes just a random building or a transport. A lot of bridges out, too. Some of the destruction's pretty old work, but not all of it. I was heading for a closer look at a fuel refinery when I realized I was being followed. I couldn't lose them, either. I guess it unnerved me a little. I was paying so much attention to *them* that I walked right into a six-pack of bugs. But faster than you can shake a drop of piss from the end of your dick, somebody cut them down—the entire patrol. And I mean, it was cold work."

The ambassador's brow furrowed. "Did you see who did it?"

Eppers snorted. "Hell, fuck, no! But they saw me. Shadowed me like pros. I've never felt so much like a mouse in a maze in my life." He paused and put on a frown. "What I can't figure out is why they didn't kill me, too. I caught the edge of a TAZ-field and went down solid for a while, but all they did was take my splinter-gun."

"They didn't take your cloak," Raine noted.

Eppers shrugged and ran a finger over the fabric. "I didn't use it while I thought they were watching. It's a new-tech emergency gimmick with a short-duration power source, but it's just a piece of cloth to most people."

Ambassador Steed faced the window again. Even through the dirty glass the flames from the palace seemed to highlight his silver hair. "Terrorists," he murmured. "A Kanamaran faction?" He turned around slowly and fixed Eppers with a hard stare. "Shadow of Darkness Falling." He said the name with angry contempt. "That's what you were really sent here for, wasn't it? To establish contact with these guerrillas!"

Eppers allowed a tight smile. "Way off the mark, Ambassador." He drew up a chair, settled down in it, and propped his feet on the desk. "It's time I told you both a little fairy tale about the first Terran colonists on Ghora. This planet wasn't always in Kanamaran hands, you know. But first—you keep anything to drink around here?"

Scowling, Ambassador Steed reached into a drawer and extracted a bottle of bourbon. But as he slammed it down on the desk, a blast shook the warehouse. The window exploded inward, filling the air with shards of glass. Covering his face, Eppers threw himself down in front of the desk. Raine screamed and fell over the chair where she'd been sitting. From the grounds below came the sounds and blue flickerings of TAZ-rifles.

Eppers scrambled through glass fragments to the shattered window. Without rising, he peered over the broken sill and cursed. A score of bug-grunts and unarmored Kanamarans were in the compound. Where the gates had been, there was only a gaping, smoke-filled hole. The wall had been breached in other places, too. He watched a bug-grunt leap the structure, firing his TAZ-rifle wildly.

The ambassador lay sprawled across his desk. Blood oozed from countless wounds. His back was riddled with glass, and a large, knifelike shard protruded from his neck. The old man had taken the main force of the explosion and probably saved Eppers' life by doing so. His fingers were still wrapped around the upright bottle of bourbon. Eppers snatched it, unscrewed the cap with a quick twist, and took a swig. Then, pushing the ambassador aside, he began yanking open the desk drawers.

"What the hell are you doing?" Major Raine raised up and leaned weakly on the desk's edge. There was a thin, bloody streak from her left ear to the corner of her chin. Odds were she'd have a lovely scar.

"The jammer," Eppers said. Snatching open the last unexamined drawer, he looked up with a grim smile and drew out a shiny metal box the size of his hand. He popped it open and made a swift adjustment to its circuitry. When he snapped it closed again, the tiniest piece of wire remained exposed. "Come on!" He headed for the door with the box and the bourbon.

Raine protested. "But Ambassador Steed . . . !" Then she seemed to look closely at the ambassador for the first time.

Without warning, an armored bug leaped through the window. Raine threw herself aside barely in time as exo-powered arms smashed the desk to splinters. Eppers caught her hand and jerked her back. At the same time, he pointed the jammer and the tiny bit of wire.

From inside the bug's helmet came an ear-splitting screech and an all-too-human scream. The Kanamaran stumbled back against the wall, then sagged to his knees, clutching his head and fumbling to get the helmet off.

Thrusting the bottle into Raine's hands, Eppers sprang forward and snatched the Peugh-model splinter-gun from the soldier's holster. Then, he gave the major a push toward the door and fired just as the helmet came off. A needle-sized rocket speared the soldier's throat. An instant later, its explosive tip took off his head.

"Go!" Eppers said, shoving the major out of the office. "We've got to clear out!"

Raine book a hasty swig from the bottle. "Medicinal purposes," she said, screwing the cap back on. "I'll take charge of it."

There was no point in heading for the barracks. They'd find nothing but bugs and Kanamarans and dead Nebula-class warriors there. Eppers thought bitterly that Ambassador Steed had got what he deserved for agreeing to an unarmed peace mission. Sure, they had plenty of firepower up in space on the *Daedalus*, the ship that had brought them to Ghora, but a fat lot of good that did his escort down here.

It was quite a surprise, then, when dashing out a loading dock door, they nearly collided with Marc Perrault. He spun on them, wild-eyed. In his hand he clutched a small splinter-gun similar to the one Eppers had lost earlier. Eppers grinned. "So I'm not the only one who can smuggle things in a toilet kit."

"Everyone's dead!" he hissed between ragged breaths. "I saw the corporal hit one of them with a chair, and they crushed . . ." He couldn't get the words out. "But I killed the one that got him! Then I just ran!" He shot a look past them into the warehouse. "The ambassador . . . ?"

A bug leaped around the corner of the building,

and spying them, raised his TAZ-rifle. Eppers fired his splinter-gun. Its silver dart punched right through the armor and exploded.

"Good shot," the major said, raising the bottle.

Eppers blew imaginary smoke from the barrel of his weapon. "Remember when the term *bug-fucker* was an insult?"

"Can we get out of here, please?" Perrault implored.

Eppers and Raine exchanged swift glances. "Who'd have thought he'd be the practical one?" she said as they ran for the wall.

Two darts in rapid succession from the gun blew a nice hole in the wall for them. They jumped through and sped up the dark street with no other thought than to put distance between themselves and the compound. The power plant explosion seemed to have taken out most of the lights in the area. At the same time, it had awakened every Kanamaran in the city.

For the first time in his life, Eppers gave thanks that Kanamarans were human. "Get rid of your jackets," he said, stripping out of his own. "Any insignia, too. Perrault, you keep that popgun out of sight. Open your shirt, Major, and try to look a little more like a woman."

"Fuck you," she whispered, but she did as he instructed.

He gave them both a quick look over and licked his lips nervously. "Now we move quick, but walk, understand? And don't fuckin' talk to anybody on the way." He folded his cloak over his arm and carried it like a blanket with his splinter-gun hidden in the folds and the jammer in his pocket.

"What do I do with this?" Raine said, holding up the bottle.

"What the fuck do you think you do with it?" He

snatched it from her and took another drink. "It's the only medicine we've got. Just keep it out of sight." He winked at her. "And you know, you've got an evil leer for somebody in a spot as tight as you're in."

She took a drink, too. "If we get out of this, I'll show you what a real tight spot is."

Perrault gave them a disbelieving look, then grabbed the bottle, sipped, and gave it back without saying a word.

Eppers led them in a northwesterly direction. When the searchlight from an air-car played over them, they waved back, and it flew on its way. When a truckload of soldiers sped by, Major Raine threw her arms around Eppers' neck, laid her head on his shoulder, and pretended to cry as she pointed toward the starport fires. It was a fine and convincing performance, made all the more poignant by the opportunity it provided for him to cop a quick feel.

Eventually, they reached the bombed out section of the city. There was no way to be inconspicuous now if they were seen. If they ran into any soldiers at all, their mere presence would draw attention, so they hugged the deepest shadows and the narrowest alleys. Finally, they reached the edge of the jungle.

"Do you mind if I button up my shirt now?" Raine asked as they plunged into the brush. She handed Perrault the bourbon to hold.

"I don't," Eppers said, although in fact he wished she wouldn't. "But our watchers might."

Raine's eyes narrowed sharply. "What are you talking about?"

"They're very good," he said, smiling, no longer bothering to whisper. "But I was expecting them this time. I can feel them. They're all around us. And they know we've got nowhere else to run."

There was a shuffling in the jungle, a rattling in

the branches above their heads, a sigh like the softest of breezes. Perrault jumped and drew his gun, and the jungle grew still again.

"Put that away, you fool," Raine ordered, and Perrault returned the gun to his pocket.

For long moments they waited, standing still, without speaking. Then the broad leaves on either side of them parted. Two figures emerged from the foliage in old-fashioned camouflage gear. Farther back, barely visible, two more stood up.

Eppers stared. He blinked. Then he reached across Raine, took the bourbon from Perrault, and knocked back another mouthful.

They were children.

The splinter-guns they held, though, were quite adult.

One of the boys stepped forward, but not so close that he couldn't fire first if any of them made a sudden move. His gun remained expertly on Eppers. His round young face was smeared with dirt, or maybe some kind of disguising stain. So were his hands. He had a crop of straight dark hair that touched the top of his ears and the back of his collar. He stood not quite four and a half feet tall, and looked all of ten years old.

"Are you really from Earth?" the boy asked quietly.

"I am," Eppers answered. He introduced himself quickly, and indicated his two companions. "Major Raine's from Shannad Dar near Proxima Centauri. The nervous Mister Perrault's from some petrie dish in a Titan laboratory. But we're all part of the Terran Union. And if you're not going to shoot us on the spot, I'd rather conduct any further conversation much deeper in the jungle."

The drone of air-car engines could be heard. They were coming nearer.

"Much deeper," Perrault emphasized.

Beckoning over the barrel of his gun, the boy spun about on his heel and gave a couple of hand signals to his three companions, who vanished once again. "Follow me exactly," he said over his shoulder. "Any deviation from the path I set could have unfortunate consequences."

His voice was pitched high, like a child's yet it was also commanding and self-assured. Something in the boy's tone and in his choice of words as he hinted at booby-traps or worse sent warning chills up Eppers' spine. But he followed. There was really no other choice.

Only one of Ghora's moons remained above the western horizon. Low in the sky, it shone through the swaying trees, occasionally eclipsed by wispy clouds or by the swift flight of night birds. The air was humid, thick to breathe, and smelled of molds and damp earth and jungle flowers. Droplets of dew fell from the leaves as they moved rapidly through the jungle.

When the forest canopy abruptly gapped, Eppers looked up, wondering if he might catch a glimpse of the floating star that would be the *Daedalus* in orbit overhead. The *Daedalus* had seen more action than any other ship or carrier in the fifty-year-long Kanamar war, but it had recently been retired from the front line and reassigned to envoy duties. It was still equipped for a fight, though, and carried a full complement of arms, crew, and technicians. No doubt they were observing the fires in Panperit. He wondered what they were making of the chaos.

The *Daedalus*. Some warriors with less superstition and a more morbid sense of humor than he had simply called it the *Dead*. For thirteen good comrades and an obstreperous old ambassador, the nickname had been prophetic.

"How did you work that trick with the jammer?" Raine asked softly, breaking into his thoughts.

He tapped the device in his pocket to reassure himself it was still there. "Normally, an alpha-model lays down a distortion blanket that turns any signal within a programmed range to gibberish. But some of my playmates at Intel recently figured out that if you make a few adjustments, turn its broadcast to maximum, and bend a particular wire for an antenna, then you've got a powerful directional transmitter that just happens to wreak all bleeding hell with the control and communications frequencies of bug armor. It sets up one hell of a screeching feedback. Imagine God Himself fucking you in your ear."

Raine made a face. "Why haven't we made a field weapon using the principle?"

"We have." Eppers glanced up at the sky and put on a carrion-eating grin as he thought of the payback Panperit's governor had coming. "And when those seven carriers get here in about five days, you can pick one out for yourself. Something in a pearl-handled model would become you."

"You, too," she replied.

He blew her a kiss. In fact, the new sonic weapon was already taking the field on half a dozen worlds. For years, bug armor had given Kanamar a superior advantage in ground combat, and the bastards had stomped across a score of star systems almost at will, seizing resources and habitable planets, and butt-flashing their might in the faces of the Terran Union. They'd been part of the Union once. Now it was like the bad son trying to put daddy in his place.

Ghora had been part of the Union, too, and its only city, Panperit, had been a thriving research colony of scientists and doctors. The jungles had proved to be a treasure trove of new drugs and plant-extract medicines. Major discoveries, new cures and treatments for all sorts of things had come fast and furious.

As it always was with science, though—hell, as it was with anything involving the human race—there had to be a dark side. When the fighting began, Ghora just naturally wanted to do its part for the cause, and some of the lifesaving research going on there just naturally and not so quietly turned to weapons. *Black biotech,* in the official jargon. New diseases, engineered viruses, mutant bacteria. The nastier, the better. And these, too, came fast and furious.

War just naturally brings out the best in everybody.

Things came to a kind of stalemate. Kanamar hit the Union worlds with their bugs. The Union worlds hit back with bug spray.

But then, ten years into all the fun, came the rumor—just a rumor—that a researcher on Ghora had developed something truly fantastic, something beyond believable, something that would finally break the stalemate and turn the course of the war. Stories about Ultimate Weapons were always being introduced and tossed around by fanatics and crackbrains and hack novelists with nothing more important to write about. But for some reason—maybe because Ghora had produced so many medical wonders already—this rumor took root. Maybe it took root because the soil had already been enriched with so much blood.

Whatever the reason, in a brief moment while the Terran Union was resting on its sword, Kanamar turned on Ghora like an angry giant, and this time when the fist came down, Ghora was the bug. The colonists were executed as war criminals. The research facilities were dismantled or destroyed, and Panperit was reestablished as a military base. In the figurative blink of an eye, the Union had lost not just a planet, but an entire sector, and worse, found itself facing the idea that all Ghora's potential might be soon turned against *them.*

No one had ever figured out why that hadn't happened. Instead of becoming a weapons factory for Kanamar, the little planet had quietly slipped from the stage altogether.

Yet still, almost half a century later, an echo of a whisper of the rumor continued to waft ghostlike among the worlds. And the Shadow of Darkness Falling found himself assigned to an idealistic ambassador's escort as a common warrior. Never mind the ambassador, though. His was a different job—to find answers to questions. Was there any truth to the rumor? Did the weapon exist? Did the Kanamarans have it? Why hadn't they used it if it existed? If it existed, could it be seized for the Terran Union?

Nothing too complicated. All in a day's work.

His bleeding ass.

Eppers stared at the back of the dark-haired boy and wondered who the child could be. Kanamaran? Probably. But the idea bothered him. Maybe, despite the reports, some of the original colonists had managed to survive, and they were staging these terrorist attacks. That seemed just as unlikely. Why would they let their children, particularly such young ones, handle the dirty work? Not that it would be the first time in Earth's history that that had happened.

He studied the boy as they traveled. That was one little bundle of determination and intensity. He couldn't help but admire the way the kid moved, how he carried his pack on his small body without bending under its weight, how his eyes swept the trail and the jungle around them.

More than anything else, those eyes impressed Eppers. They were cold, ruthless. He'd seen the look before—eyes that had seen too much. They didn't belong on a child's face.

He grabbed the bottle from Perrault and started to take a drink. He was a man who liked his liquor and liked the way it numbed him when he was tired or uncertain, and right now he was both. He'd fought the Good Fight for the Terran Union; he'd believed in the Cause and carried the banner and marched to the drum. But was this what the Good Fight had come to? Children with guns? Children with bombs? Children with killers' eyes?

He screwed the cap back on without tasting. Suddenly he wanted his mind clear. He wasn't sure what or why, but he knew he stood on the cusp of something important.

"Let me relieve you of that burden," Raine said, taking the bottle. Unbothered by questions or cusps, she took a quick drink.

By dawn, the sky had clouded over. A gray blanket of fog and misty rain fell across the jungle and soaked them to the skin. It also refreshed them, though, as the warm rivulets washed the grimy sweat from their faces. The major opened her shirt again, lifted her face, and let the rain roll down between her breasts. It was a picture that both Eppers and Perrault paused to appreciate.

"I think our young guide is getting his first eyeful," Perrault whispered, grinning.

The boy had stopped when they had stopped. He stared gape-mouthed at Raine's chest. The steely cold had faded from his gaze, and his stern expression had turned to one of pure, innocent wonder. It was a startling and amusing transformation.

Also, a brief one. When Perrault chuckled, the boy reddened and gave him a look of such animosity that it shut the aide up as effectively as a kick to the gut. Major Raine gave him a similar look and clutched her shirt together once again. "Why do I get the feeling it's your first eyeful, too," she said scathingly. "Apparently, he's not the only little boy in the jungle."

The glower on the boy's face remained. Adjusting

the pack on his shoulders, he turned around, stiffened his spine, and prepared to resume the march. Eppers considered offering to carry the pack himself for a while to take the load off those small shoulders. Its weight would mean nothing to him. But he thought better of it. Perrault or Raine had hit some sore spot, and he thought he knew what it was. *Boy. Kid. Youngster.*

"We've told you our names," he said reasonably. "Why don't you tell us yours?"

There was a long moment of silence while the boy thought it over. "DeWolfe," he answered at last. "Roland DeWolfe." He made a small show of adjusting his pack again. "We need to get moving."

Eppers fell in behind the boy, letting Raine and Perrault follow. *DeWolfe.* It wasn't a Kanamran name, and it rang a bell. He'd studied all the Union's files on Ghora before boarding the *Daedalus,* and he mentally riffled through those notes and pages now. There'd been a list of the known Terran colonists, and another of researchers and scientists, some with fat dossiers. So much information and so many names.

Another child with skin as black as onyx sprang up suddenly from the bushes directly in their path. Like Roland DeWolfe, he wore camouflage garments, but he also had a bandolier of slim, finely feathered needles slung across his small body. The rifle he held casually under one arm was like nothing Eppers had seen before. It was light, slender, no more than a wooden tube with a carved stock to fit against the shoulder. Obviously handmade.

Roland DeWolfe made quick introductions. "This is Salifu Sesay," he said.

Eppers estimated that Salifu Sesay was even younger than Roland. Eight or nine years old at most. Bending forward, he extended his hand.

Salifu Sesay looked him straight in the eye, and
the expression on his pudgy face was unyielding. "If
you came to make peace with Kanamarans, then we
have no reason to shake hands." He looked to Roland DeWolfe. "Kioshi, Michael, and Allegra are already back. Stephen and Emma haven't shown up
yet."

Roland clapped the black child on the shoulder. It
was almost a paternalistic gesture. *Or*, Eppers realized, *the gesture a leader might make to a subordinate.*
"Stay watchful, Salifu," Roland instructed in a tone
that reinforced Eppers' conclusion. "And warn everyone else to stay below today. We stirred up one hell
of a serpent's nest last night, and there might be
some air patrols."

Salifu nodded and crouched down again with his
gun, becoming effectively invisible under the thick
fronds.

"Below?" Raine repeated with a raised eyebrow.

Roland DeWolfe didn't answer. He unslung his
pack and opened it without looking at her. "I suppose you'd like this back," he said, extracting a small
splinter-gun from the contents and extending it to
Eppers. It was the gun he'd lost earlier.

He looked at the boy with a wary respect, and
perhaps even a brief spark of fear, for he glimpsed
the deactivated coil of vibro-wire in the open pack,
too, and remembered the six dead bug-grunts. "Give
it to the major," he said, exposing the larger Peugh-
model he'd been keeping concealed under his folded
cloak. "I've got this one."

Roland seemed reluctant, but at last held the gun
out to Raine. His gaze lingered on her for an instant
too long. "Thank you," she said. She made a show
of opening the splinter-clip and closing it again before she stuck the weapon in her waistband.

Avoiding her gaze, Roland unzipped a pocket on

the side of the pack and took out a flat black keypad. "You'll have to overlook Salifu's rudeness," he said as he punched in a series of numbers. "I'm afraid you won't find any peace sympathizers among us."

With no more than a hum, a five-meter crack opened in the ground, and a section of the jungle floor tilted suddenly upward to reveal a wide metallic ramp that descended deep underground. "Home sweet home," Roland DeWolfe announced as he led the way down.

"Have you considered track lighting?" Perrault said nervously when the massive door came down again, and they stood in darkness. As if in response, light panels in the ceiling activated, dim at first, then brightening.

"Lights are on a delay program at all the entrances," Roland explained. "The enemy doesn't come into the jungle often, but they do buzz the skies every once in a while, particularly after a strike. They're not much of a worry, either, but we take precautions."

The floor, walls, and ceiling were all stainless metal, and their footsteps rang softly as they followed Roland DeWolfe deep beneath Ghora's surface. Where the ramp leveled out, a pair of old transport trucks were parked, but their tires were gone, the windshields dusty, and it was plain they'd been stripped of useful parts.

The tunnel forked into three larger corridors. The centermost was lined with glass windows and steel doors. Lights blazed in some of the rooms while others remained dark. It extended as far as they could see. The left and right corridors were more dimly lit and opened into wide loading areas and warehouse space.

"What the hell is this place?" Raine muttered.

"I may be way out on a gangplank here," Eppers

answered, "but I'm guessing it's a bio-research bunker."

"You've done your homework, Mr. Eppers," Roland DeWolfe said coolly, as he led them down the central corridor. "But then, I'd already concluded you were no ordinary warrior." He waved a hand. "My father was the director of this complex. He designed it and supervised its construction."

"Your father?" Eppers pursed his lips thoughtfully as he scuffed his toe through the thick dust on the floor. Then he remembered why the boy's name had rung a bell and slapped his forehead. "Of course," he said. "Marcus DeWolfe! The guy who found the cure for the Barnard's Star plague! Where is he now?"

Perrault stopped and pressed his nose to the nearest window in an effort to see into the dark room beyond. "Where are any of the adults?" he asked.

The door to the room jerked open suddenly. A little blonde girl, perhaps seven years old, thrust her head out. Her face was shiny from recent scrubbing, and she was in pajamas. "Do you mind?" she snapped angrily. "Don't you know it's rude to stare into a room that doesn't belong to you! Haven't you heard of privacy?"

"This is Allegra Adams," Roland said formally. Then he grinned. "And she uses this room for her quarters. She set the bombs at the power plant last night." He nodded to her. "Good job, Allegra."

"You're disturbing my beauty sleep!" She slammed the door again. But through the panel she continued to yell, "Get them out of here, Roland! They don't belong, and we don't need them!" Then no more sound came from the room.

Roland DeWolfe led them on. Other doors opened, and more children looked out curiously as they passed by. He introduced each of them, speaking their names with affection and pride. Sometimes, he mentioned their accomplishments or special talents. Jono was their explosives designer. Dennis had once poisoned Panperit's water treatment system. Chin, their computer wizard, kept the Administration Palace's computers in constant disfunction by hacking into them with a light-beam.

Not all of them were present, Roland explained, but they numbered twenty.

Twenty children.

He stopped at a door and pushed it open. "You can use this apartment, Mr. Eppers," he said, stepping back. "I hope you won't mind sharing with Mr. Perrault. You'll find the rooms well appointed, if a bit dusty. Entire families used to live down here for months at a time." He opened another door on the opposite side of the corridor. "Major Raine, these rooms are yours. The showers are functional, so refresh yourselves. Our meals are communal, and breakfast should be in about an hour."

Perrault went inside, but Eppers and Raine both lingered in their doorways while Roland DeWolfe walked on down the corridor alone and opened the door to his own apartment.

Thompson Eppers watched as the cherubic little hand clutched the doorknob and twisted it with surrealistic slowness. Then as the door opened a crack, a hard, cold gaze that didn't belong on a child's face turned back and melted briefly into something warmer, and something infinitely sad. On the threshold of her doorway, unaware that she was being watched, Sharon Raine slipped the bottle of bourbon from under her shirt, tilted her head first one way and then the other as she read over the label, and finally closed her door.

With Raine gone, Roland DeWolfe's attention turned to Eppers again. His face crinkled up in a

look of annoyance. It was a look that seemed to ac-
cuse him for noticing something he shouldn't have,
and it once more turned cold.

No! Not cold. As their eyes met and locked in that
hallway, Eppers saw it with a flash of insight he
would never be able to explain. Not cold at all.

Old.

"Roland!" he said, his voice just loud enough to
stop the boy on his threshold. Roland had evaded
the question before. This time Eppers pressed it.
"Where is your father?"

Roland DeWolfe's dirty face clouded. "Dead," he
answered stiffly. "The Kanamarans killed him." His
small hand squeezed the doorknob until his knuckles
turned white. He trembled visibly, as if fighting to
control himself. "Forty years ago."

Eppers waited until the boy went inside and closed
the door. Then, left alone, he bit his lip and put a
hand on the wall to steady himself. Some part of him
rebelled against the idea. He didn't want to believe
it. But he did. The cure for the Barnard's Star plague
had been found *before* the war had even started. And
Roland was Edward DeWolfe's son!

Old minds in tiny bodies.

Twenty children who weren't children at all.

He closed the door to his room without going in,
and instead knocked on Sharon Raine's door. When
she opened it, he stepped inside without waiting for
an invitation. He spied the bourbon sitting on a coffee table in the center of the room. Uncapping it, he
took a long pull while the major stared. He took another and wiped his mouth with the back of his hand
as he settled down on her couch.

"You look like you've just been through a battle,"
she said with her back against the door.

Her clothes were still wet from the jungle rain.
Her shirt and slacks clung to her like a second skin,

revealing every curve. Her blonde, short-cut hair shimmered in the room's light. He wondered where she'd lost her beret. Probably back in the ambassador's office. Or had she cast it away later with the jacket when he'd told her to try to look more like a woman? Wasn't that a laugh?

He looked up at her face. It was a pretty face. A beautiful one, in fact, despite the thin, almost invisible cut along her jaw. Perhaps it wouldn't scar, after all. Maybe it had only been a scratch. The rain had washed away the blood and the dirt. He could barely see it.

He looked into her eyes, and for a moment, he felt a chill. It was Roland staring back at him. Not actually Roland, of course. But she had the same hard eyes, eyes that had seen too much, eyes that shone even in the quiet moments with wariness and warning. "How old are you, Major?" he asked.

A hint of a smile turned up the corners of her lips. She walked halfway toward him and stopped. "Over twenty-one," she answered.

He leaned forward, letting the bottle dangle from his hands as he leaned his elbows on his knees. "What are you doing here?"

Major Sharon Raine cocked one eyebrow and tilted her head. "I should be asking you that question, shouldn't I?"

"No, I mean, in this war, in the military, on this planet." He shook his head as he studied her. "You're a career warrior. But why?"

Her expression turned stony. She moved around the coffee table and folded her arms rigidly over her chest. "That's the one question no real warrior ever asks another," she said. "We can't count on the future, so we don't pry into the past. All we deal with is now."

He hung his head for a moment, stung. His father

had been a real warrior, but Eppers had hardly known him. "I'm sorry for the loss of your men," he said, looking up again.

"That's the past," she said icily. "Is it possible for you to deal with the *now,* soldier? Is it?"

He rose to his feet slowly and stood straight, almost as if she'd called him to attention, and in a way, she had. He stared at her wet form, at the hard curves and angles of her muscled body, and he knew what he was doing here. He'd just danced around the issue a bit, trying to take her on his terms, trying to find some softness he could probe and mold to suit his own desires.

But there was no softness in her anymore. She really was as hard and strong and tough as they came. Through and through, no facade, no pretense. Maybe the war had burned the softness out of her, or maybe she'd never been soft. He thought he saw a flash of pain in her eyes, or desperation, but maybe it was just the glint of steel, of ice.

It didn't change why he'd come here. He could deal with the *now* as well as she could. "Didn't you say something about a tight spot?"

For a moment, she just stood there with an expression that was half anger and half a frown. Then she barked a short laugh. "Well, I guess that's what passes for romance in this modern age." She came closer, took the bottle from him, and set it down on the table. With the tip of one finger she stroked his cheek. "But an officer has to stand by her word."

"Standing isn't what I have in mind," he answered.

Breakfast was a strangely subdued affair. Perrault ate ravenously, and Raine did her part, too. Eppers hadn't shared Roland DeWolfe's little revelation with them yet. He picked over the plates of fruits and berries and raw vegetables, barely noticing their taste as he studied the faces of the children seated at the long table. Only half of them were present. The others were sleeping, Roland had explained, or on watch above, or pursuing other matters.

Children. He tried not to think of them that way, but he couldn't help himself. *Little adults* just didn't fit. Adults didn't wear hair ribbons and short pants as some of these did, didn't giggle with such high-pitched voices, or whisper behind their hands into each other's ears.

They were just as interested in the three real adults. Eppers felt them watching quietly as they chewed small mouthfuls, sometimes from the corners of their eyes, sometimes with brazen directness. The boys Michael and Kioshi seemed particularly interested in Eppers' stubbled beard, and they rubbed their hands over their own cheeks when they thought no one was looking. A little brown-skinned girl named Mangansie asked to touch it, and he let her. She thanked him politely, almost shyly, before returning to her seat.

From some of them he sensed distrust or fear. They were the ones at the farthest end of the table. Their glances were surreptitious, even hostile. The blonde girl called Allegra sat with that group. Raine particularly held her attention, and when she looked at the major, it was through narrow eyes that glittered with ice. If Raine noticed, she gave no indication of it.

When Perrault finished the last bite of a pearlike fruit, he looked around with an oblivious smile as if all the dynamic of the meal had eluded him. "Well, now," he said loudly, "I wonder if anyone would care to show us around? There must be lots here to see!"

Mangansie and Emma raised their hands to volunteer.

Allegra's face purpled with rage, and she shot to her feet. "Put your hands down!" she hissed. "You're not in some damned school!"

Emma waved a hand dismissively. "What's the matter, Allegra? One of your bombs fail to detonate last night, so you have to blow up now?"

Allegra responded with a withering look, then lifted her nose and left the table.

"I suppose I should apologize for them," Roland said when the other children had finished eating and also departed. Perrault had followed, flanked by both Emma and Mangansie. "It's been a long time since any of us sat down with . . ." he hesitated, frowned as he fumbled uncomfortably for a word. "Grown-ups." He looked from Eppers to Raine. "I suppose he told you that I'm almost fifty years old?"

For a moment, Raine sat still as stone. Then she leaned back in her chair and cocked one eyebrow at Eppers. "He discussed several of his fantasies," she answered curtly. "He didn't mention that one."

"It's true," Roland assured her. "No one here is less than forty-five years old. Except yourselves, of course." He allowed a small, tight smile. "Let's go back to my apartment. I'll show you a few things along the way."

"If you don't mind, I'll beg off," Raine said with a yawn. Her voice indicated she still didn't believe Roland. "It was a long and exciting night, but I can barely keep my eyes open now."

"How thoughtless of me," Roland said, rising. "You must both be exhausted."

"I'm wide awake," Eppers answered.

"Then why don't the two of you have a little man-talk," Raine suggested through another widemouthed yawn. "I'm going to grab some sleep, then try to figure out what our next move should be."

The sound of her steps echoed as she left the room. Eppers noticed again how Roland watched her every move, how his gaze lingered on the door after it had closed and she was gone. Then, realizing he was being observed, Roland leaned back in his chair with a sigh and a wan smile.

"The gleam in my eyes isn't what you think it is," he said. He leaned forward suddenly, put his elbow on the table, and rested his chin in his hand. His expression turned puckish. "I mean, it's not the same as the gleam I see in *your* eyes when you look at her. Think about it. My mind is fifty years old, and naturally I wonder what sex is like, but my body's still prepubescent. I look at Major Raine, and I wait for something to happen, some reaction. I *hope* that something will happen." He shrugged, and his smile faded. "Well, something does—she reminds me of my mother. You know mothers are the only women that ever mean anything to a boy my age." He laughed a short, humorless laugh.

Eppers felt a tightening in his gut and even some embarrassment as he looked at the ten-year-old face across the table from him. It occurred to him to wonder if Roland DeWolfe was quite sane. But then, how could anyone in his situation remain sane?'

"We have vast databases down here, Mr. Eppers," Roland continued. "I've read all the classics of literature—the great books and plays, the finest poems." He leaned back in his chair again and ran a hand through his dark hair in a gesture of frustration. "I have a few favorites. But I confess I understand so little of it, because so much of Human literature and art is based on something I can't feel and will never experience. Passion. Love between a man and a woman."

He fell silent for a moment, and his eyes misted, though actual tears never came. "I see the way you look at Major Raine, and then I look at her, too. And you know what I feel, Mr. Eppers?"

Eppers sat riveted, his mouth dry. Some instinct

inside him urged him to reach out to this child, to comfort him somehow. But Roland DeWolfe wasn't really a child. Eppers couldn't think of anything to say, any way to respond, except to listen.

"I feel broken!" Anger and pain flashed across Roland's face, and his chair crashed backward as he sprang up and ran from the room.

Eppers followed the boy into the hallway, then stopped.

Alone, he eventually made his way back to his own apartment. Along the way, through glass windows, he dully noted laboratories with children busily at work over slides and microscopes and petrie dishes. He noted also an electronics laboratory and a worktable where another child was examining scavenged bits of bug armor, from the previous night's strike, he presumed. He passed what was obviously a computer laboratory, too, and nodded absently to the boy named Chin at work there.

He had lied to Roland when he said he wasn't tired. He felt weary to the bone. And though Roland would have laughed to hear him say it, he felt old. Raine had the right idea. He needed sleep. He'd be able to think more clearly after some downtime. There were still too many unanswered questions, too many riddles, but he didn't think he'd get anything more out of Roland today.

He reached his apartment and pushed open the door. On the sofa in the living area, Perrault sat with his head in his hands. He looked up sharply. His face was pale, and he looked like he'd jumped out of his skin and barely got back in again.

"What the hell's wrong with you?" Eppers said irritably. He really didn't want to deal with anything else right now, or anyone, especially Marc Perrault. "I thought you were getting the Grand Tour."

Perrault stared at the floor and swallowed. Then

he began to shiver. "I don't know what's going on here, Eppers!" he said, his voice thick with tension and fear. "I'm not a soldier like you. Not a particularly brave person, I know that. But I'm not the kind of man that would . . . !" He stopped and hung his head again.

"That would what?" Eppers snapped as he unbuttoned his shirt and cast it aside. "What are you spluttering about?"

"Those two little girls!" he said, looking up again. "Emma and Mangansie! They can't be more than seven or eight, but they—they tried to seduce me!" He licked his lips and fidgeted with his hands, all the while looking as if he thought Eppers might leap across the room and beat the shit out of him for what he was confessing. But he continued anyway. "They wanted me to—well, touch them! They were quite cool about it. Just as an intellectual exercise, they said. But they were very explicit!"

"Well, did you?" Eppers kicked off his boots, then unzipped his pants and stepped out of them. He couldn't say he was surprised after what Roland had told him. Fifty-year-old minds trapped in ten-year-old bodies. Ten years and less. They might not be capable of passion. But they were capable of curiosity. At least the girls were.

"Of course not!" Perrault shouted. His face was almost comic with shock.

Eppers headed for the bedroom. Later, he'd explain a few things to Perrault, but only after he'd had some sleep. "Then lock the door and relax. And don't worry—you're safe from me."

Perrault leaped to his feet. "But we need to talk!" he said. "Have you considered the possibility that these children deliberately sabotaged the peace talks?"

"It wouldn't surprise me at all," Eppers answered

as he pushed Perrault back into the living room.
"They've sabotaged everything else on this fucked-
up planet. Now I'm going to bed."

But Eppers didn't sleep well. He tossed and
turned, dreamed vague nightmares of his own child-
hood, and of his father, a warrior lieutenant killed
by the Kanamar in the Battle of Mentaka Prime. And
he dreamed of Sharon Raine, of loving her, savoring
her flesh, only he saw himself as a boy, and she held
him too tightly, pressing his small face between massive, smothering breasts, stone cold and oblivious to
his struggles. And he was Roland, and Salifu, and
even Allegra killing Kanamar, wielding vibro-wire
like a whip while explosions detonated around him
like blossoming flowers of flame filling the night.

He woke up in a cold sweat, threw back the blanket, and swung his feet over the side of the bed. He
dressed in his uniform slacks and shirt, thinking of
his father again as he did so. He wasn't a warrior.
On him, the uniform was nothing but a costume,
another disguise in a long series of disguises.

Introspection had never been one of his strengths.
It didn't pay in his business to question his own actions and motives. He was a spy. Entire battles had
turned on information he'd uncovered. But was there
any honor in it? He thought of Roland DeWolfe and
the rest of the children. No matter how old they
were, he couldn't stop thinking of them that way—
as children.

The rumor had been true. He'd found the Ultimate
fucking Weapon he'd been sent to look for. He'd
known it all along, but his dreams had made it clear
to him. He still didn't have all the answers, but they
were here in this bio-tech bunker. All he knew for
certain was that something monstrous had been done
to these kids. They'd been used somehow as lab rats
and guinea pigs, and most likely by people they'd
trusted, perhaps even by their own parents.

War was hell, someone had said. But hell didn't even begin to describe it.

He found Perrault napping on the couch. The jammer from Eppers' pocket was sitting out on the coffee table beside the Peugh-model splinter-gun and the smaller weapon. The younger man snapped awake as Eppers cursed and snatched up the Peugh-model. "I just cleaned it!" Perrault said as Eppers extracted the clip and examined the weapon minutely.

"And I suppose you cleaned the jammer, too?" he slammed the clip back in place and leveled the gun on the aide.

The fear faded from Perrault's face, and he looked disgusted. "Of course not. But I couldn't sleep. I needed something to occupy me, and if you haven't noticed, the place is a little short on newspapers and magazines. So I took your jammer apart, studied it, and reassembled it for fun."

Eppers glared suspiciously at Perrault, wondering if he could trust the jammer to work should he need it again. He picked it up anyway and pocketed it, then thrust the splinter-gun into his waistband. That still left the smaller pistol on the table. When he reached for it, Perrault moved faster. "You're forgetting that this one is mine," he said, pointing it at Eppers. There was a dark hint of anger in his eyes that Eppers had seen once before, but as then, it quickly faded. Perrault dropped the weapon in his jacket pocket.

Eppers stared at the man narrowly, wondering just who or what Marc Perrault really was. The ambassador's aide was suddenly a mystery that he'd overlooked, and he didn't like mysteries. He'd have to keep a closer eye on him and remember that he had a gun.

"Get up," he said roughly. "You're my aide now. I'm drafting you for special duty. It's time we learned a lot more about these children."

Bleary-eyed and confused, Perrault followed Ep-

pers into the corridor. Eppers knocked on Raine's
door, and when there was no response, he knocked
on the door to Roland DeWolfe's apartment. No answer there, either. "You're full of surprises, Mr. Perrault," he said sarcastically. "Surprise me again. How
are your research skills?"

Perrault lifted his head proudly. "I know you don't
hold much of an opinion of me, Eppers. But if you
show me a computer, I'll make it sing and dance."

"You find me the answers I want and I just might
change my opinion." Eppers led the way to the computer laboratory. The door was unlocked, and there
was no sign of the boy named Chin. Without waiting
for an order, Perrault took a chair before a large
wafer-screen and studied an elaborate console for a
moment. Then he picked up the key-ball and, holding it between both hands, began to type.

"We're in luck," he said to Eppers, who leaned
over his shoulder. "The last user left the system running. No password, no security, no obstacle at all."
The screen flared to life, and they saw their own faces
reflected in a blue-light glare. "I'm disappointed,"
Perrault continued. "I wanted to show off for you."

"Why would you expect security?" Eppers said.
"From everything I've seen these kids are one fuck-
ing tight team. Bring up everything you can find on
Roland DeWolfe."

Perrault typed rapidly on the key-ball. A picture
of Roland's face appeared in the upper left corner of
the wafer-screen. Perrault read the information that
accompanied the image. "Son of Edward and Parris
DeWolfe. Born in Panperit . . ." He hesitated suddenly, then leaned toward the screen. "Something's
wrong here," he said. "This says his birthdate is . . ."

"He's fifty years old," Eppers interrupted. "Tell
me something I don't know. Like, *why* he's the way
he is. Why any of these children are far older than

they look. Particularly, is there any indication they were used in some kind of experiment? And find me any records of weapons research or black biotech."

Perrault stared at him, speechless. Then he turned back to the screen and began typing again. "Magic eight-ball, tell me truly," he muttered as he typed in new commands. Roland's image faded, and text information danced over the screen at a rate almost too swift for Eppers to follow. A rapid parade of faces, adults and children, flickered and disappeared at three-second intervals. "There's a complete list with biographies of all the colonists on Ghora up until the time of the Kanamar invasion," Perrault explained. "At that time the population was five thousand, three hundred, and sixteen."

Eppers was impressed. "How can you possibly catch anything at that rate?"

Perrault didn't pause or look around. "Speed reading and eidetic memory," he answered. "I only have to look at a screen or a page and I remember everything on it."

No wonder Ambassador Steed had valued Perrault as an aide. "A natural information specialist," Eppers said half-jokingly. "Have you ever considered a career in Intelligence?"

Perrault didn't answer. He leaned back with the key-ball in his lap, and his eyes took on an otherworldly glaze. He was clearly in his element. For a brief while, he didn't even seem to breathe; his expression didn't change, nor did any sound at all escape his lips.

Then, quietly and unexpectedly, he emerged from his trance. "Oh, my God," he murmured. His fingers stopped. He gripped the key-ball and leaned toward the screen where lines of text and twenty thumb-sized pictures were displayed. Eppers leaned closer, too. "They're all geniuses," Perrault whispered in an awe-filled voice. "Not one of them has an intelligence quotient under two hundred and twenty-five! Roland's the highest of them all, and Allegra's nearly with him!" The screen changed again, and he read more slowly so that Eppers could follow along. "The adults hid them down here in the bunker and destroyed all records of this facility. Then they destroyed and disguised the road that led here, too. They knew the Kanamar were coming and that they couldn't get away in time, but they made a plan to save these twenty children. A ship from the Non-Aligned Worlds was supposed to sneak in and pick them up." Perrault looked around at Eppers. "I guess their ship didn't come in."

Eppers frowned, and his voice was bitter. "Half the Non-Aligned Worlds fell to the Kanamaran fleet the same day Ghora did. It was a massive sneak-attack, and by the time it was over any planet that hadn't already chosen sides was a blasted mudball. Nobody sat on the fence after that. They knew they'd only get shot off."

There was a noise in the corridor. Three children went racing by the computer lab window, and Eppers only got a glimpse of them. They carried weapons, and their faces were angry. "Keep working," he ordered. "Roland said his father ran this hole. Find out what he did here."

He took off after the children. They led him down the main corridor to the junction of tunnels near the entrance, but they didn't speed up the ramp to the outside world. Instead, they turned left toward what he had first assumed was unused warehouse space. It was a much larger tunnel he found himself in. The stone ceiling was higher, and the lighting not as good. He couldn't see the end of it, and he could barely see the children far ahead. He poured on the speed, determined to overtake them.

He heard shouting. Then he emerged suddenly on a platform overlooking a deep and vaulted cavern. Only a steel rail saved him from plunging headlong into a black abyss. He banged his shin painfully, and nearly pitched over anyway.

The lighting was no better here, but there was no missing the sleek, gray vessel that loomed up from the cavern floor and towered over him. He gaped as he strained his neck back and his gaze roamed up to its fore-point and the roof just above it. It was an old Class-IV *Tycho* freighter, a kind of ship seldom seen anymore, once swift and powerful, but with anti-matter drive engines that were long outmoded.

It wasn't merely a cavern he was in. It was a hangar.

So their ship did come in, Eppers thought to himself. *Then why didn't the kids get on it?*

The shouting and high-pitched squeals drew his attention again. On the far side of the cavern, he spied Salifu and Emma fearlessly scrambling up a long ladder to the distant roof. Then, still higher up the ladder, he spied another pair of figures.

Almost to the rooftop, Sharon Raine climbed as fast as she could with one hand while she held Chin, ruthlessly bound and gagged, in her other arm. The boy struggled and twisted, but his small wiriness was no match for the major's size and strength. For one confused and anguished moment, Eppers hesitated, uncertain as to what he should do, but the outcries of the children compelled him. He drew his splinter-gun and took aim.

Then he lowered the weapon and cursed. What was he thinking? He could have made the shot, but the splinter's explosive tip would kill the boy, too, and if it didn't the resulting fall surely would.

And he wasn't at all sure he was ready to shoot Raine. In flashes of fractured imagery, he remembered holding her, showering with her, loving her, and they'd told each other it didn't mean anything. He'd lied.

A narrow catwalk from the platform circled the cavern. He took off running, his heels ringing loudly on the metal surface. At the base of the ladder, the boys Jono and Michael were unslinging the strange, lightweight rifles he'd first seen Salifu with in the jungle. Just above them Kioshi was beginning his climb with an oversized Peugh-model splinter-gun dangling from a strap over his shoulder.

Jono took aim with his odd weapon. Eppers heard a soft, air-powered *phhhttt,* but either the boy's feathered dart missed, or the range was insufficient. Sharon Raine was nearly to the rooftop. Above her head, he could see the dull gleam of a hatch.

"Sharon! Stop!" he called. "What the hell are you doing? There's nowhere to go! There's nothing but jungle out there!"

Her sharp laughter echoed through the cavern as she continued to climb. "You think you're the only goddamned spy in the universe, Thompson?" she shouted back. "There's a whole motherlode of electronics down there. More than enough tech to cobble together a simple transmitter. There's an air-car waiting for me up above."

Eppers pushed Jono and Michael aside and began his own frantic climb. Kioshi was in his way, but he was sure he could get over the boy. Then Emma and Salifu, too, if necessary. Chin was the one that worried him. "Let the boy go!" he shouted. "He's only slowing you down!"

"For a guy so good in bed, you're a stupid prick!" she answered, still climbing. "But I guess you don't know! You haven't tried to kill one of these murdering little bastards yet, have you? You want me to show you? You want me to put a splinter in this little shit's head for you? Or how about if I just break his neck a little? It's a real show, lover!"

"Just let him go!" Eppers shouted back. "He's slowing you down, and if I catch up to you. . . !"

She'd reached the hatch. Chin struggled and squirmed, yet she held him like a sack of treasure. With her free arm wrapped around a ladder rung, she reached into her waistband and pulled out the small splinter-gun Eppers had given her. At first Eppers feared she intended to carry out her threat to shoot Chin. But instead, she aimed the weapon straight downward and fired.

First on the ladder, Salifu Sesay leaned back as if to protect Emma and the others below him. He took the blast squarely in the chest. His scream was short as he fell away from the ladder. Eppers made a useless, desperate grab for a small arm as Salifu plummeted and smashed on the catwalk between Jono and Michael.

"No!" Eppers cried. Rage and anguish bubbled up inside him. He climbed faster, overtaking Kioshi and clambering over him, ignoring the boy's savage protests. He felt foolish and betrayed by Raine. But more, he felt responsible for Salifu. He didn't want to be responsible for Chin, too, or for Emma still above him.

"There's no place to run, Sharon!" he screamed. "If I don't get you, there are seven Union carriers on the way!"

Sharon Raine cranked the hatch wheel with one hand. "You're such a fool, Thompson," she shouted back. "Those carriers are racing into a trap. The Kanamaran fleet's already waiting for them!" She pushed back a latch. With a hiss, the oval hatch rose open. A beam of bright sunlight stabbed downward.

"By the way, lover!" Raine called as she pushed Chin through the opening. "I don't want you feeling too guilty. Take a look at the black boy!"

Eppers hesitated, suspecting she might only be trying to distract him while she took another shot at

Emma or at him. But unable to resist, he risked a glance downward. What he saw nearly caused him to lose his grip.

Salifu was not only alive, he was climbing the ladder again—and his expression was deadly.

When he looked back up, Raine was gone. Emma had reached the hatch and was climbing into daylight. He heard the harsh drone of an air-car's rotors, and over that, a sharp scream and a splinter-blast.

"Emma!" he called as he emerged from the hatch. The wind generated by the air-car pressed against him as it soared skyward, but he ignored it. Emma lay stretched on the bushes that surrounded the hatch, her body turned away from him. He ran to her, his eyes full of scalding tears.

Emma bolted upright so quickly that he fell back a step. Before he could react, she seized the Peugh-model splinter-gun from his hand and fired three quick shots after the departing air-car. The vehicle continued on unharmed, and Emma threw the weapon down in disgust.

Eppers felt the strength go out of his legs. He fell on the ground in a clumsy lotus position, his arms limp at his sides, and sat there like a broken doll. The front of Emma's blouse had been blown to tatters. He could see her thin, flat chest plainly. A star-patterned series of scars radiated across her body, all that betrayed the impact of what should have been a fatal blast. As he stared, that, too, healed and faded until not even a blemish remained.

The scratches the bush had made on her arms and legs healed even more swiftly and vanished without a trace of a wound. Unhurt, she stood with her hands on her hips, staring after the air-car and cursing a blue streak that would have made a warrior blush as she kicked at the dirt with her toe.

Kioshi climbed out of the hatch. In his childlike voice, he asked, "Emma, is Mr. Eppers injured?"

Eppers couldn't help himself. He laughed. He laughed so hard that he fell back on the ground and kept laughing. Only when he felt the children's hands trying to pull him up again did he rise onto one elbow and stare at them. Tears streamed from his eyes, although he wasn't quite sure why. They knelt beside him, Kioshi on one side, Emma on the other, and their earnest expressions touched him inexplicably.

"I'm sorry if we scared you," Emma said gently. "But when we discovered what she'd done, we had to try to stop her."

"She was too strong," Kioshi said. His voice was a boyish mixture of disappointment and disgust. "Too fast!"

Eppers sat up and gathered both kids in his arms. It was an impulsive act, and a wrong one, he knew, but also right for him. He clung to them for a long moment, surprised that they allowed it, but also glad. "We'll get Chin back," he told them. "So help me we will. I promise."

Emma gently freed herself. "You misunderstand, Mr. Eppers," she said, and her voice became suddenly adult. "Chin wasn't the reason we were chasing that woman."

"She copied some computer files," Kioshi explained. "She has a chip that we can't let the Kanamarans have." He grasped Eppers' larger hand with his small one. "Please get up now. We need to go back inside. Roland and Allegra are in Panperit planning another strike."

Eppers didn't feel quite ready to stand yet. "Everyone in the Union has wondered why Ghora hasn't played a larger role in the war." He looked from Emma to Kioshi and tried to see them as something more than children—but he just couldn't. "You kids have kept this planet tied in knots, haven't you? And Governor Teshak has never even suspected?"

"Nor his predecessors," Emma affirmed. "In the first few years, we let them believe a few of our parents had survived their genocide and that they were taking revenge. That drove them nuts for a while, because they thought they'd murdered all the Terrans on Ghora. After that, we made them think their own people were staging the attacks, some disgruntled cell of renegade Kanamarans."

Kioshi grinned. "It's easy to move among them. We're just children. Nobody looks twice at us, unless it's to pat us on the head and say how cute we look. Certainly they never suspect such cute kids to be dropping bombs down their chimneys at midnight."

"Once," Emma continued, "we plastered the city with stickers saying 'Join the Rebellion—Stop Aggression!' And we spread leaflets everywhere. The enemy didn't know *who* they were fighting, only that their power plants and fueling facilities and government buildings and everything else were blowing up every time they turned around."

"Or their water was being poisoned, or some virus was being released in the city," Kioshi added. "At any given time, a good third of their population was probably locked up for *suspicion*." He giggled.

Eppers shook his head and finally got to his feet. He smiled as they both took his hands and guided him to the hacth. Protectively, Emma climbed down before him, and Kioshi came after.

Michael, Jono, and Salifu were waiting below. Salifu regarded him smugly, his shirt shredded, his body uninjured. "Do you still want peace with the Kanamarans?" he demanded.

He had the same hard eyes that Roland had and bristled with the same ingrained hatred. Eppers felt an ache inside as he looked from one face to the next. Behind Emma's quick smile and Kioshi's shy grin, behind Jono's quiet silence and Michael's patient reserve, he saw that same hard hatred, easier to read in some than others, disguised sometimes, but there.

Not all the scars were healed. Not all the scars would ever heal.

War is hell. He hoped the man who said that was burning there.

"The Kanamarans killed my father, too," he told them gently. "Still, I want peace. It just looks like it won't be possible today."

Slowly, Salifu extended his hand. "I'll shake now if you want," he said, his face still stern. "I didn't have much hope when Roland first showed up with you. But I think you're finally growing up."

The children laughed. But as they led him back along the catwalk and out of the cavern to the bunker's main corridor, they grew silent and grim once more. Sharon Raine had finally shown the Kanamarans the true face of their enemy. If not their lives, their home was in danger. Any moment now, the area might be overrun with bugs. For the first time, they had suffered a blow, and they knew it. And their leader wasn't there to tell them what to do.

Perrault was waiting for him in their apartment. "Some of the kids threw me out of the computer lab," he said, rising to his feet. "But I found what you wanted. Roland's father was doing bio-research for the war effort all right. He genetically modified an extract from a jungle plant to produce a substance he called the *Prometheus Enzyme*. It was supposed to accelerate the healing process to fantastic rates and make a soldier in the field nearly invulnerable." He spoke rapidly, obviously excited by what he'd learned—and obviously horrified. "But it didn't work. He discovered that the human body produced a natural blocking agent that interfered with the enzyme. *Gonadatropin*. It's a hormone produced by the adrenal-pituitary system that activates at puberty and triggers the development of the sexual organs. It's present in both men and women, so the sex of the soldier didn't matter. There were other drugs, of course, that could block the production of *gonadatropin*, but that resulted literally in chemical castration. . . ."

"Which in turn resulted in a more passive soldier," Eppers said. "Not desirable at all. So the bastards experimented on their kids!"

"Of course they didn't!" Roland DeWolfe stood on the threshold with his hand still on the doorknob. He was dressed in fatigues and covered with dirt, and there was a look of weariness on his small face. "Our parents loved us. We did this to ourselves." Drawing a deep breath, he paced across the living room and sat down on the couch. "For the first month or so we didn't even venture out of the bunker. Our parents and families were dead. We knew we were alone. But we had plenty of supplies and our computers. We schooled ourselves as we always did, and tried to preserve the illusion of normalcy. I'll never forget, though, how the youngest ones cried at night. You could hear them through the whole complex."

Eppers interrupted. "There's a ship in a hangar bay," he said. "Why didn't you leave when they came for you?"

A smile, surprising in its cruelty, flashed over Roland's face. "That's what set us on our course," he said. "The ship arrived later than it was supposed to. How the captain avoided detection, I don't know. But he had a crew of four with him. Instead of smuggling us out, they'd come to loot the place. There was a lot of equipment and technology down here worth money, not to mention the bacterial and viral weapons or the research itself. They wanted it all. But they didn't want us."

"You killed them," Perrault whispered. "You were just children!"

"We were geniuses," Roland reminded him. "And once we discovered how easy it was to kill, we realized how much we all wanted to make the Kanamarans pay for what they'd done! So we swore an oath to take revenge." He leaned forward and smashed his tiny fist down on the coffee table. "We couldn't even find our parents' graves!"

"What has that to do with the enzyme?" Eppers asked in a quieter tone. "When did you decide to take it?"

Another voice spoke from the doorway, and they turned. Allegra held out her right arm as she walked into the room. "When a bomb went off prematurely," she said. "In my hand. We didn't know much about demolitions then. We had to learn—sometimes the hard way."

"We thought Allegra was going to die," Roland continued. "So we brought her back here. I remembered the drug my father had been working on. The *Prometheus Enzyme*. You know the story about Prometheus, how a vulture ate his liver every day and how every night it grew back? My father told me that story over and over again. He used to keep me in the lab with him, and he'd even talk about his work with me. We were close, and he knew I was bright."

He paused and looked at Allegra with a strange sadness in his gaze. "I gave it to Allegra to save her life. Three injections, and she began to heal almost immediately. Her arm even grew back." He hesitated, held his hand out to her, and they intertwined fingers. "Allegra was the only one of us who didn't get to choose. The rest of us saw what the enzyme could do, and we chose to take it, because we knew it would make our own private little war with the Kanamarans that much easier. But we didn't know then—and I don't think my father knew—the far-reaching effects of the enzyme, that it would make us practically immortal."

"We can't be harmed, and we don't get sick," Allegra said. "But we don't grow, and we don't age either. We're trapped forever in these immature bodies." She glanced toward the door. All the other children had gathered in the hallway and were listening.

"Have you tried injecting yourselves with *gonadatropin* to counter the enzyme?" Perrault asked. He wore a pained, desperate expression as he sat down beside Roland.

"The effect doesn't seem to be reversible," Allegra said. "At least, not in pre-pubescent children with no real naturally occurring hormone in their bodies. And besides, the enzyme really has been our greatest weapon against our enemies."

Roland rubbed a thumb and forefinger over his eyes, then glanced up at Eppers. There was that look of weariness again, and of unnatural age. "But we've been talking among ourselves," he said softly. "We're tired of fighting. The enemy knows who we are now, and they know where we live. We can't stay here."

Salifu Sesay came into the room. "We want you to take us to the Union ship in the sky."

Emma appeared behind Salifu. "The ship in the hangar is fueled," she said. "We just don't know how to fly it." She flashed a smile. "No piloting lessons in our computers."

"To the *Daedalus?*" Eppers said. It was an idea he'd thought of himself already. He just hadn't thought the kids would go along with it. But then, they weren't really kids, he reminded himself. What other choice did they have?

"We've fought the fight," Roland said, rising to his feet, taking Allegra's hand again. "It's time to retire from the field."

Eppers and Perrault looked at each other, and Eppers ran a hand through his hair. "Then we go now," he said. "Before anyone changes their mind. The jungle's probably already crawling with bugs."

"What about Chin?" Perrault said, standing.

"Don't worry about him," Allegra said. "Once we get everyone else safe, we'll figure out some way to come back for him. We can give your soldiers information that will help."

Perrault plainly didn't like the idea of leaving a boy behind, but Eppers was a practical man. Save nineteen now—come back for the last. Hell, he didn't like it either. But what else could he do? He couldn't take on a whole bug-army with a splinter-gun and the jammer in his pocket.

They started for the ship, and before long they broke into a run. Everyone seemed to feel the urgency of a swift getaway. They reached the hangar and boarded the old *Tycho*. Eppers and Perrault took the command chairs. The children huddled on the floor around them, hugging and holding each other.

Eppers studied the controls with a dubious eye. "You said you could make a computer sing and dance," he said to Perrault, "and this crate runs on computers. Now's your big chance to really impress me."

Perrault's brow furrowed in concentration. The console was out of date, older than Perrault was. But he ran a hand over a panel, and it flared to life. "We won't need the anti-matter engines," Eppers told him. "Just find the lifters. And it would be nice if you could open the rooftop doors, too."

Perrault didn't speak. He had that glaze in his eyes again, as if he somehow intuited the controls without really looking at them. Displays flickered to life as his hands moved, and the ship began to rise.

"You did open the doors, didn't you?" Eppers asked nervously.

Perrault didn't answer, but apparently he had. The vessel climbed from the cavern darkness into the bright blue of Ghora's sky. Then a deeper darkness closed about them once more as they achieved the edge of space.

Roland appeared behind Perrault. He gazed with a rapt expression at the field of stars and at the *Daedalus* as the carrier came into view, still only a distant object, but growing in the antiquated viewscreen. He also watched with open admiration the way that Perrault worked the console. He put one hand on the aide's shoulder and stood quietly for the remainder of the trip.

The rest of the children, even Allegra, fell silent once more. They seemed reluctant to let go of each other and made no effort to get up or move about the ship. It was their first time in space, Eppers reasoned, and their first time away from home. He couldn't guess what any of them were feeling. Relief? Apprehension? Fear? All of that, he suspected.

They hailed the *Daedalus* as soon as Perrault deciphered the communications program. Eppers gave his code-name and an identification number. "Warn the carriers that they're heading into a trap," he told the *Dead*'s captain. "The Kanamaran fleet is lying in wait for them."

Guided and advised by *Daedalus*' command crew, Perrault performed the docking maneuver with ease. With little more than a thump, the old freighter nestled against the underside of the larger carrier. Eppers gave a sigh as he rose from his seat. With a smile at the children and a sense of homecoming, he moved to the forward air lock and opened it.

Without any warning at all, a dozen pairs of hands pushed him through. He tripped and fell to the metal deck, and before he could rise, the air lock hissed closed. He pressed the interior control to open it again, but the instant it did, Perrault was thrust inside by Kioshi and Jono and Salifu. Eppers pushed the aide out of his way, angry and afraid at the same time.

Then he saw the splinter-gun in Roland's hand. It was leveled at him, and the boy's face was adamant. So were the faces of the children behind him. "Sorry, Mr. Eppers," Roland said. "But there's something we left behind."

"We'll go back for Chin, I promise!" Eppers shouted.

"Yes, Chin," Roland continued. "But more importantly, that data chip Major Raine took. I'm afraid it has all my father's research on it. We won't let the *Promoetheus Enzyme* fall into the hands of the Kanamarans. In fact, we've decided that no one should have it ever again." Roland slapped the air lock control, and the door hissed shut and locked. Eppers banged uselessly on the air lock with his fists. He had a clenching, terrible feeling in his gut as he pressed his face against the metal. His heart hammered as the faintest vibration shivered through the hull. The *Tycho's* lifters came to life again.

"Roland! Emma! Allegra!" Eppers shouted. "Don't do this! Let me in!"

The *Daedalus'* hatch opened suddenly behind them, and uniformed crewmen dragged them out. "It's decoupling!" someone shouted frantically in Eppers' ear. "Get away, man!"

There was no resisting, and he was pulled forcefully into the safety of the carrier. "Get me to the bridge!" he demanded. "Tell your captain to raise a com-link with that ship now!"

A pair of warriors guided him. When someone tried to stop Perrault from following, Eppers set them straight with a sharp command. Together, they arrived on the bridge. The captain greeted him formally, but Eppers ignored the man as his gaze fastened on the huge viewscreen.

The old *Tycho* was heading right back to Ghora.

"They were only dropping us off!" Perrault said at Eppers' side. His face was white as he watched the screen, and his voice grew quiet. "It's my fault. I taught him the controls without even knowing it. He stood right beside me and watched everything I did."

"Roland!" Eppers shouted, knowing the com-link was open as he'd ordered. "Answer me!"

After a moment, the boy's voice came back with an icy calm that sent tremors through Eppers. "I liked you from the beginning, young man," Roland answered. "The way you moved through the shadows like you owned them. You were practically one of us—just bigger."

Eppers could barely control himself. "Whatever you're you doing, Roland, please stop!"

"We can't, Thompson. They have the chip, and they have Chin. We won't let them keep either."

Eppers' mouth was dry. He felt Perrault squeezing his arms as the *Tycho* gained acceleration. But there was nothing to say! Nothing he could do!

Roland's voice came back over the com-link. "Don't feel bad, Thompson. Nor you, either, Mr. Perrault. Who knows? We may walk away."

"I'll look for you," Eppers answered. "For all of you."

"Do you remember I told you that I'd read all the classics, Thompson? The great books and plays and poems? I have a favorite poem, you know, by Robert Browning. I particularly like the ending."

Eppers licked his lips. "Tell me."

He listened as the *Tycho* flashed toward Ghora, straight for Panperit, like a spear toward an enemy heart. As it hit the atmosphere, the anti-matter engines flared with a brilliant fire, hot and white, and purifying. Eppers winced, but didn't cry out when the explosion came, an explosion visible all the way to the *Daedalus*.

Allegra would have been proud.

They they stood, ranged along the hillsides, met
To view the last of me, a living frame
For one more picture! in a sheet of flame
I saw them and I knew them all. And yet
Dauntless the slug-horn to my lips I set,
And blew 'Childe Roland to the Dark Tower came.'

CJ Cherryh

Classic Series in New Omnibus Editions

THE DREAMING TREE
Contains the complete duology *The Dreamstone* and *The Tree of Swords and Jewels*.   0-88677-782-8

THE FADED SUN TRILOGY
Contains the complete novels *Kesrith*, *Shon'jir*, and *Kutath*.   0-88677-836-0

THE MORGAINE SAGA
Contains the complete novels *Gate of Ivrel*, *Well of Shiuan*, and *Fires of Azeroth*.   0-88677-877-8

THE CHANUR SAGA
Contains the complete novels *The Pride of Chanur*, *Chanur's Venture* and *The Kif Strike Back*.
                                                              0-88677-930-8

ALTERNATE REALITIES
Contains the complete novels *Port Eterntiy*, *Voyager in Night*, and *Wave Without a Shore*   0-88677-946-4

To Order Call: 1-800-788-6262

Julie E. Czerneda

Web Shifters

"A great adventure following an engaging character across a divertingly varied series of worlds."—*Locus*

Esen is a shapeshifter, one of the last of an ancient race. Only one Human knows her true nature—but those who suspect are determined to destroy her!

BEHOLDER'S EYE
0-88677-818-2
CHANGING VISION
0-88677-815-8

Also by Julie E. Czerneda:

IN THE COMPANY OF OTHERS
0-88677-999-7
"An exhilarating science fiction thriller"—
Romantic Times

To Order Call: 1-800-788-6262

Tanya Huff

The Confederation Novels

"As a heroine, Kerr shines. She is cut from the same mold
as Ellen Ripley of the *Aliens* films. Like her heroine,
Huff delivers the goods." --*SF Weekly*

VALOR'S CHOICE
0-88677-896-4

When a diplomatic mission becomes a battle for survival,
the price of failure will be far worse than death...

THE BETTER PART OF VALOR
0-7564-0062-7

Could Torin Kerr keep disaster from striking while escorting a scientific expedition to an enormous spacecraft of
unknown origin?

To Order Call: 1-800-788-6262

DAW 19